Irish author **Abby Green** threw in a very glamorous career in film and TV—which really consisted of a lot of standing in the rain outside actors' trailers—to pursue her love of romance. After she'd bombarded Mills & Boon with manuscripts they kindly accepted one, and an author was born. She lives in Dublin, Ireland, and loves any excuse for distraction. Visit abby-green.com or e-mail abbygreenauthor@gmail.com.

Louise Fuller was a tomboy who hated pink and always wanted to be the Prince—not the Princess! Now she enjoys creating heroines who aren't pretty push-overs but are strong, believable women. Before writing for Mills & Boon she studied literature and philosophy at university, and then worked as a reporter on her local newspaper. She lives in Tunbridge Wells with her impossibly handsome husband, Patrick, and their six children.

D0610354

THE VIRGIN'S DEBT TO PAY

ABBY GREEN

SURRENDER TO THE RUTHLESS BILLIONAIRE

LOUISE FULLER

MILLS & BOON

First Published in Great Britain 2018
by Mills & Boon, an imprint of HarperCollins*Publishers*
1 London Bridge Street, London, SE1 9GF

The Virgin's Debt to Pay © 2018 by Abby Green

Surrender to the Ruthless Billionaire © 2018 by Louise Fuller

ISBN: 978-0-263-93531-8

MIX
Paper from
responsible sources
FSC
www.fsc.org   FSC™ C007454

This book is produced from independently certified FSC™ paper
to ensure responsible forest management.
For more information visit www.harpercollins.co.uk/green.

Printed and bound in Spain
by CPI, Barcelona

THE VIRGIN'S DEBT TO PAY

ABBY GREEN

I'd like to dedicate this story to my go-to Equestrian Experts, Peter Commane and Nemone Routh. Any inaccuracies are all my own fault! And I'd like to thank Heidi Rice, who gave me the moment of inspiration I needed while walking down Pall Mall in London. x

CHAPTER ONE

NESSA O'SULLIVAN HAD never considered herself capable of petty crime, and yet here she was, just outside a private property, under the cover of moonlight, about to break and enter to steal something that didn't belong to her.

She grimaced. Well, to be accurate, she wasn't really going to be breaking and entering, because she had her brother's keys to his office in the Barbier stud farm offices. *Luc Barbier.* Just thinking of the owner of this stud and racing stables made a shiver of apprehension run through Nessa's slim frame. She was crouched under an overhanging branch, on the edge of a pristine lawn in front of the main reception buildings. She'd left her battered Mini Cooper a short distance away from the gates and climbed over a low wall.

Nessa's own family home was not far away, and so she knew the land surrounding this stud farm very well. She'd played here as a child when it was under different ownership.

But any sense of familiarity fled when an owl hooted nearby, and she jumped, her heart slamming against her breastbone. She forced herself to suck in deep breaths to calm her nerves, and cursed her hot-headed older brother again for fleeing like he had. But then, could she really blame Paddy Junior for not standing up to Luc Barbier—the intimidating French *enfant terrible* of the thoroughbred racing world, about whom more was unknown than known?

His darkly forbidding good looks had rumours abounding…that he had been orphaned by gypsies, and that he'd lived on the streets, before becoming something of a legend in the racing world for his ability to train the most difficult of horses.

He'd progressed in a very short space of time to owning his own racing stables outside Paris, and now he owned this extensive stud farm in Ireland attached to another racing stables, where his impressive number of successful racehorses were trained by the best in the world, all under his eagle-eyed supervision.

People said his ability was some kind of sorcery, handed down by his mysterious ancestors.

Other rumours had it that he was simply a common criminal who had grown up on the wrong side of the tracks, and had managed to climb out of the gutter to where he was now by using a fluke talent and ruthless ingenuity to get ahead.

The mystery of his origins only added to the feverish speculation surrounding him, because along with his racing concerns, he had invested in myriad other industries, tripling his fortune in a short space of time and securing his position as one of the world's wealthiest entrepreneurs. But racing and training remained his main concerns.

Paddy Jnr had talked about the man in hushed and awed tones for the last couple of years, since Barbier had employed Nessa's brother as Junior Stud Manager.

Nessa had seen him herself, once or twice, from a distance at the exclusive Irish horse sales—where there was a regular attendance of the most important names in racing from all over the world. Sheikhs and royalty and the seriously wealthy.

He'd stood out, head and shoulders above everyone around him. Inky black hair, thick and wild, touching his collar. A dark-skinned, hard-boned face and a stern expression, his eyes hidden by dark glasses. Thickly muscled arms were folded over his broad chest, and his head had followed the horses as they'd been paraded for the prospective buyers. He'd more resembled the taciturn security guards surrounding some of the sheikhs, or a mysterious movie star, than an owner.

He'd had no obvious security around him, but even now Nessa could recall the faint air of menace keeping people away. He would be well capable of protecting himself.

The only reason she was even here tonight, indulging in this hare-brained exercise for her brother, was because he'd assured her that Luc Barbier was currently in France. She had no desire to come face to face with the man himself, because on those occasions when she had glimpsed him from a distance she'd felt a very disconcerting sensation in her belly—a kind of awareness that was totally alien to her, and very inappropriate to feel towards a complete stranger.

She took another deep breath and moved forward from under the tree, across the lawn to the buildings. A dog barked and Nessa halted, holding her breath. It stopped, and she continued moving forward. She reached the main building and went under the archway that led into a courtyard, around which the administrative offices were laid out.

She followed Paddy's directions and found the main office, and used the bigger key to unlock the door. Her heart was thumping but the door opened without a sound. There was no alarm. Nessa was too relieved to wonder why that might be.

It was dark inside, but she could just about make out the stairs. She climbed them to the upper floor, using the torch app on her phone and breathed a sigh of relief when she found his office. She opened the door with the other key, stepping inside as quietly as she could, before shutting it again. She leant against it for a second, her heart thumping. Sweat trickled down her back.

When she felt slightly calmer she moved further into the office, using her phone to guide her to the desk Paddy had said was his. He'd told her that his laptop should be in the top drawer, but she pulled it open to find it empty. She opened the others but they were empty too. Feeling slightly panicky, she tried the other desks but there was no sign of the laptop. Paddy's frantic words reverberated in her head: *'That laptop is the only chance I have to prove my innocence, if I can just trace the emails back to the hacker...'*

Nessa stood in the centre of the office biting her lip, feeling frantic now herself.

There was no hint of warning or sound to indicate she wasn't alone, so when an internal door in the office opened and light suddenly flooded the room, Nessa only had time to whirl around and blink in shock at the massive figure filling the doorway.

It registered faintly in her head that the man filling the doorway was Luc Barbier. And that she was right to have been wary of coming face to face with him. He was simply the most astonishingly gorgeous and intimidating man she'd ever seen up close, and that was saying something when her brother-in-law was Sheikh

Nadim Al-Saqr of Merkazad, as alpha male and masculine as they came.

Luc Barbier was dressed all in black, jeans and a long-sleeved top, which only seemed to enhance his brooding energy. His eyes were deep-set and so dark they looked like fathomless pools. Totally unreadable.

He held up a slim silver laptop and Nessa looked at it stupidly.

'I take it this is what you came here for?'

His voice was low and gravelly and sexily accented, and that finally sent reality slamming back into Nessa like a shot of adrenalin to her heart. She did the only thing she could do—she pivoted on her feet and ran back to the door she'd just come through and pulled it open, only to find a huge burly security guard standing on the other side with a sour expression on his face.

The voice came from behind her again, this time with an unmistakable thread of steel. 'Close the door. You're not going anywhere.'

When she didn't move, the security guard reached past her to pull the door closed, effectively shutting her in with Luc Barbier. Who patently wasn't in France.

With the utmost reluctance she turned around to face him, very aware of the fact that she was wearing black tracksuit bottoms and a close-fitting black fleece with her hair tucked up under a dark baseball cap. She must look as guilty as sin.

Luc Barbier had closed the other door. The laptop was on a desk near him and he was just standing there, arms folded across his chest, legs spread wide as if to be ready for when she bolted again.

He asked, 'So, who are you?'

Nessa's heart thwacked hard. She kept her mouth

firmly closed and her gaze somewhere around his impeccably shod feet, hoping the cap would hide her face.

He sighed audibly. 'We can do this the hard way, or the harder way. I can have the police here within ten minutes and you can tell them who you are and why you're trespassing on my property…but we both know it's to get this, don't we?' He tapped the laptop with long fingers where it sat on the desk. 'You're obviously working for Paddy O'Sullivan.'

Nessa barely heard the last phrase. Totally ridiculously, all she could seem to focus on were his beautiful hands. Big and masculine but graceful. Capable hands. *Sexy hands*. The quiver in her belly became something far more disturbing.

Silence lengthened between them again and suddenly Barbier issued a low, violent-sounding curse in French and picked up the laptop, moving towards the door. He was almost there before Nessa realised that involving the Irish Gardaí would be even more of a disaster. The fact that Barbier hadn't called them yet left a sliver of hope that something of this situation could be salvaged.

'Wait!' Her voice sounded very high in the silence.

He stopped at the door, his back to her. It was almost as intimidating as his front. He slowly turned around. 'What did you say?'

Nessa tried to calm her thundering heart. She was afraid to look up too much, using the lip of her cap to keep herself hidden as much as possible.

'I said wait. Please.' She winced. As if a nicety like *please* would go over well in this situation.

There was more silence and then an incredulous-sounding, 'You're a *girl*?'

That struck Nessa somewhere very vulnerable. She knew she was dressed head to toe in black and wore a hat, but was she really so androgynous? She was well aware of her lack of feminine wiles, having spent much of her life knee deep in muck and wellies. She hitched up her chin and glared at him now, too angry to remember to try and stay hidden. 'I'm twenty-four, hardly a girl.'

He looked sceptical. 'Crawling through undergrowth to trespass on private property is hardly the activity of a grown woman.'

The thought of the kind of women a man like this would know—a world away from Nessa—made her skin prickle with self-consciousness and her vulnerability turned into defensiveness. 'You're meant to be in France.'

Luc Barbier was shocked. And he was not a man who was easily shocked. But this slip of a girl—*woman?*— was talking back to him as if she hadn't just flagrantly invaded his private property with clearly criminal intentions.

'I was in France, and now I'm not.'

He allowed his gaze to inspect her more closely, and as he did he felt something infuse his blood…*interest*. Because he could see it now. Yes, she was a woman. Albeit slim and petite to the point of boyishness. But he could see her breasts, small and perfectly formed, pushing against the form-fitting fleece of her black top.

He could make out a jaw too delicate to be a man's, and wondered how he hadn't noticed it before. He also saw a very soft lower lip, which was currently caught between white teeth. He felt a very unwelcome stirring of desire and a need to see more.

'Take off your cap,' he heard himself demand before he'd even registered the impulse.

The small chin came up and that soft lip was freed

from white teeth. He saw the tension in her. There was a taut moment when he wasn't sure what she would do. Then, as if realising she had no choice, she raised a small hand and pulled the cap from her head.

For a moment Luc could only stare stupidly as a coil of long, dark red hair fell over her shoulder from where it had been stuffed under the cap.

And then he took in the rest of her face and felt even more foolish. He'd seen countless beautiful women, some of whom were considered to be the most beautiful in the world, but right now they were all an indistinct blur in his memory.

She was stunning. High cheekbones. Flawless creamy pale skin. A straight nose. Huge hazel eyes—flashing green and gold, with long dark lashes. And that mouth, lush and wide.

His body hardened, and the shock of such a reaction to this whippet of a girl made Luc reject the rogue reaction. He did not react to women unless it was on his terms. He was reacting because she was unexpected.

His voice was harsh. 'Now, tell me who you are, or I call the police.'

Nessa burned inwardly from the thorough once-over Barbier had just given her. She felt very exposed without her cap. Exposed to the full impact of him up close. And she couldn't look away. It was as if she were mesmerised by the sun. He was simply…beautiful, in a very raw, masculine way, all hard angles and sharp lines. But his mouth was provocatively sensual—the only softness in that face. It was distracting.

'I'm waiting.'

Nessa flushed, caught out. She diverted her gaze, focusing on a picture of a famous racehorse on the wall behind him. She knew she really didn't have a choice but to give him the information. The alternative was to give it to the Gardaí and, coming from such a small, close-knit community, she knew that word would go around within minutes as to what she had been doing. There was no such thing as privacy or anonymity here.

'My name is Nessa…' She hesitated and then said in a rush, 'O'Sullivan.' She snuck a glance back at Barbier and saw that he was frowning.

'O'Sullivan? You're related to Paddy?'

Nessa nodded miserably at what a disaster this evening's escapade had become. 'I'm his younger sister.'

Barbier took a moment to digest this and then he said, with a curl to his lip, 'He's sending his baby sister to do his dirty work?'

Nessa instantly rose to her brother's defence. 'Paddy is innocent!'

Luc Barbier looked unimpressed by her impassioned outburst. 'He's made a bad situation worse by disappearing, and the facts haven't changed: he facilitated the purchase of a horse from Gio Corretti's Sicilian stud. We received the horse a week ago and the one million euros duly left my account but never reached Corretti's. It's clear that your brother diverted the funds into his own pocket.'

Nessa blanched at the massive amount of money, but she forced herself to stay strong, for Paddy. 'He didn't divert funds. It wasn't his fault. He was hacked—they somehow impersonated the stud manager in Sicily and Paddy sent the money through fully believing it was going to the right place.'

The lines in Barbier's face were as hard as granite. 'If that is the case then why isn't he here to defend himself?'

Nessa refused to let herself crumble in the face of

this man's seriously intimidating stance. 'You told him he would be prosecuted and liable for the full amount. He felt as if he had no choice.'

Paddy's frantic voice came back into her head.

'Ness, you don't know what this guy is capable of. He fired one of the grooms on the spot the other day. There's no such thing as innocent till proven guilty in Barbier's world. He'll chew me up and spit me out! I'll never work in the industry again...'

Barbier's mouth thinned. 'The fact that he fled after that phone conversation only makes him look even guiltier.'

More words of defence sprang to Nessa's lips but she swallowed them back. Trying to explain to this man that her brother had been entangled with the law when he'd gone through a rebellious teenage phase was hardly likely to make him sound less guilty. Paddy had worked long and hard to turn over a new leaf, but he'd been told that if he was ever caught breaking the law again he'd serve time and have a criminal record. *That* was why he'd panicked and run.

Luc Barbier regarded the woman in front of him. The fact that he was still indulging in any kind of dialogue with her was outrageous. And yet her vehemence and clear desire to protect her brother at all costs—even at her own expense—intrigued him. In his experience loyalty was a myth. Everyone was out for their own gain.

Something occurred to him then and he cursed himself for not suspecting it sooner. He'd been too distracted by a fall of thick red hair and a slender frame. It was galling.

'Maybe you're in on it? And you were trying to retrieve the laptop to ensure that any evidence was taken care of?'

Nessa's limbs turned to jelly. 'Of course I'm not in on anything. I just came here because Paddy—' She stopped herself, not wanting to incriminate him further.

'Because Paddy...what?' Barbier asked. 'Was too much of a coward? Or because he's no longer in the country?'

Nessa bit her lip. Paddy had fled to America, to hide out with her twin brother, Eoin. She'd entreated him to come back, tried to assure him that his boss couldn't be such an ogre. Paddy's words floated back.

'No one messes with Barbier. I wouldn't be surprised if he's got criminal links...'

For a moment Nessa had a sickening sensation. What if Barbier really *was* linked to—? She quickly shut that thought down, telling herself she was being melodramatic. But then a sliver of doubt entered her mind— what if Paddy *was* guilty?

As soon as that registered she lambasted herself, aghast that she could have thought it for a second. This man was making her doubt herself, and her brother, who she knew would never do something so wrong, no matter what his trangressions had been in the past.

Nessa's jaw was tight. 'Look. Paddy is innocent. I agree with you that he shouldn't have run, but he has.' She hesitated for a second, and then mentally apologised to her brother before saying, 'He has a habit of running away when difficult things happen—he ran away for a week after our mother's funeral.'

Barbier looked utterly remote and then he said, 'I've heard the Irish have a gift for talking their way out of situations, but it won't work with me, Miss O'Sullivan.'

Anger spiked again. 'I'm not trying to get out of anything.' She forced herself to calm down. 'I was just trying to help by retrieving his laptop. He said that he could prove his innocence with it.'

Barbier picked up the slim silver laptop and held it up. 'We've looked at the laptop extensively and there is no evidence to support your brother's innocence. You've done your brother no favours. He now looks even guiltier and you've possibly implicated yourself.'

Luc watched as colour washed in and out of the woman's expressive face. That in itself was intriguing, when so many people he encountered kept their masks firmly in place. He couldn't recall the last time he'd felt free enough, if ever, to allow his real emotions to be seen.

Still, he wouldn't believe this award-worthy display of innocence. He'd be a fool if he did and her brother had already taken him for a fool.

Nessa sensed any sliver of hope dwindling. Barbier was about as immovable as a rock. He put the laptop down and folded his arms again, settling his hips back against the desk behind him, legs stretched out, for all the world as if they were having a civil chat. There was nothing civil about this man. Danger oozed from every pore: Nessa just wasn't sure what *kind* of danger. She felt no risk to her personal safety, in spite of Paddy's lurid claims or the security man outside the door. It was a much more personal danger, to the place that throbbed with awareness deep inside her. An awareness that had been dormant all her life, until now.

Barbier's tone was mocking. 'So you really expect me to believe that you're here purely out of love for your poor innocent brother?'

Fiercely she said, 'I would do anything for my family.'

'Why?'

Barbier's simple question took her by surprise and Nessa blinked. She hadn't even questioned Paddy when he'd called for help. She'd immediately felt every protective instinct kick into place even though she was younger than him.

Their family was a unit who had come through tough times and become stronger in the process.

Their older sister Iseult had kept them all in one piece—pretty much—after the tragic death of their mother, while their father had descended into the mire of alcoholism. She had shielded Nessa and her two brothers from their father's worst excesses, and had slowly helped him to recovery even as their stud farm and stables had fallen apart around them.

But Iseult wasn't here now. She had a much deserved happy life far away from here. It was up to Nessa to shoulder this burden for the sake of her brother, and her family.

She looked at Barbier. 'I would do anything because we love each other and we protect each other.'

Barbier was silent for a long moment. Then he said, 'So now you're admitting that you'd go so far as to collude in a crime.'

Nessa shivered under the thin covering of her fleece. She felt very alone at that moment. She knew she could contact Sheikh Nadim of Merkazad, Iseult's husband and one of the richest men in the world. He could sort this whole thing out within hours, if he knew. But she and Paddy had agreed they wouldn't involve Iseult or Nadim. They were expecting a baby in a few weeks and did not need to be drawn into this mess.

She squared her shoulders and stared at Luc Barbier, hating his cool nonchalance. 'Don't you understand the concept of family and doing anything for them? Wouldn't you do that for your own family?'

Barbier suddenly looked stony. 'I have no family, so, no, I'm not familiar with the concept.'

A pang of emotion made Nessa's chest tighten. No family. What on earth did that mean? She couldn't fathom the lack of a family. That sense of protection.

Then he said, 'If your family are so close then I will go to whoever *is* capable of returning either your brother or my money.'

Panic eclipsed Nessa's spurt of emotion. 'This just involves me and Paddy.'

Barbier raised a brow. 'I will involve whoever and whatever it takes to get my money back and ensure no adverse press results from this.'

Nessa's hands clenched to fists at her sides as she tried to contain her temper and appeal to any sense of decency he might have. 'Look, not that it's any business of yours, but my sister is going to have a baby very soon. My father is helping her and her husband and they don't have anything to do with this. I'm taking responsibility for my brother.'

I'm taking responsibility for my brother.

There had been a tight ball of emotion in Luc's chest ever since she'd asked if he understood the concept of family. Of course he didn't. How could he when his Algerian father had disappeared before he was born, and his feckless, unstable mother had died of a drugs overdose when he was just sixteen?

The closest he'd ever come to family was the old man next door—a man broken by life, and yet who had been the one to show Luc a way out.

Luc forced his mind away from the memories. He was beyond incredulous that this sprite of a girl—*woman*—was insisting on standing up to him. And that she wasn't using her beauty to try and distract him, especially when he couldn't be sure that he'd hidden his reaction to her. He hated to admit it, even to himself, but he felt a twinge of respect.

She was defiant, even in the face of possible prosecution. If she was calling his bluff she was doing it very, very well. He could still have the police here within minutes and she would be hauled off in handcuffs with the full weight of his legal team raining down on her narrow shoulders before she knew what was happening.

But it wasn't as if the police were ever first on Luc's list of people to turn to in this kind of situation. Not because he had more nefarious routes to keeping the law—he knew about the rumours surrounding him, and as much as they amused him, they also disgusted him—but because of his experiences growing up in the gritty outskirts of Paris. Surviving each day had been a test of endurance. The police had never been there when he'd needed them, so to say he didn't trust them was an understatement.

He liked to take care of things his own way. Hence the rumours. Added on top of more rumours. Until he was more myth than man.

He forced his mind back to the task at hand. And the woman. 'Where do we go from here, then, Miss O'Sullivan? If you're prepared to take responsibility for your brother, then perhaps you could be so kind as to write me a cheque for one million euros?'

Nessa blanched. One million euros was more money than she was ever likely to see in her lifetime, unless her career as a jockey took off and people started giving her a chance to ride in big races and build her reputation.

She said, as firmly as she could, 'We don't have that kind of money.'

'Well then,' Barbier said silkily, 'that gets us precisely no further along in this situation. And in fact it gets worse. Thanks to your brother's actions, I will now have to hand over another one million euros to Gio Corretti to ensure that he doesn't ask questions about why he hasn't received the money yet.'

Nessa felt sick. She hadn't considered that. 'Maybe you could talk to him? Explain what happened?'

Barbier laughed but it was curt and unamused. 'I don't need to fuel the gossip mill with stories that I'm now claiming fraud to renege on payments.'

Nessa wanted to sit down. Her legs were wobbly again and she felt light-headed.

'Are you all right?' Barbier's sharp question was like a slap to her face. She sucked in a deep breath. He'd taken a step towards her and suddenly the room felt even smaller. He was massive. And so dark. Possibly the most intimidating person she'd ever met.

She couldn't fight this man. He was too rich, too successful. Too gorgeous. She swallowed. 'I wish I could hand you over your money right now, Mr Barbier, believe me. But I can't. I know my brother is innocent no matter what his actions look like.'

Nessa wracked her brains as to what she could do to appease Barbier so he wouldn't go after Paddy. At least until Paddy had a chance to try and prove his innocence. But what could she offer this man? And then something struck her. 'Look, all I can do is offer my services in his absence. If you have *me*, then can't you accept that I'm willing to do all I can to prove his innocence?'

For a moment, Nessa's words hung in the air and she almost fancied that she might have got through to him. But then he straightened from the desk and the expression on his face darkened. He spat out, 'I should have known that veneer of innocence was too good to be true.'

That unnervingly black gaze raked her up and down, disdain etched all over his face. 'I must admit, I might have felt differently if you'd come via the front door dressed in something a little more enticing, Miss O'Sullivan, but even then I can't say that you'd be my type.'

Nessa struggled to understand—he couldn't possibly mean…but then she registered what she'd said and how it might have sounded. And, she registered that he was looking at her with disgust, not disdain. Her gut curdled as a wave of mortification rushed through her whole body, along with hurt, which made it even worse. She burned with humiliation and fury.

'You know I did not mean *that*.'

He raised an imperious brow. 'What did you mean, Miss O'Sullivan?'

Nessa had started to pace in her agitation and she stopped and faced him. 'Please stop calling me that— my name is Nessa.'

His voice was hard. *'Nessa.'*

The way he said her name impacted her physically, like a punch to her gut. She instantly regretted opening her mouth but *Miss O'Sullivan* was beginning to get under her skin. This man. This…*meeting*…was veering so far off course that she wasn't even sure what they were talking about any more, or what was at stake.

She tried to force herself to stay focused, and calm. 'What I meant, Mr Barbier, is that I will do everything in my power to convince you that my brother is innocent.'

CHAPTER TWO

LUC STARED AT Nessa O'Sullivan.

I will do everything in my power to convince you that my brother is innocent.

What kind of an empty suggestion was that? And why had it given him such an illicit thrill to see her act so shocked when he'd called her bluff? She'd blatantly offered herself to him—and then pretended that she hadn't!

He wanted to laugh out loud. As if she were an innocent. There was no innocence in this world. Perhaps only in babies, before they grew up to be twisted and manipulated by their environment.

His conscience smarted to think of how he'd told her she wasn't his type. He couldn't deny the pounding of his blood right now. He told himself it was anger. Adrenalin. Anything but helpless desire.

Luc knew he should have walked away long ago and left her at the mercy of the authorities, no matter what he thought of them. He had enough evidence now to damn her, and her brother. But he knew that wasn't necessarily the best option. Not for *him*.

She was staring at him, as if bracing herself for whatever he was going to say. She was throwing up more questions than answers and it had been a long time since anyone had piqued Luc's interest like this.

What did he have to lose if he contained this himself? It wasn't as if the local law enforcement could do any better than the private security company he'd already hired to investigate the matter and track down Paddy O'Sullivan.

One thing was clear. This woman wasn't going to be walking away from here. He didn't trust her. Not one inch of her petite form. Not after he'd seen how far she was prepared to go. And she wasn't going anywhere until he had his money returned and he knew there was no damage to his reputation. If she was involved in this crime, then keeping her close would surely lead him back to the thief.

He folded his arms and saw the way her body tensed, as if to steel herself. In that moment she looked both defiant and vulnerable, and it caught at Luc somewhere he wasn't usually affected. More acting. It had to be. He would not allow her to make a fool of him.

'You say you want to convince me your brother is innocent?'

Nessa still felt sick to think that Barbier had taken her words to mean that she was offering herself up, like some kind of— She forced the thought out of her head. Of course this man would never look at someone like her in that way, but she didn't need to be humiliated.

She tipped up her chin. 'Yes.'

He was looking at her with unnerving intensity. She really couldn't read him at all. Her mouth felt dry and instinctively she licked her lips. His gaze dropped to them for a second and her insides flipped. She ignored it, telling herself her reaction to him was due to the heightened situation.

His eyes met hers again. 'Very well, then. You're not leaving my sight until your brother accounts for his actions and my money is returned.'

Nessa opened her mouth but nothing came out for a moment. Then she said, 'What do you mean, not leaving your sight?'

'Exactly that. You've offered your services in place of your brother, so until he or my money returns you're mine, Nessa O'Sullivan, and you will do exactly as I tell you.'

Nessa struggled to comprehend his words. 'So you're going to hold me as some kind of…collateral? As a prisoner?'

He smiled but it was mirthless. 'Oh, you're quite free to walk out this door, but you won't make it to your car before the police catch up with you. If you want me to believe that you have nothing to do with this, *and* that your brother is innocent, then you will stay here and do your utmost to make yourself useful.'

'How do you know about my car?' Nessa asked, distracted for a moment and not liking the way panic had her insides in a vice grip.

'You were tracked as soon as you parked that heap of junk outside my perimeter wall.'

Fresh humiliation washed over Nessa to think of her stealthy progress being watched in some security room. 'I didn't hear any alarms.'

He dismissed that with a curl of his lip. 'Security here is silent and state of the art. Flashing lights and sirens would unsettle the horses.'

Of course it would. Hadn't Nadim insisted on installing a similarly high-tech system on their own farm?

Nessa searched in vain for some way to avoid being forced to spend an unknown amount of time under this man's punitive command, even though she'd all but asked for it. 'I'm a jockey and I work at our family farm—I can't just walk away from that.'

Barbier's black gaze flicked dismissively over her body again before meeting her eyes. 'A jockey? Then how have I never heard of you?'

Nessa flushed. 'I haven't run many races. Yet.' In recent years she'd gone to university and got a degree, so that had taken her out of the circuit for some time. Not that she was about to explain herself to Barbier.

He made a scathing sound. 'I'm sure. Being a jockey is gritty, hard work. You look as if a puff of wind would knock you over. Somehow I can't really see you rousing at dawn and putting in a long day of the back-breaking training and work that most jockeys endure. Your pretty hands would get far too dirty.'

Nessa bristled and instinctively hid her hands behind her back, conscious of how *un*pretty they were, but not wanting to show Barbier, even in her own defence. She still felt raw after his stinging remark, *I can't say that you'd be my type.*

The unfairness of his attack left her a little speechless. Her family had all worked hard at their farm for as long as she could remember, getting up at the crack of dawn every day of the week and in all kinds of weather. Her family had certainly never lived a gilded life of leisure. Not even when Nadim had bought them out and pumped money into their ailing business.

'Who do you ride for, then?'

She forced down the surge in emotion and answered as coolly as she could, 'My family stables, O'Sullivans. I'm well used to doing my share of the work, believe it or not, and I've been training to be a jockey since I was a teenager. Just because I'm a woman—'

He held up a hand stopping her. 'I have no issue with female jockeys. What I do have an issue with are people who get a free pass on their family connections.'

If Nessa had bristled before, now she was positively apoplectic. She'd had to work twice as hard to prove herself to her own family, if not even more. But she was aware that to really prove herself she'd have to get work with another trainer. It was a sensitive point for her.

'I can assure you,' she said in a low voice full of emotion, 'that my being a jockey is not a vanity project. Far from it.'

She might have laughed if she were able to. Vanity—what was that? She couldn't remember the last time she'd worn make-up.

Barbier looked unimpressed. 'Well, I'm sure the family farm will cope without you.'

Nessa realised that she was damned if she walked out the door and and damned if she didn't. But there was only one way of containing the situation and making sure that the rest of her family weren't dragged into it, and that was doing as Barbier said. She wished she could rewind the clock and be safe at home in bed...but even as she imagined that scenario something inside her rejected it. Rejected the possibility of never having had the opportunity to see this man up close. The shock of that revelation made her stop breathing for a second, its significance terrifying to contemplate.

But the fact was that Nessa's blood was throbbing through her veins in a way she'd never experienced before. Not even after an exhilarating win on a horse.

Shame bloomed deep inside her. How could she betray her own brother, her family, like this? By finding this man so…compelling? Telling herself that stress was making her crazy, she asked, 'What will I be doing here?' She tried to quash lurid images of herself, locked in a tower being fed only bread and water.

Barbier's eyes flicked up and down over her body as if gauging what she might be capable of. Nessa bristled all over, again.

'Oh, don't worry, we'll find something to keep you occupied, and of course any work you do will be in lieu of payment. Until your brother resurfaces, his debt is now yours.'

Barbier straightened up to his full intimidating height and Nessa's pulse jumped.

'I will have Armand escort you back to your home to retrieve what you need. You can give me your car keys.'

This was really happening. And there was nothing she could do about it. Nessa reluctantly reached into her pocket for her keys and took the car key off the main ring, all fingers and thumbs. Eventually she got it free, skin prickling under the laser-eyed scrutiny of Barbier.

She handed it over, a little devil inside her prompting her to say, 'It's a vintage Mini. I doubt you'll fit.' Even the thought of this man coiling his six-foot-plus frame into her tiny battered car was failing to spark any humour in the surreal moment. She really hadn't expected the night to turn out like this…and yet she could see now that she'd been supremely naive to assume it would be so easy to infiltrate the Barbier stud.

He took the key. 'It won't be me retrieving your car.'

Of course. It would be a minion, despatched to take care of the belongings of the woman who was now effectively under house arrest for the foreseeable future.

Not usually given to dramatics, Nessa tried to quell her nerves. She was within five kilometres of her own home, for crying out loud. What was the worst this man could do to her? A small sly voice answered that the worst he could do had nothing to do with punishment for Paddy's sins, and everything to do with how he made her feel in his presence. As if she were on a roller coaster hurtling towards a great swooping dip.

Barbier turned away and opened the office door to reveal the huge burly man still standing outside. They spoke in French so rapid that it was beyond Nessa's basic grasp of the language to try and understand what they were saying.

Barbier turned back to her, switching to English. 'Armand will escort you home to collect your things and bring you back here.'

'Can't I just return in the morning?'

He shook his head, looking even more stern now, and indicated for her to precede him. Mutely, Nessa stepped over the threshold and followed the thick-set security man back out the way she'd come. In the courtyard there was a sleek four-by-four car waiting. Armand opened a car door for her.

For a second Nessa hesitated. She saw the entrance to the courtyard and a glimpse of freedom, if she moved fast. From behind her she heard a deep voice. 'Don't even think about it.'

She turned around. Barbier was right behind her and looked even more intimidating in the dark. Taller, more austere. His face was all hard bones and slashing angles. Not even the softness of that provocative mouth visible.

Nessa put her hand on the car door, needing something to hold onto. 'What happens when I come back?'

'You'll be informed when you do.'

Panic made her blurt out, 'What if I refuse?'

She saw the gallic shrug. 'It's up to you but you've

made it clear you don't want to involve your family. If you refuse to return I can guarantee that *that* will be the least of your worries. You would be an accessory to a crime.'

Nessa shivered again in the cool, night-time air. She had no choice, and he knew it. Defeated, she turned and stepped up into the vehicle, and the door closed behind her.

The windows were tinted and Nessa was enclosed in blackness as the bodyguard came around the front of the vehicle and got into the driver's seat. Barbier strode away from them towards the main building and she felt suddenly bereft, which was ridiculous when the man was holding her to ransom for her brother. *You put yourself up for that ransom*, a voice reminded her.

As they approached the main gates Nessa reluctantly gave Armand directions to her own home. They passed her lonely-looking car on the side of the road and she sucked in a deep breath, telling herself that if she could endeavour to persuade Paddy to return to prove his innocence, and prevent anyone else from getting involved, then this—hopefully!—brief punishment at the hands of Barbier would be worth it.

Nessa tried to call up her usually positive disposition. Surely if Barbier saw how far she was willing to go to prove her brother's innocence, he'd be forced to reconsider and give Paddy a chance to explain, wouldn't he?

But why was it that that seemed to hold less appeal than the thought of seeing Luc Barbier again? Nessa scowled at herself in the reflection of the tinted window of the car, glad she wasn't under that black-eyed gaze when her face got hot with humiliation.

When Nessa returned a short while later the stud was in darkness and quiet. Armand handed her over to a middle-aged man with a nice face who looked as if he'd just been woken up, and he was not all that welcoming. He introduced himself as Pascal Blanc, Barbier's stud and racing stables manager, his right-hand man, and Paddy's one-time immediate boss.

He said nothing at first, showing her to a small spartan room above the stables. Clearly this was where the most menial staff slept. But still, it was clean and comfortable, when Nessa had almost expected a corner of the stables.

After giving her the basics of the Barbier stud schedule and informing her that, naturally, she would be assigned to mucking out the yard and stables, and to expect a five a.m. wake-up call, he stopped at her door. 'For what it's worth, I would have given Paddy the benefit of the doubt based on what I thought I knew of him. We might have been able to get to the bottom of this whole nasty incident. But he ran, and now there's nothing I can do except hope for his sake and yours that he either returns himself or returns the money. Soon.'

Nessa couldn't say anything.

Pascal's mouth compressed. 'Luc… Mr Barbier… does not take kindly to those who betray him. He comes from a world where the rule of law didn't exist and he doesn't suffer fools, Miss O'Sullivan. If your brother *is* guilty, then Luc won't be gentle with him. Or you.'

Somehow these words coming from this infinitely less intimidating man made everything even bleaker. But all Nessa could find herself doing was asking, 'You've known Mr Barbier for long?'

Pascal nodded. 'Ever since he started to work with Leo Fouret, the first time he came into contact with a horse.'

Nessa was impressed. Leo Fouret was one of the most respected trainers in racing, with hundreds of impressive race wins to his name.

'Luc didn't grow up in a kind world, Miss O'Sullivan. But he is fair. Unfortunately your brother never gave him that chance.'

Luc didn't grow up in a kind world... The words reverberated in Nessa's head for a long time after she'd been left alone in the room. She eventually fell into a fitful sleep and had dreams of riding a horse, trying to go faster and faster—not to get to the finish line but to escape from some terrifying and unnamed danger behind her.

What on earth did she have to laugh about? Luc was distinctly irritated by the faint lyrical sound emanating from his stableyard, which was usually a place of hushed industry in deference to the valuable livestock. It could only be coming from one person, the newest addition to his staff: Nessa O'Sullivan.

Her brother had stolen from him and now she laughed. It sent the very insidious thought into Luc's head that he'd been a total fool. Of course she was in on it with her brother and now she was inside the camp. It made him think of the Trojan Horse and he didn't find it amusing.

He cursed and threw down his pen and stood up from his desk, stalking over to the window that looked down over the stables. He couldn't see her and that irritated him even more when he'd deliberately avoided meeting her since her arrival, not wanting to give her the idea that their extended dialogue the other night would ever be repeated. Now he was distracted. When he couldn't afford to be distracted.

He'd only just managed to convince Gio Corretti that the slight delay in money arriving to his account was due to a banking glitch.

Luc's reputation amongst the exclusive thorough-bred racing fraternity had been on trial since he'd exploded onto the scene with a rogue three-year-old who had raced to glory in four consecutive Group One races.

Success didn't mean respect though. He was an anomaly; he had no lineage to speak of and he'd had the temerity to invest wisely with his winnings and make himself a fortune in the process.

Everyone believed his horses were better bred than he was, and they weren't far wrong. The rumours about his background merely added colour to every other misconception and untruth heaped against his name.

But, as much as he loved ruffling the elite's feathers by making no apology for who he was, he *did* want their respect. He wanted them to respect him for what he had achieved with nothing but an innate talent, hard work and determination.

The last thing he needed was for more rumours to get around, especially one suggesting that Luc Barbier couldn't control his own staff. That he'd been stupid enough to let one million euros disappear from his account.

Even now he still felt the burn of recrimination for finding Paddy O'Sullivan's open expression and infectious enthusiasm somehow quaint. He should have spotted a thief a mile away. After all, he'd grown up with them.

Luc tensed when he heard the faint sound of laughing again. Adrenalin mixed with something far more ambiguous and hotter flooded his veins. Nessa O'Sullivan was here under sufferance for her brother—and that was all. The sooner she remembered her place and what was at stake, the better.

'Who were you talking to?'

Nessa immediately tensed when she heard the deep voice behind her. She turned around reluctantly, steeling herself to see Barbier for the first time since that night. And she blinked.

The skies were blue and the air was mild but, in that uniquely Irish way, there seemed to be a mist falling from the sky and tiny droplets clung to Barbier's black hair and shoulders, making him look as if he were… sparkling.

His hands were placed on lean hips. Dark worn jeans clung to powerful thighs and long legs. He was wearing a dark polo shirt. The muscles of his biceps pushed against the short sleeves, and the musculature of his impressive chest was visible under the thin material.

He couldn't look more virile or vitally masculine if he tried. Nessa's body hummed in helpless reaction to that very earthy and basic fact.

'Well?'

Nessa was aghast at how she'd just lost it there for a second, hypnotised by his sheer presence.

She swallowed. 'I was just talking to one of the grooms.'

'You do realise you're not here to socialise, don't you, O'Sullivan?'

Tendrils of Nessa's hair escaped the hasty bun she'd piled on her head earlier, and whipped around her face in the breeze. Her skin prickled at her reaction to him and irritation made her voice sharp. 'It's hard to forget when I've been assigned little more than a cell to sleep in and a pre-dawn wake-up call every day.'

She was very conscious of the unsubtle stench of horse manure clinging to her. And of her worn T-shirt tucked into even more worn jeans. Ancient knee-high boots. She couldn't be any less his *type* right now.

A calculating glint turned his eyes to dark pewter. 'You assured me you were accustomed to hard work and you did offer your services in the place of your brother—if this is too much for you…' He put out a hand to encompass the yard around them.

Nessa stiffened at the obvious jibe. He was clearly expecting her to flounce out of here in a fit of pique. And yes, the work was menial but it was nothing she hadn't done since she'd started walking and could hold a broom. That, and riding horses. Not that he'd believe her.

She squared her shoulders and stared him down. 'If you don't mind, the yard has to be cleaned by lunchtime.'

Barbier looked at the heavy platinum watch encircling his wrist, and then back to her. 'You'd better keep going then, and next time don't distract my employees from their own work. Flirting and gossiping won't help your brother out of his predicament or make things any easier for you here.'

Flirting? For a second Nessa's mind was blank with indignation when she thought of the groom she'd been talking to—a man in his sixties. But before she could think of anything to say in her own defence, Barbier had turned his back and was walking away.

In spite of her indignation, Nessa couldn't stop her gaze following his broad back, seeing how it tapered down to those slim hips and a taut behind, lovingly outlined by the soft worn material of his jeans. He disappeared around a corner and Nessa deflated like a balloon. She turned around in disgust at herself for being so easily distracted, and riled.

Feeling thoroughly prickly and with her nerves still jangling, Nessa turned the power-hose machine back on and imagined Barbier's too-beautiful and smug face in every scrap of dirt she blasted into the drains.

'She's totally over-qualified, Luc. She's putting my own staff to shame, doing longer hours. I shouldn't even be saying this but the yard and stables have never been so clean.' Luc's head groom laughed but soon stopped when Luc fixed him with a dark look.

'No, you shouldn't. Maybe you need new staff.'

Simon Corrigan swallowed and changed the subject. 'Can I ask why we're not paying her? It seems—'

'No, you can't.' Luc cut him off, not liking the way his conscience was stinging. He was many things, but no one had ever faulted him on his sense of fairness and equality. But only he and Pascal Blanc knew what was behind Paddy O'Sullivan's sudden disappearance, and he wanted to keep it that way.

Nessa had been working at his stables for a week now. She hadn't turned tail and run or had a tantrum as he'd expected. He could still see her in his mind's eye— standing in the yard the other day, her back as straight as a dancer, face flushed, amber-green eyes bright and alive. That soft lush mouth compressed. Long tendrils of dark red hair clinging to her hot cheeks as she'd obviously struggled to keep her temper in check.

Her T-shirt had been so worn he could make out the shape of her breasts—small, lush swells, high and firm.

He could also remember the feeling that had swept

through him when he'd heard her carefree laugh. It hadn't been anger that she might be up to something. It had been something much hotter and ambiguous; a sense of possessiveness that had shocked him. It wasn't something he felt for anything much, except horses or business acquisitions.

'Where is she now?' Luc asked Corrigan abruptly.

'She's helping to bring the stallions in from the paddocks. Do you want me to give her a message?'

Luc shook his head. 'No, I'll do it.'

But when Luc got to the stallions' stables Nessa was nowhere to be seen and all the stallions had been settled for the evening. Feeling a mounting frustration, he went looking for her.

'You are a beautiful boy, aren't you? Yes, you are… and you know it too. Yes, there you go…' The three-year-old colt whinnied softly in appreciation as he took the raw carrot from Nessa's hand and she rubbed his nose.

She knew she shouldn't be here in the racing section of Barbier's stables, where the current thoroughbreds resided, but she hadn't been able to resist. She felt at peace for the first time in days, even as her body actually ached with the need to feel a horse underneath her with all that coiled power and strength and speed. But she wouldn't be riding again for a while.

'You were told to stay away from this area.'

And just like that Nessa's short-lived sense of peace vanished and was replaced by an all-too predictable jump in her heart-rate. She turned around to see Barbier standing a few feet away, arms folded. He was wearing a white shirt, and it made his skin look even darker. His hair touched the collar, curling slightly.

'I'm on a break,' she responded defensively, wondering if he was this autocratic with all his employees. But she had to admit that, so far, everyone seemed pretty content to be working here. She'd found out that the employee who'd been fired on the spot had been smoking weed and she'd had to concede that he would have suffered a similar fate on their own stud farm. Barbier had also enrolled the employee on an addiction course. It was disconcerting to realise that perhaps he wasn't as ruthless as she'd like to believe.

Barbier moved now and closed the distance between them before she could take another breath. He snatched the rest of the carrot out of her hand, frowning. 'What are you feeding Tempest?'

'It's just a carrot.' She pulled her hand back into her chest disconcerted by the shock his fleeting touch had given her.

He glared at her, and he was far too close, but Nessa's back was against the stall door and the horse. She was trapped.

'No one is allowed to feed my horses unless they're supervised.'

Her mouth dropped open and then she sputtered, 'It's just a carrot!'

He was grim. 'A carrot that could contain poison or traces of steroids for all I know.'

Nessa went cold. 'You think I would harm your horses?'

His jaw was as hard as granite. 'I'm under enough scrutiny as it is. I don't need the possible accomplice of a thief messing around with my valuable livestock. I don't know what you're capable of. How did you know that this is the horse?'

Nessa struggled to keep up. '*What* horse?'

Now Barbier was impatient. 'The horse I bought from Gio Corretti.'

Nessa swallowed. 'I had no idea, I just came in for a visit. He seemed agitated.'

Barbier's gaze went from her to the horse behind her and she took the opportunity to slide sideways, putting some distance between them. He put out a hand and stroked the side of Tempest's neck, murmuring soft words in French. Nessa's gaze locked onto his big hand stroking the horse, and she had to struggle not to imagine how that hand might feel on her. She'd never in her life imagined a man stroking her—she must be losing her mind.

The horse pushed his head into Barbier's hand and Nessa glanced at Barbier to see his features relax slightly. For a heady moment she imagined that there was no enmity between them and that he might not always look at her as if she'd just committed a crime. She wondered what he'd look like if he smiled and then she glanced away quickly, mortified at herself and afraid he would read her shameful thoughts on her face.

Barbier said, 'He's been agitated since he arrived, not settling in properly.'

Welcoming the diversion from her wayward imagination, Nessa replied, 'He's probably just pining for his mother.'

Barbier looked at her sharply, his hand dropping away. 'How would you know such a thing?'

Nessa flushed and kept avoiding his eye. How could she explain the weird affinity for horses that she shared with her sister and father? She shrugged. 'I just guessed.'

Barbier's voice was harsh. 'Gio Corretti told me and your brother that we might have issues settling the colt because he hadn't been separated from his mother until recently, which is unusual. That's how you know.'

Nessa looked at Barbier and saw the condemnation and distrust in his eyes. How could she defend a gut feeling? She shrugged and looked away. 'If you say so.'

Without realising it, Nessa's hand had instinctively lifted up to touch the horse again, until suddenly Barbier reached out and took it. Nessa jumped at the weird electricity that sparked whenever they got too close. She tried to pull her hand back but his grip was too firm. And warm.

He was holding her palm facing upwards, and asked grimly, 'What is this?'

She looked down and saw what he saw: her very *un*pretty hands, skin roughened from her training as a jockey and blistered from the last few days of hard work. Humiliated at the thought that he'd see this as proof she wasn't used to work, she yanked her hand back and cradled it to her chest again. 'It's nothing.'

She backed away towards the entrance. 'I should go—my break is over.' She turned and forced herself to walk and not run away, not even sure what she was running from. But something about the way he'd just taken her hand and looked so disapproving to see the marks of her labour made her feel incredibly self-conscious and also a little emotional, which was truly bizarre.

Nessa couldn't recall the last time anyone had focused attention on her like that. Her sister had done her best but she wasn't their mother. Their father hadn't been much use while he'd drowned his sorrows.

So they'd had to fend for themselves mostly. She hadn't even realised until that moment how much another's touch could pierce her right to the core. And for it to have been Luc Barbier was inconceivable and very disturbing. She didn't have an emotional connection with that man—the very notion was ridiculous.

Luc watched as Nessa walked quickly out of the stables and around the corner with an easy athletic grace that made him wonder what she'd be like on a horse. *Excellent*, his instincts told him, as much as he'd like to ignore them.

He was still astounded at the apparent ease with which she'd calmed Tempest, who was one of the most volatile horses Luc had ever bought. But also potentially one of the best, if his hunch about the colt's lineage was right. Certainly Gio Corretti had asked for top dollar, so he'd clearly suspected potential greatness too.

Luc turned back to the horse, who pushed his face into Luc's shoulder, nudging. Did Luc really believe Nessa would poison the horse? He held up the innocuous, gnarled carrot and eventually fed it to the horse with a sigh.

The answer came from his gut: no, she wouldn't poison his horse. She'd looked too shocked when he'd said it. But the fact was that, until her brother reappeared or the money did, the jury was out on Nessa O'Sullivan and he had to keep her under close scrutiny. He'd be a fool not to suspect that brother and sister were working in tandem.

Luc told himself it was for this reason, and *not* because her raw hands had twisted something inside his gut, that he was about to move her to where she could be kept under closer scrutiny.

CHAPTER THREE

'I'M MOVING YOU out of the stables and into the house.'

Nessa looked at Luc Barbier where he stood behind his desk. She'd been summoned here a few minutes ago by the head groom, Simon Corrigan, and she'd tried not to let the understated luxury of the grand old Irish country house intimidate her.

This was where Barbier's suite of private offices were based and now she stood on thick sumptuous carpet and was surrounded by dark oak panelling. Books filled floor-to-ceiling shelves. In contrast to the rather conservative decor, there was modern art on the walls that tickled at Nessa's curiosity. And behind Barbier, a massive window where Nessa could see the training gallops in the distance. An amazing view and one that made her yearn to be on a horse.

But she dragged her attention back to what he'd said. 'Excuse me?'

'I said, I'm moving you into the house.' He enunciated the words slowly, which only made his accent more noticeable. Nessa still couldn't get over the raw, untameable energy that emanated from the man, in spite of the luxe surroundings.

She felt a bit dense. 'Why?'

'My housekeeper has lost one of her household assistants and so I told her you would fill in.'

'Household assistant,' Nessa said slowly as it sank in. 'You mean a cleaner?'

Barbier grimaced faintly. 'I think they prefer the term household assistant.'

A faint burn of humiliation washed up through her body. 'This is because I went to see your racehorses.'

Barbier's jaw tightened. 'I'm not so petty.'

Nessa thought of being cooped up indoors cleaning floors and already felt claustrophobic. 'You accused me of potential sabotage.'

Barbier's jaw got even tighter. 'At this point in time I have no idea what you're capable of. You've put yourself in this position in a bid to convince me your brother is innocent. Mrs Owens, my housekeeper, needs someone to help her out—'

'And I'm just the handy house-arrest guest you can move about at will to wherever it suits you,' Nessa interrupted, feeling frustrated and angry.

'You're the one who is here by choice, Nessa. By all means you're free to walk out this door at any time, but if you do I won't hesitate to involve the local police.'

Nessa tipped up her chin, feeling reckless. 'So why don't you do it, then? Just call them!'

Barbier didn't look remotely fazed at her outburst. 'Because,' he said easily, 'I don't believe it serves either of our interests to involve the law at this point. Do you really want to drag your family name into the open and inform everyone of what your brother has done?'

Nessa went cold inside when she thought of the lines of pain already etched into her father's face. Indelible lines that would never fade even in spite of his much better mental state. She thought of Iseult's frantic worry and her husband, Nadim, who would undoubtedly storm in to take over—just weeks before their baby was due.

Nessa looked at the man in front of her and hated him at that moment. Hated the way he was able to hold her to ransom so easily, and then that hatred turned inwards. She only had herself to blame. And Paddy.

She had taken responsibility and she couldn't crumble now.

She forced down an awful feeling of futility and said, 'No, I don't want anyone to know what has happened. If I stay and do as you ask, can you promise that you won't report what Paddy has done?'

Barbier inclined his head slightly. 'Like I said, it serves us both to keep this to ourselves for the time being.'

Nessa wondered why he was so reluctant to let this get out, but then she realised that he would hardly like it to be known that payment for a horse had gone astray. It would put off potential sellers everywhere.

For a fleeting moment Nessa considered threatening to leak this news in return for Barbier's assurance that Paddy wouldn't be prosecuted. But she realised, without even testing him, that Barbier was not a man who could be so easily manipulated.

Apart from which, she didn't have the stomach for blackmail, and there would be no way that Paddy's reputation could remain unsullied. He might never get the chance to prove his innocence, and with the stain of possible theft and corruption on his record he'd never get a job in the industry he loved again. It would ruin him. Not to mention the disappointment of their father and sister...

As if privy to her thoughts, Barbier said, 'You're the only insurance Paddy has at the moment. His only guarantee of any kind of protection. You walk out of here and that's gone, along with any sliver of doubt I may have about his guilt.'

Nessa's heart thumped hard at that. So there *was* a chance that Barbier might believe in Paddy, if she could just convince him to return and explain what had happened. She had to cling onto that.

Not even sure what she wanted to say but wanting to capitalise on any sliver of mercy she could, she started, 'Mr Barbier—'

'It's Luc,' he cut her off. 'I don't stand on ceremony with anyone, not even a suspected thief.'

He didn't trust her as far as he could throw her, yet he would still allow her to call him by his first name. Nessa didn't like how his bad opinion of her affected her. She'd never done a dishonest thing in her life— apart from creeping onto this property on that fateful night.

She told herself that she just didn't like anyone thinking badly of her—and that Barbier's opinion of her wasn't important. But that felt like a lie.

'Fine, I'll work in the house.'

The corner of his mouth tipped up ever so slightly in a mocking smile. 'I like how you give yourself the illusion of having a choice.'

Nessa controlled her facial expression, not wanting to let him know how much he got to her. 'Was that all?'

Now he looked slightly frustrated, as if he'd expected something else from her. After a moment he just said coolly, 'Yes, Mrs Owens will send for you and show you what she needs. You'll move into one of the staff bedrooms here.'

So she was to be completely removed from the realm of the stud farm and racing stables. Her heart contracted at the thought of being away from the horses, but at the same time an illicit fizz started in her body at the realisation that she'd be sleeping under the same roof as Barbier—*Luc*.

She'd never be able to say his name out loud; it felt far too intimate.

And not that she'd even see him, she assured herself. Not that she *wanted* to see him! She'd probably be confined to cleaning bathrooms and vacuuming hallways. Nessa left his office with as much dignity as she could muster.

En route back to her own quarters, she diverted and went to the paddocks where the stallions idly grazed the lush grass.

One of the huge beasts came over and whinnied, pushing his face into Nessa's shoulder. She dutifully pulled out the ubiquitous carrot she always carried and fed it to him, stroking his soft nose and feeling ridiculously at sea.

Being sequestered indoors and kept away from the bucolic expanse and the animals was more of a punishment than mucking out stableyards and stables ever could be. But Nessa couldn't convince herself that Barbier was doing it out of spite. He really didn't seem that petty.

Instead, she couldn't stop thinking about how he'd taken her hand in his and looked at her rough skin so fiercely the other day. She'd felt self-conscious ever since then. She curled her hands inwards now and shoved them back into her pockets, backing away from the horse.

As she walked back to the main buildings she told herself it was ridiculous to imagine for a second that Barbier had moved her away from the stables for any other reason than just because she was bound to serve out her time here however he willed it.

The man couldn't care less about her labour-worn hands, and, anyway, hot soapy water and housework were hardly going to be any less taxing or more gentle! She just had to get on with it and make the best of this situation until they could prove Paddy's innocence.

It took a long time for the heat in Luc's body to die down after Nessa had left his office. He'd had to battle the urge to push his desk aside and take that stubborn chin in his thumb and forefinger, tipping it up so that she presented her lush mouth to his. Silencing her in a way that would be unbelievably satisfying.

It was confounding. And irritating as hell. Especially as she was wearing nothing more provocative than a worn T-shirt, jeans and boots, hair pulled back in a messy ponytail and no make-up. Yet there was something very earthy and sensual about her that made her all woman.

That, and the defiant tilt of her jaw and the look in her eyes, effortlessly enflamed him. He had the same impulse when he was around her that he had with an unbroken horse. A desire to tame it, and make it bend to his will.

He'd never before become so interested in one woman. Women had never enthralled Luc beyond the initial attraction, and it usually waned quickly. He'd be the first to admit his experience of women hadn't been the most rounded. His mother had shown only the briefest moments of motherly love, before her addictions had swallowed her whole.

The girls in his milieu had been as gritty and tough as him, broken by their surroundings and circumstances. And if they weren't broken then they got out and went far away, exactly as he had done.

Sometimes, the women who frequented the social sphere he now inhabited reminded him of the girls and women of his youth. They were hard and gritty too, but hid it under a shiny, expensive sheen.

But Nessa was none of those things, which intrigued him in spite of his best instincts. And she was out of bounds, for many reasons, not least of which was her suspected collusion with her brother.

He knew without arrogance that she was attracted to him. He saw it in her over-bright eyes and pink cheeks, her taut body that quivered slightly in his presence. He felt fairly sure she must know that he was attracted to her—in spite of his words that first night. *I can't say that you'd be my type.* Apparently she was.

Yet she wasn't testing him by using their chemistry to try and leverage any advantage. He didn't think a woman existed who wouldn't. Unless she was playing some game. *That* was far more probable.

He stood at his window now, the view encompassing the gallops in the distance where his thoroughbreds were being exercised, and the stud farm just out of sight on the other side.

He had both sides of the industry here—racing and breeding. It gave him immense satisfaction to see it all laid out before him, except today, for the first time, there was a slight dilution of that satisfaction. As if something had taken the sheen off it. As if something was reminding him that he hadn't made it yet. Not really.

Luc scowled. He knew he hadn't made it yet, not completely. No matter how many winners he had or sired with his stallions.

He wouldn't have made it until he was respected by

his peers, and not looked at with varying degrees of suspicion.

It was the only fulfilment he wanted. He had no desire for the things most normal people wanted—family, security, love. What was love anyway? It was a foreign concept to Luc that came far too close to believing in trust, and such notions as fate and chance.

He couldn't understand Nessa's blind defence of her brother—unless she was getting something out of it too. It was inconceivable she was doing it out of pure affection or loyalty.

All that existed for him were the solid successes he'd manifested out of sweat and dogged ambition. The legacy he would leave behind would tell a different story from the one he'd been handed at birth. His name would endure as a gold standard in racing.

And yet now, for the first time, he had the disquieting suspicion that even if every one of his peers were to look him in the eye with the utmost respect, he'd still feel less than them.

A movement to the far right in the stud stableyard area caught Luc's eye and he welcomed the distraction. He turned his head just in time to catch a flash of dark red hair coiling down a slim back before Nessa disappeared around a corner. His reaction was instant and intense, making him scowl even harder at his body's lack of control.

His body pulsed with need. He should be pushing this woman further away, leaving it to his staff to keep her in check. But instead he was bringing her closer.

He was experiencing a kind of hunger he'd only felt once before, when he'd had his first taste of the wider world outside the gloomy Parisian suburbs and had made the vow to never end up back there again. He'd taken that hunger, and used it.

This hunger, however, would be crushed. Because it could do nothing to enhance his success, or his life. Resisting her would be a test of his will to not demean himself.

'Here—last job of the day, love, go up and do the boss's private suite. He's due back from Paris later this evening and I never had a chance to get around to it, what with the preparations for the party this weekend.'

Nessa took the basket containing cleaning products from Mrs Owens and hated that her skin got hot just at the mention of *the boss* and that he was returning soon. He'd been at his Paris stables for the past three days, which hadn't felt as much of a respite as Nessa had thought it would.

Angry with herself for still being so aware of him when he wasn't even here, she focused on feeling relieved that the day was nearly over. There was something particularly soul-sucking about doing housework all day, every day, and as Nessa had polished the silver earlier she'd revised her opinion that Luc Barbier wasn't petty.

They'd also been busy preparing for a huge party that was being thrown at the house that weekend, to launch the most prestigious racing event in the Irish season.

Just as the homely housekeeper was turning away she stopped and said, 'I've left fresh bedlinen in his room, so just strip the bed and remake it. Once you're done with that you're off for the evening.'

Nessa went upstairs to the second floor of the villa-style country house, still marvelling at the opulence.

It was about two hundred years old. All the bedroom suites were on the second floor. The first floor was taken up with Barbier's—*Luc's*—office and a gym. There was also a vast media room with a private cinema and informal meetings rooms.

The ground floor held the grand ballroom—prepared for the party now—with French doors opening out onto exquisite manicured gardens. It also had the main, and less formal, dining rooms and reception rooms.

The basement was where the vast kitchen and staff quarters were laid out. All in all a very grand affair. It certainly put Nessa's family farmhouse to shame, even though it too had been refurbished to a high standard since Iseult had married Nadim. It was a far more modestly sized house, though.

Nessa reached the second floor, and walked to the end of the corridor past all the guest rooms to where Luc's rooms were based. He had one entire wing, and she found she was holding her breath slightly as she opened the door.

His scent hit her instantly. Woody and musky. It curled through her nose and deep into the pit of her belly. Cursing herself for her reaction, she strode into the main reception room, dumping the basket of cleaning supplies and resolutely opening the sash windows to let some air in. She told herself the room was musty, not musky and provocative.

Still, she couldn't help but look around. The room was huge and open plan, with soft grey furnishings in muted tones. The same stunning modern art that she'd seen in his office was dotted around the walls, along with sculptures, huge coffee-table books on photography, art, and movies. More books than she'd ever seen in her life, ranging from thrillers to the classics.

The decor and objects reflected a far more cerebral man than Nessa would have guessed existed under Barbier's brooding, sexy exterior.

She had to force herself to remember why she was here and not give into the impulse to pluck out a book from the shelves and curl up on one of the sumptuous couches to read. She realised that she was more weary than she'd realised—the stress of the situation and hard work, mixed with nights of fitful sleep, wasn't a good combination. But she wasn't a wilting lily, and normally worked harder than most, so it annoyed her to find herself feeling tired now.

She scooped up the cleaning supplies and set to work dusting and cleaning. Eventually, as if she'd been putting it off, she went into the bedroom area. She opened the doors and the first thing that hit her eyeline was the bed. It was massive, dominating the room. Much like the man.

It was a modern bed with a dark grey headboard that reminded her ridiculously of his eyes and how they could turn dark silver. A detail she shouldn't even be aware of.

Apart from the bed there were some built-in wardrobes, a sleek chest of drawers and bedside tables. What was striking was the absence of anything of particularly personal value. No photos. No *stuff*. Just some clothes draped on one of the chairs and the rumpled bedsheets, which she avoided looking at.

Then she spied two more doors that revealed a walk-in closet and a luxurious bathroom complete with wet-room shower and a tub that looked big enough to take a football team.

Nessa set about cleaning the bathroom, trying not to breathe in his scent, which was everywhere. She picked up a bottle of cologne and guiltily sniffed it before putting it down again hastily.

Disgusted with herself, she finished cleaning and went back into the bedroom, pulling off the crumpled sheets and trying not to imagine that they were still warm from his body. *Would he sleep naked? He seems like the kind of man who would...*

Nessa stopped dead for a moment, shocked at the vivid turn of her imagination, and at the way she suddenly hungered to know what he would look like—imagining the sexy naked sprawl of that big bronzed body all too easily, and knowing her imagination probably fell far short of reality. Her pulse became slow and hot.

She had to face the unpalatable fact that Luc Barbier had succeeded where no other man had. He'd awoken her hormones from their dormant state. *Their virginal state.* And it was beyond humiliating that the first man she should feel lust for was the last man who would ever look at her like that.

She'd often wondered why she'd never felt particularly roused by other boys' kisses at university, and her lack of response had earned her a reputation of being standoffish. She'd closed inwards after that, choosing to avoid exposing herself and risk being mocked.

Nessa made the bed as clinically as she could, ignoring the faint dent near the centre that indicated where he slept. When she was done she made one more sweep of the rooms to make sure she hadn't missed anything and collected all the cleaning materials. She stepped inside the bedroom one last time to run her eye over the now-pristine bed and was about to step back out and shut the door when something caught her eye outside.

She went over to the window, putting the basket down for a moment. The view took her breath away; the sun was setting over the gallops, bathing everything in a lush golden light. There were no horses being exercised now, but Nessa could remember how it felt to harness a thoroughbred's power as it surged powerfully beneath her. There was a wide window seat and Nessa sat down, curling her legs underneath her, enjoying the view for an illicit moment.

Nessa suspected that she knew exactly why she had avoided physical intimacy until now. Their mother's death had profoundly affected everyone in her family: Iseult had grown up overnight to become their mother and much more, and the boys had gone off the rails in their own ways but had always turned to each other. Even though Nessa was a twin to Eoin, they'd never had that bond people spoke of.

Their father had gone to pieces.

But Nessa had been too young to do much but internalise all of her own pain and grief, too acutely aware of everyone else's struggles to let it out. She'd always been terrified of what might come out of her if she did. It had been easier to retreat emotionally, and concentrate on her dreams of being a great jockey.

But sometimes the pain in her chest—her unexpressed grief—took her breath away. And sometimes, when she looked at her sister Iseult with her husband and she saw their incredibly intimate bond, she felt envious of that relationship, even as it made her heart palpitate with fear. She couldn't imagine ever allowing herself to love someone that much, for fear of losing them. For fear of the devastation the loss would cause.

Up until now she'd avoided sex because getting close

to someone had seemed like too high a price. And yet, when she thought of Luc Barbier, the last thing on her mind was the emotional price.

Luc was tired and frustrated. He'd spent the last three days working intensively with one of his brightest hopes, a horse called Sur La Mer. He was due to race in a few weeks in France but none of his jockeys seemed capable of getting the horse to perform to his maximum ability. Luc would ride the horse himself if he weren't six feet four and two hundred pounds.

Luc was also frustrated in a far more difficult area—sexually. It was not a state he was used to. He didn't do sexual frustration. He desired a woman, he had her and he moved on.

But only one woman had dominated his thoughts in France. Nessa O'Sullivan. He'd gone to a glitzy charity auction in Paris that was abounding with beautiful women. Not one had piqued his interest. Instead he'd found himself wondering what Nessa would look like out of those jeans that seemed to be shrink-wrapped to her taut thighs. Or the series of worn T-shirts that did little to conceal her lithe body and firm breasts. Or what her hair would look like teased into luxurious waves, rippling down a bare back.

Dieu. He cursed himself as he strode down the corridor to his bedroom, relishing the prospect of a cold shower and bed.

But when Luc opened the door to his bedroom all of his instincts snapped onto high alert. An old habit from when his environment had spelled danger from sunrise to sunset.

He saw the basket of cleaning supplies first, on a table near the door. And then he saw *her* and his breath stopped in his chest. He wasn't entirely sure he wasn't hallucinating.

She was curled up on the wide window seat, fast asleep. Her knees were leaning to one side, and her head was leaning against the window as if she'd been looking at the view of the gallops.

He moved closer and his hungry gaze tracked down over her body—he was disappointed that she wasn't wearing the jeans and T-shirt combination that had enflamed his imagination. She was wearing the plain black trousers and black shirt that all his household staff wore. Flat, functional sneakers.

The shirt had untucked from her trousers, and he could see the tiniest bare patch of her waist and her paler than pale skin. Blood roared to his head and groin in a simultaneous rush.

He was incensed at her effect on him, and at his growing obsession with her.

As if finally becoming aware of his intense scrutiny, she shifted slightly and Luc looked at her face to see long dark lashes fluttering against her cheeks for a moment before her eyes opened sleepily. He watched as she slowly registered where she was, and who was in front of her.

Her cheeks flushed and those huge eyes widened until all he could see was dark, golden green. He wanted to slip right into those pools and lose himself...

A tumult raged inside him as she looked up and blinked innocently, as if butter wouldn't melt in her mouth. He might have almost believed for a second that she hadn't planned this little set-up.

'Well, well, well, what do we have here?' He looked her over slowly and thoroughly, fresh heat flooding his veins when he saw the thrust of her breasts against the shirt. It made his voice harsh. 'You would have been much more comfortable and made it easier for both of us if you'd stripped naked and waited in my bed.'

CHAPTER FOUR

NESSA LOOKED UP at Luc Barbier, who was towering
over her with a dark scowl on his face and stubble on
his jaw. For a blessed foggy moment, just before the
adrenalin kicked in, his words hung harmlessly in the
air between them.

His hair was tousled, as if he'd been running a hand
through it, and he was wearing a white shirt, open at
the neck, revealing a glimpse of dark skin. Awareness
sizzled to life, infusing her with an urgency she felt
only around him.

And then his words registered. It was like an electric shock or a slap across the face. Nessa was wide
awake, and she scrambled off the window seat to stand
on wobbly legs.

Her hair was coming loose from where it had been
piled messily on her head to keep it out of the way. She
was thoroughly rumpled, she smelled of cleaning products and he really thought…? Bile rose in her throat.

'How dare you insinuate such a thing?' Her voice
was scratchy from sleep and she was burningly aware—
even as she said that—of how bad this looked. She
cursed herself for allowing her weariness to get the
better of her.

Luc's head reared back, arms folded across his chest.

'I walk into my bedroom and find a woman, pretending to be asleep, waiting for me…like I said, they're usually in my bed and wearing a lot less but the message is essentially the same. They're here for one thing.'

Nessa was speechless at his sheer arrogance. Eventually she managed to get out, through waves of indignation and far more disturbing physical reactions, 'Well, I hate to burst your ego bubble but that was the last thing on my mind. I was cleaning your room, then I sat down for a minute and I fell asleep. I apologise for that. But I did not come here to…to…'

He raised a brow. 'To seduce me?'

Before she could respond to that, he continued as if she hadn't spoken. 'I might as well tell you now that kinky role-play doesn't really do it for me. I'm a traditionalist that way. When I make love it's intense, thorough and without the need for embellishment.'

A flash of heat went up Nessa's spine to imagine just how intense his lovemaking would be. Little beads of sweat broke out between her breasts and in the small of her back. Anger rose too. Anger that it was him who was firing up all her nerve-endings.

'I am not here to *make love* with anyone. My only crime was to fall asleep on the job and if you'll excuse me now I'll leave you in peace.'

She went to step away and out of his orbit but he caught her arm after muttering something that sounded very French and rude under his breath. His hand encircled her whole upper arm and his fingers were brushing the side of her breast. Nessa's pulse rocketed, and in the dim lights of the room—*night had fallen outside…just how long had she been asleep?*—all she could see were the forbiddingly gorgeous lines of Luc's face.

'Peace?' He almost spat the word out. 'I've had precious little peace since your brother absconded with one million euros and then his temptress of a sister turns up to play sidekick. Just what is your agenda, Nessa? What game are you playing here? Because I warn you now that you will get burned if you think you can play with me and get away with it.'

His dark intensity was totally intimidating, but somehow Nessa managed to pull her arm free and step away. Shakily she said, 'I'm not playing any games. I wouldn't know how. I really didn't come here with some nefarious intention to seduce you.'

She bit her lip to stop a semi-hysterical giggle from emerging. She wouldn't know how to seduce her way out of a paper bag, never mind a man like Luc Barbier. The very notion was ridiculous.

His mouth thinned. 'You really expect me to believe that you fell asleep like Sleeping Beauty in the fairy tale, waiting for her prince?'

Heat rushed into her cheeks—she *had* been mooning about his suite like some lovelorn teenager earlier. It wasn't like her at all. 'I don't believe in fairy tales,' she said stiffly. 'And don't worry, I know you're no prince.'

He put two hands on her arms now, swinging her around to face him properly. His eyes had turned to cold steel. 'What's that supposed to mean?'

'I…' Words got stuck in Nessa's throat. She couldn't seem to concentrate on anything but Luc's face above hers. The sensual lines were mesmerising. 'I didn't mean anything.'

Except she had, she realised. She'd just articulated it badly. This man was no prince, he was a marauding sultan, or a king. Uncultivated and suave all at once. Infinitely hard but also soft, as when he'd put a hand to his horse.

His mouth twisted. 'I might never be a prince, but you're in no position to look down on me, the sister of a common thief who thought she could seduce her way to paying back her brother's debt. Like I said, you could have saved a lot of conversation if you'd been waiting in my bed naked instead of playing out this elaborate charade of innocence.'

Nessa's hand had lifted and connected with Luc's cheek before she even realised what she'd done. Shock coursed through her system as the sting registered on her hand and Luc's face turned from the blow. All her anger drained away instantly.

He turned back slowly, face even darker now, a livid handprint showing on his cheek. Horrified, Nessa used his name for the first time. 'Luc, I'm so sorry. But I didn't mean it like that, and Paddy's not a common thief. He's really not—'

'Stop talking, you little hellcat, I don't want to hear another word.' His voice was rough.

Before Nessa could even think of uttering another word, Luc had pulled her right into him, so that her body was welded to his. All she could feel was whipcord strength and heat.

All she could see were his eyes, fathomless and like molten steel. She realised he was livid and yet she felt no fear. She only felt an intense excitement. She opened her mouth but he said, 'Not another word.'

And then his mouth covered hers, and words were the last thing on Nessa's mind as heat fused with white light and poured into every vein in her body to create a scorching trail of fire.

Shock rendered her helpless to Luc's savage sensuality and her own immediately rampant response.

Luc's arm went around her back, arching her into

him even more, and his mouth began to move over hers. But this was no gentle exploration, and it left any other kisses she'd shared with boys in a far distant universe. This did not leave her cold, or unmoved. This was igniting her very soul.

It was mastery, pure and simple. And domination. And punishment. And yet despite all those things that should have had Nessa tensing and squirming to be free, she strained to be even closer, raising her arms to twine them about Luc's neck. If she could have climbed into his skin, she would have.

She opened her mouth under his, instinctively seeking a deeper kiss, wanting to taste him with every fibre of her being. His fingers threaded through her hair, catching her head, angling it so that he could give her exactly what she wanted, but on his terms.

He consumed her, demanding nothing less than total surrender, and Nessa knew only one thing: that she wanted to surrender, with no doubt or hesitation in her mind. It was as if every moment in her life had been building up to this conflagration.

She was drowning in liquid heat and could feel it, slippery, between her legs. Luc's mouth left hers and she heard a soft moan emanating from her mouth. He trailed kisses over her jaw and down her neck. Her head fell back, too heavy.

The only sounds in the room were harsh breathing and the *thump thump* of her heart. Luc's hand was on her shirt, deftly opening the buttons. Cool air hit her bare skin and her nipples drew into tight, hard points.

The world tipped on its axis and Nessa only realised moments later that Luc had sat down on the edge of the bed, bringing her with him so that now she sat on his lap. She was dizzy, and thought that this must be how it felt to be drunk: light-headed and euphoric.

He was pushing her shirt open, and she looked at him and saw an almost feral expression on his face. He cupped one of her lace-covered breasts. Breasts that had always felt very inadequate to Nessa. But now when she looked down she could see how she perfectly filled his palm. As if she'd been made for his hands alone.

He pulled down the lace cup, baring her flesh, and she bit her lip to stop from moaning, pleading. His thumb skated over one small hard nipple and it sent electric shocks through her whole body.

He looked at her and smiled and Nessa realised that he hadn't smiled at her once until now. And it was as devastating as she'd suspected it might be. Wicked, seductive, gorgeous and irresistible.

Lust and need cocooned them from reality, and for one wild second Nessa could almost convince herself that perhaps she was still asleep and this was all just a very vivid dream.

But she knew it wasn't a dream, and she knew that it was very important that she stand up and stop this.

Luc's head was dipping towards her breast and Nessa had never wanted anything more than to surrender completely to this moment, but something within her, some small sane voice, broke through. She put her hands on Luc's shoulders and levered herself off his lap, feeling like a foal trying to stand for the first time.

Luc just looked at her as if he couldn't quite believe she'd moved away, and Nessa realised she was half naked. She pulled at her shirt, scrambling to do up at least one or two buttons. The bare flesh of her breast chafed against the material, sensitised by his touch.

She forced out, through the clamour of her own desire, 'I didn't come here for this. I really didn't.'

Luc's body was hard and throbbed with a need to claim and possess, things he'd never felt for a woman before. Nessa was looking at him with wide eyes and flushed cheeks, and hair coming loose.

I didn't come here for this. Something slid into Luc's mind: the very rogue possibility that she *had* just fallen asleep while on the job. And then he dismissed it. She was playing with him and he would not be manipulated like this. He'd already exposed himself far too much. And the fact that she'd been the one to pull away, signalling she was more in control than he was, was even more exposing.

Luc forced his blood to cool, and stood up in a fluid motion. Nessa took a step back. The thought that she was stepping back from him in case he touched her again sent something dark into his gut. And something far more unwelcome: a feeling of vulnerability, something that Luc had rejected long ago. He was invulnerable.

'Sleeping with me isn't going to improve your, or your brother's, situation. I told you already that I don't play games, Nessa, so unless you're willing to admit that we both want each other with no strings attached then get out of here.'

His voice was so cold and remote it skated over Nessa's skin like ice. She hated his obvious cynicism, and wanted to deny his claim that she would manipulate him to gain favour for her brother, but self-preservation kicked in at the last moment. She fled, taking the basket of cleaning supplies with her.

When Nessa finally made it back to her room she closed the door behind her and rested against it. Her heart was still thumping out of time, and her whole body ached for a fulfilment she'd never needed before.

And she reeled with the knowledge that she'd almost lain back for Luc Barbier and handed him something she'd never handed anyone else. Her innocence. She'd almost tipped over the edge of allowing Luc to see her at her most vulnerable. A man who had shown her nothing but disdain and distrust.

Thank *God* she'd pulled back from the brink. She shivered now at the prospect of Luc looking at her when he'd discovered her virginity. She could already imagine the mocking look on his face, and how he would spurn her with disgust.

But then she thought of how he'd said, *Unless you're willing to admit we both want each other with no strings attached*, and she shivered again. But this time it wasn't with trepidation or humiliation. It was with an awful sense of illicit excitement.

Luc had turned the shower to cold, but that still hadn't cooled the lingering heat in his body. He couldn't believe how close he'd come to stripping Nessa O'Sullivan bare and taking her in a haze of lust.

She'd been the one to pull back. And even though Luc hadn't imagined the chemistry between them, it still got to him somewhere very vulnerable that she'd had more control than him.

He couldn't trust her, and yet he'd been about to sleep with her, complicating an already complicated situation even more. He shuddered to think of the hold she could have had over him after sleeping together. He hadn't yet known a woman who didn't try to capitalise on intimacies shared, even when they were only physical. And he had no doubt—in spite of her protestations otherwise—that she'd had an agenda.

He looked at himself in his bathroom mirror and scowled. If she thought that she could whet his appetite like this, and he would come running after her like a dog in heat, she was mistaken. Luc wouldn't be caught offguard again. She *was* resistable. Even if the pounding of his blood told him otherwise.

He pulled a towel around his waist and knotted it roughly, finding his mobile phone and picking it up. Within seconds he was issuing a terse instruction to the security firm he'd hired to seek out Paddy O'Sullivan, to step up their efforts.

Afterwards he threw the phone down and surmised grimly that the sooner they found Paddy and his money, the sooner he could get rid of the all too distracting Nessa O'Sullivan too.

Two nights later, Nessa was holding a tray full of champagne flutes filled to the brim, serving them at Luc's glitzy party. She was dressed in a white shirt and black skirt. The uniform of waiters everywhere. Hair up in a tight bun.

She could appreciate the breathtaking scene even as her arms felt as if they were about to drop out of the shoulder sockets. The unusually mild Irish spring day was melting into a lavender-hued dusk. Candles imbued the guests and room with a golden light.

She smiled in relief as some guests stopped and helped themselves to drinks on her tray, lightening her load marginally. And then her gaze tracked back inevitably to where one man stood out from the crowd—dark head and broad shoulders visible from every corner of the room.

Her main objective was to avoid coming face to face with Luc Barbier at all costs. The enormity of what had almost happened still sent shock waves through her body every time she thought of it. *So did the thought of a no-strings encounter,* added a wicked voice.

And even though she was trying to avoid him, she couldn't look away. Much like most of the women in the room, she'd noticed with a spurt of something suspiciously…possessive. He was dressed in a tuxedo and he was simply breathtaking. He was the epitome of virile beauty, but with that undeniable edge of something dark and dangerous.

As if reading her mind, two women stopped nearby and, in that way of seeing but not seeing Nessa, because she was staff, they were whispering loudly enough for Nessa to catch snippets.

'Apparently he's an animal in bed…'

'They say he was found on the streets…'

'Petty crime…'

'Only got to where he has because he slept with Leo Fouret's wife and the husband bought him off to keep him quiet…'

Nessa went still at that, something cold trickling down her spine. She hadn't heard that final, particular rumour before. Although, he *had* apparently left Leo Fouret's stables under less than amicable circumstances, before blazing a trail on his own.

The women moved away and then more guests approached Nessa, relieving her of her remaining drinks. She was only too happy to escape back to the kitchen to stock up. Just before she left, she cast one last glance in Luc's direction, but his head was bowed towards someone in conversation.

Lambasting herself for having listened to gossip, no

matter how inadvertently, Nessa forged a path through the crowd and away from Luc. She told herself that she wasn't remotely interested in what the women had been saying. And that she was truly pathetic to be feeling the tiniest bit sorry for him that he was surrounded by such fervent gossip in the first place.

There was no smoke without a fire, as her father loved to say on a regular basis. And from what she'd seen of Luc in action, she could almost forgive a married woman for falling under his spell.

'What on earth is Nessa O'Sullivan doing serving drinks at your party, Barbier? I'd hardly think she's short of a few bob!'

It took a second for Luc to register what the man beside him had said and when he did his wandering attention snapped into sharp focus. 'You know her?'

The man snorted. 'Of course I do—you forget Ireland is a small place. Her father is Paddy O'Sullivan, one of this country's best trainers—at one time. Before he hit the bottle and almost lost everything. Now of course they're back on top of the world, although I don't think Paddy will ever repair the damage to his reputation. Still, he doesn't need to now, not with the goldmine he's sitting on thanks to his son-in-law.'

Luc usually had an aversion to gossip but not this time. 'What are you talking about?'

Percy Mortimer, a well-known English racing pundit, turned to Luc. 'Nessa O'Sullivan is related to royalty—her older sister—who incidentally is also a very talented amateur trainer—is married to the supreme Sheikh Nadim Al-Saqr of Merkazad. He bought out their stud a few years back. Nessa's not a bad rider.

I've seen her in a couple of races over the years, but she doesn't seem to have made a proper impression yet.'

What the hell? Luc barely heard that last bit. Sheikh Nadim was a very serious contender in racing circles, and a billionaire. And Luc had had no idea that he owned a stables just down the road. *Nessa's family stud.* He reeled, although he didn't show it.

Percy was saying something else but Luc wasn't listening. His gaze was already scanning the crowd for a dark redhead. He'd seen her earlier—looking once again as if butter wouldn't melt, dressed in her white shirt and skirt. Even that small glimpse had been enough to cause a spike in his heart-rate.

Damn. Where was she, anyway?

Luc tried to move away but saw a group headed for him with Pascal leading the way. The look on Pascal's face told Luc that he had to stay exactly where he was.

Nessa would have to wait, for now. But he would track her down and this time there would be no games. Only answers to his questions. Like what the hell was she playing at, working for nothing to pay off her brother's debt when presumably she could ask for a handout from her billionaire brother-in-law?

Nessa's feet and arms were aching, and she knew she shouldn't be here, but after the party had finished and they'd been released, she found herself gravitating towards the stallions' stables. As if pulled by some magnetic force. As if that could help to ground her and fuse her scattered energies back together.

She'd been acutely conscious of Luc's every movement, all evening.

At one stage she'd caught his eye and it had seemed as if he was trying to communicate something telepathically. From the grim look on his face it hadn't been something particularly nice. And then, even though she'd skirted around the edges of the room, keeping far out of his orbit for the rest of the evening, she could have sworn she felt his dark gaze boring into her periodically.

She came to a stop in the middle of the stables when she realised that they were empty. She looked around and remembered belatedly that the stallions had been moved up to different paddocks and stables for a few days while these were being repainted and renovated.

There were white sheets piled high in a corner along with painting and cleaning paraphernalia. Nessa told herself it was just as well as she turned around to leave. The last thing she needed was to be caught again in the wrong place—

Her heart stopped when she saw the tall broad figure blocking the doorway, with only the moon behind him as a silhouette. Too late. *Luc.*

She could see that his bow-tie was undone and top button open, his jacket swinging loose and his hands in the pockets of his trousers.

He moved forward into the stables and she saw his stern expression revealed in the dim lighting. Immediately the space felt claustrophobic. Nessa's body tingled with awareness as he came close enough for her to see that there was also barely leashed anger in his expression.

She swallowed. 'I know I shouldn't be here—'

'That's not important. We need to have a little chat.'

Surprise robbed her voice for a moment and then she said, 'About what?'

Luc folded his arms. 'About why you've omitted to mention the not inconsequential fact that your sister is married to Sheikh Nadim Al-Saqr of Merkazad, *and* that he owns your stud farm.'

He continued, 'I'd imagine one million euro is short change to Sheikh Nadim Al-Saqr, so what the hell is Paddy doing jeopardising his career for a handout he could've begged off his brother-in-law, and why didn't *you* just pick up the phone to Nadim to sort this mess out?'

Nessa went hot and then cold as the significance of this sank in, and the realisation that someone must have recognised her at the party.

She said carefully, 'I didn't think it was relevant.'

Luc looked even more stern. 'Not good enough.'

Nessa swallowed. She knew she couldn't avoid an explanation. 'Nadim *did* buy our farm but he put it back into our name as a wedding gift for Iseult, my sister. It's ours again, he's just one of the shareholders. And I didn't want to involve him because this has nothing to do with Nadim or Iseult. My sister is due to have a baby in a couple of weeks and they don't need the stress.'

Luc stepped closer but Nessa was trapped, with a stable door at her back and nowhere to go. She was acutely aware of his tall, lean body and his scent.

'There's more to it than that,' he said. 'You and your brother avoiding asking for help just proves you're both involved in something that's gone beyond your control. I'm guessing Nadim wouldn't approve, and you don't want to bite the hand that feeds you.'

In a fierce low voice Nessa replied, '*No*. It's nothing like that. Why must you be so cynical and mistrustful?'

'Because,' he answered smoothly, 'I was born that way and nothing I've experienced has ever proved me wrong. Life favours the opportunistic. I should know.'

I was born that way. Nessa couldn't stop a rush of

curiosity and pity. The second time she'd pitied him this evening. But then she crushed it. Luc Barbier was the last man on the planet who needed anyone's pity.

He said, 'You could be free to walk away if you asked Nadim for help.'

Luc heard himself say the words even as something inside him rejected it immediately. Let her walk away? A hot surge of possessiveness rose up inside him. *He wanted her.*

She was looking at him, eyes huge, and for a second he could almost have imagined that she looked...*hurt*. A ridiculous notion.

Nessa shook her head and some long tendrils of red hair framed her face. 'No. I will not take the easy way out and cause my family distress. I promised Paddy that I wouldn't go to Nadim or Iseult.'

Luc was intrigued by this apparent loyalty. 'Give me one good reason why I shouldn't go to Nadim myself.'

An expression of panic crossed her face. 'I thought you didn't want this news to get out either!'

'I don't. But from what I know of the Sheikh, I think he would appreciate the need for discretion on his family's behalf. It would affect his name and reputation too.'

Nessa wrung her hands in front of her and it only drew Luc's attention to where the shirt strained slightly over her breasts. He dragged his gaze up.

'You have no right to involve them.'

Now he really wanted to know why she was being so stubborn on this. 'Give me one reason, Nessa, and make it a good one.'

She looked at him as if he was torturing her and then she answered with palpable reluctance. 'When our mother died Iseult was only twelve; I was eight. Our father couldn't cope with the grief. He went off the rails, and developed a drink problem. Iseult went to school, but she did the bare minimum so that she could take care of the farm, the horses and all of us.'

Nessa glanced away for a moment, her face pale. Luc felt at an uncharacteristic loss as to what to say but she looked back at him and continued. 'If it wasn't for Iseult shielding us from the worst of our father's excesses and the reality of the farm falling to pieces, we never would have made it through school. She shouldered far too much for someone her age…and then Nadim came along and bought the farm out and she felt as if she'd failed us all at the last hurdle.'

Nessa drew in a breath. 'But then they fell in love and got married, and for the first time in her life she's really secure and happy.'

'Married to a billionaire, conveniently enough.' The cynical comment was said before Luc had even properly thought about it, and it felt hollow on his lips.

Nessa's hands clenched to fists by her sides. 'Iseult is the least materialistic person I know. They love each other.'

Luc was a bit stunned by her vehemence. 'Go on.'

She bit her lip for a moment, and he had to stop himself from reaching out to tug it free of those small white teeth.

'My sister is truly happy for the first time in a long time. The only responsibility she now bears is to her own family. They had problems getting pregnant after Kamil so this pregnancy has been stressful. If she knew what was going on she'd be devastated and worried, and Nadim would do everything he could to help her. He might even insist on coming all the way over here, and she needs him with her now.'

She added impetuously, 'If you do talk to Nadim,

I'll leak it to the press about the money going astray. Maybe they'll be easier on Paddy than you've been.'

Luc just looked at Nessa for a long moment, and he had to admit with grudging reluctance that her apparent zeal to protect her family was very convincing. He'd never seen a mother bear with cubs, but he had an impression of it right now. And he didn't like how it had affected him when she'd mentioned her sister's happy family. For a second he'd actually felt something like envy.

It reminded him uncomfortably of when he'd been much younger and he and other kids from the flats would go into Paris to pick pockets or whatever petty crime they could get away with. Stupid kids with nothing to lose and no one at home to care what they got up to.

One day Luc had been mesmerised by a family playing in a park—a mother, father and two children. The kids had looked so happy and loved. An awful darkness had welled up inside him and he'd tasted jealousy for the first time. And something far more poignant— a desire to know what that would be like.

His friends had noticed and had teased Luc unmercifully, so he'd shoved that experience and those feelings deep down inside and had vowed never to envy anyone again. And he wasn't about to start now.

But eclipsing all of that now was the carnal hunger building inside him. He'd thought of little else but that incendiary kiss the other night. When he'd sought Nessa out after the party he'd told himself he could resist her. But the thick sexual tension in the air mocked him.

She called to him, even in those plain, unerotic clothes. She called to him, deep inside where a dark hunger raged and begged for satisfaction.

Suddenly it didn't matter who she was related to. Or if she was playing mind-games. She threw up too many questions, but there was only one question he was interested in knowing the answer to right now, and that was how she would feel when he sank deep inside her.

Luc closed the distance between them, and reached out to slide a hand around Nessa's neck, tugging her closer. Her eyes went wide and her cheeks bloomed with colour. She put a hand up to his and said, 'What are you doing?'

Luc's gaze was fixated on her mouth and he had to drag it away to look into those huge hazel eyes. 'Do you really expect me to believe that you're just an innocent who would do anything for her family? And that the other night was pure chance and chemistry?'

For a taut moment, Luc held his breath because he realised that some small kernel of the little boy he'd once been, yearning for something totally out of his orbit, was still alive inside him. He waited for Nessa to gaze up at him with those huge eyes and move closer, to tell him in a husky voice, *Yes, I'm really that innocent.* The worst of it was, he wasn't entirely sure that he wouldn't believe her.

But she didn't. She tensed and pulled back, jerking free of Luc's hand. Glaring up at him. 'I don't *expect* you to believe anything, Luc Barbier. You've got eyes in your head and if you choose to view the world through a fog of cynicism and mistrust then that's your prerogative.

'As for the other night—it was madness and a mistake. You won't have to worry why it happened because it won't happen again.'

Nessa had almost moved past Luc when his shocked brain kicked into gear and he caught her hand, stopping her. Every cell in his body rejected what she'd just said. She was walking away again. A savage part of himself rose up, needing to prove that she wasn't as in control as she appeared.

He pulled her back in front of him. 'You want me.'

She bit her lip and looked down. She shook her head. Luc tipped her chin up feeling even more savage. 'Say it, Nessa.'

She looked at him, eyes huge and swirling with emotion but Luc couldn't draw back now. Eventually she said with a touch of defiance, 'I might want you but I don't want to.'

Something immediately eased inside him. She glanced down again as if by not looking at him she could avoid the issue.

'Look at me, Nessa.'

For a long moment she refused but then she looked up, eyes spitting golden sparks, and it ignited the fire inside him to a burning inferno of need. He pulled her closer again. She put her hands up to his chest. 'No, Luc. I don't want—'

But he stopped her words with his mouth and used every ounce of his expertise to show her how futile her resistance was. Whatever else was happening around them, whatever she was saying, he could trust that this was true at least.

CHAPTER FIVE

NESSA WANTED TO resist Luc—she really did. She hated
that he still patently believed she'd orchestrated the
other night. And that he most likely didn't believe what
she'd told him about her family.

But it was hard to think of all of that when his mouth
was on hers and he was sliding his tongue between her
lips and possessing her with such devastating ease. Big
hands moved down her back to her buttocks, cupping
them and bringing her in close to where she could feel
the bold thrust of his arousal. For her. Not for one of
the stunningly beautiful women at the party. *Her.* Nessa
O'Sullivan.

He drew back then and Nessa realised she was
welded to him. Arms and breasts crushed against his
chest. One arm kept her clamped to him, not letting
her escape for a moment. He undid her hair so that it
fell around her shoulders. He looked at it for a moment
as if mesmerised and something inside Nessa melted.

He wrapped some hair around his hand and gently
tugged so that her head came back. And then he kissed
her again, dragging her deeper and deeper into the pit
of a fire that she knew she couldn't walk away from
again. She'd barely been able to the last time.

He pulled her skirt up until she felt cool air skate over

her heated skin. He palmed the flesh of her buttocks and the place between her legs burned with damp heat.

She broke away from the kiss, breathing rapidly, and looked at him. Her heart was racing. She couldn't look away from his eyes. They held her to account and she couldn't lie.

'What do you want, Nessa?' His fingers moved tantalisingly close to the edge of her panties. Her breathing quickened. One finger slid under the material, stroking. Her legs were weak.

'Do you want me to stop?'

No! shouted every fibre of her being. Nessa couldn't explain it and wasn't sure if she even wanted to investigate it, but she realised at that moment that she trusted him. She wasn't sure *what* she trusted exactly. Maybe it was that he wouldn't lie to her or spout platitudes. And so she convinced herself that if she said yes to this... whatever it was...she'd be under no illusions that emotions were involved.

He drew back marginally. 'Nessa?' And there it was—a glimmer of concern, showing a side to this darkly complex man that she suspected not many people ever got to see. She knew he would let her go if she insisted, even if his pride demanded her capitulation. Even as they both knew she would capitulate all too easily. But, she wanted this man with every cell in her body. She'd never wanted anything as much.

'Don't stop,' she whispered, reaching up to wind her arms around his neck again, pressing her mouth to his. Luc didn't hesitate. He gathered her even closer and backed her into the stall behind them, where she'd seen all the white sheets piled up in readiness for the work.

Nessa felt a soft surface at the backs of her legs that swiftly gave way, and she fell into the pile of sheets.

Luc looked down at Nessa, sprawled before him. Her skirt was up around her smooth thighs, and her untucked shirt strained across her chest. Her red hair spilled across the white fabric. It was probably one of the least romantic settings for lovemaking, but it was one of the most erotic sights Luc had ever seen. He was no longer aware of anything but the pounding in his blood and the need he felt in every cell of his body.

A small voice tried to get through to him, to remind him that he was no longer this uncivilised man, but it fell on deaf ears as he started to take off his clothes with the singular intention of joining their naked bodies as soon as possible.

Nessa stared up at Luc. The intense expression on his face might have scared her if she didn't feel as though she might have a similar expression on her face. He pulled off his jacket, dropping it to the ground, and then his bow tie. He started to open his shirt and Nessa's eyes grew wide as his magnificent chest was revealed bit by glorious bit until he was naked from the waist up. She could hardly breathe.

He came down over her, arms bracketing around her body, and his head dipped to hers, mouths fusing again in a series of long, drugging kisses that made Nessa want more, much more.

By the time he was opening her shirt, she was arching her back towards him in silent supplication. He pushed apart the material and pulled down the lace cups of her bra, exposing her breasts to his dark gaze as he rested on one arm beside her.

'Si belle...' he murmured before dipping his head and surrounding one tight peak in wet heat. Nessa might have screamed, she wasn't sure. She just knew that Luc's mouth on her bare flesh was almost more than she could bear. And he was remorseless, ignoring her pleas for mercy.

His mouth moved down over her belly, and he pulled up her skirt so that it was ruched around her waist. He stopped for a moment and looked at her in the dim light, watching her expression as his hand explored under the waist of her panties before gently pushing them down her legs.

Nessa sucked in a breath. This was more exposed than she'd ever been in her life, and yet it didn't scare her. She felt exhilarated.

Luc's gaze moved down her body and his hand rested between her legs, cupping her. Slowly, he started to move his hand against her and Nessa gripped his arms like an anchor.

He watched her again as one finger explored in a circle, through her secret folds of flesh and then right into the heart of her. Nessa's back arched and she squeezed her eyes shut. It was sensory overload. Her legs were splayed and Luc's hand was a wicked instrument of torture, as one finger became two, stretching her.

She lifted her head. 'I can't…' Was that her voice? So needy and husky?

'Can't what, *chérie*?'

'Can't cope…what you're doing, it's too much…'

He smiled and it was the smile of the devil. 'It's not nearly enough. *Yet.* Come fly with me, *minou*. Come on…'

She didn't understand what he was asking, but then he flicked his finger against the very heart of her. She tumbled blindly over an edge she had no chance of saving herself from.

If Luc had ever wanted to assert his dominance, he just had. With pathetic ease.

It took a long moment for Nessa to come back to her senses. She felt undone but deliciously sated. And yet there was something deeper, throbbing with need inside her, an instinctive knowledge of something even greater to come.

'*Ca va?*'

Nessa opened her eyes to see Luc looking at her. If he'd looked smug or remotely triumphant she might have wakened from this craziness but he didn't. He looked slightly...fascinated.

She nodded. She didn't know what she was but it was better than *okay*.

Luc's hand moved up to cup her breast, fingers finding and pinching her nipple lightly. Immediately her body was humming again, as if she hadn't just orgasmed.

She realised that Luc's chest was within touching distance and reached out shyly to touch him. Tentative, but growing more adventurous when she felt how warm he was, and the latent steel of his body underneath.

'You really don't have to pretend, *minou*.'

He sounded slightly amused. Nessa's hand stopped and she looked at him. 'Pretend...what are you talking about?'

'Pretend to be some kind of innocent. I told you I don't get off on games. It's really not necessary. I want you, more than I've ever wanted anyone else.'

She wasn't pretending; she *was* innocent! His face suddenly looked stark, as if he hadn't meant to say those words, and treacherously it robbed her of any words of defence. Somehow she knew that if she said anything, this would all stop and she wasn't ready for it to be over.

So she did the most selfish thing she'd ever done

in her life and said nothing. She touched him again, placing her mouth over his blunt nipples and exploring with her tongue, feeling ridiculously powerful when she heard him hiss between his teeth and felt him catch her hair again, winding it around his hand as if he needed to restrain her.

It was an incredible aphrodisiac to know she had any kind of effect on Luc Barbier.

She explored further, down his body, tracing her fingers over abs so tight that her own quivered in response. And then she reached his belt. There was a moment, and then he said gruffly, 'Keep going.'

So she undid the belt, sliding it through the loops, then his button and the zip. She could feel the potent thrusting bulge under the material and her hand started to shake as she drew the zip down.

Luc muttered something in French and then he was standing up and pushing his trousers down and off, taking his underwear with them. And now he was naked and fully aroused and Nessa couldn't speak, taking in his virile majesty.

'Touch me.'

Nessa sat up and reached out, curling her hand tentatively around Luc's rigid erection. She found it fascinating—the silky skin pulled taut over all that potent strength. There was a bead of moisture at the top, and, acting completely on instinct, she leant over and touched it with her tongue, tasting the tart saltiness. Her mouth watered and she wanted to wrap her whole mouth around him but he was pulling her away saying, 'Stop...or I won't last.'

Luc's brain was so fused with lust and heat and need that it was all he could do not to thrust between the tempting lushness of Nessa's lips. All rational thought had gone. He couldn't wait. He needed to feel her whole body around him, not just her mouth.

He moved over her, between her spread legs, and for a second the way she was looking up at him, with some expression he'd never seen on a woman's face before, almost made him stop, and take a breath. This was too crazy. Too rushed. He needed to get his wits back...

But then he felt her hands on his hips as if guiding him into her and he was lost again, drowning in need.

Nessa was filled with a raw sense of earthy urgency so sharp and intense she found herself reaching for Luc, wanting to bring him closer. He knelt between her legs, spreading them wider with his hands.

Nessa was vaguely aware that her shirt was open, her breasts bared and her skirt ruched around her waist. But any selfconsciousness fled when the head of his erection nudged against where she was so hot and wet. She instinctively circled her hips up to meet him.

Nothing could have prepared her though for that first cataclysmic penetration. She felt impaled. Luc was too big. He looked at her for a moment with a line between his brows and her heart stopped. *Did he know?* But then he slid in a little further. The discomfort faded as he filled her more, all the way until she couldn't breathe.

As he started to move in and out he lifted her leg and wrapped it around his hip, making him move even deeper inside her. Nessa was clasping his shoulders, needing something to hold onto as tension wound into a tight ball deep inside her.

She'd never felt anything like the glorious glide of his body in and out of hers. She was utterly consumed with the moment and what this man was doing to her.

She wrapped both legs around him now, digging her heels into his buttocks, wanting, needing more. Sweat made their skin glisten and their breathing was harsh as they both raced to the pinnacle of the climb.

Luc's movements became faster and Nessa could only cling on for dear life as the oncoming storm hurtled towards her. He arched her up towards him and found a nipple with his hot mouth, sucking it deep, and at that moment Nessa was flung into the eye of the storm and she cried out a release that went on, and on, and on.

Luc went taut above her and she felt the warm rush of his release inside her but at that point her brain was too burnt out to think of anything else but the oblivion that extreme pleasure brought in its wake.

After a long moment, with Luc's body embedded in hers, Nessa felt as if she were claiming him. Immediately she rejected it as a ridiculous notion. Luc Barbier was not a man who would ever be claimed. That much was obvious.

She unlocked her arms from around his neck. His breath was warm against her neck. He moved then and she winced as tender muscles protested. He didn't look at her as he pulled away and stood up.

Nessa felt self-conscious and realised how wanton she must look, spreadeagled and with her clothes in total disarray. She started to pull her shirt back over her chest, and her skirt down, feeling cold. She had no idea how to behave in this unorthodox and totally new situation to her—post-sex etiquette. In a stables. On sheets.

Luc was just standing there, half turned away, like a statue. Nessa's hands stilled and she came up on one elbow. Something caught her attention, a long angry scar that zigzagged down Luc's back. She remembered feeling it under her hand in the throes of passion. But it hadn't registered fully.

She sat up. 'What is that on your back?'

Finally, he looked at her and his face was expressionless. Little alarm bells went off.

'My scar?'

She nodded, horrified to imagine him suffering such violence.

'It's a reminder from a long time ago to not forget who I am or where I came from.'

Nessa didn't like how it almost sounded like a warning. 'That sounds serious.'

Luc looked at her. 'My scar isn't serious. What is serious is that we didn't use protection.'

Nessa insides seized with icy panic when she remembered feeling the warm rush of his release. How could she have let that happen?

And then she ordered her sluggish brain to kick into gear and breathed a sigh of relief, tinged with something much more disturbing, like regret. Which was crazy. After her experience losing her mother, Nessa had never relished the prospect of becoming a mother that could die and potentially devastate her family. No matter how cute her little nephew was, or how envious she felt when she saw his special bond with her sister.

She'd taken birth control in college but had stopped soon after leaving, not deeming it necessary when it had never been necessary there. Now she felt supremely naive and foolish.

She forced herself to look at Luc. 'I'm at a safe place in my cycle.'

Luc made a mirthless, almost bitter sound. 'I'm supposed to take your word for it?'

Anger surged at herself for being so lax and at his accusatory tone. She stood up, pulling her shirt together and her skirt down, hair wild and loose. She mustered up every atom of dignity she could given the circumstances and said coolly, 'Well, you'll have to just take my word for it. There were two of us involved, so why weren't *you* thinking of protection?'

Because for the first time in a long time he'd been a slave to his base desires, and protection had been the last thing on his mind.

The realisation sent shards of jagged panic into Luc's guts. How could he have forgotten one of his most stringent rules? He, who had vowed never to have children because he had no desire for a family. Family was anathema to him. And to forget that with this woman, of all women? She was the one most likely to turn around now and use this for her own gain. He might as well have just handed her a loaded gun.

Except even now, Luc was still acutely aware of Nessa's state of déshabillé and how much he wanted to tip her back onto the sheets and take her again. He reached for his trousers, pulling them on angrily, disgusted with his lack of self-control.

He was in the grip of a tumult inside him that he didn't know how to decipher or necessarily want to. All he knew was that what had just happened between him and this woman left anything else he'd ever experienced in the dust. It hadn't just been mind-blowing sex. It had been something else. Something that had affected him on another level.

More disgust ran through him—he'd just done what he expressly forbade his own employees from doing. And now he'd made things exponentially worse by not using protection.

Nessa was looking at him and he realised she was pale. He knew he was being a bastard—it had been his responsibility to protect them. Not hers. He ran a hand through his hair. 'Look, I'm sorry. I just… I don't ever forget about something as fundamental as protection.'

She still looked pale and his chest felt tight. 'What's wrong?' *Had he hurt her?* He was so much bigger than her and the last thing on his mind had been taking care, or being gentle.

What's wrong? What's right? Nessa glanced away for a moment feeling ridiculously vulnerable, and even more so after his apology. She hadn't expected cuddles and a heart-to-heart after sex with this man—no matter how much lust had clouded her brain. But she also hadn't expected him to be so obviously angry with himself.

He hadn't even noticed that she was a virgin. He'd thought she was acting innocent.

She forced herself to look at him and for a second could have almost imagined she'd dreamed up the last hour. He was dressed again, albeit without his tie and jacket. She still felt thoroughly dishevelled and at a disadvantage, and suddenly she wanted to pierce that cool disdain and self-recrimination.

'I don't know what this is between us but I'm not proud of myself,' she said.

Luc looked at her with no discernible change in his expression, but then she saw the merest flash of something almost like hurt cross his face. He stepped closer, and she could see his eyes burning and a muscle jumping in his jaw.

'You might be related to royalty but if you were seated at a banquet table right now and dressed head to toe in couture, you would still want me. Lust makes great levellers of all of us. As does crime,' he answered.

It took a second for Nessa to absorb what he'd said. She couldn't believe he'd misunderstood her. He turned away at that moment and, in spite of the turmoil she was feeling, she reached out, wrapping a hand around his arm. 'Stop.'

He turned around.

She swallowed. 'I didn't mean that I wasn't proud because it was *you*. I meant that I'm not proud because I feel like I'm betraying my family.'

His lip curled. 'It's just sex, Nessa. Don't overthink it.'

She immediately felt silly for opening her mouth. She let his arm go and stepped back. 'Forget I said anything.'

She was about to step around him and make her exit to lick her wounds and castigate herself for being so weak but this time he took her arm, stopping her and asking harshly, 'What is that?'

Nessa looked around and for a second couldn't see what he was looking at behind them. But then she noticed the unmistakable stain of red on the white sheets. Her blood. Her virginal blood.

She went icy cold, and then hot with humiliation. Quickly she stood in front of it. 'It's nothing.'

He moved her aside and looked closer. If the ground could have opened up and swallowed Nessa whole she would have jumped right in.

He looked at it for so long Nessa wished she'd taken the chance to escape. But then he moved back, and there was such a mix of expressions on his face that she was stunned into silence.

Luc couldn't believe what his eyes had just told him, and yet he couldn't stop thinking about all the moments when he'd thought she was putting on some act with the shy tentative kisses, the self-consciousness, and the way she'd run the other night.

But what beat at his brain most of all had been that

moment, when he'd felt her body clamping tight around him. It had made him stop, and look at her, but the question had barely formed in his mind before her muscles had been relaxing to let him go deeper, and he'd conveniently blocked the half-formed question out, too desperate to sate himself.

She'd been a *virgin*.

That knowledge filled him with too many things to untangle now. One of which was a fierce feeling of satisfaction that he'd been her first. It was something he'd never imagined feeling in a scenario like this.

'Why didn't you tell me?'

She opened her mouth and closed it again, and that only brought Luc's attention to those lush lips and how they'd felt on his body.

'Well?' he snapped. She flinched minutely and Luc bit back a curse at himself. He felt unmoored, boorish. Out of control.

A hint of defiance came into her eyes and it comforted him. This woman was no wilting lily.

'I didn't think it was relevant. Or that you'd notice.'

Luc burned inside at that. He had noticed but had dismissed it. 'I don't sleep with virgins.'

Nessa folded her arms and said tartly, 'Well, you just did.'

He felt the burn of more self-recrimination. 'If I'd known I wouldn't have been so...rough.'

Amazingly, Nessa blushed and glanced away. 'You weren't too rough.' She hesitated. 'It was okay.'

'Okay?'

She looked back at him. 'I mean, I don't know, do I? It was my first time.'

Her words propelled Luc forward and he caught her arms in his hands. She felt unbearably slender and delicate all of a sudden. He was acutely aware of how petite she was. 'It was more than *okay*. I felt your body's response, and not everyone has that experience for their first time.'

She blushed even more now but she stared at him. 'I'll have to take your word for it.'

Luc was torn between laughing out loud at her sheer front and tipping her back onto the sheets to remind her exactly how unbelievably good it had been. But she'd be sore, and frankly he didn't like the strength of the emotions running through him. This was not a post-sex scenario he had ever experienced before. Usually there was a bare minimum of conversation before he left. Right now it was hard to let her go.

In fact, he was afraid that the longer they stood there, the more likely it was that he *would* take her again. Especially when she was looking at him with those huge pools of amber and green. Her face flushed and hair wild. Clothes in disarray.

Doing something he'd never done before—exhibiting any kind of post-sex tenderness—he put his hands to the buttons of her shirt and did them up, gritting his jaw when he felt the swells of her breasts underneath the material.

He stood back. 'You should go. Take a bath. You'll be tender.'

She swallowed and for a moment looked endearingly unsure. And unbelievably sexy.

'*Go*, Nessa,' Luc growled, aware of the tenuous grip on his control.

She looked around at the sheet and made a gesture. 'I should take—'

'I'll take care of it.' This was unprecedented territory for Luc.

Finally, she left and Luc watched her walk out, slightly unsteadily. Her skirt was still at an angle and all he could see were those slim legs and remember how they'd felt clamped around his hips. She was a lot stronger than she looked.

Luc tried to make sense of what had just happened but it was hard. One thing was sure, though: Nessa O'Sullivan had just managed to impact somewhere no one had touched him in a long, long time. And if he was to consciously allow her to gain any more advantage, then he'd be the biggest fool. What just happened…it couldn't happen again. No matter how much he wanted her.

Nessa stayed in the bath until the water cooled and her skin had started to pucker. There was tenderness between her legs but also a lingering buzz of pleasure.

She couldn't quite believe the sequence of events that had led to that frantic coupling on sheets in a stables with Luc Barbier.

Her whole body got hot just recalling how quickly they'd combusted. How easily she'd given in, and given away her innocence. And, how easily she'd justified it to herself. *And you'd do it again right now if you could*, whispered a wicked little voice. Nessa knew it was true. She wouldn't have the strength to resist Luc again, not after that. It was like experiencing paradise and then having to deny it existed.

And while he wasn't here right now, cosseting her and whispering sweet nothings in her ear, the way he'd told her to leave and take a bath, and how he'd done up her buttons for her, had made her feel pathetically cared for.

She cringed and wanted to submerge herself under

the water when she thought of how Luc had to be seriously regretting what had happened. Nessa cringed even more to think of him disposing of the evidence of her virginity.

He was a man used to sleeping with the most beautiful women in the world: experienced worldly women, not naive innocents like Nessa.

She took a deep breath as if testing for emotional pain and she let it out shakily. Her emotions were intact. Luc had impacted her on a physical level but that was all, she assured herself.

Liar, mocked a voice. Seeing those slivers of the more complex man under his stern exterior, and his gruffly tender treatment at the end had moved her more than she cared to admit.

If she saw any more evidence of *that* Luc, she wasn't so sure her emotions would remain untouched. And forming an attachment to Luc Barbier would be a lesson in futility and pain. Of that she was certain.

One thing was clear. The moment of madness just now couldn't happen again. Not that Nessa imagined for a second that Luc wanted it to. His self-recrimination had been palpable, and that suited Nessa fine. *It did*, she told herself. No matter what her newly awakened body might be aching for in secret places.

CHAPTER SIX

Luc LOOKED AT the figure riding the horse and couldn't believe what he was seeing. The boy—for it had to be a boy, he was too slight to be a man—was riding one of his prize thoroughbreds as if he'd been riding her all his life.

Jockey and horse were one entity, cutting through the air like a bullet. He'd never seen the filly perform so well. And he already itched to see what the jockey would be like on Sur La Mer, back in France. He just knew instinctively that he could be the missing link to get the best out of the horse.

Luc looked at his chief Irish trainer. 'Okay, who is he and where has he been before now, and can we retain him immediately?' Luc knew how rare it was to find raw talent like this.

Pete had come to him a few minutes ago and just said enigmatically, *You need to see this.*

Pete grinned. 'He's a *she.*'

'What the—?' Luc looked back and his skin prickled with a kind of awareness. The jockey and horse came around the nearest corner and as they thundered past him he caught a glimpse of dark red hair tucked under the cap and a delicate jawline. He recalled Percy Mortimer saying Nessa was a good rider.

Luc's nervous system fizzed immediately, even before Pete said, 'It's Nessa O'Sullivan.'

For the past couple of days Luc had been ruthlessly crushing any memories or reminders of what had happened in the stables. At night, though, when he was asleep, he couldn't control his mind: his dreams were filled with X-rated memories. He'd woken every morning with a throbbing erection and every muscle screaming for release.

He hadn't been at the mercy of his body like this since his hormones had run wild as a teenager.

It was galling; humiliating.

And here she was again, provoking him.

Pete was looking at him. 'Well?'

Luc controlled himself with effort. 'What the hell is she doing on my horse?'

Pete's grin faded. He put up his hands in a gesture of supplication. 'I've known Nessa for years, Luc. I know her whole family. They've been riding horses since before they could walk. Her sister and father are excellent trainers. I've seen Nessa race—she's not done many, granted, but she's got her licence and she's a natural. We were short a rider today and so I asked Mrs Owens if I could borrow her. I don't know what she's doing working for your housekeeper, Luc, but she's wasted there. She should be out here. All she's been waiting for is an opportunity to prove herself.'

If it had been anyone else but his trusted and very talented trainer, and if Luc hadn't seen her with his own two eyes, he would have fired Pete on the spot. And he wasn't about to tell Pete why Nessa was working at the house.

He looked back at the gallops to see the riders dismounting and walking the horses back to the stables. He spotted her immediately, the smallest of the bunch, immediately bringing to mind how tight she'd felt when he'd breached her body. *Virgin. No protection.* And he still wanted her with a hunger that unnnerved him.

Oblivious to what was going on in his head, Pete said, 'Luc, I think you should use her in the next race. Give her a chance.'

Luc looked at Pete, provocation and frustration boiling over. 'You've done enough for now. I don't care how talented a jockey she is, she knew better than to say yes to your request.'

Nessa was still buzzing with adrenalin after exercising the horse, and chatting with the other riders, some of whom she knew. They'd all been curious as to why she was here but she'd kept it vague.

She was in the changing room and had just pulled off her mud-spattered top when the door slammed open and she whirled around, holding the shirt to her chest. 'Do you mind?'

But it wasn't Pete or one of the other riders entering the ladies' changing room near the racing stables. It was Luc Barbier and he looked murderous. The door shut behind him with an ominously quiet click, and the room was suddenly tiny.

She'd deliberately avoided thinking about Luc's reaction if he found out. Apparently for good reason.

He stood before the door in worn jeans and a black polo shirt. He'd never looked more forbiddingly sexy. Nessa's insides melted even as she tried to ignore her body's response. Luc hadn't come near her for the past couple of days, making it perfectly clear that the other night couldn't have been a bigger mistake. And while

Nessa agreed on every rational level, she hated to admit that she'd been hurt by the dismissal.

Guilt lanced her now. Had she agreed to Pete's request to fill in for one of the jockeys, knowing Luc wouldn't approve, to provoke a reaction? Nessa was afraid she knew the answer to that.

'What the hell do you think you're doing?' Luc's voice was quiet, which made him sound even angrier.

Nessa lifted her chin, refusing to be intimidated, clutching her top to her chest. 'Pete was short a rider and so he asked me if I'd fill in. I was just doing him a favour.' *Liar*, mocked a voice. The thrumming of her pulse told her very eloquently why she'd done it.

'You knew very well that you weren't allowed to go near the horses. I don't let anyone that I don't personally vet myself near them.'

Nessa tried not to sound defensive. 'Pete knows me. He's seen me ride before. And it wasn't his fault,' she said hurriedly, having visions of Luc sacking him. 'I knew I should have said no…but I couldn't resist. It's my fault.'

Once again Luc was struck somewhere uncomfortable at how readily Nessa was able to take the blame from someone else. Her brother, and now Pete, who wasn't even related to her.

As if physically incapable of allowing space between them, Luc moved closer, seeing how Nessa's hands tightened on her top. He commented, 'It's not as if I haven't seen you before.'

She blushed. Amazingly. And it had a direct effect on Luc's body, sending blood surging south.

She scooted her head and arms back into her top but not before Luc had seen a generous amount of pale flesh and her breasts encased in a sports vest top. Her hair was caught at the back of her head in a bun, and he curled his hands to fists to stop from reaching out and undoing it.

She folded her arms over her chest and then said stiffly, 'I'm sorry. It won't happen again.'

Luc made a split-second decision. 'I'm afraid that's not really up to you.'

She looked at him. 'What do you mean?'

'There's a race this weekend; I want you to ride the same filly you were just riding.'

She went pale, and then colour washed back into her cheeks. It was fascinating to see someone so expressive. And then she looked suspicious. 'You don't want me near your horses. Why would you let me do this?'

'Because I'm not stupid enough to let someone as naturally gifted as you waste your talent, especially not when it might win me a race. I am, after all, running a business. And your brother owes me a million euros, which you have taken on as your debt. If you win, the money will go towards paying it off.'

Nessa was so stunned by what he'd just proposed she was speechless for a long moment. Eventually she managed to get out, 'I…well, thank you.'

Luc was brusque. 'You'll obviously work to Pete's instruction from now on.'

Then he turned to walk back out and Nessa blurted out, 'Wait.'

When he stopped at the door he turned around and she almost lost her nerve, but she forced herself to ask, 'What about what happened? The other night.' *As if he wouldn't know what she was talking about.*

She cringed inwardly. She hated that she'd felt compelled to ask. She hated that she couldn't be as nonchalant as him, and pretend the other night had never happened.

Luc looked remote. Almost like a stranger. 'What happened between us won't happen again. It was a mistake. You're here to pay off the debt through racing or until your brother returns my money, whichever happens first.'

And then he walked out and she felt as if he'd just punched her in the belly. She was breathless, and then she castigated herself. Hadn't he warned her, that first night in his room, that she'd get burned?

She had nothing to entice a man like Luc Barbier beyond that brief moment of craziness.

And here he was offering her the opportunity of a lifetime—a chance to ride for one of the great trainer/owners in the racing world. Luc might have a rogue's reputation but no one could discredit his amazing accomplishments, even if they weren't quite sure how he'd achieved them without a background steeped in the industry.

Nessa had to concede that, from what she'd seen so far, his incredible work ethic was responsible for much of his success. Without fail, he was up with his earliest employee, and probably one of the last to bed. She'd even seen him help with mucking out a stables one day, practically unheard of for someone at his level.

Nessa told herself she should be relieved that Luc had laid out in brutal terms where they now stood in terms of their short-lived intimacy. Conducting an affair with a man like him was total folly at best and emotional suicide at worst. Not to mention the guilt she'd feel.

But the most humiliating part of it was knowing that

if he'd kissed her just now, she'd have been flat on her back on the cold tile floor, showing not an ounce of restraint or control.

'I can't believe she's actually won.'

'Never fail to surprise us, eh, Barbier?'

'A female jockey? Who is she? Has anyone heard of her? Where did she come from?'

'Trust Barbier to come from left-field with a win like this...he just can't resist throwing the cat amongst the pigeons...'

Luc heard all the indiscreet whispers around him, but he was too stunned to care. Nessa had won the race. Unbelievably. On the horse with the longest odds.

She was coming into the winner's enclosure now, with Pete not far behind accepting his own congratulations. Luc caught the horse as she passed, stopping her momentarily. Nessa had a huge grin on her mud-spattered face and something turned over inside him.

He patted the horse and looked up at her, at an uncharacteristic loss for words. Her smile faded and he noticed how she tensed and something inside him rejected that. Normally he never had a problem congratulating his jockeys but this was different. It was *her*. Eventually he said, 'Well done.'

'Thank you. I can't believe it myself.'

That glimmer of uncertainty on her face reminded him of how she'd looked the other night when she'd stood before him all mussed and flushed after sex. His body tightened with need.

She was led on, and then slid off the horse to be weighed after the race. Luc watched her across the enclosure. She took off her hat and her hair tumbled down. A man behind him made an appreciative whistling sound and Luc spun around, glaring at him. The man blanched.

When Luc looked back Nessa was walking away from the podium and stewards with her saddle, presumably to go back to the changing rooms.

Pascal Blanc hurried over to him at that moment, shaking his head and smiling. 'Luc, this is incredible. Nessa is a sensation; it's all people are talking about, wondering who she is and where she came from. You've both been invited to a function this evening in Dublin, celebrating the racing industry in Ireland. I don't think I need to tell you how important this is.'

Luc knew exactly how important it was. So far the industry here had largely been closed to him socially, but one win with an outsider filly and a beautiful young female jockey and suddenly he was being granted access.

Yes, said a voice. *This is it.* And yet now that the moment had arrived, all Luc could seem to think about was not the potential for acceptance at last, but what Nessa would look like in a dress.

'Is it really necessary for me to attend?' Nessa's gut was churning.

'Yes, it is,' Luc said, looking frustrated. They'd returned to the racing stables after the race and Luc had just informed Nessa about the function in Dublin that night.

She couldn't even begin to describe the trepidation she felt at the thought of some glitzy social event. She'd never been a naturally girly girl and her few experiences of dressing up had invariably ended in failure when she'd seen how wide of the mark she was with current trends.

There'd been one memorable incident in university when she'd gone to a party and a girl had said snarkily, *I didn't know it was a fancy dress party.* After that, Nessa had given up trying to fit in. She wasn't cool, or fashionable, or blessed with any innate feminine wiles or sensuality. Luc had proved that in no uncertain terms.

'I don't have anything suitable to wear to an event.'

Luc glanced at his watch. 'I've asked a stylist to come from a local boutique with a selection of dresses. She's also bringing someone to look after hair and make-up.'

Nessa felt as if a noose were tightening around her neck. Luc was still dressed in a three-piece suit, in deference to the dress etiquette of the races. It was distracting to say the least, especially in the way that it seemed to be moulded to his muscles.

'Why is it so important that I go? I'm just the jockey. They won't know who I am.'

Luc took out his mobile phone and, after a few seconds of swiping, handed it to Nessa. She gasped. It was a headline on an online racing journal. *Two gorgeous fillies triumph at the Kilkenny Gold Stakes!* And there was a photo of a beaming Nessa astride the horse, being led around the winner's enclosure.

'Unfortunate headlines aside, you're a sensation. Everyone could see, just from that race, how talented you are.'

Nessa handed the phone back, feeling a little sick. She'd wanted to do well, but she'd never expected this level of attention. The euphoria of the win was draining away to be replaced with anxiety. She'd never liked being front and centre, and certainly not in an environment outside her comfort zone.

Her sister Iseult had struggled with this kind of thing

too, but she'd since blossomed into a poised and elegent Sheikha of Merkazad. Even so, she had confessed to Nessa that she still found it hard sometimes to pretend that she was comfortable with dressing up.

But Nadim loved her no matter how she looked or what she wore. A pang lanced Nessa to think of their bond. She felt very alone all of a sudden.

'What's wrong?'

Luc's question jolted Nessa out of her reverie. He was frowning down at her, and she hated the thought of him seeing an ounce of the vulnerability she felt. She was being ridiculous. It was just an event.

She tipped up her chin. 'Nothing is wrong. What time should I meet the stylist?'

'They'll be here within the hour. I've asked Mrs Owens to move you to a bigger bedroom suite to accommodate you getting ready. We may have more events like this to go to. I'll meet you at the front of the house at seven p.m.'

Nessa looked at herself in the mirror and blinked. *Was that her?* She felt the same inside, but on the outside she looked like a stranger. Her hair was pulled back on one side and trailed over her other shoulder in a rippling cascade of glossy waves. She wore a shimmering black dress that clung to her shoulders in a wide vee, and showed what felt like acres of pale flesh.

It was gathered under her breasts and fell in a swathe of material to the floor. Under the dress she wore spindly delicate high heels that made her walk with her chest out and with an unnatural arch in her back.

Her make-up was discreet, at least, but it made her eyes look huge. Her lips glistened with flesh-coloured lipstick.

The stylist stood back and looked at her critically. 'You look stunning, Miss O'Sullivan.'

'Call me Nessa, please,' Nessa said weakly, feeling like a fraud.

The stylist looked at her watch as the hair and make-up girl tidied up her things.

'It's almost seven p.m. You should go down to meet Mr Barbier.' The stylist winked. 'What I wouldn't give to swap places with you right now. He is *gorgeous*.'

The make-up girl giggled, clearly of the same opinion. Nessa forced a smile and desisted from saying that she'd be more than happy to swap places. But they wouldn't understand.

She made her way downstairs, careful in the high-heels. When she got to the hallway the door was ajar and she went out. Luc was standing with his back to her on the steps, his hands in his pockets, the jacket material pulled taut across his back. It reminded her of the scar she'd seen and how he'd dismissed it so enigmatically.

For the brief moment before he turned around Nessa could almost imagine she was one of those beautiful women who populated his world, and that this was a date. But then he turned around, and those dark eyes raked her from head to toe without an ounce of emotion or expression on his face and Nessa didn't feel beautiful any more. She was remembering how he'd told her that first night that even if she'd come via the front door and dressed to impress, she still wouldn't be his type...

For a second Luc almost didn't recognise Nessa. His chest tightened and his whole body went taut with the need to control his instantaneous response.

She looked beautiful. She surpassed anything he could have possibly imagined, and yet there was nothing showy about her. She oozed understated elegance in the long black dress. His body lit on fire when he registered the low-cut vee and saw how much of her skin was exposed, including the pale swells of her breasts.

He dragged his gaze back up, feeling a little dizzy. He saw her biting her lip, and looking anxious. 'Is it okay?' she asked.

Luc was a little incredulous. Did she really have no idea how gorgeous she was? His reaction to her, and his instincts urging him to believe this wasn't an act, made his voice curt. 'It's fine. We should go.'

Nessa tried not to feel disappointed by Luc's reaction as he turned away and went down the steps, towards where a sleek four-wheeled drive was parked. The other night was a mistake, not to be repeated, and this was *not* a date.

She made her way across the courtyard after him in the vertiginous heels, praying she wouldn't sprain her ankle. He was holding a door open and she got in gingerly, holding the dress up so it wouldn't get caught.

Luc walked around the bonnet. Nessa couldn't help observing how good he looked in the tuxedo. When he was behind the wheel he drove them a few short miles to where a helipad was located, away from the racing stables and stud.

'We're going in a helicopter?'

He looked at her. 'It's an hour's drive to Dublin. The event starts in half an hour.'

Nessa tried her best to look nonchalant and not shocked. When she stepped out of the car, though, she stopped. The grass was soft and damp after recent rain and she wasn't sure how to navigate the terrain in her shoes from here to where the helicopter was waiting.

Luc came around the front of the car and saw her, obviously assessing her predicament. Nessa was about to bend down and take the shoes off, but before she could do so Luc had lifted her into his arms effortlessly and was striding towards the helicopter where a pilot was waiting by the open door.

Nessa clung to his neck breathlessly, burningly aware of his hard chest and strong arms. Luc however showed no such similar awareness when he deposited her into the seat with a grim expression and did up her seat belt before she could object. His hands glanced off her bare skin as he adjusted it and Nessa's blood fizzed.

She was glad when he sat in the front beside the pilot because she didn't want him to decipher what she was thinking. He couldn't have made it more glaringly obvious that she was just someone he was tolerating, until such a time as she ceased to be a thorn in his side.

When they'd put on their headphones he turned around. 'Okay?'

She nodded rapidly and forced a bright smile wanting to leave him under no illusion that she was anything other than *okay* and completely unmoved by what had happened between them.

They took off and, as much as she hated Luc Barbier right now, she couldn't help feeling emotional when they swooped low over the River Liffey in Dublin's city centre and she saw the capital city glittering like a jewel in the dusky evening light. It was magical.

They landed, and Nessa was saved the ignominy of being carried again as she was able to walk to the car waiting for them. Luc sat in the back with her, and the plush interior, which looked huge, felt tiny with him so close to her.

The journey to Dublin Castle took ten minutes and soon they were pulling up in the majestic forecourt. Lights shone out onto the cobbles as a glittering array

of people were disgorged from sleek cars. And Nessa—
who had just won her first prestigious race on a thoroughbred horse—had never felt more terrified in her
life.

Luc got out and came around to help Nessa out. She
looked at his hand for a moment, hesitating, and then
took it, letting him help her. As soon as she was standing, though, she let go as if burned.

Luc figured that he couldn't blame her after his less
than gracious reaction to how she looked. He'd never
been less charming. With other women he at least put
on a show of being civilised. But with Nessa, he didn't
know where to put himself.

When he'd picked her up to carry her over the grass
to the helicopter it had been purely for expediency, but
it had been torture to feel her slender frame curling into
his, her arms around his neck. He'd been as hard as a
rock for the entire journey.

It irritated the hell out of him that he'd made it more
than clear that what had happened between them was
a one-off mistake, and she didn't seem in the least inclined to try and change his mind.

Mind you, in a dress like the one she was wearing,
she didn't have to do much. He was already aware of
men around them looking at her twice. He was also
aware of the way he felt inclined to bundle her back
into the car, and take her straight to some private place
where he could lay her out on a bed and make love to
her as he *hadn't* done the first time.

Her first time. Surely, whispered a wicked little voice,
she deserves to know what it can really be like?

Luc shut it down and put out his arm for Nessa to
take. He had the feeling when she slipped her arm

through his that she was only touching him to stay upright in those vertiginous heels. They added inches to her height and only made him more aware of how much closer her mouth would be to his.

Then he noticed how pale she was. He stopped just before they walked into the pool of golden light spilling out onto the beautiful enclosed courtyard of the castle. 'Is something wrong?'

She shook her head and glanced at him briefly, shooting him a fake smile. 'Everything is fine. Why wouldn't it be?'

'Because you look like you're about to walk the plank rather than walk amongst your peers at one of the highest profile society events of the year.'

She made an inelegant snorting sound. 'Peers? Don't make me laugh.'

Luc was shocked at the bitter tone to her voice. He'd never heard it before. But before he could ask her what she meant, a young officious woman in a long violet gown was coming forward to greet them. She was the PR lady. 'Mr Barbier, Miss O'Sullivan, we're so grateful you could both join us at short notice. Please, do come this way.'

They were led through the marbled foyer into a huge ceremonial room where the drinks reception was being held before the dinner. Luc noticed people turning to look, and how their eyes widened when they saw who it was. He usually would have wanted to snarl at them that he had as much of a right to be here as they did. But for the first time, he found himself not really caring how they were looking at him.

He was too distracted by the woman by his side.

They were served with champagne and Nessa took her arm out of Luc's. Perversely he wanted to take it back. She was looking up at him with a minute smile playing around her mouth. He said, 'What?'

'You said I looked as if I was about to walk the plank but you look as if you're about to take someone's head off.'

Luc relaxed his features, unnerved she'd read him so well.

'Haven't you been to this event before?' she asked.

Luc took a healthy swig of champagne and shook his head. 'No. They've never deigned to invite me. I was too much on the edges of acceptability for them.'

'So you don't want to be here?'

Luc looked out over the crowd and noted the furtive glances he drew. 'Whether or not I want to be here is beside the point. I've worked as hard as anyone here, harder, perhaps. I deserve to be respected and not stared at like an exhibit in a zoo. I deserve to be here.'

As soon as he'd spoken, he was shocked he'd let the words spill out. In a bid to divert Nessa away from asking more questions, he turned to her. 'What was that outside…? You made a comment.'

She flushed and took a sip of her own drink. Luc noted that her hands were tiny, with short, functional nails and clear varnish, unlike the elaborate claws many women sported. He also noticed that her hands looked softer already. His body thrummed with an arousal he was barely able to keep in check, especially when his taller vantage point gave him an all too enticing view of her cleavage.

'I didn't mean anything by it.'

Luc's gaze narrowed on her. 'Nessa…'

She rolled her eyes. 'I don't count these people as my peers, not really.'

'Why? You come from the same world. You have

a family lineage in racing to rival any one of these guests.'

'Perhaps. But that counts for nothing when you're losing it all. When my father got ill and the stud started to go downhill, most of these people turned their backs on us, as if we were cursed. See that man over there?'

Luc followed her eyeline to a portly man with a face flushed from drink. The man caught Nessa's eye and went even redder, sidling out of sight like a crab disappearing under a rock.

'Who is he?' Luc asked.

'He's P J Connolly. Used to be one of my father's oldest friends. They grew up together. He runs the state-owned stud. He was in a position to help us out but he never did. It was only when Nadim bought us out and the farm started to recover that we became personae gratae again.'

Luc was stunned. He hadn't expected to feel any sort of affinity with Nessa. He'd assumed she'd be air-kissing old friends and acquaintances within minutes, but she too knew how the cold sting of rejection felt.

She turned back to him then and looked up. 'How *do* you know so much about horses? I can't believe it was just through your work with Leo Fouret.'

Luc balked at her question. Most people were usually too intent on believing one of the many rumours about him to ask him such a question directly.

'Didn't you hear?' he said with a lightness he didn't feel. 'I'm descended from gypsies.'

Nessa just looked at him and cocked her head to one side as if considering it. 'I don't think so.'

A weight lodged in Luc's chest at her easy dismissal of such a lurid claim. At that moment the PR lady came back to them, smiling widely. 'Mr Barbier, Miss

O'Sullivan, there are a few people who would love to congratulate you on your win today. Please follow me.'

The weight in Luc's chest didn't abate as the woman led them further into the room. No one had ever looked at him as Nessa just had, without any guile or expectation for a salacious story.

CHAPTER SEVEN

Nessa was still irritated by the interruption earlier. Luc had looked as if she'd delivered an electric shock rather than asked an innocuous question. She was also still mulling over how he'd been deliberately ostracised from this milieu, and how it had obviously affected him.

They had just finished the sumptuous dinner when Nessa snuck a glance to where Luc was seated opposite her. He was talking to an older woman on his right-hand side, and as Nessa looked at him his eyes met hers and a shaft of sensation went straight into her gut.

She quickly looked away and put her napkin to her mouth, almost knocking over her glass in the process, in a bid to disguise that she'd been staring. When she could risk another glance, she saw the tiniest smile playing around the corners of his mouth, and it couldn't have been due to what the woman was saying because she looked all too serious.

Damn him. Nessa wanted to kick him. He must know exactly what his effect on her was—he'd been the one to awaken her, after all. She felt intensely vulnerable and averted her eyes from then on. Then the chairman got up to make a speech, so thankfully she could focus on that and not Luc. She tuned most of it out except the bit where he said, '…and we'd like to say welcome to our newest import, all the way from France. Luc Barbier stunned the crowds today with a spectacular win…'

Nessa looked at Luc and saw him incline his head in acknowledgement of the chairman's gushing praise. The expression on his face was cool, not for a second revealing anything. Nessa wondered what he was thinking. She was surprised at the affront she felt on his behalf that he hadn't ever been invited before now.

Then she got a mention too and her face flamed bright red as everyone in the room turned their attention to her.

When the speech was over the guests got up to go to a different room where soft jazz was playing. Nessa felt awkward standing alone, not sure if Luc was going to leave her to her own devices now that everyone was lining up to speak to him. She longed to take off the shoes, which were killing her, but to her surprise Luc came straight around the table and walked up to her.

'So, what was making you look so angry during the chairman's speech?'

Nessa blanched. She was far too expressive for her own good, useless at hiding anything. The thought of him noticing her reaction was beyond exposing. Luc wasn't budging, waiting for her reply.

She blurted out, 'Well, it's not as if you're *new* to the scene here, is it? You've been here for a couple of years, had plenty of horses in races and won more than your fair share, not to mention your accomplishments in France.'

Luc's tone was dry. 'This community is a tight-knit one. They don't allow entry purely by dint of your owning a stud and racing stables.'

'That's ridiculous. You have as much right to be here

as anyone. You have a brilliant reputation. Paddy—'
She stopped abruptly and bit her lip.

Luc arched a brow. 'Paddy *what*?'

She cursed her loose tongue. 'Well, you probably won't believe me, but Paddy idolises you. You're all he talked about for the first few months he was working for you. To be honest I think part of the reason he's in hiding is because he's so mortified that he let you down...'

Luc looked at Nessa. He knew vaguely that he should be working the room, capitalising on being welcomed into the fold, but he was more intrigued by this conversation. Disturbingly he did seem to recall Paddy Jnr's rather puppy-like manner and the way he'd followed Luc around for the first few weeks. When Paddy had first disappeared Luc had recalled his slavish devotion and had seen it in a more suspicious light. But now...

Nessa went on. 'He thinks you're a maverick, and he admired your unorthodox methods.'

Luc battled with the urge to trust what Nessa was saying. 'You say one thing but his actions say something else. They're nice words, Nessa, but I don't need staff idolising me. I just need people I can trust.'

'Who *do* you trust?'

'Almost no one,' Luc answered and for the first time in his life it didn't feel like something to be proud of. Disgruntled at the turn in conversation, and not liking how Nessa's affront on his behalf made him feel, he took her arm and led her into the other room where couples were already dancing.

But as soon as they approached the dance floor she became a dead weight under his hand. He glanced at her and she was pale and had a terror-struck expression on her face. Something sharp lanced him in his chest. 'What's wrong?'

She shook her head. 'I can't dance.'

'Everyone can dance. Even me.' He hadn't actually intended on dancing but now he was intrigued.

She started to pull away. 'No, really, I'll just watch. There have to be any number of women here who'd love to dance with you.'

Luc couldn't say he was unaware of the fact that a few women seemed to be circling, but apparently he was with the only woman in the room who *didn't* want to be with him. It was a novelty he didn't welcome.

He moved his hand down her arm to her hand and gripped it firmly and tugged her very reluctant body onto the dance floor.

Nessa felt sick. This was her worst nightmare. She hated dancing in public with a passion and could already hear the laughs and jeers of her brothers ringing in her ears. *Come on, Ness, you can't actually trip over your own feet—oops, she just did!*

'Really, I would rather just—' But her words dried up in her throat when Luc pulled her into his chest and put an arm around her back, then took her hand in his, holding it close to his chest.

Suddenly they were moving, and Nessa had no idea how her feet were even capable of such a thing, but suddenly she was being propelled backwards. No one was staring. Well, they were, but it was at Luc, not her.

Her tension eased slightly but then she became aware of how it felt to be so close to his body. Her eyeline was somewhere around his throat. She was still a full foot smaller than him, even in heels, and she felt very conscious of the taller and more swanlike women that glided past with their partners.

The more she thought about it, the more she had

to wonder if she'd hallucinated what had happened in the stables. Right now, aside from her own thundering heart-rate and physical awareness of him, Luc could have been a total, polite stranger.

And then he looked down at her and said, 'I never really congratulated you on your win today. If you perform like that again, you could be the face of a new generation of women jockeys.'

Had that been today? It felt like years ago. Nessa blushed, not expecting praise from this man. 'It could have been a fluke. If I do badly at the next race it won't help your reputation, or my career.'

Luc shook his head. 'You handled her beautifully. Where did you learn to ride like that?'

Nessa swallowed. The air suddenly felt thicker. She looked at Luc's bow tie. That seemed safer than looking up into the dark eyes that made her feel as if she were drowning.

'My father, before he got too ill. But mainly Iseult; she's got the real talent. I was never off a horse really, as soon as I got home from school and then every weekend when I came home from university—'

'You went to university?'

Nessa looked up. 'Iseult insisted we all go. She knew I wanted to be a jockey and she helped me, but she made sure I had something else to fall back on. The world of racing for female jockeys isn't exactly…easy.'

'What did you study?'

'Business and economics.'

Luc arched a brow. 'That's a little removed from racing.'

Nessa felt self-conscious. 'I know, and it kept me off the scene for a few years. But I didn't mind, really.

I wanted to learn how to take care of our business if anything happened again.'

'Even though your brother-in-law is a sheikh and rich as Croesus?'

Nessa gave him a withering look. 'None of us expect handouts from Nadim. Not even my sister, and she's married to him! And anyway, Iseult hadn't met Nadim by the time I began university, so things were still pretty grim. I knew I didn't have the luxury of doing what I wanted and following a precarious career path.'

Luc had to admit to a grudging respect for Nessa and what her family had obviously been through. Unless of course it was all lies designed to impress him. But as much as he hated to admit it, he didn't think it was.

Since he'd discovered she was a virgin and wasn't putting on some innocent act, it had shifted his perception whether he liked it or not. Also, he could verify her story pretty easily if he looked into it.

She looked up at him again and he saw something like determination in her eyes. 'You never did answer my question earlier…how you came to know so much about horses.'

Luc cursed the fact that they were so close and surrounded by couples. No escape. But then, what did he have to hide except a very banal answer?

'An old man lived in the apartment next to my mother's. He paid me sometimes to do odd-jobs for him, shopping, things like that. He used to be a champion jockey as a young man but an accident had ruined his career. I was always fascinated by his stories and the fact that every thoroughbred today is descended—'

'From just three Arab stallions,' Nessa finished. 'I know, that's always fasincated me too.'

'Pierre became a chronic online gambler but in spite

of knowing everything about every single horse's lineage and form he always lost more than he won. He taught me almost everything, including how to invest prudently, which was ironic because he never took his own advice.'

Nessa felt ridiculously emotional to think of a young Luc Barbier spending all that time with an old injured jockey. 'He sounds like an amazing person. Is he still alive?'

Luc suddenly looked more remote. He shook his head. 'He died when I was a teenager. Before he died, though, he gave me Leo Fouret's number and told me I should call him and impress him with my knowledge of racing, and that if I did he might take me on.'

Which he obviously had. Nessa was a little stunned. But before she could ask Luc any more questions she felt him pull her in much closer to avoid colliding with another couple. She'd almost forgotten they were on a dance floor, surrounded by people.

And then she felt it. The press of his body against her lower abdomen. His arousal.

She looked up, eyes wide, cheeks flaring with heat. Luc arched a brow in silent question as they kept moving, which only exacerbated the situation.

Nessa could hardly breathe. The previous conversation and revelations were forgotten. All she could think about now was the way he'd been so cold the other day in the changing rooms. *What happened between us won't happen again.*

She'd thought he'd meant he no longer desired her. 'I thought you said it wouldn't happen again.' Nessa had just assumed that her virginal state was a huge turn-off.

'I meant what I said,' Luc answered now.

Nessa was confused, and aroused. 'But…' She couldn't articulate it.

'But I still want you?'

She nodded dumbly, feeling completely out of her depth and clueless as to how to handle this situation.

Something stark crossed Luc's face. 'Just because I want you doesn't mean I have to act on it. I don't have relationships with staff.'

Nessa wanted to point out she was hardly staff, as she was working for free, but she was afraid it would sound pleading.

It was torture to be this close to him, knowing that he did want her but could act so cool about it. She was not cool. She was the opposite of cool. Her insides were going on fire and between her legs was hot and slippery.

Emotion was rising and bubbling over before she could stop it. She felt especially vulnerable after hearing his story about the old jockey. She pulled free of his embrace. 'You said you don't play games but maybe you lied, Luc. I think you're toying with me as a form of punishment. You know you're more experienced than me so maybe this is how you get your kicks.'

Nessa walked quickly off the dance floor—as quickly as she could in the heels. To her horror, she felt tears prick the backs of her eyes and she was almost running by the time she reached the foyer.

A man stepped forward. 'Miss O'Sullivan?'

It took her a second to recognise the driver. And then his eyes lifted to something, or someone, behind her. *Luc.* Nessa composed herself, aghast that she'd run like that. The last thing she wanted was for him to know he affected her emotionally.

The driver melted away again and Nessa turned around reluctantly. Luc caught her arm and tugged her over to a discreet corner. He was grim. 'I told you before that I don't play games. And I don't get off by denying myself, believe me—this is new territory for me.'

Nessa felt slightly mollified by that. Maybe she'd overreacted. And now she was embarrassed. If anything she should be rejoicing that he wasn't taking advantage of her lack of control around him.

She pulled her arm free, avoiding Luc's eye. 'It's late, and I promised Pete I'd be up early to train for the next race tomorrow.'

Eventually Luc just said, 'I'll have Brian drive you home. I have a meeting to attend tomorrow morning here in town so I'll stay the night.'

Nessa hated herself for the betraying lurch she felt, as if she'd been hoping that Luc might have said something else, like *stay*. She stepped back. 'Goodnight, Luc.'

He called Brian on his mobile phone and the driver reappeared. Within seconds of Luc delivering his instructions Nessa was in the back of the car, being driven swiftly away from Dublin Castle and back out to Luc's racing stables.

She cringed with humiliation the whole way because, whether he'd intended it or not, Luc had just proven that he might still want her, but she was the last woman on earth he'd take into his bed again. She might've felt like Cinderella going to the ball tonight, but wearing a pretty dress and dancing with a prince wasn't enough to make her a princess.

A short time later, Luc stood with a towel slung around his waist on the balcony of his opulent hotel suite. The moon reflected off the River Liffey where it snaked its way through Dublin city centre. He could hear late night revellers' shouts drifting up from the street. He took a sip of the finest Irish whiskey, but nothing could put a dent in the levels of his arousal. Not even the cold shower he'd just taken.

What the hell was he thinking denying himself the pleasures of female flesh? Even if it was Nessa O'Sullivan and she came with a million and one complications.

Because of the way she looks at you...and because of the questions she asks that reach right down to a place you don't care to analyse.

Luc cursed. He'd told her about Pierre. Pierre Fortin had been one of Luc's saving graces while growing up, teaching him about this fantastical world of horses and racing.

Luc had called his very first racehorse Fortin's Legacy, after his friend.

He never spoke about Pierre. It was too personal, too close to the bone. Sometimes grief for his old friend resurfaced, taking him by surprise with its intensity. But, for the first time, he felt as if he'd done a disservice to his friend by not talking about him more.

Luc cursed again. Tricky questions or no tricky questions, he still wanted Nessa. He realised now that denying himself the carnal satisfaction of taking her to bed again was doing nothing but messing with his head.

He wanted her on a physical level. That was all. And maybe if he reminded her of the physical, it would dissuade her from thinking about anything else. Like asking awkward questions that he wasn't interested in answering or thinking about.

Nessa came second in the next race. Not a win but very respectable all the same. Pete was ecstatic. As for Luc—his reaction, Nessa couldn't figure out, because his expression was always so unreadable and he'd given nothing away when she'd seen him on the sidelines after she'd finished the race.

A few days had passed since the function and she'd hardly seen him. Apparently he'd been in Dublin for meetings, and he'd also visited Paris in the meantime.

Nessa told herself that she didn't care, as she checked herself in the mirror of the VIP guests' bathroom. She pulled at the cream lace pencil skirt she was wearing, feeling overdressed. It had a matching top. Pascal had told her she'd need to dress up for the press, so she'd brought some of the clothes that the stylist had left for her from the night of the function.

She'd pulled her hair back so it looked as sleek as possible and had it in a low bun at the back of her head, and she wore one of those ridiculous-looking fascinator hats, set to the side of her head. She sighed, hoping she looked presentable, and made her way to the VIP room to meet Pascal.

When she got to the plush suite, however, it was empty. There were some refreshments lined up on a table but Nessa ignored her growling stomach and helped herself to some water, not wanting to be caught with a bun in her mouth and crumbs all over her clothes.

The room had an enviable view of the track where races were still being run, but it was blocked off from the other suites, making it very private.

She heard the door open behind her and turned around to greet Pascal and whatever press he'd brought with him but it wasn't Pascal. It was Luc, in his three-piece suit. Looking like the most uncivilised civilised man on the planet.

His dark gaze swept up and down and Nessa's skin

prickled with self-consciousness and awareness. 'Pascal told me to dress appropriately for the press.'

'You look very…*appropriate*,' Luc said. Nessa heard the unmistakable turning of the lock in the door, and her heart-rate increased as Luc prowled into the room like a predator approaching his prey.

Nessa took a step back and said nervously, 'Pascal and the press are going to be here any minute.'

Luc shook his head. 'He's keeping them busy elsewhere for a little while.'

Nessa felt confused. 'Why did you lock us in here?'

Now he was in front of her and looked very tall. And fierce, and sexy. Her body was reacting in spite of her best intentions to try and remain immune to his appeal.

'I locked us in here because I'm done denying myself where you're concerned.'

Luc put his hand around the back of her head, and before she knew what was happening she could feel her carefully constructed bun being undone and her hair was falling down her back. The silly, frivolous hat ended up on the floor.

'Luc, what are you doing?' Why did she sound so breathy?

In a silent answer, he pulled her into his body, tipped her face up and kissed her. Nessa had no defence for this sensual ambush. Her whole body ignited as if it had just been waiting for his kiss and touch.

Luc was like a marauding warrior, leaving no space to think about what was happening. All she could do was *feel*. Succumb. She'd wanted to experience this again so much, and now that it was happening she never wanted it to stop.

Before she could control herself her arms were lifting to wrap around his neck and she was arching her body into his, straining to get closer. His hands moved up and down her back, tracing her waist, going under her top to find the bare skin between that and her skirt.

But, like a cool wind skating over her skin, reality intruded, and she mustered up every ounce of strength she had to pull free.

Nessa was breathing as if she'd just run a marathon. Luc's eyes were burning and she belatedly noticed the stubble on his jaw. She could feel the burn on her skin like a mocking brand.

'What's wrong?'

'What's wrong?' Nessa wrapped her arms around herself defensively. 'You said this wouldn't happen again.'

His face was stark. 'I thought I could resist you, Nessa…but I can't. This will burn up, but then it'll fizzle out. It always does. Let me be the one to teach you how it can be, for as long as we want each other.'

She shivered inside. He'd already done a pretty good job of teaching her how it could be. There was something very illicitly enticing about the prospect of burning up with this man and then letting it *fizzle out*. But she had to be strong. She shook her head. 'I don't think this is a good idea.'

His jaw tightened. She spoke again before he could. 'I'm not just some convenient plaything you can discard and pick up again when it suits you.'

'Believe me,' he growled, 'there's nothing convenient about how I feel about this, or you.'

Nessa smarted. 'Well, I'm sure there are plenty of women who would be far more *convenient* than me.'

He shook his head and closed the distance between them, reaching out to cup her jaw, a thumb moving against her skin hypnotically.

'The problem is that I don't want any other woman. I only want *you*.'

Nessa's throat went dry. Luc Barbier telling her he wanted only her was more than she could handle. Treacherously, she could feel her resistance weaken.

Her heart thumped unevenly. As if trying to soothe a nervy foal, Luc gently cupped her face with his hands, tipping it up to him. He filled her vision.

'I want *you*, Nessa.'

Her mind raced. Could she really handle another intimate encounter with this man? He was already sliding under her skin in a way that mocked her for thinking she could separate her emotions from the physicality.

Dark grey eyes held her captive. 'This is just physical. Don't overthink it. It has nothing to do with your brother or the debt. This is just for us.'

He was saying all the right things to make her weaken even more. *Just physical*. She could keep her emotions out of it if he could.

Nessa was afraid she could no more refuse what Luc was offering than she could stop taking her next breath. She reached up and traced the hard sensual line of his mouth with her finger, overwhelmed that he wanted her so much.

A sense of fatality filled her. She knew she couldn't resist. She reached up and pressed her mouth against his in a silent gesture of capitulation, unable to articulate it any other way.

Luc didn't like to acknowledge the surge of triumph he felt when Nessa's mouth touched his. He didn't like to think of the swirl of emotions he'd just seen in her expressive green eyes. But it wasn't enough to stop him.

He wrapped his arms around her and backed her up against the wall so that he could fully explore that lush and sexy mouth that had been haunting his dreams for days now.

She was as sweet as he remembered. Sweeter. Her small tongue darted out to touch his, and went back again. He captured it, sucking it deep, making her squirm against him. His aching flesh ground into her soft contours and Luc knew that there was no stopping this now. He had to have her with a hunger that was unprecedented.

Somehow a sliver of cold realism entered his head and he took his mouth off Nessa's for a moment. 'I need you, here, right now…'

She looked up at him, eyes molten pools of desire. Slightly glazed. She bit her lip. 'Okay.'

Luc took his hands off her even though it was the hardest thing. 'Take off your clothes.'

Nessa shivered, feeling vulnerable for a moment, but then Luc started to disrobe and she couldn't take her eyes off him as he cast aside his jacket, waistcoat, tie, shirt, and unbuckled his belt.

In a bid to try and keep breathing, Nessa reached for the zip at her neck, but her fingers fumbled and were clumsy. Luc was bare-chested, his trousers open, showing the trail of dark hair that led down into his underwear. She couldn't function.

He stepped forward and said, 'Turn around.'

She did. His hand came to her zip, pulling it down, and then the top slid off from her front. He opened her bra and turned her to face him, pulling it off completely. The crowds outside the VIP box roared as another race was won, but Nessa barely noticed.

Luc discarded his trousers and she could see where the material of his underwear was tented over his erection. Her mouth watered.

'Your skirt. Take it off, now.'

The rough quality of his voice made the flames lick even higher. Nessa knew she should be feeling more self-conscious as she shimmied out of the skirt but she felt emboldened under Luc's appreciative gaze.

For the first time in her life she felt a very feminine thrill of power. It was heady to know she had this effect on a man like Luc Barbier, who was normally so in control.

As soon as the skirt pooled at her feet, she kicked off her shoes and dropped a few inches in height. Luc yanked down his underwear, freeing himself, and pulled her close, wrapping his arms around her and hauling her up and into him as his mouth landed on hers and he devoured her.

She loved the feel of his hard body next to hers. It made her feel delicate and soft. Her arms twined around his neck as she lost herself in his kiss and she wasn't even aware that he'd carried her over to a seat until the earth tilted and she realised he was sitting down and she was straddling his lap.

His hands felt huge on her back and his mouth was on a level with her breasts. He surrounded one hard peak in hot, wet, sucking heat and Nessa's head fell back. When his teeth teased her tender flesh she sucked in a breath, tensing all over.

His erection was thick and long between them. She reached down and touched him, feeling the bead of moisture at the tip. He hissed a breath and she heard the sound of foil being broken before Luc set her back slightly to roll protection onto his length.

He reached for her again, putting his hands on her hips. 'Sit up slightly...that's it...'

As he manoeuvred her into position over his body,

Nessa had never felt more animalistic, or earthy and raw. Luc ripped the side of her panties so they were no longer an impediment, and she felt the thick, blunt head of his erection against her slippery folds.

She had a moment of remembering the brief pain of his first penetration, but as if he were reading her mind his hand soothed her, up and down her back, and he said, 'Trust me, *minou*…it won't hurt again, okay?'

She nodded, bracing her hands on his shoulders as he slowly joined their bodies. Nessa couldn't look away from his eyes as, inch by inch, he filled her so completely that she couldn't breathe.

'You dictate the pace, *ma belle*…'

Luc's voice sounded strained and Nessa felt that rush of feminine power again as she experimented by moving up and down on his body, rolling her hips.

He huffed a laugh against her breast. 'You're going to kill me…'

But Nessa was too distracted by the building tension at her core and how, by moving faster, she could make it build and build. Luc was pressing kisses all over her bared skin, his teeth and mouth teasing her breasts unmercifully. Nessa's movements became wilder, more desperate, as she sensed the shimmering peak approaching. She was losing control. But just as she thought that, Luc took over, demonstrating his experience and mastery.

He clamped his hands onto her hips, holding her still as his body pumped up into hers, stronger and harder and deeper than before.

Sweat glistened on their skin, black eyes burning into hazel. Nessa couldn't hold on. She thought she might die, and then with one cataclsymic thrust she did, but it was an exquisite death that brought with it rolling wave upon wave of pleasure. It was so intense that she had to bite his shoulder to stop herself from screaming out loud and informing the entire racetrack what was happening in this room.

In the aftermath, Nessa couldn't have said how long she was slumped against Luc's body, wrapped in his arms. Her body pulsated rythmically around his, and it sent new shivers of awareness through her.

He gently tugged her head back. She was too sated and exhausted to care how she looked.

'Next time, we make it to a bed and do this properly.'

Next time. More shivers went through her body. *This is only just beginning.*

'Next time?' She injected her voice with a lightness she didn't feel.

Luc smiled and it was wicked and sinful and gorgeous. 'Oh, yes, there'll be a next time and one after that too…and possibly even one after that.'

He punctuated his words with hot, open-mouthed kisses along her bare shoulder. Weakly, Nessa blocked out all of the voices trying to burst the amazing afterglow bubble surrounding her and told herself that she could handle this. She could handle anything, as long as he didn't stop kissing her.

CHAPTER EIGHT

'THERE'S A HORSE at my stables in France that I'd like you to try riding. He's tricky and none of my jockeys there seem to be able to handle him.'

Nessa looked over at Luc from where she was brushing down Tempest, who she'd just been riding out on the gallops. Luc was dressed in his casual uniform of worn jeans and a long-sleeved top with boots. He leaned nonchalantly against the stable door, arms folded. He took her breath away all too easily and she had to focus to remember what he'd said. It had been two days since the X-rated interlude in the VIP suite at the track and her body still felt overly sensitised.

'Ok.'

Luc straightened up. 'When you've finished here go and pack—we'll leave in a couple of hours. We'll stay in my Paris apartment tonight for the function and go to the stables tomorrow.'

Nessa swallowed as she absorbed this information. 'The function?'

He nodded. 'We've been invited to the annual French sports awards. Apparently you're a sensation outside of Ireland too. Everyone wants to see you up close.'

Nessa quailed at that and distracted herself by asking, 'You said we'd stay at your apartment, is that appropriate?'

Luc came towards her and he said, 'It's very appropriate. What part of *next time* didn't you understand?'

He slid his hand around the back of her neck under where her hair was gathered in a messy ponytail and tugged her towards him, saying in a low voice, 'Maybe you need reminding...'

The stable and horse were blocked out as Luc's mouth covered hers. It was so explicit that all she could think about was heat and desperate need. She was barely aware of the brush falling to the ground or the horse moving slightly, jostling them.

Luc lifted his head after a few moments and it took a second for Nessa to open her eyes. *Damn.* She was toast, as well as being well reminded.

With a smug look on his far too gorgeous face, Luc backed out of the stable and walked away, leaving Nessa standing there feeling as if a bolt of lightning had just gone through her body.

She knew that it wasn't a good idea to allow Luc to affect her like this, for many many reasons, not least of which was self-preservation. But the thought of going to Paris with him was just too seductive to resist.

A few hours later, Nessa increasingly felt as if she were in a fairy tale. She'd been to Paris before, on a school trip, but it had been nothing like this. They'd flown in by private jet and then been whisked from the airport into the centre of Paris.

Nessa had noticed that, as they'd passed the graffiti'd high walls on the motorway on the outskirts of the city, Luc had seemed to tense and had looked resolutely out of the window at something she couldn't see.

But was there a more beautiful city than Paris, with its distinctive wide boulevards and soaring magnificent buildings? Especially at this time of year, on the cusp of summer and when spring's blossoms lined the ground like a multicoloured carpet. Not to mention the iconic structures of the Arc de Triomphe and the Eiffel Tower that Nessa could see through the open doors of her bathroom right now.

When they'd arrived at Luc's apartment, at the very top of one of those massive ornate buildings on a wide boulevard, he'd disappeared into a study to take some calls, and a friendly housekeeper had shown Nessa into a guest bedroom suite.

She'd shown her a dressing room that was full to the brim of a stunning array of clothes. Nessa hadn't really known how to react to the fact that Luc was evidently always prepared for his female guests, but it had certainly been sobering. It had been just as well, she'd told herself stoutly, as she hadn't even thought to pack a dress before leaving Ireland.

Now Nessa stood in her bathrobe on the small terrace outside the French doors, and pushed everything out of her head but *this* glorious magical view. Dusk was claiming the skies and the lights of the Eiffel Tower were just beginning to twinkle to life. As if someone had been waiting especially for her.

Nessa smiled and realised with a pang that it had been a long time since she'd felt such uncomplicated happiness. The minute she thought that, though, the smile slid off her face. *How* could she be feeling happy when her brother was still probably worried sick at the thought of ever showing his face again?

She'd tried calling him earlier but his phone had been

off, as it was every other time she'd tried. And her other brother, Eoin, was equally hard to track down.

Just then there was a light knock on the main bedroom door. Nessa's heart was pounding at the thought that it might be Luc, but when she opened the door, it was the housekeeper with two other women. Nessa breathed out.

'Mr Barbier has arranged for these ladies to help you get ready for this evening.'

Nessa forced a smile, the thought of the function making her feel slightly ill. Dublin was one thing. This was Paris. She would definitely need help. 'Thank you, Lucille.'

As the women set to work, Nessa tried to block out the insidious thought of all the other women Luc had had in this exact same spot, being preened especially for him.

'Luc, it's PR gold. They love her. The fact that she's so naturally talented makes her even more interesting. There hasn't been a buzz like this about a female jockey in years. The press have also discovered her family connection to Sheikh Nadim and his wife so now there's even more heat. Invitations are flooding in—you're officially accepted into the inner sanctum now. How does it feel?'

How did it feel? The conversation he'd just had with Pascal on the phone replayed in his head, as did that question. How did it feel to finally be experiencing a measure of the acceptance and respect he'd long since craved?

Curiously anticlimactic, if Luc was brutally honest. Even this view, which took in an exclusive slice of glittering Paris, left him feeling a little hollow.

Just then he heard a noise and turned around to see Nessa in the doorway of the room. And his heart stopped. She'd been beautiful before but now she was... *stunning.*

She wore a long, shimmering green gown. She was covered up from neck to toe and it had long sleeves, but it hugged every delicate curve of her body, highlighting her lithe sensuality. Her hair was up in a chignon and she wore simple diamonds in her ears.

She walked into the room looking nervous. 'I'm ready to go.'

There was a quality to her this evening that made her seem very vulnerable. Luc could tell how out of her depth she was, and he felt a very alien need to say something to reassure her.

Far too gruffly he said, 'You look very beautiful, Nessa.'

As she blushed and smoothed the dress at her hip, he noticed the slight tremor in her hand and it tugged on something very raw inside him. This woman could ride and master a thoroughbred horse, and yet *this* made her tremble?

'I'm not beautiful. You don't have to say that.'

He closed the distance between them in two long strides and tipped up her chin, searching her eyes. 'If you were anyone else I'd say you're fishing for compliments, but I think you really mean it. Who ever made you believe that?'

She pulled her chin free. 'Growing up with two brothers makes it hard to explore your feminine side, and our mother died when I was eight, so I never really had that influence.'

'What about your older sister, Iseult?'

Nessa shrugged. 'She was a tomboy too. And she was always so busy.'

Luc tried to contain his surprise. He'd never known a beautiful woman to not make the most of her assets, until now. Nessa was all the more refreshing for it. He felt in serious danger of taking her by the hand and leading her back to the bedroom to undo all that pristine hair and make-up. He felt unmoored.

He stepped back. 'We should go. The driver will be waiting for us.'

As they descended in the lift Nessa found it hard to douse the ball of warmth Luc's words had created in her chest. *He thought she was beautiful.* She knew he wasn't a man to make empty compliments, and for the first time in her life she actually felt something close to beautiful.

She took deep breaths to quell her nerves and tried not to be too aware of Luc in the small space. But he took up so much of it, effortlessly.

Their eyes met in the mirror of the door and any benefits of the calm breathing Nessa had been doing were gone in an instant. His eyes were like molten black pools, and there was a gleam so explicit that she couldn't breathe.

Everything tightened inside her and she wished she knew how to react in this situation. She could imagine that his other lovers—the ones who had also chosen dresses from the vast array he had—would turn to him now and twine their arms around his neck and say something sultry and confident.

They would take control. They might even press the Stop button and initiate an X-rated moment. Maybe he was waiting for her to do that? Overcome with insecurity, mixed with arousal, Nessa gabbled the first thing that came into her head. 'It was lucky that you're so prepared for your…er…women friends. There were a lot of dresses to choose from.'

His brows snapped into a frown at the same time as the doors opened. She stepped out and he took her arm, stopping her in her tracks. 'What's that supposed to mean?'

Nessa felt inevitable heat climb up from her chest to her face and cursed her colouring and lack of sophistication. 'The clothes in the dressing room. You obviously keep it stocked so your lovers aren't caught short.'

'Those clothes were for you. I had a stylist deliver them before we arrived. I don't entertain women at my apartment and I certainly don't keep a ready supply of clothes for them.'

Nessa was momentarily speechless. There was also a very dangerous fluttering feeling near her heart. He didn't entertain women at his apartment and yet she was here. She finally managed to get out one word. 'Oh.'

Luc looked grim, as if he'd just realised the significance of that too. He said nothing but just propelled her towards the entrance where the car and driver were waiting.

The journey to the hotel where the function was being held was taken in silence. Nessa was afraid of what else might come out of her mouth, so she kept it shut and drank in the view of Paris as they swept through the streets.

She had to remind herself that whatever overwhelming intensity she was feeling for Luc, it wasn't remotely the same for him. He was interested in her for a relatively brief moment, for some bizarre, unknown reason. If she hadn't burst into his life in such dramatic fashion out of a desire to protect her brother, there was no way she would have ever been sitting in the back of his car, dressed in a gown worth more than her annual income.

The sooner she kept reminding herself of that, the better. Because once Paddy sorted out this issue of the missing money, Nessa had no doubt she would be out of Luc Barbier's life so fast her head would be spinning.

A few hours later, Nessa was waiting for Luc in the foyer of the hotel. He was a couple of feet away, conducting a conversation with a man who had just stopped him. Nessa was glad of the brief respite. Luc had been right by her side all evening and she'd been embarrassingly aware of him, and even more acutely aware of every tiny moment he'd touched the base of her back or her arm.

Just then an accented voice said close to her ear, 'Isn't he the most beautiful thing you've ever seen?'

Nessa jumped and looked around to see an older but carefully preserved woman with blonde hair, her blue eyes fixated on Luc. There was something about the nakedly hungry gleam in her gaze that sent a shiver through Nessa.

'I'm sorry, do I know you?'

The women dragged her gaze off Luc and looked Nessa up and down disparagingly. 'You're this new jockey they're all talking about, I gather.' Her eyes narrowed. 'You're sleeping with him, aren't you?'

Nessa flushed. 'I don't think that's any of your—'

But the women grabbed her arm in an almost painful grip. She hissed at Nessa, 'He won't be tamed, you know. A magnificent beast like him will never be tamed.'

Nessa pulled her arm free and looked at the woman, feeling a hot surge of anger and something far more ambiguous. A fierce protectiveness. 'He's not an *animal*. He's a man.'

'Celeste. What a pleasure.'

Nessa's head whipped around to see Luc right behind her, looking sterner than she'd ever seen him, his glaze so black it was obsidian. Clearly it *wasn't* a pleasure.

The woman all but thrust Nessa out of the way and stepped close to Luc. 'Darling…it's been so long.' She laid a hand on his arm and a wave of revulsion went through Nessa to see the long red nails. It made her think of blood.

Luc picked off her hand and took Nessa by the arm, pulling her back beside him. 'Good evening, Celeste.'

He turned and they walked out. Nessa resisted the urge to look back at the woman. She had to be one of Luc's ex-lovers, but the thought of him with her made Nessa's stomach roil.

The car pulled away from the kerb and Luc reeled. He didn't like how it had made him feel to hear Nessa speak those words to that woman. *He's not an animal.* She'd looked ferocious, disgusted on his behalf. She'd had a similar expression on her face when she'd defended her brother so vociferously when they first met.

It impacted Luc in a very visceral way to think of Nessa standing up for him. He didn't need any of that.

He looked at her now and she was pale. His voice was harsh. 'You didn't need to say that. I can fight my own battles.'

She looked at him. 'She was talking about you as if you're not even human. How could you have ever been with her? She's awful.'

Luc felt disgust move through him. 'We were never lovers, even though she did everything in her power to seduce me. She's Leo Fouret's wife. I found her naked in my bed one night and she threatened to accuse me of rape if I refused to sleep with her. That's why I had to leave the stables. Leo Fouret knew what she was like and he offered to pay me off to leave and say nothing. I refused his money but I did take a horse.'

And why the hell had he just let all of that slip out? He didn't owe Nessa any explanations.

Nessa said slowly, 'That's why you reacted the way you did when you found me in your room.'

She continued, 'I'm sorry I opened my mouth but I couldn't help myself. You're *not* just some object.'

No one had ever jumped to Luc's defence before. A disturbing warmth curled through his gut. His anger was draining away. He said, 'In the end she actually did me a favour. If I hadn't had to leave Fouret's stables I might still be working there. That horse became my fortune.'

Nessa shook her head. 'I don't think so. I think you would have always made your fortune.'

Luc looked at her intently. 'You're like a fierce tigress.'

Nessa's cheeks got hot. She didn't know how to respond to that. She regretted letting that woman get to her, but the relief she felt to know that he hadn't been intimate with Celeste was almost overwhelming.

A thousand more questions were on Nessa's lips but then Luc said, 'You did well this evening.'

Nessa shrugged slightly, embarrassed. 'I felt like a bit of a fraud, to be honest. A couple of well-run races does not merit all that attention.'

Luc shook his head. 'You have a natural ability that anyone can see from a million miles away, and you're a beautiful young woman. It's quite a combination.'

She smiled wryly. 'I've been riding in races for a few years now and no one has ever commented before. I think the fact that I'm riding for you is the key. People are fascinated by whatever you do.'

Luc's jaw tightened. 'Fascinated in that way that drivers are when they pass a crash and have to look at the carnage.'

Nessa instinctively wanted to deny that but she knew he wasn't saying it for effect or sympathy. She'd seen how the guests had looked at him all evening. And no wonder, with that woman in their midst. It had to be exhausting, constantly having to prove himself.

Afraid he might see too much on her face, Nessa looked out of the window. They were driving along the Seine and Nessa noticed all the amorous couples. It tugged on a yearning inside her.

She couldn't imagine Luc stopping the car and taking her by the hand to walk along the Seine, and it shook her to realise she'd even thought of that. Whatever was between them wasn't about romance or emotions or love. But even as Nessa thought of that word, *love*, her heart pounded unevenly and she felt cold and clammy. Sick.

Oh, God. She was falling for him.

'Have you ever been to Paris before?'

Nessa jumped at his question and looked at him. *She wasn't in love with him. She couldn't be.* She forced down the panic she was feeling, assuring herself that the romance of Paris had infected her brain momentarily.

She said, 'Only once, a long time ago, on a school trip. I always wanted to come back some day—I've never seen anywhere more beautiful.'

Luc's gaze narrowed on Nessa's face. She'd been a million miles away just now, gazing wistfully out of the window.

His body was in an agony of sexual frustration after an evening standing by her side as countless people, mainly men, he'd noticed, had come and stared as if they'd never seen a woman before. He'd had to control the urge to snarl at everyone so he could pull Nessa into a quiet corner and muss up that far too tidy chignon and peel that dress from her luscious body.

And even though all he wanted right now was to drive straight to his apartment so he could do just that, he found himself leaning forward and instructing his driver to take a small detour.

Nessa looked at him when they came to a stop a few minutes later, after climbing the winding narrow streets as far as they could go in the car. 'Where are we?' she asked.

Luc was already regretting the impetuous decision even as he said, 'Montmartre. Come on, I want to show you something.'

He got out of the car and came around to help her out. Her hand slipped into his, and he had to grit his jaw at the surge of desire even that small, chaste touch provoked.

They walked the small distance up towards Sacre Coeur cathedral. It was late but there were still small knots of people milling around. Luc opened his bow tie and the top button of his shirt. He noticed Nessa shiver slightly in the cool evening air. He took off his jacket and draped it over her shoulders and she looked at him. 'Oh, thank you.'

They came around a corner and the full majesty of the iconic cathedral was revealed. Nessa stopped in her tracks. 'Wow. I'd forgotten this existed. It's so beautiful.'

'You came here on your trip?'

Nessa nodded, her eyes gleaming. 'Yes, but not like this. It's magical.'

He led her around to the front and then down the steps to the lookout points. Nessa sucked in an audible breath. Paris was laid out before them like a glittering carpet of jewels.

Luc realised how long it had been since he'd been here.

'This is stunning. Thank you.'

Luc was ridiculously pleased, which was ironic because over the years he'd presented women with far more tangible and expensive trinkets and had felt nothing when they'd expressed gratitude.

He gestured towards the view. 'I used to come here when I was younger, around age ten, eleven. We'd come in from the flats during the summer, peak tourist season. We used to take advantage of people's absorption with the view to pick their pockets, steal watches, that kind of thing.'

She turned to face him. His coat making her look even more petite, her hair a dramatic splash of red against the night sky.

'Were you ever caught?'

He shook his head. 'That's why they sent us in at that age. We were small and fast, able to disappear in seconds.'

'Who would send you in?'

'The gangs, older kids. We'd bring the haul back to them and if we'd creamed anything off for ourselves they'd know immediately.'

'So you grew up in the suburbs?'

Luc looked out over the city that had been witness to his single-minded ascent out of his grim circumstances. He nodded. 'Where I grew up is about as far removed as you can get from this view. It was a basic existence in not very pretty surroundings. School was a joke and gang life on the streets was our education.'

He looked at her, expecting to see that gleam women got in their eyes when they spied an opening to invite further intimacies but she just looked at him steadily. 'Is that when you got your scar?'

Luc's insides clenched when he remembered the stinging pain. He nodded. 'A rival gang surrounded me, and knives came out. I was lucky to escape with just a scar.' That had been the moment he'd realised that if he didn't get out, he might die.

'You said before that you had no family—did you really have no one?'

Luc's chest tightened. 'My mother died of an overdose when I was sixteen, and my father appeared for the first and last time to get a handout once he saw that I had money. I had no brothers, no sisters. No aunts, uncles, or cousins. So, no, there was no one.'

'Except for Pierre Fortin,' Nessa said quietly.

The tightness in Luc's chest increased. 'Yes. Pierre saved me. He died shortly after I'd received the beating that led to the scar and I took his advice to get out and contact Leo Fouret. If I hadn't done that, I think I might be dead by now.'

Nessa shivered at that. She could tell he wasn't being melodramatic. 'I'm sorry he's gone.' Her voice was husky.

He turned then to face her and for a second there was an expression of such rawness on his face that she was surprised he was letting her see it. And then he reached out and rubbed his knuckles along her jaw. Her breathing quickened in an instant.

'You're very sweet, Nessa O'Sullivan, or else you're a better actress than I've ever seen in my life.'

A sharp pain lanced her to think that even now he still distrusted her. She took her chin away, afraid of the emotion clogging her throat. 'I *am* sorry for your loss. You deserved to have someone in your corner and I'm glad he was there for you.'

Nessa felt exposed but refused to break eye contact. She was determined to show Luc her sincerity even if she had to brand it onto his brain through sheer will.

And then he reached for her, hands sliding under her arms and tugging her towards him until their bodies were flush and she could feel his arousal pressing against her.

Instantly words were forgotten. She got a sense of how much he'd been leashing his desire all evening and bizarrely felt comforted. Because he'd seemed completely in control and unaffected. But he hadn't been. He was just better at disguising it.

He said, 'I think we've talked enough. I've wanted to do this all evening.'

Before she could ask *what*, he'd started taking the pins out of her hair, until the heavy mass fell down around her shoulders and he dropped the pins to the ground.

He ran his hands through her hair and then cupped her face, tilting it up to his. In the split second before their mouths met, Nessa felt something incredibly poignant move through her as she realised she was one of those kissing couples she'd been so envious of earlier. And then Luc's mouth was on hers, his tongue was mating with hers and she could only clutch at his shirt to try and stay standing. She wasn't even aware of his jacket falling to the ground from her shoulders. She was burning up.

After long, drugging moments Luc pulled back and emitted a curse. 'I could take you right here, right now, but next time we make love it will be on a bed.'

He took her hand to lead her back the way they'd come, to the car. She grabbed his jacket up off the ground as they went, and her cheeks burned. If Luc had decided to make love to her there and then against that wall, she wouldn't have had the ability to stop him.

When they returned to the apartment Luc gave her no time to think. He led her straight to his bedroom. There was one small light burning in the corner, throwing everything into long shadows. His face was stark with need. Exactly how she felt.

He pushed his jacket off her shoulders to the ground and instructed, 'Turn around.'

She turned around, presenting him with her back. He pushed her hair to one side so that it fell over one shoulder, and then he pulled the zip down all the way to where it ended just above her buttocks. He undid her bra. She shivered with anticipation as he ran the knuckles of his fingers up and down her spine.

Then he pushed the two sides of the dress off her shoulders and down and it fell away from her chest. He turned her around again and peeled off her arms so that she was naked from the waist up.

Her nipples stiffened under his gaze, and when he brushed his fingers across the sensitised tips she had to bite her lip to stop from crying out.

He took his hand away. 'Undress me.'

Luc saw the almost drugged expression on Nessa's face. Sweat broke out on his brow at the effort it was taking not to rip the rest of Nessa's dress off her body, throw her onto the bed and sink himself so deep inside her he'd see stars. He had to exert some control before he lost it completely.

She lifted her hands to his shirt and undid each button with an air of concentration that he found curiously touching, tongue trapped between her teeth.

She pushed his shirt off and put her hands to his belt, then the button, and the zip. He was so hard he hurt. When she pushed his trousers down he stepped out of them.

'Your dress and panties. Take them off.' He sounded as rough as he felt, uncouth and desperate.

She pushed the dress down and it landed at her feet in a shimmering green pool. Then she pushed down her panties, revealing the enticing red-gold curls between her legs. She was blushing and not meeting his eye. He tipped up her chin until her eyes met his. 'You're beautiful, Nessa.'

'If you say so.'

'I do. Lie down on the bed.'

She crawled onto the bed and Luc bit back a groan at the sight. Then she lay down on her back. 'Open your legs.'

Shyly she did so and he could see where she glistened with arousal. It undid him. Luc tore off his own underwear and put his hands to her thighs, pushing them apart even more. He knelt between her legs and the scent of her almost drove him wild.

He kissed her inner thighs, and they quivered under his hands. Then he spread apart the lips of her sex and put his mouth to her, getting drunk on her essence. He'd never tasted anything sweeter.

She was moaning and trying to speak. 'Luc, what are you...? *Oh, God.*'

He smiled against her when he could feel the way her body was responding: melting, shivering, tensing. He was remorseless, ignoring her pleas to stop, but not stop. He thrust a finger inside her and she orgasmed around it, muscles clamping down so hard that he had to exert every ounce of self-control not to explode himself.

He sheathed himself and came over her. She looked up at him, dreamy and unfocused. 'That was…incredible.'

For a second, in spite of the raging hunger inside him, Luc stopped. There was something so open and unguarded in her eyes that he couldn't bear it. He felt as if she was looking all the way into the depths of his soul with that steady gaze—in a way no one had ever looked at him before. She was seeing too much.

'Turn over,' he commanded. When she blinked and a look of hesitancy came over her face he felt a sharp tug in his chest. He ignored it. Pushed it down.

He ran his hand down her body, cupping between her legs where she was so damp and hot and fragrant. 'Turn over, *minou*.'

She did and Luc pulled her back until she was on her knees. The delicate curve of her spine and buttocks was breaking him in two. She looked at him over her shoulder in an unconsciously erotic pose. 'Luc?'

He put his hands on her hips and pulled her right into his body. He saw her eyes widen and flare when he pressed against her. And then he was breaching her body as slowly as he could afford to go without going mad, feeling her snug muscles clamp around him and then relax to let him push deeper and deeper.

She let out a low groan, coming down on her elbows, bowing her head. Her hair was a bright fall of red against the white sheets. He saw her curl her hands to fists in the sheets, knuckles white as he drove into her again and again.

But as Luc could feel Nessa's body quickening towards her climax, he felt hollow inside. His own release was elusive. He realised he couldn't do it like this, no matter how exposed the other way made him feel. He pulled out, his whole body screaming in protest.

He turned Nessa around again so she was on her back. She was panting, skin gleaming with perspiration. 'Luc…'

'Look at me.'

She did, her eyes wide and trusting. Desperate for the release that he was withholding. He thrust into her again, just once, and that was all it took to send them both hurtling over the edge.

When Luc was capable of movement again he pulled free of Nessa's embrace, and went into his bathroom to dispense with the protection. He placed his hands on the sink and bowed his head. He felt momentarily weak, as if some of his strength had been drained away during sex.

He grimaced at the fanciful notion of Samson and Delilah. It was just the after-effects of extreme pleasure. *But*, a small voice reminded him, *you weren't able to climax until you were looking in her eyes. You needed that connection.* Luc had never sought that kind of connection before.

He went cold. The events of the evening flooded his mind and an icy finger danced down his spine.

He'd told Nessa more than he'd told anyone. He'd blithely let most of his sad history trip off his tongue without a moment's hesitation. He went even icier when the full significance of that hit him.

He'd lost sight of who she was. And what she could *still* be: an accessory to theft.

A hard knot formed in his gut. He'd become so blinded by lust for her that he'd lost sight of a lifetime of lessons, teaching him to trust no one. Luc's heart beat fast to think of how close he'd come to— He shut that thought down. He didn't trust her. They'd had sex. That was all.

He had to admit that since she'd been riding for him, the turnaround in public perception was phenomenal. That was the important thing here. Not his lust for her. That was a base instinct he couldn't afford to indulge again.

He also had to acknowledge the fact that, in spite of the reasons why she was there, she was a boon to his business. But she owed him this. Her brother had stolen from him and she had taken on the debt for herself.

A familiar feeling of ruthlessness settled over Luc like a well-worn coat. In spite of Nessa's innocence or apparent sweetness, he still couldn't trust that she wasn't taking advantage of his desire for her.

He would not be weak again.

CHAPTER NINE

NESSA COULD HEAR Luc in the bathroom. The shower was turned on. She opened her eyes in the dim light of the bedroom, unable to stop imagining water sluicing down over that powerful body. Between her legs ached pleasurably as she recalled the breathtaking feeling of Luc's body driving into hers over and over again.

She got hot when she thought of how he'd made her turn over, taking her from behind. There'd been something so raw and animalistic about it. It had also felt erotic, but she'd felt slightly unsure, out of her depth. She hadn't liked not being able to see his face, or his eyes. Until he'd turned her back and said *look at me*, and that was all it had taken to send her shattering into a million pieces.

The bathroom door opened and Nessa instinctively pulled the sheet up over her body, suddenly shy, which was ridiculous after what had just happened.

Luc stood in the doorway with nothing but a small towel hooked around his waist. Droplets of moisture clung to his sculpted muscles and Nessa's mouth watered.

'You should go back to your own bed now.'

Nessa sat up, holding the sheet to her chest. Humiliation rushed through her. Of course. What had she expected would happen? That Luc would come back to bed and take her in his arms again, whisper sweet nothings in her ears and want to cuddle?

'I don't sleep with lovers,' he said, as if he might not have been clear enough.

Nessa looked at him, unable to stem the blooming of hurt inside her. 'It's fine. You don't need to explain.'

She scooted to the side of the bed feeling awkward as well as humiliated as she searched for her dress, which lay on the ground a few feet away in a pool of shimmering green. She was just wondering how to get there without exposing herself even further when Luc appeared in her eyeline holding out a robe.

'Here.' He sounded gruff.

Nessa took it and pulled it on while trying to stay as covered up as possible. She hated herself for feeling so hurt by Luc's dismissal, by the confirmation that she was no different from his other lovers. *But you want to be different.* She stood up, belting the robe around her, squashing that thought. She didn't want to be different. *Yes, you do.*

Before Luc might see any evidence of the tumult of her emotions, Nessa plucked the dress up off the floor and walked to the door, avoiding his eye. She forced herself to stop, though, and turned around. 'Thank you for this evening. I had a nice time.'

Nessa had walked out of the door before Luc had a chance to respond. He waited for a sense of satisfaction that he'd made it clear that he had boundaries, but it wouldn't come. He thought of how awkward she'd looked just now at the door, avoiding his eye, clutching her dress. She wasn't like the women he knew. He felt like a heel now. Not satisfied at all.

If he was brutally honest with himself, he already regretted saying anything. He wanted to go after her, bring her back to bed and continue where they'd finished.

Luc bit off a savage curse and went back into the bathroom to take a cold shower. Damn Nessa O'Sullivan for sliding under his skin like this. The sooner his people tracked down her brother, the better.

Nessa couldn't sleep when she went back to her bedroom. She went out to the balcony and sat on the chair by the small table, looking at the view. She was such a naive fool. To have imagined for a second that Luc's opening up to her earlier that evening had meant anything.

It had meant nothing. He'd been on a trip down memory lane and she'd happened to be there.

It hit her then, with a cold, clammy sense of panic. She really was falling for him, and it was already too late. She had stood up for him in front of Celeste Fouret the way she would stand up for any of her loved ones. The thought that Luc might have interpreted her defence as devotion, and that had been why he'd sent her back to her own room, made her feel nauseous.

She knew now, with an awful sense of impending doom, that whatever emotional pain she thought she'd ever felt before would pale into insignificance once this man cast her aside. As surely as he would.

Because Celeste Fouret had been right, after all. Luc Barbier would never belong to anyone. And certainly not Nessa. She was a brief interlude. A novelty for a cynical and jaded man, and she knew now that she had to protect herself before she got in any deeper.

The following morning Nessa got washed, dressed and packed before going in search of Luc. She heard movement coming from the main living area and walked into the room to see the dining table set and the housekeeper serving breakfast.

Sunlight streamed through the huge windows but it all paled into insignificance next to the image of Luc wearing a dark suit, sipping coffee and reading a newspaper, clean shaven. He looked every inch a titan of industry, and as remote as a rock in the middle of the ocean.

His dark glance barely skimmed over her, and Nessa was glad as it would give her the strength to do what she knew she had to for her own self-preservation.

Lucille told her to take a seat and that she'd bring her some breakfast. Nessa smiled her thanks, relieved that she wasn't entirely alone with Luc.

He put down the paper as she sat down. She felt self-conscious in her daily uniform of jeans and a T-shirt. She'd hung the glittering dress back up in the closet and had pushed down the dangerous spurt of emotion when she remembered Luc telling her she was beautiful.

'Did you sleep well?'

She looked at him and it almost hurt, he was so gorgeous. She nodded and told a white lie. 'Very well, thank you. Your apartment is beautiful. You're very lucky.'

Lucille came back and placed a plate down in front of Nessa with perfectly fluffy scrambled eggs with spring onions, salmon and buttered toast. Ordinarily her mouth would have watered but for some reason she felt nauseous. Not wanting to insult the Frenchwoman, she spooned a mouthful and ate, murmuring her appreciation to the beaming woman. When they were alone again Nessa put down her fork and took a sip of coffee, willing the faint nausea away.

Luc said, 'Luck had nothing to do with me having this apartment. It was success born out of hard work.'

Nessa shouldn't have been surprised that Luc didn't believe in things like luck, or chance. She hadn't either for a long time after their mother's death had rent their world apart. Until fate had stepped in, bringing Nadim into her sister's life, transforming their fortunes.

The hurt she still felt made her want to pierce a little of Luc's stark black and white attitude. 'Well, I do believe in luck. I believe there's always a moment when fate intervenes and you can choose to take advantage of it or not. Not everything is within our control.'

Luc's mouth tightened. 'Apparently not.'

Nessa wasn't sure what that meant. Incensed now, she said, 'Don't you consider Pierre Fortin to have been fateful for you?'

Luc looked at her. 'He gave me an opportunity and I made the most of it.'

Nessa resisted making a face at Luc's obduracy and made a stab at eating some more of the delicious breakfast, and tried to ignore the churning of her stomach.

Luc said, 'I have some meetings to attend in Paris today. My driver will take you to my stables just outside the city this morning, where you'll meet with François, my head trainer. He's expecting you. He'll see how you go on Sur La Mer and, depending on what he thinks, you'll ride him in the race next week. Or not.'

Nessa put down her fork. 'What if I don't perform well on Sur La Mer?'

Luc shrugged minutely. 'Then you'll go back to the stables in Ireland.'

She felt like a pawn being moved about at Luc's will. Into his bed, out of it…it was time to claim back her independence. She took a deep breath.

'Luc, I—'

'Look, Nessa—'

They both spoke at the same moment and stopped. Luc said, 'You go.'

Nessa's heart hammered. She swallowed. 'I just wanted to say that I don't think we should sleep together again. I'm here to do a job. I'd like to focus on that.'

Luc looked at her, eyes glittering like two black unreadable jewels. She'd never know what this man was thinking in a million years. He was too well protected. As she should be.

'I agree. I was going to say the same thing.'

'That's good,' Nessa said quickly, even as something curled up inside her. Some very pathetic part of her that had hoped that he might refuse to agree.

Then Luc stood up and walked over to the window. Nessa stood too, still feeling that nausea in her stomach. It got worse.

He turned around, hands in his pockets. 'As you said, you're here to focus on a job, a job that you've proven to have a great talent for. That's the most important thing now.'

Of course it was, because it was bringing the Barbier name respect and success. And as Nessa had learnt, Luc's business and reputation were everything to him. She couldn't begrudge him that. Not after everything he'd been through. But it was clear that he had no interest in anything outside that. Certainly not a personal life, with love, fulfilment, or family.

As if reading her mind, he said, 'My life isn't about relationships, Nessa. I don't have anything to offer you except what we've shared. There are other women who understand that and can accept it. You're different and, believe me, that's a good thing. But I don't do fairy-tale endings. For me…the novelty has worn off.'

The novelty has worn off. The sheen had gone from his naive virginal lover. Nessa should be thanking him for being so brutally honest, but she just felt incredibly sad, and sick.

She lifted her chin. 'I'm not as naive as you might think, Luc. And I don't believe in fairy tales either.' *Liar…* whispered that voice. Nessa ignored it.

'I'm ready to leave now, if you want to let your driver know.'

For a long moment there was silence and Nessa felt tension rise in the room. Eventually Luc said, 'Of course, I'll call him now and let him know you're coming down.'

So polite. So civil. So devastating. *So over.*

Nessa turned and left the room and when she reached her own bathroom she couldn't keep the nausea down any longer. She looked at herself in the mirror afterwards and saw how pale she was.

It was time to get a grip on herself again and forget anything had happened between her and Luc. Do the race, win the money, pay off Paddy's debt. That was her focus now. Nothing else.

Four days later Nessa was tired and aching all over from training so hard. François appeared at the door to Sur La Mer's stall where Nessa was rubbing him down and trying hard *not* to let her mind deviate with humiliating predictability to Luc Barbier.

She'd almost hoped that when she first sat on Sur La Mer, he'd throw her off. But he'd been a dream to ride and she'd connected with him immediately. François had been ecstatic.

Luc hadn't appeared once at the gallops to watch them train, but then one of the other jockeys had pointed to the CCTV cameras and told her that Luc often watched remotely from screens in his office.

Nessa knew he was at the stables because he'd returned from Paris the day after she'd arrived. The thought that he was watching her progress but avoiding any more personal dealings with her slid through her ribs like a knife, straight to her heart.

François was looking at her as if waiting for a response and Nessa blushed to have been caught out daydreaming. 'I'm sorry, did you want me for something?'

'It's Luc—he wants to see you in his office. It's in the main house on the first floor.'

The roiling in her gut intensified. The ever-present nausea that never seemed to quit. Nessa dusted her hands off and patted Sur La Mer before following François back out, careful to lock the stall door behind her.

He left her at the main door of the house and she went in, making her way up to Luc's office. The door was closed and she took a deep breath, hating that she felt so jittery and on edge at the thought of seeing him again.

She knocked lightly.

'Come in.'

She pushed the door open and Luc was standing behind his desk in jeans and a T-shirt. For a moment Nessa felt so dizzy and light-headed she thought she might faint. She clutched the doorknob like a lifeline.

'You wanted to see me?'

It was only then that she noticed he was on the phone. And he looked grim. He held the receiver towards her. 'It's Paddy.'

For a second she just looked at him. Her brain felt sluggish. 'Paddy...?'

Now he looked impatient. 'Your brother.'

Nessa moved forward feeling as if she were under water. Weighed down. It was shock. She took the phone and Paddy's familiar voice came down the line. 'Ness? Are you there?'

Luc moved away to the window.

Nessa turned away to hide the tears blurring her vision to hear her brother's familiar voice. 'Paddy, where are you? What's going on?'

Her brother sounded happy. 'Ness, it's all been cleared up. Well, not the money, I'll still owe Mr Barbier but he knows now it wasn't my fault. He's agreed to give me my job back and I'll start paying him back out of my wages every month. I'm going to do a course in cyber security too so we can prevent this happening again. He told me you're riding for him in a big race tomorrow—that's fantastic news, Ness! Look, I've got to run. I'm catching a flight home tonight. I'll call you when I get back and tell you everything. Love you, Ness.'

And the phone connection went dead. It was all over, just like that.

She looked at the phone for a long moment trying to gather herself and when she felt a bit more composed she turned around. Luc was standing in front of his window, arms folded. Nessa put the phone receiver back in the cradle.

She forced herself to meet his gaze. 'Can you tell me what's going on?'

He was still grim. 'It was Gio Corretti who realised what was happening, because it happened to him with another horse. Someone had hacked into his computer system so they could impersonate Gio's stud manager. They would then say something about a slight change in bank account details and the buyer would send the money to the hacker's account. That's what happened to Paddy. He'd suspected something, but by the time he'd figured out what had happened the money was gone and couldn't be traced. Then he panicked.'

Luc continued, 'Shortly after speaking to Gio Corretti, my security firm tracked Paddy down to the United States. He was staying with your twin brother.'

Nessa flushed with guilt.

Luc continued, 'I got in touch with Paddy to let him know he could come back. I told him never to do such a foolhardy thing like running away from a problem again.'

Nessa could feel Luc's barely leashed anger and almost felt sorry for her brother.

Luc unfolded his arms then and ran a hand through his hair. Nessa realised it was messier than usual and he looked tired. Stubble lined his jaw. She felt a spurt of pain when she wondered if he'd already taken a replacement into his bed. Someone whose novelty wouldn't wear off so quickly. Someone who knew the rules. Someone who didn't want the fairy tale.

He put his hands on his hips and looked at her. 'Obviously you're now free to go. I'd like you to run the race tomorrow on Sur La Mer but if you'd prefer not to, I will accept that. It's only fair. You have no obligation to me any more.'

Nessa blinked. She hadn't considered that. She felt a little panicky. 'But what about Paddy's debt? He said he still has to pay that back.'

'I told him the debt would be forgiven but he's insisting on paying it back for having been lax enough to be taken in by the hackers. Nothing I said would make him change his mind.'

Nessa's heart squeezed. Luc had been prepared to let the debt go. One million euros.

She made a decision, even though a part of her wanted nothing more than to turn around and walk away right now and go somewhere private where she could lick her wounds and try to get on with her life. She had to be professional about this and the race tomorrow was a huge opportunity for her.

'I'll run the race tomorrow. But if I win, or place, and there's any prize money I'd still like it to go towards the debt.'

'You wouldn't take it for yourself?'

Nessa shook her head. 'No. I don't want anything. I don't need anything from you. Are we done here?'

Every bone in Nessa's body ached with the need to be closer to this man. Have him touch her. It was agony.

Eventually Luc said, 'Yes, we're done.'

Nessa turned and walked to the door, but at the last second he called her name. For a heart-stopping moment she thought she'd heard some inflection in his voice and she couldn't control the surge of hope.

But when she turned around he was expressionless. He said, 'Wherever you go, or whatever you want to do in the future, you'll have my endorsement. I would retain you as a jockey at my stables here or in Ireland but I don't think you would welcome working for me.'

The thought of working alongside Luc Barbier every day for years to come, and seeing him lead his life as the lone wolf that he was, taking and discarding women as he went, was unthinkable. And it just drove home how unaffected by her he was.

She lifted her chin. 'Frankly, after tomorrow, Luc, I hope I never see you again.'

* * *

The following day before the race, Nessa was sick with nerves. Literally. Her breakfast had just ended up in the toilet bowl of the ladies' changing room at the racetrack. She cursed Luc Barbier as the source of all her ills and forced herself to just concentrate on getting through the race in one piece.

She'd booked herself on a flight back to Dublin later that night. Soon this would all be behind her.

She weighed out and made her way to the starting gate to line up with the rest of the horses and jockeys. She was oblivious to their curious looks. They were led into the stalls one by one. One horse started kicking and it took about three men to get him into position.

As Nessa waited on Sur La Mer, feeling his restlessness underneath her, she pushed all thoughts of anything else but the task at hand out of her head.

She took a deep breath. And then the gate snapped open and she unleashed the power of the horse beneath her.

As was becoming a familiar refrain, François said beside Luc, 'I don't believe it. She's going to win, Luc.'

An immense surge of pride and something much more tangled made Luc's chest swell and grow tight.

He watched as Nessa approached the last furlong, moving through the air like a comet. She looked tiny on the horse and something else moved through him, stark and unpleasant. Fear, for her safety.

When she'd stood before him in his office the day before, it had taken all of his control not to drag her into his bedroom like a Neanderthal and strap her to his bed so she could never leave.

He was going mad. She wasn't out of his system.

His system burned for her. But it was too late. This was it. She'd be gone within hours. *I hope I never see you again.*

He'd ruthlessly contemplated seducing her again, but he knew he couldn't do it. Much to his own surprise, it would appear he did have something of a conscience. Nessa wasn't like the other women. She was strong, yes, but soft. Her eyes held nothing back. She might say she didn't believe in fairy tales but he knew that, in spite of the obvious trauma of her mother's death and its effect on their family, there was still something hopeful about her.

She deserved someone who could nurture that hope. Never before had Luc been made so aware of his malfunctioning emotions.

But, as much as he could tell himself that he was doing this to protect her, he had the insidious suspicion that it was also himself he was protecting. He wasn't even sure from what, though.

'Luc, *look*! She's won!'

Luc saw Nessa shoot past the post and the usual sense of achievement and triumph when one of his horses won was tinged with something darker. '*Merde*, Luc, that horse is out of control...'

Luc went cold. He saw the other horses thundering over the line and spotted one that was riderless. It was going berserk. And it was heading straight for Nessa, who had slowed down and was turning around. Even from here Luc could see the huge smile on her face. A tendril of red hair falling from under her cap. Everyone was cheering.

But it was as if he were stuck under water and everything happened in slow motion. He saw the riderless horse rear up in front of Sur La Mer. Another jockey, still on his horse, tried to calm that horse down, but Nessa somehow got stuck in the middle. Sur La Mer bucked. There was a blur of movement, a huge collective gasp from the crowd and Nessa was off the horse and lying on the ground. Underneath the three horses.

Luc wasn't even aware he'd vaulted over the fence. All he could see was a horrifying tangle of horseflesh, hooves, and Nessa inert underneath it all.

The ambulance and paramedics were attending her by the time he got there and he only realised someone was holding him back when François' voice broke through the pounding of blood in his head.

'Luc! Leave them alone. They're doing all they can. Sur La Mer is fine. Someone has him.'

'I'm afraid I can only give out information to family or loved ones, Mr Barbier.'

Loved ones. That struck Luc forcibly, but he pushed down its significance. He was desperate to know if Nessa was all right and her family weren't here. *No,* said a voice, *because you took her away from them.*

Luc ignored the admonishing voice, and his growing sense of guilt. 'I'm not just her employer. We've been lovers.'

The doctor looked at him suspiciously for a moment but there must have been some expression on Luc's face because then he said, 'Very well. If you're intimately acquainted, then there's something you should know. Injury-wise, she was a very lucky young woman. She escaped from under those horses with just a badly bruised back. It could have been a lot worse.'

Luc felt sick when he thought of how much worse it could have been, how vulnerable she'd looked.

The doctor sighed heavily. 'However, there was

something else. I'm afraid we weren't able to save the baby. She wasn't even aware she was pregnant so I'm guessing it's news to you too. It was very early—just a few weeks. There's no way of saying for sure why the miscarriage happened; it could have been the shock and trauma, but equally it could have just been one of those things. Having said that, there's no reason why she can't get pregnant again and have a perfectly healthy baby.'

Luc stood outside the hospital a few minutes later, barely aware of the glances he was drawing. He was reeling. In shock. *Pregnant. A baby.*

He couldn't breathe with the knowledge that he'd almost had a family and in the same moment it was gone.

He'd spent so long telling himself a family wasn't for him that it was utterly shocking now to find himself feeling such an acute sense of…loss and grief.

He'd only ever felt like this a couple of times in his life. When he'd found his mother's dead body, and when Pierre Fortin had died. He'd vowed to himself he'd never let anyone close enough to hurt him again.

But this caught him unawares, blindsiding him.

The grief he felt for this tiny unborn child told him he'd been lying to himself for a long time. He'd blocked out the thought of children, not because of his own miserable upbringing, but because of the potential pain of losing someone again.

He might have believed he'd crushed the dream of a family. But it had remained, like a little kernel inside him. Immune to his cynicism. Immune to his attempts to control his life by creating so much wealth and success that he would never feel at the mercy of his environment again.

Family. Nessa had been pregnant with his child, and she'd almost died under those horses' hooves. He felt clammy at the thought of how close she'd come to serious injury. She'd been pregnant with his child because of *his* lack of care in protecting them both. She was his family now, in spite of the loss of the baby.

The doctor's words came back: *there's no reason why she can't get pregnant again.*

There, on the steps of the hospital, Luc was aware of his whole world view changing. The vision he'd always had for his life and legacy had been far too narrow. He could see that now.

Everything had just changed in an instant and he knew there was only one way forward.

Nessa was one big throbbing ache that radiated out from her back and all over her body, but most acutely in her womb. The place where her baby had been. A baby she hadn't even been aware of.

It was a particularly cruel and unusual thing to be told you're pregnant, and, in the same breath, that you're not.

How could she be feeling so much for something that had been so ephemeral? *Because it was Luc's. And because you do want the fairy tale. And because as soon as the doctor told you you'd been pregnant, you pictured a small child with dark hair. A child who would grow up secure and loved and who would take all of that dark cynicism out of his eyes. A child who would take away the terror you've always felt at the thought of your world collapsing around you again...*

Nessa squeezed her eyes shut at the surge of emotion that gripped her. She felt a tear leak out. But before she could wipe it away there was the sound of the door, and her heart clenched because she knew instantly who it was.

'Nessa.'

She quickly dashed the tear away, keeping her face turned towards the window. When she felt slightly more composed she opened her eyes and turned her head. And she knew straight away that he knew. The doctor had told him.

His suit was crumpled, tie undone, shirt open at the top. He came in and stood near the bed, eyes so dark that Nessa felt as if she might drown in them.

'I didn't know about the baby,' she said, hating the defensive tone in her voice.

'I know.'

The emotional turmoil of the past few hours and weeks and Luc's inscrutability made Nessa lash out. 'Do you? Are you sure I didn't do it on purpose to try and trap you?'

Something fleeting and pained crossed Luc's face but Nessa felt no triumph to have pierced that impenetrable wall. 'Once,' he admitted, 'I might have suspected such a thing but I know you now.'

He did. She'd let him right into the heart of her. And she resisted that now even though it was far too late. 'No, you don't. Not really. You have no idea what I want.'

Luc sat down on a chair near the head of the bed and sat forward. Suddenly he was too close.

'What do you want, Nessa?'

You, came the automatic response. She looked away from that hard-boned face. 'I want you to leave, Luc. My brother is coming from Dublin to help take me home first thing tomorrow.'

She heard a curse and movement and the bed dipped

as Luc sat down. Nessa couldn't move without extreme pain so she was trapped. She glared at him, seizing on as much anger and pain as she could to protect herself.

He looked fierce. 'We just lost a baby, Nessa. We need to talk about this.'

More pain gripped her. '*I* lost a baby, Luc. Don't try to pretend you would have ever welcomed the news.'

He stood up, eyes burning. 'What are you saying? That you would have never told me?'

Nessa was taken aback. 'I don't know. I didn't have to make that decision.'

'Would you have got rid of it?'

Nessa's hands automatically went to her belly and the answer was immediate and instinctive. '*No.*'

Luc seemed to relax slightly. He paced away from the bed for a moment, running his hand through his hair. Nessa's gaze couldn't help taking in his unconsciously athletic grace, even now.

He turned to face her again. 'I won't pretend I wasn't shocked by the news, and I can't blame you for thinking I wouldn't welcome it. I've never made any secret of the fact I don't want to have a family. I never wanted to be a father because my own was absent, so how would I know what to do?

'But now,' he said, 'things are different.'

Nessa's mouth was suddenly dry and her heart thumped. 'What do you mean?'

She had no warning for when Luc said in a very determined tone, 'I think we should get married.'

CHAPTER TEN

NESSA JUST LOOKED at Luc in shock. Finally she asked, 'Are you sure you didn't receive a head injury?'

He shook his head. He stood at the end of the bed, hands on the rail. 'I'm serious, Nessa. We would be having a very different conversation right now if you hadn't lost the baby.'

Sharp pain lanced her. 'Do you think it was my fault? I didn't know… I felt nauseous all last week but I thought it was just—' She stopped. She'd thought it was due to emotional turmoil. Not pregnancy.

Luc came and sat down near the bed again. 'No, Nessa. Of course it wasn't your fault. The doctor said these things happen. But the fact is that we almost had a baby and if you *were* pregnant there is no way we wouldn't be getting married. No child of mine will be born out of wedlock. I was born that way and I won't inflict the same unsure existence on my child.'

Nessa was desperately trying to read Luc, to absorb what he was saying. 'But I'm not pregnant, so why on earth would you want to marry me?'

As if he couldn't be contained, Luc got up and paced again. He stopped. 'Because this experience has made me face up to the fact that I'm not as averse to the thought of family as I thought I was. Having a child, an heir, it's something I'd always rejected. But I can see the benefits now.'

Nessa shrank back into the pillows. 'That all sounds very clinical.'

Luc came to the end of the bed again. 'I would love it to the best of my ability. I would give it a good life, every opportunity. Brothers, sisters. Like your family.'

It. Something in Nessa shrivelled up.

'What about me?' she forced herself to ask. 'Would you love me to the best of your ability?'

He waved a dismissive hand. 'This isn't about love—that's why it would be a success. We'd be going into this with eyes open and no illusions. I still want you, Nessa. And I can offer you a commitment now.'

He went on. 'We're a good team. These last few weeks have been a success for both of us professionally. We can expand on that, create an empire.'

'Just a few days ago you told me *the novelty had worn off.*'

'I didn't want to hurt you.'

'Well, you did,' Nessa said bluntly. She felt sick all over again at this evidence of just how far he was willing to go in a bid to achieve his ultimate ambition.

'As flattered as I am that you would consider me a good choice to be your wife and mother of your children, I'm afraid I can't accept.'

Luc's brows snapped together. 'Why not?'

'Because I don't love you.' *Liar.*

He didn't miss a beat. 'We don't need love. We have amazing chemistry.'

'Which you said would *fizzle out,*' Nessa pointed out.

A muscle pulsed in Luc's jaw. 'I underestimated our attraction. I don't see it fizzling out any time soon.'

'But it *will,*' Nessa all but wailed. 'And then what?

You take mistresses while our children see their parents grow more distant?'

She shook her head. 'I won't do it, Luc. Before my mother died my parents had a blissfully happy marriage. I won't settle for anything less. I'm very pleased for you that you've figured out what you want, but I'm not it. Go and choose one of the women who understand your rules. I'm sure one of them can give you everything you need.'

His words mocked her. *This isn't about love.* But it was. For her. And now that she'd broken her own rules and fallen in love, she knew she couldn't settle for anything less than what her parents had had and what she saw in her sister and brother-in-law's relationship. True selfless devotion. Trust.

Surely that was worth the fear of losing the one you loved? Even knowing that for a short time?

'Nessa—'

'I'm sorry, sir, you'll have to leave. She needs to rest now. Her blood pressure is going up.' A nurse had come in and neither of them had noticed.

Suddenly Nessa felt very weary. 'Luc, just go. And please don't come back. I can't give you what you've decided you need.'

For a long moment she thought he was going to refuse to leave. He looked as if he was about to pluck her from the bed. But then he lifted his hands up in a gesture of surrender. It was a very *un*-Luc gesture. 'I'll go, for now. But this conversation isn't over, Nessa.'

Yes, it is, she vowed silently as she watched him walk out.

The nurse came over and fussed around Nessa, checking her stats. She winked at Nessa and said, 'If you can't give him what he needs, just send him my way.'

Nessa forced a weak smile and laid her head back on the pillow. It was throbbing with everything Luc had just proposed. *Luc had just proposed.* But he hadn't. It wasn't a real proposal. He'd proposed a business merger. No doubt he saw the benefits of being related in marriage to Sheikh Nadim; it would place Luc in an untouchable place. Finally he would have all the respect and social acceptance he craved. And Nessa would be a side benefit of that. His wife, the jockey, who could be trotted out at social events as a star attraction. For as long as she won those races, of course.

And then bear his children, who he'd suddenly decided would be a convenient vehicle to carry on his name.

In a way she envied Luc—that he could be so coolly calculating and detached. She wanted to be detached. Not in love.

The nurse left the room. Just then Nessa's phone rang on the bedside table and she picked it up, expecting it to be Paddy. But it was Iseult, calling from Merkazad. She sounded frantic. 'Ness, what on earth happened? Are you okay?'

Nessa forced it all out of her head and told her sister everything. Everything, except how she'd fallen stupidly in love with Luc Barbier and lost his child.

It had been a week since Luc had seen Nessa in Paris and he'd since returned to the stables in Ireland.

He'd gone back to the hospital the day after their conversation to find her room empty and ready for the next patient. She'd already left for Ireland, with her brother. He'd since found out that her brother-in-law had arranged a private jet for them to go back to Kildare.

The image of Nessa being taken back into the bosom

of her protective family was all too vivid for Luc's liking. He hadn't liked the spiking of panic and the feeling of being very, very out of control.

He had to admit now that he'd had it all so very wrong. Paddy hadn't been a thief, and Nessa hadn't been an accessory. They were just a close-knit family.

Luc hadn't pursued her since then because she needed to recuperate, and he knew she also needed time to go over his proposal.

But there was no way that she was refusing his proposal the next time. Damn the woman anyway. From the very first moment he'd laid eyes on her she'd challenged him, thwarted him and generally behaved in exactly the opposite manner to which he expected. His blood thrummed even now as he looked out over the gallops and expected to see a head of dark red hair glinting in the sunshine.

It was inconceivable that he wouldn't see her here again, that she would turn him down. The chemistry between them was still as strong as ever. He would seduce her, and convince her to agree to his proposal. The alternative was not an option.

'What do you mean she's not at home?'

Luc glared at Paddy, who gulped. Luc had summoned the young man to his office to ask for directions to the O'Sullivan farm. It was time to bring Nessa back.

'She's gone to Merkazad. Iseult needed some help with the new baby. It's due any day now.'

Luc's blood pressure was reaching boiling point. 'But she's injured!'

Paddy looked sheepish. 'She said she felt much better already.'

He could imagine that all too well. Her sister said

she needed her, and Nessa jumped, without a thought for herself.

Luc made an inarticulate sound and dismissed Paddy. He paced his office, feeling like a caged animal. He needed Nessa *now*, and she was on the other side of the world.

A cold, clammy sweat broke out on Luc's brow and he stopped dead as the significance of that sank in. *He needed her.* When he'd never needed anyone in his life. Not even Pierre Fortin had impacted Luc as hard, and that man had given him a whole new life.

Luc assured himself now that he just needed her for all the myriad reasons he'd told her that day at the hospital. That was all. But the clammy feeling wouldn't recede.

He went to his drinks cabinet and poured himself a shot of whisky. He felt as if he were unravelling at the seams. He took another shot, but the panic wouldn't go away.

Eventually Luc went outside to the stables and staff scattered as he approached when they saw the look on his face. Pascal bumped into him and stepped back. 'Woah, Luc. What's wrong? Has something happened?'

Luc all but snarled at him and strode off. He went to the stables and saddled up his favourite horse, cantering out of the yard and up into the fields and tracks surrounding his land. He came to a stop only when the horse was lathered in sweat and heaving for breath. Like him.

He slid off the horse and stood by his head, holding the reins. This was the same hill he'd come to when he'd bought this place. He could remember the immense sense of satisfaction to be expanding his empire into one of the world's most respected racing communities.

Finally, he'd thought then, *I'll be seen as one of them. I'll no longer be tainted by my past.*

But as he stood in exactly the same place now, Luc realised his past was no further away than it ever had been. It was still as vivid as ever. He expected to feel frustration or a sense of futility because he knew now he'd never escape it. He waited, but all he did feel, surprisingly, was a measure of peace.

For the first time, Luc could appreciate that his past had made him who he was and there was a curious sense of pride in that.

Yet, this revelation left a hollow ache inside him because he had no one to share it with. He knew now that there was only one person he would want to share it with, and she was gone. A sense of bleakness gripped him.

Nessa had returned to the protection of *her* home, *her* family, and Luc had no place there. He had no right to claim her. For a brief moment they could have been together, but it had been taken away and he had no right to that dream with her.

She didn't love him, and if he had an ounce of humanity left he would not take advantage of their attraction to persuade her otherwise. She deserved someone far better than he would ever be.

The horse moved restlessly beside him, ready to return home, and Luc felt the bitter sting of irony. He wanted to go home too, but the home he wanted to go to didn't exist, because he'd spent his whole life denying that it could exist, or that he needed it. And now it was too late.

'Nessa, if you had told me about the baby I never would have let you come all the way here.'

Nessa's emotions bubbled up under the sympathetic

gaze of her older sister, who was sitting with her in one of Merkazad castle's beautiful courtyards. They'd just been served afternoon tea, which had remained untouched as Nessa had spilled out the last few weeks' events under the expert questioning of her concerned sister, who had noticed something was off.

Much as Nessa might have guessed, Iseult had already vowed to pay off Paddy's debt to Luc Barbier, and Nessa was glad she hadn't told Iseult before now. She would have been far too worried and insisted on getting involved. At least this way it was all over; whether or not Paddy would let Iseult and Nadim take on the debt was for him to deal with now.

'It's fine, Iseult. I'm glad I came. Really.' She adored her nephew, Kamil, a dark-haired imp of five going on twenty-five, who was as excited about the imminent birth as everyone else.

Iseult reached for her hand now, squeezing it gently. 'And what about Luc?'

Nessa sighed. 'What about Luc? He proposed marriage as a business merger, not out of romance or love.'

'But you do love him?'

Nessa desperately wanted to say no. But in the end she nodded, feeling her heart contract with pain.

Her sister sat back again, placing a hand over her rotund bump that looked ready to pop under her kaftan. Just then Kamil burst into the courtyard, holding his palm tablet and saying excitedly, 'Look, Auntie Ness, I found you on the Internet!'

He jumped up onto Nessa's lap and started playing the video of Nessa's last race. Iseult suddenly realised the significance and reached across, saying, 'I don't think Auntie Ness wants to see that one, Kami. Let's find another.'

But Nessa shot a smile at Iseult even as her heart was thumping. 'It's fine. I wouldn't mind seeing it anyway. I haven't looked back at it yet.'

The tablet was propped on the table and Kamil squealed with excitement on Nessa's lap as the race drew to a close and she won.

When Kamil wriggled off her lap to run off again Nessa barely noticed. And she didn't see the concern on her sister's face. Her eyes were glued to the screen and the aftermath of the race. She saw the riderless horse and then a flurry of movement, Sur La Mer bucking and then herself disappearing underneath the horses.

She had no memory of the actual incident, so it was like watching someone else.

A blur of movement entered the frame from the right. A man, pushing his way through, throwing people out of his way and shouting. The camera focused on him, zooming in. Nessa realised with a jolt that it was Luc, and that he was being held back by Francois while the medics cleared a space and worked on her.

Francois was saying something indistinct to him and then Luc turned around with a savage look on his face and shouted very clearly, *'I don't care about the damn horse, I care about her.'*

The video clip stopped then, frozen on Luc's fierce expression.

Nessa looked warily at Iseult, who arched a brow. 'That does not look like a man who is driven by ambition to marry a woman he sees only as a business opportunity, now, does it?'

'He's in the gym on the first floor, love. He's in there for hours in the morning and every evening. It's like he's trying to exorcise the devil himself.'

Nessa smiled her thanks at Mrs Owens. Her heart was palpitating—she'd come here straight from Dublin airport. Iseult had insisted she come home, all but bundling her onto the plane herself saying fiercely, *'You'll always regret it if you don't find out for sure, Ness.'*

Nessa had known herself that even if Luc did feel something for her, he wouldn't come after her. He'd been too hurt by his past. He'd never had anyone to depend on. Not really. And anyone he'd felt anything for had died.

It had only dawned on Nessa then that they actually had more in common than she'd ever appreciated. Fear of loss. Grief.

The difference was that she'd had a family around her and he'd had no one.

She stopped outside the door to the gym. It was too late to worry about how she looked in worn jeans and a long-sleeved top. No make-up. Hair up in a loose top-knot. Impulsively at the last second, she undid it and her hair fell down around her shoulders.

All she could hear from behind the door was a low and muffled-sounding rhythmic *thump thump.*

She took a deep breath and opened the door into the vast room. All Nessa saw at first were a hundred complicated-looking machines. But Luc wasn't on any of those.

He was at the other end of the room punching a heavy bag, dressed in sweats and bare-chested. He was dripping with perspiration, a fierce frown on his face, hair damp. The scar on his back was a jagged line and Nessa's heart squeezed.

He gave the bag a thump so hard that Nessa felt the reverberations go through her own body. And then he stopped suddenly. She realised that he'd seen her in the mirror.

He turned around, chest heaving and gleaming. Nessa was breathless. She'd never seen him looking so raw. Unconstructed. Suddenly the thought of never being with this man again left her breathless with pain. She couldn't do it. Even if he didn't really love her.

He stood with an arrested expression on his face and she walked towards him slowly. As she came closer the expression was replaced with a smooth mask. He pulled off his gloves and picked up a towel, running it roughly over his face and the back of his neck. He pulled on a T-shirt.

'I thought you were in Merkazad.'

Nessa stopped a few feet away. 'I was. I came back.' *Brilliant, Nessa. As if that weren't patently obvious.*

He shook his head. 'Why did you go there? You'd just lost our baby, but you jumped to your sister's bidding with no thought of the pain it might cause you?'

Our baby. Not *it*. Nessa's heart clenched. 'It wasn't like that. Iseult didn't know about the baby, and I thought it would be a good idea to help out.'

'You were afraid I'd propose again.' Luc sounded grim.

Nessa nodded slowly. 'Part of me was afraid you'd insist…' And that she wouldn't be able to say no.

'Was my proposal so unwelcome?' There was a bleak tone to his voice now.

Nessa nodded, watching his expression carefully. Something flashed in his eyes and she recognised pain. As much as she hated to see it, it also sent hope to her heart.

She moved closer and saw a wary look cross his face now.

'But not because of why you think. I couldn't bear the fact that it was such a clinical proposal. To merge two names. To bolster your reputation and success. And just because you'd had a revelation about wanting a family.'

He shook his head and when he spoke his voice was rough. 'It wasn't just that.'

He looked at her, and the pain in the depths of his eyes was unmistakable now. 'I'm sorry for everything. You just tried to help your brother and I treated you as if you'd stolen from me yourself. Then I seduced you, when I had no right to take your innocence, an innocence that I didn't believe in until it was too late. I had no right to disrupt your life like that.'

He went pale. 'When I saw you lying under those horses, I thought I'd killed you…and then the baby. It's my fault you lost the baby, Nessa. If I hadn't asked you to ride in the race it wouldn't have happened. You were innocent of every charge I levelled at you.'

Suddenly Nessa felt cold. She put a hand to her mouth, horror coursing through her. 'You feel responsible? That's why you were so upset when you saw the accident. I thought…'

Nessa felt sick and turned away before he could see her. She'd never felt like such a fool. She tried to walk away as quickly as she could but a hand on her arm stopped her.

'You thought what…?'

Nessa blinked back tears and turned around, avoiding Luc's eye. 'I watched the race online. You ran over, and you shouted at Francois that you cared about me, and not the horse.' But now Nessa realised that of course Luc would care about any one of his jockeys more than a horse.

That was all it had been.

His hand tightened so much on her arm that she looked up at him. When she saw the look on his face she stopped breathing.

'You thought I just felt responsible for you?'

Nessa's humiliation turned to anger. 'Didn't you?'

His eyes were burning and she saw the same volatile emotion she was feeling reflected in their depths. But she didn't trust it.

'Believe me,' he said grimly, 'I wish that what I felt for you was just a sense of responsibility.'

'What's that supposed to mean?'

He dropped his hand from her arm as if suddenly aware he might be hurting her.

'I proposed to you in the hospital because I was too cowardly to admit that I nearly lost my whole life when I saw you lying under that horse. Of course I felt responsible, but I was also terrified.'

He took a deep breath. 'I was terrified I was about to lose the only other person I've ever truly loved in my life, but I couldn't admit that to myself even then.'

Nessa's heart stopped. She was afraid she might be projecting words from her heart onto Luc's lips. 'What are you saying?'

He took a step closer. He looked uncharacteristically vulnerable. 'I'm saying that I love you, Nessa. I think I've loved you from the moment we met, when I knew that I didn't want to let you out of my sight. But I know you don't love me and I told myself I wouldn't stoop low enough to seduce you again because you deserve more. I brought nothing but more loss into your life.'

Nessa shook her head, almost too afraid to move in case she shattered this delicate moment. 'First of all, it's no one's fault we lost the baby. It was just one of those things. Secondly, I lied to you. I *do* love you. So much that it scares me. And third of all, you brought nothing but richness into my life. You awakened me. You made me believe I was beautiful, you gave me the chance to be a jockey, you showed me Paris. That's where I knew I loved you.'

He reached for her and drew her to him as gently as if she were spun glass. 'Do you mean this?'

She nodded. 'I mean it with every bone in my body. When I told you I didn't love you at the hospital it was because I thought you were just consolidating your empire with a marriage of convenience.'

He shook his head, drawing her in even closer so their bodies were touching. A wave of need surged through Nessa. Luc's voice was full of self-recrimination. 'None of this means anything without you. I said it wasn't about love because I didn't know what love was. Until I went back the next day and you were gone. I was so sure I could persuade you…seduce you. And then I realised I wanted so much more.

'I want it all, Nessa. A real family. Even though it terrifies me. How do I know how to have a family when I've never been part of one?'

Nessa reached up and put her arms around Luc's neck. She felt stupidly shy all of a sudden. 'I can show you.'

He looked down at her, a suspiciously bright glint in his eye. 'It might take a lifetime.'

'I wouldn't settle for anything less.'

Luc suddenly looked serious. He framed her face with his hands. 'Nessa O'Sullivan, I'm never letting you out of my sight, ever again. Will you marry me?'

She nodded, a surge of joy spreading from her heart

to every part of her body. Tears made her vision blurry. 'Yes…yes, I will. I love you, Luc.'

'I love *you*, *mon amour*.'

Luc could feel Nessa's heart thumping in time with his, and as her mouth opened under his and he pulled her even closer he knew that this wasn't just a mirage, and that, finally, he'd found peace, love, and his true home.

EPILOGUE

'AND IT'S NESSA BARBIER, riding to glory again in the Kilkenny Stakes on Sacre Coeur, owned by her husband and brother-in-law...'

A short time later Luc watched as his wife rode into the winner's enclosure, mud-spattered face beaming. She wore the colours of the newly announced Barbier-Al-Saqr racing consortium—green and gold, a nod to Ireland and Merkazad.

His heart-rate finally returned to normal to see her in one piece. She saw him and her smile got even wider. She jumped off the horse gracefully and handed it to a groom before coming over to where he was standing with their two-year-old son, Cal, in his arms.

Flashes of light went berserk around them—the press still couldn't get enough of Luc and Nessa ever since their fairy-tale romance had become news. They'd been married almost two years ago in a modest ceremony in an old chapel on Luc's stud farm grounds in Kildare, and then they'd celebrated with a more lavish reception in Merkazad.

'You do know that every time I watch you race it takes about a year off my life?' Luc grumbled good-naturedly as he handed over his son, who was reaching for his mother with chubby arms.

Nessa cuddled him close and looked up at Luc. She had an enigmatic glint in her eye and then said *sotto voce*, 'Well, if it's any consolation it looks like this will be my last race for about a year, if not longer.'

Luc looked at her. The only other time she'd stopped racing was when they'd fallen pregnant with Cal, and even though the doctor had assured them that Nessa should be fine to race early in her pregnancy they'd both agreed that she wouldn't, in deference to what had happened when she'd first been pregnant.

A surge of emotion rushed through Luc as he reached for her. 'You're...?' He stopped, mindful of waggling ears.

She nodded, eyes shimmering with emotion. 'I'm late, so I don't know for sure yet, but I'm pretty certain.'

Luc pulled her and Cal into him, her free arm wrapped around his waist and his son snuggled up between them. His heart was so full he was afraid it might explode. He finally knew the true meaning of wealth and success and it had nothing to do with professional respect or money. It was *this*.

And then over Nessa's head he saw Nadim and Iseult with their two children walking towards them. Iseult was pregnant again with baby number three. *His family.* Luc finally felt like he belonged to something he'd never had the courage to hope for, and it still felled him sometimes. How lucky he was. How blessed he was. And now this, the seed of a new life in Nessa's belly.

Nessa looked up at him and for a brief moment before they were enveloped in their family, and congratulations, they shared a look of pure love and understanding. 'I love you,' he said, not caring about hiding his emotion.

'I love you too...'

The kiss they shared at that moment with their son between them was the picture used on the front pages of the newspapers the next day under the headline: *Love at the races...a true family affair.*

* * * * *

SURRENDER TO THE RUTHLESS BILLIONAIRE

LOUISE FULLER

To Millie. For always smiling. Even when I'm really annoying. And for making me laugh. Love you lots.

And to Nic. For reading, rereading, reassuring me and generally being the best editor. Thank you.

CHAPTER ONE

DOWNSHIFTING THROUGH THE GEARS, Luis Osorio slowed his vintage Ducati motorbike to a standstill and let the engine idle in neutral. As he gazed down the hill at the city illuminated in the late afternoon sunlight his heart did a *paso doble* inside his chest.

Segovia. Finally he was home.

He had deliberately left the motorway some twenty minutes earlier in order to enjoy this moment—a moment of private communion with the city of his childhood.

A city he loved.

A city he'd shunned for five years.

Five years that had felt like a life sentence.

Although really he'd got off lightly...

His breath caught in his chest and he felt a twisting rush of guilt that made his hands tighten painfully around the handlebar grips.

It was the same guilt that had almost stopped him from coming home. But this time he'd had no choice. His mother's sixtieth birthday was a celebration he couldn't miss, whatever the consequences to himself, and so he'd reluctantly agreed to fly in the morning before her party then catch a flight back to California at the weekend.

Her actual birthday was just over a week later, and he knew that his parents had been hoping he would stay. He'd wanted to, and he would have done so only—

Only that would mean forgetting the past and trying to celebrate a present none of them had ever imagined, much less wanted. There was no way he could face that. Nor could he imagine being able to keep his emotions locked down for longer than a couple of days.

It would be better—easier and less painful—to go to the party, so that was what he'd agreed with his parents.

His jaw tightened. He knew they were disappointed but he could live with that. His mouth thinned. In fact he welcomed their disappointment, for he deserved it more than they knew.

But then without telling them he'd changed his mind and instead he'd flown to Athens a month earlier than planned, bought this bike and taken the road trip across Europe that he and his brother, Bas, had promised to do together.

It was the best, the only way he could think to honour Bas's memory.

His head swam and he felt the same surge of guilt and loneliness that came whenever he thought about his brother. Bas—Baltasar—his best friend as well as his brother. And now he was gone.

On the flight over he'd told himself that it was the right time to come back, that five years of self-imposed exile would be long enough. Only now that he was here he knew that he'd been kidding himself. That nothing—no words, no gestures—could atone for what he'd done.

But he couldn't just sit there, trapped in the endless maze of his thoughts. Soon enough he was going to have to face his past—but not yet. First he wanted just one last night—not of freedom but of fantasy. A chance to cheat time…to forget who he was and what he'd done.

He breathed out slowly, listening to his heartbeat, and then, twisting the throttle, he leaned forward, feeling the bike move beneath him as he accelerated down the road.

After the wide emptiness of the motorway the city streets seemed narrow and busy. Braking gently to avoid an elderly couple crossing the road, Luis glanced up at the five-star Palacio Alfonso VI hotel. It was tempting to book a room there. Despite his dishevelled appearance, he had no doubt that the roll of banknotes in his back pocket would ensure a warm welcome.

But right now he needed more than a generous-sized bed and a power shower. He wanted anonymity. And he wouldn't get that in a hotel like the Alfonso VI.

Scooting down the side streets, he found what he was looking for twenty minutes later. This hotel only had two stars, and it was not central. But it was clean and unobtrusive, and the *dueño* was a keen biker himself. Not only did he have a lock-up for the bike, he offered to pressure-wash it too.

Two hours later, having showered and changed into his cleanest pair of jeans and a plain black T-shirt, Luis walked back out onto the street. The *dueño* had obviously kept his promise—aside from a couple of scratches to the metalwork, his bike looked just as it had when it had left the showroom and, climbing on, he set off towards the city centre.

It was warm enough for him not to need his battered leather jacket, but over the last few days he'd grown comfortable wearing it—he particularly liked the way it seemed to discourage anyone from trying to make conversation.

Although, remembering his reflection in the hotel bathroom's small mirror, it seemed unlikely that would be a problem anyway. The dark, rough stubble shadowing his jaw and the coolness in his equally dark grey eyes would probably deter all but the most persistent or thick-skinned of people from talking to him.

Outside, the light was starting to fade as he made his way through the crowds spilling off the pavements. He had no real idea of where he was going, and yet for once he didn't care. He was happy to drift through the streets for it felt so familiar—the warm night, the buzz of chatter and laughter, the smell of oranges and exhaust fumes.

It was as though the last five years had never happened. If he closed his eyes he could almost imagine that Bas was there beside him, that at any moment he would slap him round the shoulder and tell him to lighten up, because tonight was the night he would meet the woman of his dreams.

Lost in thought, he stared dazedly across the square.

As a child, the four years between them had felt vast. Then his big brother had been so much taller than him, handsome, sporty. The coolest person on the planet, in fact. Of course he'd got older and grown taller himself, until finally they were the same height. But in his head nothing had changed. Bas had always been his big brother, always at the centre of everything, his dark eyes pinballing across the room to whatever beautiful girl had caught his attention.

Whatever beautiful girl had caught his attention...

The words were still echoing inside his head as he sidestepped carefully through the groups of people pacing the pavements like glossy thoroughbreds in a paddock when from nowhere his gaze collided with a pair of soft brown eyes the colour of *dulce de leche.*

For a fraction of a second heat—unexpected and all-consuming—burned his skin. He registered traffic-stopping red hair, a husky laugh and long golden limbs. And then, just like that, she was gone, swallowed into the crowd funnelling through the doorway into a nightclub.

He stared after her, motionless, another ripple of heat that had nothing to do with the air temperature thrumming across his skin. And then moving swiftly, he did something he'd never done before. He followed her.

Inside, the club was exactly the kind of place he loathed and normally avoided. Hot, loud and crowded, with a dress code and a VIP area. The men were sleek and groomed, the women doubly so.

But he spotted her as soon as he stepped through the door.

How could he not?

Even without the warning beacons of that striking auburn hair and those matching crimson lips, the young men congregating around her like a pack of hungry coyotes made her impossible to miss.

He gritted his teeth. It was easy to see the attraction.

Her feminine curves promised the kind of pleasure that men would fight for with their fists, and she was beautiful and confident in her charms in a way that reminded him painfully of his brother. But that was where the similarity ended, for Bas had never sought the attention he'd received, whereas this woman was deliberately using her beauty and her body to seduce.

His groin tightened as his eyes swept over her.

Okay, maybe that wasn't completely fair.

Her bright yellow top covered her arms and breasts, and her shorts were actually modest in comparison to those worn by most of the women in the club. But they still revealed an inordinate amount of long golden legs—legs that ended in some of the highest heels he'd even seen. And in fact, now that he was closer, he could see that her top was actually transparent!

His face hardened. Basically, she was sexy and she knew it.

So not his type at all—and yet he had followed her.

Still not entirely sure why he had done that, but somehow reluctant to leave, Luis shrugged off his jacket and pushed his way to the front of the bar.

'Una sin.'

At least that was something that had changed for the better in the five years since he'd been away. Alcohol-free beer was widely available now, and an acceptable substitute for the real thing.

Not that it would have made any difference if it hadn't been. He would drink dishwater rather than break his vow. Never again would he risk that loss of control that had ripped his world apart.

Staring straight ahead, he lifted the glass to his lips. He had deliberately chosen to sit with his back to the red-haired woman, and she should have been out of sight and out of mind. But, despite not actually being able to see her, he could still sense her every move. Could picture her hand reaching up to tuck her hair behind her ear, almost hear that soft, sexy laugh that hinted not just at fun and flirtation but at a fantasy come true.

Annoyed with the direction of his thoughts, but unable to stop himself, he looked up at the mirror above the bar, his eyes fixing on her reflection. Instantly he regretted his lack of self-control, for she was laughing at something one of the men was saying, her hand brushing against his arm as she leaned in closer to him.

Luis scowled. No doubt he was her boyfriend—for now. The rest were just watching and waiting. Or maybe *she* was watching and waiting to see which of the men in the room were prepared to make a move.

His eyes narrowed and he felt a swirling anger mingle with his desire as he realised that he himself was included in that demographic.

Why, then, did he find her so damn desirable?

It didn't make any sense that someone like him would be attracted to someone like her—especially not now. Tonight of all nights he needed to stay detached. Yet, like a bull mesmerised by that flash of red, he could feel himself being drawn to her.

He ran his hand wearily over his face. It must be tiredness…or the heat.

Right, he mocked himself. Or maybe, like every other man within a five-mile radius, he wanted what she was offering.

Glancing over his shoulder at the group of men, he felt his chest tighten. Even from here he could feel their longing, spilling into the dark club.

Like it or not, he was no different.

His heartbeat slowed. Except that he was.

Sure, he'd had girlfriends. No one special, though. And nor was there likely to be any time soon, for more than anything he needed to be certain—and certainty was not a part of the dating equation. Chasing women was definitely not his thing either. It was Bas who had loved the thrill of the chase.

His hand tightened involuntarily around the glass.

The thrill of the chase—even just thinking the words made him feel slightly sick and, tilting his glass, he gazed down at the swirling contents and tried to distract himself from the guilt and remorse building inside his chest.

It didn't work. And suddenly he knew that it was time to leave. That his little adventure was over.

Keeping his eyes low, he breathed out softly, then still clutching his glass, he turned and—

The glass slammed against his chest, beer slopping down his T-shirt.

He heard a soft cry of surprise, and then the reflexes honed by years of riding motorbikes kicked in. Reaching out, he grabbed the arm flailing in front of him just as his startled brain realised that it was *her*—the red-haired woman.

Cristina Shephard gasped.

One moment she'd been taking a selfie on her phone—the next she was falling forward. Her one conscious thought was, *I knew I shouldn't have worn these heels,* and then suddenly, out of nowhere, she was being pulled upright, strong hands curving around her wrist and waist.

She breathed out in a rush as those same hands spun her round. 'Sorry...'

Why was she apologising? she thought dazedly, almost forgetting to breathe. He'd walked into *her*. But she knew why, and as her fingers curled into warm, hard muscle she gazed up at the man in front of her.

All evening she'd been aware of him. How could she not be? He dominated the whole club—and not just because he was handsome in a way that made you look twice...actually, three times. First to check you weren't seeing things. Then to marvel at such blatant perfection. And finally just to savour his extraordinary masculine beauty.

He was just so cool. With or without the leather jacket, he had an aura of calm assurance that suggested he was bigger than the sum of his problems. Or hers.

Although obviously not *hers*. She might never have shared them with anyone, but she knew her problems were too much for most people to handle. Or maybe it was her that was the problem. Her last boyfriend had more or less told her that—shortly after she'd found him in bed with her flatmate.

Her stomach clenched and, pushing aside that thought, she said quickly, 'Thank you for catching me—and sorry about your beer.'

Luis stared at her. Up close, she was more than beautiful. She was devastatingly lovely. Her huge, melting *turrón*-coloured eyes with their fringe of probably fake eyelashes were perfectly offset by her flushed cheeks and the scarlet bow of her mouth. He wondered just how soft the skin was on her throat, and then instantly wished that he hadn't as his brain began tugging him on an imaginary tour beneath her clothing.

Imposing an indifference he didn't feel onto his features, he shrugged. 'I was leaving anyway.'

Looking down into her beautiful, curious face, he couldn't actually remember why that was the case. In fact he appeared to be having trouble remembering how to do a lot of things—like breathing and speaking. It was her fault, though, he thought irritably. Her beauty kept catching him off guard, so that each time he looked at her he forgot what he'd been planning to say.

As the silence grew, Cristina felt her lungs contract.

What was she doing here?

Tomorrow was going to be the biggest day of her life and she should be back in her hotel room, having a quiet night in on her own—just as she'd promised her mum. Only 'quiet and alone' were not a great combination, for that was when the thoughts came creeping into her head—thoughts that left her breathless with misery and doubt.

And so she'd come out, bumped into some people at a bar, and ended up here.

With him.

Her mouth felt dry and her breath was suddenly scratchy in her throat. It actually hurt to look at him.

She'd been surrounded by men all evening, but none of them had felt real. They were like chameleons—constantly changing according to their environment. It had made her feel nervous and unsteady, as though the solid floor of the club was actually quicksand.

Her heart tripped in her chest.

And then there was this man.

She liked it that he had ignored the dress code. Liked it, too, that he was happy with his own company. Not that he needed to be. She wasn't the only women in the club who'd clocked him—for obvious reasons.

He definitely ticked all the boxes in the 'tall, dark and

handsome' category. In fact his hair was almost black, and so long it curled loosely over the collar of his now damp T-shirt. Stubble that was definitely not 'designer' shadowed the clean lines of his jaw, and he had a small infinity tattoo on his wrist.

How on earth had he got past the *gorilas* on the door? she wondered distractedly. Even *she'd* had trouble getting in.

But probably he'd just walked straight in. Men with his kind of aura didn't stop for doormen.

Aware suddenly that she had been staring at him for what felt like for ever, she glanced down at his almost empty glass and said quickly, 'Please. Have mine.'

She held out the bottle but he shook his head.

'Okay, then let me buy you another one? To make up for spilling yours.'

Pulse racing, she reached into her bag, pulled out her purse and—

'Oh.'

Groaning inwardly, she gazed down at the handful of coins. She'd meant to go to the cashpoint on her way out but she'd forgotten.

'It really doesn't matter.'

He spoke quietly, but there was a firmness to his voice that cut through his casual manner and made her breathing accelerate in time with her heartbeat.

'It does.' She cleared her throat. 'Look, Tomás will buy you one. He won't mind.'

Luis gazed at her incredulously. He could hardly believe what she'd just said.

Seriously? She was going to ask her boyfriend to buy him a drink?

His face hardened. 'There's no need, really,' he said tersely.

He didn't care about the drink. Or his T-shirt. Or the

fact that she had a boyfriend. He definitely didn't care about that, he thought angrily. So why, then, did he feel so wound up?

And then, catching sight of the phone in her hand, he felt a warm surge of relief. She'd been taking a selfie—that was why she'd bumped into him.

Wasn't it enough that every man in the room was drooling all over her? Did she have to drool over herself too?

Reaching around her, he snatched up his leather jacket from the bar stool.

'I don't want another drink,' he said quietly. 'But just do yourself and everyone else a favour and look where you're going next time you come over all narcissistic.'

She gazed up at him as if she couldn't quite believe what he was saying. Probably she couldn't. With lips and legs like hers she'd almost certainly never had to take responsibility for her actions before.

Her mouth curled. 'I *was* looking where I was going because I was standing still. *You* walked into me.'

It was true. He had walked into her. But somehow the knowledge that he was technically in the wrong just antagonised him more.

His voice cold, and clipped with a fury he didn't fully understand, he shrugged his arms into his jacket. 'You were taking a selfie in the middle of a nightclub. You weren't concentrating. And that's how accidents happen.'

He watched her eyes darken to the colour of burnt sugar, her face stiffening with shock and then a fury that doused his.

'Well, don't worry—next time I spill a drink all over you I'll make sure I do it on purpose.'

She stared at him fiercely and then, lifting her chin, turned and stalked off towards the dance floor.

For a fraction of a second Luis stared after her, his

heart ricocheting inside his chest. Then, biting down on the frustration rising inside his throat, he turned and strode towards the stairs.

Out in the street, he felt his fury fade in the still night air. Gazing up at the dark sky, he breathed out slowly.

He hated conflict of any kind. Rarely lost his temper or provoked a fight. Yet tonight he'd almost done both—and with a woman. Gritting his teeth, he cursed softly. He'd been obnoxious and childish—and frankly he'd deserved everything she'd thrown at him and more.

In fact he was lucky she hadn't thrown her own drink at him too, he thought savagely as he began walking across the square.

The pavements were empty now, almost like a ghost town, and he felt a wrench of loneliness as he unlocked his bike. He missed Bas so much. Living in California, it was easy to rationalise his brother's absence from his life. All he had to do was pretend that back in Spain Bas was doing just what he always did—teasing their mother, eating *empanadas* by the plateful, partying until dawn with his friends.

Here, though, it was impossible to pretend.

And it would be even harder tomorrow—he glanced at his watch and frowned—or rather later today, with his parents. His stomach twisted with guilt and grief, and suddenly he knew that he had to move.

Straddling the bike, he pushed the key clumsily into the ignition. It would better once he was moving. On the open road, with the sound of the engine mingling with the beat of his blood, his feelings would spin away into the darkness like the dirt beneath his wheels.

He eased the bike forward and turned the ignition. Pulling in the clutch, he thumbed the starter button—and then frowned as the engine sputtered and died.

Damn it!

He tried again, and then again, over and over, feeling a tic of irritation start to pulse in his cheek. What the hell was wrong with the damn thing? It made no sense.

Trying to stay calm, he leaned forward and took a deep breath. He would check the blindingly obvious. And then...

And then nothing. For anything else he'd need pliers, a wrench, a screwdriver—

'Do you need any help?'

He sensed movement behind him and, turning, he felt his breath catch in his throat as she took a step closer.

She was watching him warily. Her auburn hair was now tied up into some kind of messy ponytail and she'd changed her shoes. Glancing at the black military-style boots on her feet, he almost smiled. Good job she hadn't been wearing those earlier or he might not have made it out the club.

He shook his head. 'Not sure you can,' he said carefully. Holding her gaze, he gestured towards the high-heeled shoes dangling from her hand. 'Unless those transform into some kind of toolkit. Or are you planning on throwing *them* at me too?'

Cristina stared at him in silence.

She had hesitated before coming over. He'd been so patronising and rude to her. But then she had spilled his drink over him, so maybe that made them equal. It was a pretty lame argument, but before her brain had had a chance to object she had already been walking across the square.

'I didn't plan on throwing your drink over you—as you yourself pointed out. Now, do you want my help or not?'

Luis stared at her for a long moment. Her voice was husky—distractingly so. Was this some kind of trick? Or a joke.

'You want to help me?' he said slowly. 'I'm—'

'Touched?' she suggested. 'Grateful? Pleased?'

'Actually, I was going to say surprised. And a little nervous maybe.' He glanced over at her shoes.

Her mouth twitched. 'Well, I probably would have broken my leg or my neck if you hadn't caught me, so I guess it's only fair.'

'It's more than fair. It's magnanimous, given that I not only walked into you but then failed to apologise for doing so.' His grey eyes were level with hers. 'I'm sorry. I was the one who wasn't looking where I was going.'

As his gaze held hers Cristina felt her heart thud against her ribs. Even though it had been a little awkward, she liked that he had picked up where they had left off. Liked that he was honest enough to admit that he'd been wrong.

And, although he might not say much, she liked that he meant what he said.

'Don't you need to get home?'

Home. The word made her breathe in sharply. She shrugged.

'Right now, I don't really have one. I'm just travelling.'

Feeling suddenly horribly self-conscious, she glanced down at the Ducati.

'I don't know this model, but I'm almost sure you don't need a toolkit to fix it.'

Watching his mouth turn up at one corner, she felt a rush of heat tighten her skin. It was impossible not to imagine what he would look like if he smiled properly, or what it would be like to be kissed by that mouth.

Feeling his gaze on her face, and terrified that her thoughts might somehow be visible, she frowned. 'Did I say something funny?'

'No, I'm just tweaking my mental picture of you. I had you down as a party girl, not a back-warmer.'

She took a step towards him, her eyes narrowing. 'Is

that right? Then maybe what you need isn't a toolkit but a little imagination. Or perhaps a little less prejudice. Women ride motorbikes on their own these days, and guess what? They don't even do it side saddle.'

Meeting her gaze, Luis felt something soft and dark stir inside in his blood as she took another step closer and touched the fuel tank between his legs.

He sighed. 'You're enjoying this.'

She nodded. 'A little. You were pretty mean to me.'

Watching her fingers stroke the warm gleaming metal, he felt his stomach tense.

'Is this some kind of hands-on healing?'

Her fingers stilled and she cleared her throat. 'Your bike is really clean. In comparison to your boots, I mean.'

They both looked down at his scuffed and dust-covered boots.

Despite himself, he was interested now. 'Okay, Nancy Drew, I got my bike washed this evening. And, no, it's not something I do very often but I have done it historically and I've never had a problem. And besides, it worked fine when I rode over here tonight.'

'Was it washed by hand?'

He frowned. 'No—pressure-wash.'

She nodded. 'Okay…well, I could be wrong, but water might have got into the ignition switch. It probably just needs a spritz of some kind of water-displacer.'

He stared at her, his pulse jumping with excitement, his hands tightening in a gesture of pure possession. He wanted her as he had never wanted any woman. Only the fact that, however deserted it appeared to be, they were still in a public place stopped him from reaching out and—

Stomach clenching with desire, he pushed aside an image of her splayed against the gas tank and said dryly, 'That's good to know. But as I don't have any—'

He broke off in disbelief as she opened up her handbag and pulled out a small spray can.

'I know how this must look, but I don't normally carry this stuff around with me,' she said quickly. 'It's just that the window in my hotel room is so squeaky that I can't sleep. Anyway, I complained, and when I was going out this evening the guy in reception gave me this.' She held out the can. 'It's worth a try.'

Luis wanted to ask her to rewind and repeat everything she'd just said, but instead he took the can and sprayed the ignition switch. He waited a moment, and then turned the key. He grinned as the snarl of the engine punctured the silence in the square.

Cristina blinked, and then smiled too. It was impossible not to. For, even though it was a dark and starless night, his smile made her feel as though the sun was rising and it was a new dawn.

She felt her heart skip a beat.

No wonder she'd tripped earlier.

Since finding Dominic, her on-off boyfriend of several months, in bed with her flatmate, she'd sworn off men. But there were men and then there was fate.

And surely that was why she had spilt his drink over him. Why his bike had failed to start. And why she'd ended up booking the worst hotel in Segovia, possibly in Spain.

'Thank you.'

He was holding out the can to her.

'It's okay. You can keep it.'

'But your window—'

'It's fine. I probably won't sleep tonight anyway. My mattress is really hard, and I think it's going to storm later. It's so hot and humid now.'

Luis felt his body tense. *Hard. Hot. Humid.* Why did every word she said make him think of sex?

Gritting his teeth, he ignored the blood pounding through his veins and forced himself to speak. 'So how did you know what was wrong?'

Cristina hesitated. *Good question*. However, the completely truthful answer was not one she was about to share with a perfect stranger—no matter how tall, dark and handsome.

It would take too long, and—her skin tightened over her cheekbones—it would be too humiliating to reveal the mend-and-make-do life she and her mother had been forced to live for so many years. But, just as she always did, she would tell him one truth.

Her eyes met his. 'My dad had a motorbike. Not like this one, but I took it over for a bit and I got to hang out with bikers—and they can't shut up about ignitions and sparks.'

She winced inside. What was she doing, rambling on about bikers as if she was some kind of Hell's Angel?

'Anyway...' She glanced up at the sky. 'I should probably be going. It's late, and I want to get back to my hotel before it starts to rain.'

That wasn't true. The thought of her bedroom, dark and quiet, filled her with dread. She didn't want to be alone. But tonight was not the night to mess up, and how could taking this handsome stranger back to her room be anything but a risk not worth taking?

She held out her hand. 'Goodbye,' she said woodenly.

He took it, and at the touch of his fingers heat flared inside of her—and something bittersweet. A sense of what might have been if they'd met at some other time.

'Let me give you a lift. Please. It's the least I can do.'

His voice jolted her back to reality and, swallowing down the ache in her throat, she shook her head.

'No, really—it's fine.' She pointed at one of the side streets off the square. 'My hotel is literally down there.'

He looked at her for the longest time, then frowned.

'I don't even know your name.' He sounded surprised.

'It's Cristina.'

He nodded. 'Lucho.'

There was a low rumble of thunder overhead, and as they both looked up at the sky she took a deep breath. 'You should go or you'll get soaked.'

He nodded and dropped her hand, and quickly, before she could change her mind, she turned and began to walk away as the rain started to fall.

At first it was soft and light like tears but then almost immediately it changed. Heavy, fat droplets hammered her head and shoulders so that in seconds she was soaked and the pavement was awash with water.

Don't look back, she told herself. *This wasn't meant to be. Just keep walking.*

But she couldn't just walk away. And, really, what difference would it make if she took one last look?

She turned, and suddenly her heart was hammering louder than the rain.

He was still sitting there, watching her, rain running down his face.

Cristina shivered.

He was waiting.

For her.

For a moment she hesitated.

Don't—don't go back. It's just because you're nervous about tomorrow, and when you get nervous you make stupid decisions.

Her heart kicked against her ribs, and then she walking, running back across the square, and what she was feeling wasn't nervousness but relief. And then he was pulling her against him, his mouth seeking hers, his hands sliding beneath the soaking fabric of her top.

They left the bike where it was, and ran to her hotel.

Ignoring the startled glance of the receptionist, they stumbled up the stairs and into her bedroom.

He kicked the door shut and, bending his head, he took her mouth again. Rising on tiptoe, she kissed him back, her fingers tugging at his T-shirt, her mouth meeting his with urgent, frantic hunger.

'No—' Her eyes darkened with frustration as he broke away from her mouth and yanked his T-shirt over his head.

He was so gorgeous—all sleek, hard muscle and smooth skin, and a line of soft dark hair disappearing into the waistband of his jeans.

Reaching out, she ran her fingers lightly over the hair, watching his muscles tremble, and then she breathed in sharply as he took hold of the zip on the front of her jacket and slowly pulled it down.

Leaning forward, he rested his forehead against hers, the dark grey of his eyes almost black. For an endless moment he stared at her, his breathing ragged, and then, lowering his mouth, he began to kiss her again—lips, neck, throat—each kiss leading on to the next one and the next.

As he buried his face against her neck she moaned softly, sliding her fingers up through his hair. Her head was spinning…heat was slipping over her skin as his hands slid under her top, under the bandeau she was wearing underneath and over her damp breasts, his thumbs caressing the hard peaks of her nipples.

For the second time that night her legs crumpled beneath her, and her fingers tightened in his hair.

She heard a hiss as he breathed in sharply, and then he was tugging down her shorts, lifting her up, his hands curving beneath her as he pinned her against the door with his body. She shifted against him, panting, seeking relief for the ache building inside her, until suddenly she couldn't bear it any longer and her fingers clawed at his belt and zip, pushing his jeans down.

'Wait…' he muttered, and she felt her breath catch as he fumbled in his pocket and slid a condom on.

For a moment he held her gaze, and then, groaning, he forced her mouth back to his. Pushing aside the fabric of her panties, he thrust inside her. She arched against him, her nails biting into his arms, and then her muscles clenched and she cried out with pleasure as his body shuddered and slammed into her.

CHAPTER TWO

EVEN BEFORE SHE opened her eyes Cristina knew that Lucho was gone.

Shifting down beneath the duvet, she gazed up at the ceiling. From the sharpness of the light creeping beneath the curtains, and the buzz of traffic in the street, she guessed that it was probably time to get up.

And she *would* get up—only not just yet. For getting up would mean having to accept that what had happened last night was over, and she wasn't quite ready to do that.

Closing her eyes, she rolled on to her side.

Her body felt pleasurably blurred at the edges, and her lips were still tingling. Lifting a hand to her mouth, she touched it lightly, feeling her lips curve into a smile as she remembered everything.

A wild, breathless happiness was swirling inside her. She could hardly believe that any of it was real. Meeting him in the club, spilling his drink, following him outside and his bike refusing to start—

Groaning, her cheeks suddenly burning, she buried her face in the pillow, remembering how she'd pulled that can from her handbag...

Her pulse stumbled.

And then the storm had started. Thunder—and rain like a monsoon.

He'd been soaked to the skin.

But he had waited for her.

The heat on her cheeks spread as another memory

came to her. Of her body anchored to his…and of his dark, steady gaze watching her until the moment he'd buried his beautiful face in her neck and shuddered deep inside her.

She shivered, remembering, her thighs pressing together, pressing against the warmth and the tenderness there.

That had been the first time…

Later, after she'd lost count of the number of times and ways they'd made love, he'd pulled her against him, his eyes still dark, but soft with sleep, and kissed her gently.

She bit her lip. His intensity, his stamina, his skill hadn't surprised her. But that kiss had. Or maybe her response to it was what was so surprising.

She'd never felt like that with any man before. She had wanted him so badly. Her need for him had been fierce and absolute and unstoppable—like a river breaking its banks. And he had needed her too. She had never felt so wanted, so desired.

Opening her eyes, she bit her lip. Or so certain.

Normally, even the thought of intimacy with a man triggered a loop of self-doubt and distrust inside her head, so that she was already questioning her behaviour and possible responses before anything had even happened.

Her mouth twisted. And for good reason.

She'd only had a handful of relationships, but they'd all ended the same way—with whatever boyfriend it had been telling her that she was too difficult, too demanding. In other words nothing like the carefree young woman they had fallen for.

After what had happened with Dominic she'd given up. It was easier that way. Easier and less exhausting than caring about someone only to be inevitably let down.

And she'd stuck to her pledge.

Until last night.

But she didn't regret it. Lucho had been a great lover. He had made her feel desirable and sexy. Okay, he hadn't said much, but she was glad about that for last night she hadn't wanted to talk.

And if they had talked she would have been busy now picking over his words.

Rolling over, she pulled one of the pillows towards her and hugged it against her stomach, the faint lingering scent of his cologne making her think of night and heat and rain about to fall.

Lucho hadn't needed to talk. To big himself up. Why would he?

He was gorgeous. All lustrous golden skin and lean muscle, and those dark eyes that had seemed to swallow her whole.

And she liked the fact that he had been happy to communicate through touch, his fingers writing poems on her body, his warm breath against her throat a wordless promise of infinite pleasure. His silence had nothing to do with laziness or shyness, but contentment. He was one of those rare people who was happy living in the moment, without expectations or regrets and with nothing to prove.

Unlike her.

Picturing the remote expression on her father's face, the distance in his eyes, she curled her fingers into the pillow. He had not only managed to deny her existence, he'd replaced her too.

Her stomach flip-flopped as beneath her pillow the alarm buzzed on her phone. Reaching round, she switched it off, glancing at the screen. There were several missed calls, all from a number she didn't recognise, and for one brief moment she considered calling back.

But now was not a good time. For a start, she needed to shower, pack and get dressed, and she also wanted to check in with her boss. She trusted Grace—not just professionally, but on a personal level too—and she wanted to see if she had any last-minute advice for her.

And anybody who mattered would call her back if it was important. Not that whatever he or she was calling about was likely to be life-changing.

Rolling out of bed, she grabbed a towel and walked into the bathroom.

In another bathroom, on the other side of the city, Luis stepped out of the shower and wrapped a towel around the taut muscles of his stomach. Ignoring the mirror on the wall, he ran his hands slowly through his hair, smoothing the tangles with his fingers.

He released a slow breath, remembering how just hours earlier Cristina had done more or less the same thing. Except her hands had been urgent, frantic. Almost as frantic as her mouth.

His lungs emptied slowly. And she'd tasted so sweet... sweeter than molasses.

It was supposed to have been just sex—a carnal union designed to delight and, more importantly, to distract him from his thoughts. Except that now he couldn't stop thinking about her. And even though he knew she was in a hotel on the other side of the city, her presence was so strong in his memory that he kept turning to look at the bed, expecting to see her there.

Watching Cristina in the club had been one of the most confusing experiences of his life. She had dazzled him. Even just looking at her in those heels and that top, those shorts, had made a pulse of excitement beat beneath his skin. He had wanted her—and yet he'd almost hated her too. For she was *too* beautiful, *too* sexy, and an attention-seeker to boot. In other words, everything he loathed in a woman.

And so he'd got up to leave—

Gazing at his reflection, he felt his face grow warm.

She might have spilt his drink but she'd been right. It had been his fault. He'd been so desperate to leave that he hadn't been thinking about anything but getting as far away as possible from her gravitational pull. He certainly hadn't been looking where he was going.

Breathing in sharply, he ran his hand slowly over the stubble grazing his face.

Only instead of apologising he'd acted like a jerk.

His heartbeat slowed. He had lost her then, and that might have been the end of it—would have been if his bike hadn't refused to start.

He stared at his reflection, steadying himself, pushing aside the thought of what might have happened, or rather *not* happened, if his bike hadn't been washed or she hadn't come outside.

But she had, and she'd rescued him.

He swallowed.

Rescued him and then kissed him.

Or were they one and the same thing?

Glancing out of the window, he felt his heartbeat accelerate. He was naturally cautious by nature, but even if he hadn't been life had taught him in the most brutal and devastating way not to act impulsively. He didn't do spur-of-the-moment or random.

Yet last night he'd done both. Only instead of regret or shame he could feel a kind a radiance inside his chest. It took him a moment to realise that it was happiness, and that for the first time since stepping off the plane in Athens he was ready to face his past.

Picking up his phone, he punched in a number.

'Carlos. It's Luis...'

Having settled his bill, he made the hotel's owner day by giving him his bike, and then, having finally extricated himself from the man's grateful and disbelieving embrace, he strolled down the street towards the *peluqueria*.

It was just opening, and the old guy who ran it seemed slightly astonished to have a customer so early, but he was happy to do what Luis asked.

Thirty minutes later Luis stepped out into the sunshine, his dark hair cropped close to the head, his face smooth. Catching sight of himself in the window, he felt a flicker of panic. He looked so young. Almost as though the last five years had never happened.

Only so much *had* happened. So much he could never change. He ran his hand slowly over his jawline. The last time he'd been clean shaven had been for his brother's funeral.

It hadn't been a conscious decision to stop shaving—he'd just found it so hard to look at himself as life—*his life*—had carried on.

He had set up a hedge fund, a lucrative, global business. And he'd bought a house—several, actually. He'd even had the occasional girlfriend.

But none of it had mattered. None of it had felt real. Without Bas there to tease him about his tie, or drag him out at the end of a busy week, he'd felt empty, hollow.

Until last night.

With Cristina.

Picturing her beneath him, her eyes darkening as he'd thumbed her legs apart, he almost lost his footing on the pavement. Her passion had been primal; it had blindsided him, left him grappling for breath and self-control.

Over his shoulder, he felt rather than saw a dark saloon car peel away from the opposite side of the square and head towards him. For a moment he carried on walking, and then, slowing down, he turned and waited as the car drew up beside him.

Before it had even come to a stop a thickset man wearing a dark grey suit stepped out onto the pavement and pulled open the back passenger door. Luis nodded at him and climbed inside.

'Thanks for picking me up, Carlos,' he said softly, turning his head towards the window. 'Now, let's go home.'

The journey took less time than he remembered, but it was still long enough for his stomach to turn over and inside out. As the car passed slowly beneath a large stone arch and into a courtyard he had a familiar glimpse of yellowed walls and tall windows, and then he was stepping onto the cobbled paving.

Trying to rein in the beating of his heart, Luis made his way through his childhood home. It might be five years since he'd been back, but he knew exactly where his parents would be waiting.

But he was wrong.

As he walked into the sitting room he frowned. It was empty.

It looked the same, though. He stared round dazedly, barely taking in the opulent interior with its beautiful tapestries and paintings by Goya and Velázquez. Only where were his mother and father?

Behind him a door opened softly and, turning, Luis felt his heart squeeze with a mixture of love, respect and dismay as a silver-haired man walked into the room.

His father, Agusto Osorio, might be nearly seventy, but he was still handsome. And his dark, austere grey eyes and upright bearing were a reminder that he was a man who was used to demanding and getting his way.

But although he was still tall, and immaculately dressed, there was a hesitancy and unsteadiness in his manner that hadn't been there before. Unable to watch his father's faltering progress any more, Luis crossed the faded Persian carpet and embraced the older man gently.

'Papá!'

His heart gave a lurch as he hugged the older man. His father smelt of shaving soap, and that old-fashioned cologne his mother loved, and there was a reassuring familiarity to his father's shoulders. As a child he'd loved to be carried up there; for a long time it had been the only way he could be taller than Bas.

His chest tightened as Agusto released him and smiled.

'We were expecting you earlier. Your mother was worried until she got your text. She misses you. We both do,' he said simply. 'It's good to have you home, Luis, even if it is just for a week.'

Trying to suppress the ache inside his chest, Luis nodded. 'It's good to be back, Papá. And I'm sorry I can't stay longer—'

His father patted him on the arm. 'We understand.' He gestured towards a trio of sofas and armchairs. 'Sit! I'll ring for coffee.'

Watching his father's face crease in pain as he turned and tentatively lowered himself into one of the chairs, Luis held his breath. As a child, Agusto had seemed to him like one of the mythical knights in the books he'd used to read to his sons. A man of honour, vital, inviolate and invincible.

Now, though, his father looked frail and tried—smaller, somehow. Only it wasn't just the passing of time that had caused these changes, but the pain and grief of losing his oldest son.

He felt another stab of guilt and, glancing past him, said quickly, 'Where's Mamá? Should I go and find her?'

'You don't have to, *mi cariño*, I'm right here.'

Across the room, his mother Sofia was standing in the doorway. Before he'd even realised what he was doing he was on his feet and moving. As they embraced he felt a tug at his heart, for he could sense that she had changed more than his father. Not physically—she was still beautiful, slim and elegant—but her sadness was palpable. It seemed to seep into him so that he was suddenly struggling to breathe.

'Luis, you look so well. Doesn't he, Agusto?' She turned to her husband.

Smiling, Agusto nodded as the housekeeper arrived with a tray. 'Yes, he does, *querida*! Ah, here's the coffee. *Gracias*, Soledad. Just there will be perfect.'

Luis waited until they were alone again, and then, turning towards his mother, he smiled. 'So, how many people are coming to the party?'

'Sixty, of course—that's why we had to arrange it for tomorrow. It was the only date everyone could make. '

Picking up his coffee cup, Agusto cleared his throat. 'But we can always squeeze in one more if there's someone special you'd like to bring along.' He glanced over at his son. 'We did wonder if you might bring Amy.'

Shaking his head, Luis met his father's gaze with resignation. 'That's not going to happen, Papá. I haven't dated her in about a year. We're friends now—that's all.'

His father frowned at him. 'But you're seeing someone else?'

'No one serious.'

He held his breath, waiting for the conversation to continue as he knew it surely would. His parents had met at his mother's *quincañera*. It had been love at first sight, and they had both believed—assumed, really—that their sons would find a partner just as effortlessly.

Only with Bas gone all their attention was now focused on him, so that every conversation, no matter how it started, always seemed to turn inevitably to Luis's relationships. But he didn't—couldn't—trust his feelings. Believing that someone loved and desired you was stupid and dangerous. It lulled you into a dream state, made you careless.

And he was never careless. Never took risks. In fact he'd spent most of his adult life doing his damnedest to minimise risk, doing everything in his power to control the world around him. It was one of the reasons why he'd set up his business. Hedge funds were by definition speculative. However, by using algorithms to calculate the optimal probability of executing a profitable trade, he'd eliminated not just fear and greed but risk. Risks that were not worth taking—

His body stilled, his breath catching in his throat as he pictured Cristina, with those ludicrous heels dangling from her hand, as he'd kissed her up the stairs to her hotel room.

She'd been a risk worth taking.

He felt suddenly exhilarated, and a flurry of anticipation rose up inside him.

A risk worth repeating.

He would call her hotel after lunch.

Feeling calmer, he glanced over at his father. 'Life is different in California, Papá. The people are different there. They don't care about—'

'About what? Love? Commitment? Family?'

He could hear the confusion in his father's voice, and the hurt. About everything that was left unspoken. The past. His brother. And, of course, the family business.

His father was coming up to seventy. He wanted to retire and he wanted Luis to take over from him. But he wasn't going to. He couldn't step in for his brother. Sit at the head of that massive oak table in the boardroom. It just wasn't going to happen.

Glancing at his father expression of frustration and his mother's stricken face, he wanted to apologise for letting them down. For not being the son they deserved. But to do so would mean having to explain his reasons, and that would mean losing their love for ever.

His father shook his head. 'Thank goodness we're only

being photographed for this article,' he muttered. 'I can't imagine how I'd explain the fact that my only son and heir has turned his back on his birthright.'

Luis felt his skin tighten across his face, his brain locking on to the one word in his father's remark that was designed to trigger alarm bells in his head.

'What article?'

Sofia leaned forward. 'It's for a magazine. We're meeting the photographer before lunch, just to have a little chat. I have her CV here...'

Reaching across, she picked up a folder from the table, and handed it to Luis.

He didn't open it.

'But what's the point of the article?' He could feel his hackles rising.

His father raised an eyebrow. 'I know you're not interested in the family business, Luis. But I would have thought that even *you* might have remembered it's the bank's four hundredth anniversary this year.'

Luis cursed silently. Of course it was. Agusto had mentioned it to him several months back. Believing it to be some kind of entrée into discussing his return to the family business, he'd pushed it away.

Gritting his teeth, he forced himself to speak calmly. 'I hadn't forgotten, Papá,' he said slowly. 'I just didn't connect the dots.' He frowned. 'I get that the anniversary is a big deal, but Banco Osorio's reputation is built on our discretion. We never talk to the media. So why go public now?'

'It was my idea.' His mother looked up at him, her face suddenly anxious. 'Do you think I made a mistake, Luis?'

Damn right he did. He didn't trust any journalists or photographers.

But he could hardly explain the reason for that to his parents.

His spine stiffened, his body tensing as memories filled his head. Memories of the night his brother had died.

He hadn't even wanted to go to that party, only Bas had insisted and his mother had backed him up. She knew that Luis needed his big brother in order to socialise, and Bas needed Luis to rein in his excesses.

But the party had been so not his style. Wall-to-wall trust fund brats, drinking and whining about their parents.

Watching Bas work the party, Luis had felt one of his occasional twinges of envy. His brother was so charming. With Bas there he always felt like a spare part—particularly around women. Then, out of nowhere, he'd spotted her. And she had been looking at *him*.

Unlike all the other women in the room, she'd looked at ease with herself. Jeans, boots, hair loose to her shoulders. They had talked and talked, shouting at first, over the noise of the party, and then later more quietly out on the balcony. She had liked the same artists he did, hated parties, and had had an older sister who was much cooler than she was.

He had felt as though she knew him inside out.

It was only later that he'd realised why that was.

Much later.

After he'd slept with her.

After he'd learnt that she was a *paparazza* and after he'd accidentally let slip where Bas was going to be staying that night.

After her colleagues had chased his brother to his death.

Striving for calm, he looked up at his mother. 'So when is this photo shoot happening?'

'Next week. The day after you go back to California.' Sofia bit her lip. 'Your father wasn't sure, but he's worked so hard and I wanted to do something—'

He squeezed his mother's hand gently. 'It's a lovely idea.'

He felt a fist of tension curl inside his stomach.

He couldn't stay. It would be unbearable, and unfair to his parents, for he knew they would begin to talk wistfully of his moving back to Spain.

But how could he leave them to face some unscrupulous photographer alone? They were so otherworldly, so trusting.

'I know you don't like the press,' his mother said tentatively. 'But we'll have final say over the photos. And your father made it clear that we won't be answering personal questions.'

There was a knock on the door. It was Soledad.

'The photographer is here, Señor Osorio. She's waiting in the *salón azul*.'

'Thank you, Soledad.'

Taking his mother's hand, Luis helped her to her feet. 'I feel bad about making such a fuss, Mamá. Let me come with you—please. I might even be some help. I deal with the media a lot back in California, so I'm pretty sure I can handle anything they throw at me.'

His words were still reverberating around his head as he followed his father into the *salón azul* and came face to face with Cristina.

He stared at her in silence, his heartbeat deafeningly loud, a thousand questions bombarding his brain.

Had he just looked at her clothes he might not have recognised her. Gone were the denim shorts and that insane transparent top. Instead she was wearing tailored navy trousers and a blue-and-white-striped matelot top. Only her hair was the same—still tumbling over her shoulders in a mass of glossy red waves.

Slowly the events of the night before began to whirl in front of his eyes, spinning over and over until finally they lined up alongside one another like fruit on a slot machine.

Drink. Bike. Kiss.

Jackpot.

His breath felt sharp in his throat as he realised that it had all been a set-up. Right from the moment he'd walked into that club he'd been played. Everything that had felt so random, so spontaneous—their eyes meeting in the mirror, her banging into him and spilling his drink, even her having that stupid can of oil in her bag—all of it had been planned.

Flipping open the folder his mother had given him, he read swiftly through her CV, his stomach knotting with fury both with her and himself.

What was wrong with him? After what had happened with Bas did he really need another opportunity to prove how naive and complacent he was?

Apparently he did.

Apparently he had already forgotten that a beautiful woman always had an agenda of her own.

He was on the verge of striding across the room and dragging her lying, manipulative little body out of the building, when his mother stepped past him, smiling.

'You must be Cristina. Welcome to our home.'

Sliding to her feet, Cristina held out her hand.

Her editor, Grace, had warned her that the Osorios were old-school and preferred to keep things on a formal footing, so she'd tried to dress in a way that implied she was professional, yet creative. But her heart was still beating like a startled horse as the beautiful grey-haired woman crossed the room towards her.

'Señora Osorio. Thank you so much for meeting me today.'

'Please…' Sofia smiled. 'You must call me Sofia. This is my husband, Agusto, and my son, Luis. He's over on a visit from California. Flew in this morning.'

Cristina shook Agusto's hand, and then, finally registering the second, taller, darker-haired man, she turned to Luis.

She smiled. Or tried to. But her lips wouldn't work. Her whole body seemed to be numb. Around her the room was dissolving into a mist the same grey as his eyes—*Lucho's* eyes—as silently she racked what was left of her brain for some kind of practical response to what was happening.

Only Grace's notes had said nothing about coming face to face with your one-night stand. Or finding out he was the son of the people you were meant to photograph.

As he held out his hand she took it mechanically.

It couldn't be.

Except that it was, and suddenly she thought she might faint.

Sofia was staring at her. 'Are you all right, my dear? You look pale.'

'I'm fine.' She smiled stiffly. 'Too much coffee, I'm afraid. I should probably try decaffeinated, but it's so disgusting. I prefer a simple *espresso*—Arabica bean, black, no sugar.'

Agusto beamed at her. 'Ah, a coffee connoisseur. I'm trying to cut back too, but it's hard when the alternatives are such poor substitutes.'

Cristina nodded, and then, sensing Luis's cool, dismissive gaze, she felt a rush of anger. 'I agree. I *hate* things that aren't what they appear to be.'

A warning flag of anger flared in his grey eyes, but she didn't care.

Lucho—Luis—whatever he called himself—was a phony, happy to offer different versions of himself in order to get what he wanted.

In this case her.

He was just like her father—and she should have known that.

A familiar feeling of doubt and panic was slipping over her skin. She felt her eyes tugged towards the door and escape.

Her pulse jerked. Escape from *what*? She had come here to put the past behind her. It was why she'd fought so hard to win this assignment. To make the world, and more particularly her father, sit up and take notice. And that was what would happen when she sent him a copy of the magazine with her byline beneath the photographs. Lifting her chin, she smiled at Agusto.

'I'm sure you didn't invite me here to discuss coffee. How about I talk you through the production process for the shoot? And then if you have any questions I'll try and answer them.'

'*I* have some questions.'

Luis's voice cut through her smile.

'You do?' She forced herself to meet his gaze. 'That's great,' she said stiffly.

'You seem very young. I'm just wondering about your experience.'

His mother frowned at him. 'I gave you Cristina's CV, *cariño*.'

'And I read it. It seems very light. Does it cover all your talents?'

He watched her beautiful light brown eyes widen.

'No, not all of them.' She looked at him calmly. 'I worked in a cake shop when I was fifteen, so I can make a mean *crème pâtissière* if you're tempted.'

'I'm not.' He held her gaze. 'Not any more, anyway.'

After the interview was over, and Cristina had left the room, Sofia glanced at her husband and son and said quickly, 'Well, I thought that went well. I know she's young, but she seemed very genuine—and quite charming.'

Luis felt his stomach twist. Oh, she was charming, all right—but *genuine*?

Breathing in, he said as calmly as he could manage, 'She did seem charming. But wouldn't you prefer someone with a little more gravitas?'

He was speaking to his mother, but it was his father who answered the question.

'Not really. Unless you have a particular reason to doubt this young women?'

Luis hesitated. *Say it*, he ordered himself. *Tell the truth.*

But how? He could hardly tell his mother that he'd had sex with Cristina. For a start, she thought he'd flown in that morning. Nor could he reveal that his fears lay rooted in a mistake he'd made five years ago—a mistake that had cost his brother his life and his parents a son.

Looking at their faces, he made up his mind. He didn't trust Cristina, but he didn't need to admit that or explain why. He just needed to be around to keep tabs on her.

Slowly, he shook his head. 'No, I don't. All that matters to me is that you're happy. And besides, I can help. You know how much I love photography.'

His mother looked at him in confusion. 'But, *cariño*, you won't be here—'

Luis picked up his mother's hand and pressed it to his mouth. 'I can be, Mamá. And I *want* to be.'

His mother's tears of happiness made him feel guiltier than ever. But he would do whatever it took to protect his parents. Even lie to them.

'I think it would be a good idea if we did the photo shoot on the island,' he said firmly.

La Isla de los Halcones had belonged to the Osorio family for over one hundred years. It was isolated—only accessible by motorboat—and best of all communication with the mainland was limited to a landline.

It's completely private, and much more relaxed.' He smiled reassuringly at both of them. 'It'll be perfect, and I'll be there to supervise the whole thing.'

And if that meant keeping a close eye on Cristina then so be it.

CHAPTER THREE

'IS THERE ANYTHING else I can get you, Ms Shephard? More coffee?'

Closing her laptop, Cristina smiled up at the air stewardess and shook her head. 'No, thank you. I'm good.'

The stewardess smiled back at her. 'Okay, but just let me know if you need anything.'

Watching the woman move gracefully away down the cabin, she resisted the urge to pinch herself again, and instead gazed out of the window at the cloudless blue sky.

She'd never flown business class before, and frankly it would probably be a long time before she did so again. But the Osorios had insisted, and it was a treat to have the extra legroom and a lunch that was actually edible.

The Osorio name had helped in other ways too. She'd been fast-tracked through baggage and security, and a limousine would be waiting at Valencia airport to take her to the marina.

It was all very civilised. But then people like Agusto and Sofia didn't queue for taxis or hang around waiting for luggage. The rich and the powerful valued their time almost as much as their privacy, and unlike normal people they only did what they wanted to do.

As she knew from experience.

She felt her face stiffen, the muscles tightening involuntarily, and, reaching down, she picked up her cup—china, not cardboard—and took a sip of coffee.

What other reason could there be for her father never bothering to get in touch with her?

Still gazing listlessly out of the window, she thought about how at the beginning she'd tried to make sense of his actions. Husbands divorced wives, not children, so why didn't he want to see her?

At first she'd made excuses for him, and then she'd blamed her mother. Later, though, there had been only one explanation. Her father didn't love her and he probably never had.

Frowning, Cristina flipped open her laptop and gazed determinedly down at the screen. She wasn't going to let her father's rejection ruin this moment for her. This was her last chance to do her final preparation before the photo shoot, and she wasn't going to waste it brooding about the past.

She began scrolling through the background notes that Grace had emailed to her. It didn't take long. It was mostly historical facts about the Osorio banking dynasty. Personal, biographical details about the family were frustratingly sparse.

Her heart gave a lurch. Panic was beginning to uncoil inside her stomach. It wasn't the first portrait that she'd taken—Grace wasn't *that* trusting. But it was the most important to date, and she wanted it to work. Not just for the magazine but for herself. She so badly wanted to prove that she could do this.

Her fingers shook slightly above the keyboard.

No, that wasn't true. She wanted more than that. She wanted to matter, to be somebody, to be noticed. And not just by her peers.

Only how could she do that if she couldn't find *the key to their story*?

She felt her stomach clench.

It was her job as a photographer to seek the truth—that

was why she'd so foolishly become a *paparazza*. But with portraits the truth was elusive. In the intimacy of a studio-style setting people grew guarded, and of course there was always an obstacle between her camera and the sitter. It wasn't just a matter of point and click; the shutter was like a tiny little door that she needed to open.

And that required a key.

She had hoped to find one, talking to Agusto and Sofia. But although they had been polite, and helpful, they had fairly conservative ideas about what they wanted from the photo shoot—and, looking down at the pictures that Grace had sent her, she could see why.

To her photography was magic. But the Osorios were clearly intensely private people who simply wanted a record of a particular moment.

She needed to see beyond the staged poses. She needed to do a little supplementary research of her own. But as she typed in the Osorio name she felt heat spread over her cheeks as the screen filled not only with photos of Agusto and Sofia, but Luis too.

She stared at them greedily.

There were a couple of him as dark-eyed teenager, watching the polo at Sotogrande with his parents and brother. Another as a student in America, rowing at Harvard. And then, leaping forward several years, there were several more of the adult Luis. Publicity shots of him in his role as CEO of the quantitative hedge fund he'd founded.

Clearly turning his back on one fortune had been no obstacle to amassing another. His business was less than three years old but it had already made him a billionaire.

The thought of Luis behind a desk, with some glossy PA hovering over his shoulder, made her feel as if she was pressing on a bruise. But now that she knew the truth about him his career choice made perfect sense.

He enjoyed taking risks, was able to keep his emotions in check, and clearly didn't mull over the consequences of his actions. Crucial qualities not just for succeeding in the high-stress, high-reward culture of the stock market, but for managing multiple lives.

So what if he was rich? Money wasn't everything.

Except when you didn't have it.

She gritted her teeth, familiar nausea cramping her stomach as she remembered the years of struggle after her father had deserted them.

He had left them penniless, and that had not been all. With no money coming into the house, and a terrifying number of bills to pay, there had been no time to deal with their shock and grief and anger.

But he'd probably never even given them or their feelings a thought. Why would he? After all, he'd relocated to America and just carried on as if nothing had happened.

As if *she* had never happened.

She had felt so unimportant. So insignificant.

Until last week, when Luis had walked into his parents' palatial living room and the expression on his face had confused and frightened her so much that she had forgotten to breathe.

She'd thought the shard of misery inside her chest would split her in two.

Luis Osorio was a liar. And a fake.

But—and it was an important 'but'—he also lived in California. And, despite barely managing to hold all the pieces of herself together during that awkward interview in Segovia, her brain had registered the fact that he was returning to the States at the end of the week—today, in fact.

Her shoulders straightened. She'd been right about him the first time in that club. He was a mistake. But now he was in her past. Here, in the present, it was just her and her camera.

Half an hour later the plane landed in Valencia. Feeling like a minor celebrity, she was whisked through the airport to the promised limousine, and then twenty minutes later was stepping onto a sleek, white motorboat.

Inside, the decor was all smooth, pale wood, cream leather upholstery and discreetly tinted glass. As she sat down in one of the armchairs she suddenly remembered that Agusto had referred to the boat as a 'dinghy'. Suppressing a smile, she was just about to pull out her camera when her phone rang.

'Chrissie, darling? It's not a bad time, is it?'

As usual, the tentative note in her mother's voice made her heart beat faster with love—and remorse.

Over the years she had been such a brat. More than anything she wanted to make amends, to show her mother how much she loved her. And if she did well with this assignment then finally it might be possible to do that with more than words. She might actually be able to give her mum the security of a home instead of just a couple of rooms that went with her job.

Clearing her throat, she said brightly, 'No it's a great time, Mum. I'm just on the boat now. On my way to the island.'

'How long does the ferry take?'

Her spine stiffened, her mother's innocent question catching her off-guard.

She hadn't lied—didn't lie, full-stop, not even about stupid, insignificant things. As far as she was concerned it was better to say nothing than to lie, and over the years she'd got really good at deflecting or misunderstanding anything that got too close to the bone.

So, no she hadn't lied, but she'd been reluctant to hint at the Osorios' insane wealth. With her history of messing up, she'd been scared of jinxing herself. But, knowing how excited her mother would be, she couldn't resist pressing the phone against her face, and whispering, 'It's their island, actually, and I'm not on a ferry. I'm on their motorboat.'

'A motorboat *and* a private island.' Her mother laughed. 'Oh, darling, it sounds like something from a film.' She hesitated. 'And will you be staying with the family?'

'Yes, they have a house there.' Actually Agusto had called it a fortress, but had he been speaking literally? 'I can't send you any pictures, though, Mum.'

'Of course not. I wouldn't—'

Cristina's phone buzzed. She frowned. Someone was trying to ring her.

She glanced at the screen, her eyes narrowing.

Unknown number. *Damn!* Agusto had given her his private number but she hadn't had a chance to put it into her phone yet. Fumbling with her bag, she tried to find the notepad where she'd written it down.

'Mum, I'm going to have to go. I've got another call—'

'Oh, of course. Well, I'll hang up, then. Bye, darling, bye…'

Tucking the phone under her chin, Cristina cleared her throat.

'Cristina Shephard.'

But there was only silence. She cursed silently. She must have just missed it.

'Ms Shephard?'

Turning, her mind still on the mystery caller, she saw that it was one of the crew.

'We're just about to dock now. If you could stay seated until I return?'

Nodding, she managed a quick, tight smile.

Should she call back? No, she wouldn't—not now. It would only distract her, and she needed to concentrate. Besides, if it was important they'd ring back, wouldn't they?

Stepping onto a short wooden jetty, she felt a flicker of

anticipation ripple over her skin. She could taste the salt in the air, and as a slight breeze lifted her hair she couldn't stop herself from smiling.

Another limousine was waiting for her—only it was not the sort that could be rented out by the hour. Judging by the coat of arms on the door, it was the family's own private car. Settling back against the soft leather seating, she felt almost giddy with excitement. It was like being Cinderella.

Or maybe not Cinderella, she thought a moment later. There would be no fairy godmother or glass slipper to help her achieve her happy-ever-after. It was up to her to make this work.

Which was fine. She had the talent and the determination, so what could possibly stand in her way?

Turning her head, she gazed eagerly out of the window. For such a small island, there was quite a mix of landscapes. Inland, green hills covered with grass blended into dust-brown olive groves, like paint on a palette, while along the coastline clumps of pine trees ended in vertiginous drops down to the water. As the road twisted upwards she could see that the cobalt blue sea splashed foam up onto both shining dark rocks and sand the colour of clotted cream.

There was a tiny church on one of the smaller hills, and some rustic-looking cottages—and then suddenly, as the car slid round a corner, she saw it.

Her mouth dropped open.

It really was a fortress.

Gazing up at the castellated stone walls, she felt her heartbeat accelerate.

It was huge. The Osorios' beautiful home in Segovia seemed modest in comparison, but even the fortress was dwarfed by the six-sided tower that rose up from the centre of the building.

Feeling almost hollow with shock and envy, she was

vaguely aware of the limousine stopping, and then she was stepping out of the air-conditioned cool into heat and sunlight. A middle-aged woman wearing a cream linen dress greeted her with a smile.

'Ms Shephard? Welcome to Fortaleza de Moya. My name is Pilar, and I'm in charge of housekeeping. I'll be taking care of you during your stay.'

Reining in her nerves, Cristina smiled. 'Thank you. It's lovely to meet you.'

She glanced across at her shabby luggage, but before she had a chance to move Pilar stepped towards her.

'Javier will take your bags to your room. I'm sure you want to freshen up after your long journey, but Señor Osorio was hoping you'd have a coffee with him first.'

Cristina held her gaze. It was difficult not to be intimidated by the opulence and glamour of the Osorios' world and their cool, crystalline confidence. Particularly when she dressed so casually.

But remembering Luis's cool dissection of her CV, she felt a rush of defiance. Now, more than anything, she wanted to get started. To prove that she could hold her own with these people.

Lifting her chin, she smiled. 'What a lovely idea. I could do with a coffee.'

She followed the other woman through a series of gorgeous, glamorous rooms out onto a stone balcony overlooking the sea. Coffee and some petit-fours were arranged on a marble-topped table, and after Pilar had left she picked up a small crescent-shaped biscuit and nibbled it—more for something to do than because she was hungry.

There was a slight breeze and, leaning forward against the balustrade, she drew up her mass of hair, enjoying the sensation of cool air on the warm skin of her neck.

Hearing footsteps behind her, she let her hair fall. Reminding herself to call him by his first name, she turned, smiling warmly.

'It's a beautiful view, Agusto. You must be so happy to see it—' she began.

But her words dried to dust in her mouth. For it wasn't Agusto standing there. It was his son, Luis, and he was looking anything but happy.

Luis stared at her, his heart pounding. Walking onto the balcony, he'd flinched. But not because of the glare of sunlight. It was looking at Cristina that had momentarily blinded him. With her auburn hair spilling down over her bare arms, her mouth open in an O of shock, she was easily as beautiful as the view she'd been admiring.

He felt a shot of anger; he wasn't sure if it was with her or with himself. But he was grateful that she was on the other side of the flagstones, for it took every step towards her for him to compose himself.

Although, to be honest, she looked more stunned than he felt.

Her words confirmed that fact as she said shakily, 'What are you doing here? Your father—'

'Isn't here.'

Her beauty felt like a punch to the face, but he held her gaze, forcing himself to look at her—*really* look at her— until the pain subsided to a dull ache.

'They arrive tomorrow. Something came up at the bank, so I offered to come along and hold the fort.'

Cristina stared at him mutely. If that was a joke, it wasn't funny. But then humour was pretty low on her list of responses right now. Mostly she was in shock at coming face to face with him. And then there was the shock of his beauty.

Her pulse gave a twitch. She was used to beauty—had photographed numerous celebrities. None of them, though, had ever made her heart beat like a metronome. But then none of them had had a clear gold profile that could cut through the dusk of a summer evening.

He took a step towards her, his eyes drifting towards the biscuit in her hand.

'Making yourself at home, I see,' he said softly. 'Don't get too comfortable. You won't be staying.'

It took a moment for his words to sink in. Back in Segovia she'd thought he was warning her off, but this was the first time he'd made it clear.

'I'm pretty sure that's not up to you,' she said stiffly.

'Then you've been misinformed—or you have made an assumption based on ignorance, not fact. When I want something to happen, it does.'

'And let me guess...' She glared at him. 'You don't ask twice.'

She felt a chill slide over her skin as he shook his head, his grey eyes dark with hostility.

'I don't ask.' His gaze drifted dismissively over her face. 'You've had a nice all-expenses-paid trip. And now it's over.'

Holding on to her temper by a rapidly fraying thread, she raised an eyebrow. 'I don't work for you, and you have no say in what I do or where I do it. I do what my editor—'

'Really? Your editor told you to sleep with me?'

His face was cold and harsh.

Cristina gaped at him. Leaning over the balcony, lost in the sound of the waves and the heat of the mid-afternoon sun, she had been expecting a pleasant if slightly formal welcome from Agusto.

But Luis was neither pleasant nor welcoming. Nor did he bear any resemblance to the hard-muscled lover who had pulled her against him time and again during that night in the hotel. Instead he was staring at her in a way that made the solid stone beneath her feet feel flimsy.

'You surprise me. I've met your boss, and Grace White-
ley doesn't strike me as the kind of woman who'd pimp
out her staff.'

'That's not I meant and you know it.' She was almost
blindsided with outrage and fury. 'How dare you suggest
that—?'

'That what? That you seduced me?'

Luis could feel the rage rolling beneath his skin. He'd
wanted this opportunity to confront her with what she'd
done, and back in Segovia it had all seemed so straightforward, so logical. Without his parents there to intervene
he would summon her, punish her, and then dismiss her.

Now that she was here, though, he wanted to teach her
another kind of lesson completely. One that had nothing to
with logic and reason and everything to do with lust. His
eyes wandered over her beautiful face, dropping over her
small rounded breasts to the temptingly smooth bare skin
of her stomach. And as for dismissing her—

Breathing in sharply, he ignored the longing constrict-
ing his groin and dragged his gaze up to meet hers. 'Please
don't treat me as though I'm stupid. Or naive. You'd be
wrong on both counts. And you can stop all the wide-eyed
outrage. I read your CV, Ms Shephard. I know exactly how
your type operates and you set me up. All that business of
spilling my drink…'

His mouth curled, contempt flaring in his eyes.

'I should have known something was up when you fixed
my bike.' He shook his head. 'You only knew how to fix
it because you'd broken it.'

And that expression on her face when she'd turned and
looked back at him—it hadn't been doubt but relief. Relief
that he was still there. His skin prickled with shame. Still
there, fool that he had been, not struggling or fighting, just
watching and waiting for her to reel him in.

Cristina stared at him in confusion. Her mind was completely empty, spotless—bare like a blank piece of paper. But it wasn't just his words that had robbed her of the power of thought. She just couldn't match the cold-eyed stranger in front of her with the man who had made love to her with such passion and intensity.

With an effort, she tried to marshal her brain into some kind of order. 'I don't know what you're talking about.'

Luis stared at her coldly. She was a good actress. *Really* good. The shaking hands were a particularly nice touch. He might have been tempted to believe her had he not been stung so badly before.

Five years ago he had been young, naive and insecure. The reporter back then had been older than him, pretty and persuasive, and he'd been flattered—

Until the moment when he'd woken up and heard her talking to her colleague.

His stomach quivered, dread pooling low down as he remembered how it had felt—not just the shock of discovering who she was, but the creeping recollection of what he'd said to her. Even now it still had the power to wake him some nights, sweating and yet cold, breathing heavily in the darkness.

A storm was building in his chest, and he knew his feelings must be showing on his face, but he didn't care. The proficiency of her performance only served to feed his anger.

'I told you not to treat me like an idiot. You might have fooled me once with those eyes, that mouth, but I learn from my mistakes—and *you* are a mistake I've no intention of repeating.'

Cristina felt familiar panic twist her stomach.

Meeting Luis with his parents had been a shock. But that had been all about his lies. This—here, now—was about his contempt. Her throat tightened, misery, dark and impenetrable, crowding out the breath in her lungs as his words ricocheted inside her head.

A mistake.

Suddenly it wasn't Luis's voice she could hear but her father's, and the words were those he had spoken to her eight years ago in a hotel foyer in London.

Her mouth felt bone-dry, and for a moment she thought she was going to throw up.

A week ago Luis had turned her body into a quivering mass of desire, his gaze, his touch, his kiss had made her feel as if she was the only woman in the world for him. Now, though, it was as if he could see inside her. See that she was a fake, a failure, with no place in the world—especially *his* world.

Watching the colour drain from her face, Luis felt something crack inside him.

She looked stunned—sick, even—and the fact that *he* was the one who had upset her made his heart beat painfully hard. He was never brutal—not even in business, and especially not to women.

But Cristina had lied to him. She'd let him believe that she wanted him, when all she'd really wanted had been to get the inside story on his family.

His mouth thinned. She didn't deserve gentleness or mercy.

He took a step closer. 'You lied to me. You knew who I was and you deliberately set out to seduce me. You followed me into that bar and then you made damn sure I noticed you. Hell, you even walked into me so that I'd spill my drink.'

That wasn't what had happened, she thought, striving to stay calm as a swirl of anger and frustration rose up inside her.

'Is that right, *Lucho*?' she snapped. 'You see, the way I remember it, you walked into *me*. Oh, and remind me again—which one of us was using a false name?'

Luis could barely contain his rage. It wasn't a false name.

It was his childhood nickname. Even now his mother still used it sometimes, and Bas had always called him Lucho.

At the thought of his brother, the last thin thread of his temper snapped.

His eyes narrowed. 'You know, you're wasting your talents, Ms Shephard. You should really be on the other side of the camera. Or is that what this is all really about? You selling some kiss and tell story to the newspapers?'

Cristina stepped forward, her hands curling into fists, frustration arrowing through her blood. 'For the last time—I didn't know who you were—'

'And I didn't know who *you* were.' His eyes met hers, dark grey with contempt and retribution. 'But I do now. I know exactly who and what you are. You're a cold-hearted, self-serving parasite.'

She could hardly breathe. 'And *you're* a phony. A fake. A fraud. Sneaking around, playing at being a biker, when really you're a CEO—'

'I was *not* sneaking.'

'Oh, really?' she snarled. 'Is that why your mother thought you flew in that morning? Why your father has no idea you ride a motorbike?'

A solid, choking anger filled his lungs. 'This is between you and I. It has nothing to do with my parents.'

'You're right. It did have nothing to do with your parents. Or my editor. It was just us.'

Just us.

The words spun out of her mouth, whirling between them like sparks—bright, luminous, impossible to ignore.

They were inches apart.

Luis could feel his body responding to her words, to the darkness of her pupils, to her mouth tipped up towards his—

Somewhere in the house a door slammed, and they both jumped.

Cristina stared past him, concentrating on the horizon. She felt weightless; as if the pulse beating between her thighs was all that remained of her body. It had been so hard not to reach out and touch him. But she hadn't, and soon he wouldn't be here to tempt her.

'And now it's over,' she said quickly, turning to face him. 'Look, I'm just here to work. So why don't you go back to California and let me get on with my job?'

Luis stared at her in silence. He was still reeling from what had just happened. His pulse shuddered. What had *nearly* just happened—and would have done if that door hadn't slammed, and brought him to his senses.

Senses that clearly needed to step up a level.

Stepping past her, he picked up the coffee pot and carefully filled two cups. 'Interesting hypothesis. But I'm not going back to California. Coffee?'

He held out a cup, and she shook her head. 'But you said—'

'Something I didn't mean, Ms Shephard. How does it feel to be on the receiving end of that for once?'

His eyes locked onto hers.

'I don't trust you. I certainly don't trust you in *my* home with *my* parents. So while you're here I'm going to be here too. And every day I'm going to be watching you, waiting for you to mess up, and when you do I'm going to ruin you. But until that moment you're stuck with me.'

Staring past her, he gazed coolly at the sunset.

'You know your way out, don't you?'

CHAPTER FOUR

LEANING FORWARD, CRISTINA grabbed a handful of grass and hauled herself over a small outcrop of rock. The hill had looked quite gentle from a distance, but up close she had quickly realised that, like a lot things in life, its appearance was deceptive.

Scowling, she breathed out slowly.

It was yet another reason for her to loathe Luis Osorio, for she wouldn't even be up here if it wasn't for him. But after a restless night spent dissecting his remarks she had woken feeling just as tense and furious as when she'd gone to bed.

Back in London she would have distracted herself by going out and merging with the noise and the crowds, blending with friends and strangers at pubs and parties across the city, blanking out her brain with noise and laughter.

Only how could she do that stuck on a private island? There *were* no people or parties.

But there was no way she could just sit alone with her thoughts in that huge, beautiful bedroom, so she'd opted for her other go-to solution: exercise. After grabbing a bottle of water from the fridge, she'd headed towards the hill, expecting a walk and a view.

But of course nothing connected with Luis was what it seemed.

Her jaw tightened as his cool, hostile soundbites replayed inside her head.

Out of all the men in that club, she'd had to go and sleep with him.

The sun was high in the sky now, but despite its heat a familiar damp clamminess was creeping over her skin. She felt numb. It would be easy to say it was just bad luck. That she was the victim of some massive cosmic conspiracy. That she had simply been in the wrong place at the wrong time.

But what would be the point?

She knew what had really happened. When he'd collided with her in the club it hadn't rendered her helpless or incapable of thought. The truth was that even before she'd felt the lean, hard muscles of his chest, or the power in his arms as he'd stopped her falling, she had wanted him.

Having sex with him had been her choice.

And his choice too.

She could feel the blood trembling beneath her skin.

Only he'd already distanced himself from that part of the equation. Distanced himself from her too. Just as her father had done.

Her father—

She felt a sting of pain in her chest. Why did everything always begin and end with her father? A man who thought so little of her that he had found it easy—effortless, really—to walk away. Nor had he felt any need to keep in touch. No letter telling her that he cared, no phone call to explain or justify his actions. Not so much as a backward glance. But then why *would* he look back? she thought dully. He already had a whole other life mapped out— another future—and it was easier to delete her and her mother, to rewrite history. Just as Luis had.

She shivered.

And that wasn't all they had in common.

Just like with her father, she had now given him the power to jeopardise her future.

Thinking back to what it had been like after her father had left, she took a breath, trying to steady the panic lurching in her stomach.

His desertion had, of course, devastated her thirteen-year-old self, but it had impacted on the future Cristina too. Angry and hurt, and with the cause of her anger and pain absent, she had turned on those who remained.

She had messed up her education, lost her friends, and lashed out at the one person who had consistently and unfailingly loved her—her mother.

It had taken years to get her life back on track, and this photo shoot was her chance finally to be a part of something. Only now, just like always, she had managed to mess it up.

Her body stilled. It was awkward enough that she'd had sex with Luis—she couldn't even imagine what Grace would say if she found out—but there was also the matter of Luis wanting her gone.

Her insides tightened. Surely that wouldn't be up to him?

She bit her lip. Except that, like any normal parents, Agusto and Sofia were clearly devoted to their son. If he came up with a convincing enough excuse to end her contract it was inconceivable that they would take her side against him.

She felt her heart thud against her ribs. So the real question, then, was how far would he go to make good on his threat?

'That's great, Señor Osorio. If you could maybe lean in a little towards your wife. That's wonderful. Perhaps just a little bit closer. Wonderful.'

Cristina swallowed. At some point in the future she would look back to this day and see it as some sort of baptism of fire. A rite of passage that she might refer to in her memoirs. Right now, though, she just wanted it to be over.

She had probably taken hundreds, if not thousands of photographs over the last two years, but today nothing was working.

In theory it didn't matter. Today's shots were supposed to be 'fun'. Really they were just about making Agusto and Sofia feel comfortable around her, but instead they were making her question her ability to do the job.

She shivered on the inside. Maybe Grace's faith in her had been a little premature. Or, worse, could Luis's scathing remark about her experience actually be true?

Hating the way he had already managed to undermine her, she tried unsuccessfully to block his words from her head.

Only it was hard to do when the man himself was lounging negligently on a sofa to her left.

The sun was already high in a sky the colour of forget-me-nots, and both she and the Osorios were dressed for the heat—short sleeves, cool, pale fabrics. Luis, though, cut a sombre figure. Wearing a beautifully cut dark grey suit that made his eyes look almost black, a pale blue shirt and dark blue knitted tie, he looked as though he was about to preside over a full board meeting rather than sitting in on an informal photo shoot.

She felt a flicker of irritation.

His choice of clothing was obviously a deliberate attempt to sabotage the relaxed atmosphere she had been trying to create. And it didn't help either that he seemed determined to prove she was a scurrilous, manipulative hustler. Not only did he seem to be constantly there, policing her every move, he treated any attempt she made to engage him or his parents in conversation as some kind of an inquisition.

Aside from that he ignored her completely, immersing

himself in his work so that she couldn't actually imagine him without his laptop.

Glancing furtively over to where he sat—one hand hovering over the keyboard, the other tracking a line of numbers on a paper printout—not for the first time she wondered how Luis 2.0 could be the same man who had stripped her naked and taken possession of her feverish body.

A memory of the earlier version of the man sitting opposite her dropped into her head—his mouth rough and urgent against hers, his eyes darkening as he lowered her onto the bed—and suddenly her mind went blank.

All she could think was how perfect it had felt…how perfect it had been.

When he'd banged into her in the club she had been blown away, knocked off her feet—not just literally but metaphorically. The attraction between them had been instant, inescapable.

She gritted her teeth. And now he was inescapable again, unfortunately…

Feeling completely exposed, she glanced back down at the camera, steadying herself. Then, staring at the photos, she felt her pulse start to accelerate. The composition and light were fine, but—

They said the camera never lied, and if that was true in this case her job had just got about a million times harder.

Agusto looked tense. Everything from the set of his shoulders to the tightness around his mouth suggested that he was not enjoying the photo shoot at all. But it was his wife's expression that made a knot form in Cristina's stomach.

Sofia was looking not at the camera but through it, her eyes focused on some distant point, as though she was searching for something that wasn't visible. She looked sad—hollowed out, almost.

Keeping her head bent over the camera, Cristina forced herself to click through the images on the screen, all the while making encouraging noises.

It wasn't just the sadness in the older woman's eyes that had caught her off guard, it was her own unintended intrusion into it.

Head spinning, she took a breath. She felt grubby, tainted. Just as she had when she'd caught that actress, with her philandering husband of three weeks, in a restaurant. Even now she could remember the thrill of it. She had thought being a *paparazza* was like being some kind of avenger. A truth-chasing, justice-seeker on a bike, with a camera as her weapon of choice.

But watching that actress, who'd been younger than she herself was now, go into meltdown had made her feel physically sick. It could have made her a lot of money. It wasn't every day that an A-lister stripped down to her underwear in public. But instead it had been the reason she had quit chasing celebrities.

'Is there a problem?'

At the sound of the cool, clipped voice, she felt her fingers curl instinctively around the camera. Given his low opinion of her, Luis Osorio was the last person she wanted to talk to when she was feeling like a *paparazza* with his mother. But then he was pretty much the last person she wanted to talk to, or see, in *any* situation.

Although judging by the way her skin now felt as if it was on fire, it appeared that her body might have missed that particular memo.

Gritting her teeth, she trained an expression of what she hoped looked like serenity onto her face, and looked up at him.

At first, when she'd found him talking with his parents in the ornate sitting room the Osorios had chosen as a backdrop for the photos, she had assumed he would leave once she began to work. However, it had become clear almost immediately that he was keeping his promise to her. That not only was he going to watch her every move, but he was going to do so with an expression of utter contempt on his handsome face.

'Not at all,' she lied. 'It's all just part of the process.'

'Really? So all this playing with the light settings and changing lenses actually leads somewhere? That's good to know,' he said softly. 'To us amateurs it just looks like you don't know what you're doing.'

He held her gaze, and she felt her stomach tighten like a fist.

'By "amateurs" he means his mother and I,' Agusto said drily. 'Luis has a great interest in photography. He has a quite a collection now.'

It was true. She had seen them around the fortress. His photographs ranged from Bauhaus Expressionism to nineteen-thirties social documentary, and were of a calibre normally not seen outside of galleries and museums.

Cristina kept her expression neutral. 'I know. I've noticed them.' She had admired them too, although no amount of waterboarding would have persuaded her to say so.

Turning, Sofia smiled fondly at her son. 'And he's met quite a number of the photographers personally—haven't you, *mi cariño*?'

Watching her son's face stiffen at the endearment, Cristina stifled a smile. But her amusement faded rapidly as Luis said slowly, 'I'm sure Ms Shephard doesn't want to hear about that now, Mamá. She is an artist at work, and we wouldn't want to interrupt her muse.'

For a moment she couldn't reply—she was too busy loathing the way he could say one thing and mean something entirely different. She knew definitively that he hadn't even looked at her work, and that he thought her 'muse' was Lady Luck.

Meeting his gaze, she felt her heart skip a beat as his dark grey eyes swept over her face.

'I'm happy for any interruption that includes an espresso, Señor Osorio,' she said sweetly.

Agusto laughed. 'I agree.' His earlier tension seemed to have shifted. 'Luis? Why don't you go and ask Pilar if she will bring us some coffee?'

'Isn't it a little early, Papá? It's barely ten o'clock.'

His father ignored him. 'And some of those *rosquillas* that she makes so well.'

Cristina held her breath as Luis stood up, his eyes steady on her face. If looks could kill, she might not be dead but she would be seriously maimed.

'I'll be right back,' he said stiffly.

Watching him stalk out of the room, Cristina released her breath. It was a relief to be free of his baleful presence— even it was only going to be a short respite. But she had no time to enjoy her small victory, as from inside her pocket she felt her phone vibrate. Normally she would never have answered it—particularly not with Luis looking for any opportunity to hint at her unprofessionalism—but it was the third time it had rung that morning, so it was probably someone from the office checking up on her.

'Excuse me, Señora Osorio. Would you mind if I took this call? It's the magazine.'

'Of course, my dear.' Sofia smiled. 'Agusto and I are just going to stretch our legs.'

Turning, Cristina walked quickly out of the room and swiped across the screen. 'Hello?'

'Hello? Is that Cristina? Cristina Shephard?'

The voice at the other end of the phone was a little breathless, as though the owner was nervous, or wasn't sure she was doing the right thing.

It didn't sound like anyone from the magazine, but then who else knew how to get hold of her? She had only just switched phones, and so far had only given her new number to the magazine, the Osorios and her mum.

Had something happened to her mother?

It seemed unlikely, but she couldn't stop the fear, sharp and irrational, spiking inside her.

'Hello, yes—who is this?' She flinched at the sound of her own voice. It sounded strange, taut and too high.

'You don't know me—well, you do, sort of…'

The woman hesitated. She sounded young—probably around her age—and in fact her voice sounded familiar. Cristina wondered why that should make her hand suddenly grow clammy against the phone—

'Only we've never met. I know you know about me, though, because you came to the hotel that time…' She hesitated again, and then gave a small, nervous laugh. 'I'm Laura.'

Laura.

It wasn't just the name that made her heart vibrate painfully inside her chest. Laura was a reminder of everything she'd lost and everything she'd failed to be.

Ice was slipping over her skin. It was lucky there was a wall behind her, she thought dazedly as she took a step back, pressing her spine against the cool plaster. Her legs felt like blades of grass and her mouth was dry.

The hotel.

Out of a lifetime of mistakes, that had probably been one of the worst.

And she wasn't about to repeat it now.

'I don't want to speak to you— I don't— I can't—'

'Please don't ha—'

She disconnected the call, her pulse racing. With trembling fingers she switched the phone to silent and stuffed it into her pocket.

Laura—

'Ms Shephard? Is there a problem? Not bad news, I hope?'

Cristina flinched. Hell—where had he come from?

For so many years she had imagined speaking to Laura. But not like this. And not now. Not with Luis Osorio staring at her, his dark gaze picking at the loose threads of her composure. He had already written her off, and she wasn't about to give him even more reason to despise and distrust her.

Forcing herself to meet his gaze, she shook her head. 'Sorry to disappoint you. It was just my editor,' she lied. 'I had a few ideas that I wanted to run past her.'

'Really? That's strange. I just got off the phone with her myself.'

Cristina swallowed. Of all the lies she could have picked, why had it been *that* one? And why did *he* have to be the one to catch her out in the lie?

The air between them was suddenly vibrating with tension.

'Actually, we got cut off,' she said quickly. 'I'll call her back later.'

Luis stared at her in silence. She had just lied to his face, and now she was doing it again. If she'd been cut off she would have looked irritated, or annoyed. But when he'd caught sight of her, slumped against the wall, the expression on her face had been not frustration but fear.

His pulse twitched. In fact she had looked distraught. So distraught that for a moment he had forgotten that she was the enemy. Forgotten that she couldn't be trusted. All he had wanted to do was reach out and— His brain paused. And what?

Hold her? Pull her close? Say something to wipe that look off her beautiful face?

He had been on the verge of doing it, but then she'd looked up at him and lied.

Just like that.

His anger simmered dangerously. How many times was she going to have to prove him right before he actually accepted the facts? That she had used him and that she was dangerous.

In two long strides he was in front of her, his arms on either side of her body, boxing her in against the wall.

'Don't take me for a fool, Ms Shephard. You might think that running with a pack of slobbering hyenas has made you tough. But you need to be *very* careful.'

His eyes locked with hers.

'I'm watching you. And the next time you lie to me will be the last.'

With the barest turn of his head, he pushed away from the wall and spun round.

'Pilar—let me take that tray.'

After lunch, Luis took a phone call of his own, and after he'd stepped out of the room Cristina felt her heartbeat return to normal again. It had been stupid to lie to him like that, for all she'd succeeded in doing was confirming his bad opinion of her.

But why did she care what Luis Osorio thought of her anyway? After this photo shoot she would never see him again. But for some reason she *did* care. Maybe it was because, just like her father, he found her wanting, and she so badly wanted to prove him wrong. Or maybe, after Laura's phone call, her defences had been down.

Either way, this was *not* the time to crumple.

She looked up and felt her heart contract. Agusto looked tired, but Sofia seemed drained.

'Señora Osorio, I was wondering…would it be possible to have a little look around the fortress? Just to get a feel of the place. I know how important it's been to your family.'

'Of course.' Sofia glanced at her husband. 'That would be fine—wouldn't it, Agusto?'

He nodded. 'Does that mean you don't want to take any more photographs today? Only...' his face softened as he looked at his wife '... I think Sofia and I could both do with a break.'

Cristina smiled. 'You deserve one. Most people find photo shoots exhausting and very stressful.'

'Pilar will be happy to show you around.' Sofia smiled.

'Or Luis could show you?' Agusto took a sip of his coffee. 'He knows all there is to know. He was even born here.'

'Oh, no, please—your son is a very busy man,' she said quickly. 'He doesn't need me interrupting his work.'

Her head was spinning. There was no way she was going to be stuck with Luis on her own.

Agusto shook his head. 'What my son needs is to realise that work isn't everything. That other things matter more.'

Catching sight of the pleading expression on his wife's face, he frowned.

'Just ignore me, Cristina. As usual, my wife is right. Pilar is the best person to show you around.'

Pilar would have made an excellent tour guide, Cristina thought an hour later. She was very knowledgeable, patient, and obviously passionate about her subject matter.

'So, did the family buy the island or the fortress first?'

'The island.'

They were climbing the steps to the tower. There were one hundred and twelve, which hadn't sounded like a lot until they'd reached just over halfway and the backs of Cristina's calves had started to burn.

'This is like a workout,' she said breathlessly on step ninety-one.

They finally reached the top.

'It is.' Pilar smiled. 'But you don't get this view with a normal workout.'

Turning slowly, Cristina gazed in silence at the view. 'It's incredible,' she murmured. 'You can see for miles.'

The housekeeper nodded. 'That's why the tower was built. To spot pirate ships.'

'Pirates? I thought they were from the Caribbean.'

Pilar laughed. 'Some were. But we had our own pirates here. From Africa. They were very determined, and ruthless. The fortress was built to keep them out.'

Cristina nodded. *Determined and ruthless.* Unprompted, a picture of Luis's beautiful, masculine face came into her head. Instantly she felt a tingling heat travel slowly over her skin, her body responding with indecent speed to the idea of Luis gazing out to sea, his grey eyes dark with predatory intent.

Yes, he would probably make a great pirate, she thought irritably. *And you would be the first person he'd make walk the plank.*

Downstairs were the family's private rooms.

'I don't need to see those,' Cristina said quickly.

'But you would like to see Baltasar's room.' It was a statement not a question.

Baltasar.

The son who had died in a car crash.

Grace had given her biographies of all the family members, but the information on Luis and his older brother had been basic—probably because her editor had believed it to be irrelevant for a photo shoot on Banco Osorio's four-hundredth anniversary.

Walking into the bedroom, Cristina realised that Grace had been wrong. Realised, too, why nothing had worked that morning. And why Agusto was so tense and Sofia so desolate.

There were many beautiful objects downstairs, but it

what was missing that really mattered. Like negative space in a sketch, or silence in a piece of music, it told the hidden story.

In her house it had been her father's possessions. The shirts and suits left hanging in the wardrobe, never to be worn again. His precious vintage motorbike in the garage. And of course the letters addressed to him that kept on coming...

In Baltasar's room the shutters were half open and the room was cool and dark and quiet, and yet it seemed to hum with memories of the boy who'd lived there.

Her throat felt tight; the feelings she tried so hard to contain were swamping her. Her legs felt so rigid she thought they would snap—and then she saw it on the wall. A painting of two boys. Brothers. The older was smiling, clearly enjoying the attention. Loving it, in fact. And suddenly she found she was smiling too, for even on canvas his smile was infectious. He was blue-eyed, like his mother, and handsome. His grey-eyed younger brother seemed less at ease, more serious.

What held her gaze, though, was not the brothers but the gap between them. Or rather the lack of it. Turning, she gazed at the collection of photographs on a beautiful inlaid chest of drawers. Some were of the two boys, some included their parents—she frowned—and grandparents, maybe an aunt and uncle. But in each photo there was that same closeness.

Her earlier panic was fading. Maybe she would be able to take these photographs after all...

Sofia was sitting on the balcony, basking in the late-afternoon sun. Beside her Agusto dozed peacefully. Looking up, she smiled at Cristina. A book lay in her lap—a thriller that promised a 'breathtakingly brilliant and compulsive read'. But Cristina knew that it would be a miraculous book that could compete with Sofia's memories of her son.

'Was Pilar helpful?'

Striving for an appropriate level of enthusiasm, Cristina nodded eagerly.

'Yes, and I have an idea for the photographs. But...'

She hesitated. In her head, it seemed such a good idea. But what if she couldn't explain it properly? She had always been so bad at expressing herself—especially if it came to anything personal.

As though sensing the reason for her hesitation, Sofia patted the chair beside her. 'Start at the beginning. I find that usually works for me.'

Cristina felt some of the ache inside her chest ease.

'I was supposed to go to art college at eighteen, but I messed up.' Her mouth twisted. 'I was a bit of rebel at school, so I didn't end up going until a couple of years ago.'

Sofia nodded. 'That was a brave decision.'

Cristina shrugged. She hadn't felt brave. More like terrified. But she had wanted it so badly.

Glancing down at the cover of the book, she felt her heart start to race. Her need to learn, to improve, to be a good photographer had been compulsive.

She met Sofia's gentle blue eyes. 'I loved it,' she said simply. 'All of it except this one thing. We had to do a final project. The theme was "Legacy", and I couldn't make it work.'

Remembering her growing sense of panic, her hands tightened around the portfolio she was holding.

'Everything I tried felt fake. And then I was at home one afternoon and the post came, and there was a letter for my dad.' She hesitated. 'He was gone by then.' Gone was easier to say than left.

Sofia held her gaze, then nodded. 'And it inspired you?'

Cristina stared at her in silence.

In a way, yes. It had come almost nine years after he'd left. Nine years of silence—except that one time at the hotel, and then she had been the one doing the talking, or rather shouting.

They had probably moved six or seven times over those years. And yet there it had been, on the doormat. Her father's legacy to her—a letter from a clothing storage company, requesting payment for the two fur coats they had in cold storage.

She felt a tug on her heart. She hadn't shown her vegetarian mother the letter. But she had found inspiration for her project—a project that had been seen by Grace.

'Yes. It inspired me to take these photographs.' She held out the portfolio. 'I'd really like you to have a look at them.'

She sat with Sofia while she looked through the photographs.

Finally, the older woman closed the portfolio.

'Thank you, Cristina, for sharing these with me. I think I understand what you want to do, and I believe it will work beautifully.' Brushing a tear away from her cheek, she smiled. 'You're a very talented young woman, and your father would have been very proud of you.'

Cristina swallowed past the ache in her throat. Understandably, Sofia had thought that the photos were a memorial to her father. How could she reveal the truth?

That he had been a ghost in her life only this portfolio was not a record of his death but his absence.

That not only had he never been proud of her but he had judged her unworthy of his love and support.

She fixed a smile on her face.

'Thank you. I'll let you get back to your book.' She hesitated. 'If you don't mind, I'd like to photograph one of the paintings in your elder son's bedroom.'

For a moment Sofia didn't reply, and then, slowly, she

nodded. 'Of course. And would you mind if I held on to this for a little longer?' Her mouth twitched. 'Like most men, Agusto responds so much better to show than tell.'

Upstairs, Cristina worked quickly. She felt excited—elated, almost—and desperate to explain her concept to the Osorios. Sofia, she was sure, would understand. Hopefully Agusto would too, and then—

'What the *hell* do you think you're doing?'

The voice was familiar, but the anger rippling through it exceeded anything she had ever experienced. Turning she felt alarm shiver down her spine.

Luis was more than angry. In the gloom of the room his features were almost luminous with fury.

She felt her whole body turn to stone, her mind blanking as his gaze locked onto the camera in her hand.

'I was just—' She croaked.

'Just what? Snooping? Stealing a little private shot?'

'No!' She shook her head, knowing exactly how it must look to him. But if knew the whole story… 'If you'd just let me speak—'

'You mean *lie*.'

'You're not giving me a chance—'

Luis stared at her in disbelief. 'A chance?' He repeated the word with distaste. 'I gave you a chance to prove me wrong. I let you stay. And look how well that turned out.'

'You just want to think the worst of me.'

There was a shaken note to her voice, but he told himself that he didn't care.

'And you make it almost pathetically easy for me to do so.'

Shivering, Cristina backed away. His voice was cold. But not as cold as his eyes.

'I can explain—' she began.

But her words dried to dust in her mouth as he strode across the room towards her.

'No—stop!'

She held up her hand but he just kept on walking, as though she hadn't even spoken.

'Please. Just let me explain.'

Her body bumped against the wall and she stopped moving. Her thoughts were racing. Had she imagined this situation she would have supposed that she would be scared. And she *was* scared—but not of him...not physically, anyway.

What scared her was the way he was looking at her—as though he'd seen who she really was. A boring, mousy little girl who didn't belong anywhere but especially not in his gilded world.

He stopped in front of her and the ferocity in his eyes sucked the breath from her lungs.

'You don't need to.' His lips were curling with contempt and the hostility of his gaze was giving her skin trauma. 'Your actions speak for themselves. I read your CV, remember? Once *paparazzi* always *paparazzi*.'

'No, you don't understand—'

It was the wrong thing to say. She knew that instantly as his expression hardened to stone.

'Oh, I understand. I understand that you're a leech. A parasite. You latch on to people and bleed them dry. Well, not this time. And not with my parents.'

Before she had a chance to register what he was doing his fingers had curled around her camera, tugged it out of her hand.

'First I'm going to wipe this clean—'

'You can't do that. It's my camera.'

'And this is my home.' His eyes narrowed. 'And I want you gone from it. So first I'm going to wipe this clean, and then you're leaving—

'That's not your decision to make.'

She made a grab for the camera but he held it out of

reach, his other hand capturing hers. Then he jerked her against him.

'And yet I'm making it. So I suggest you lose that martyred expression or—'

'Or what?' She struggled against his grip, her fingers splaying ineffectually against the muscles of his chest. 'Oh, let me guess. This is where I get to choose between the hard way and the easy way?'

His grey eyes bored into her. 'You're wrong twice over. You don't get to choose. And there *is* no easy way.'

She jerked her hand free, her throat tightening. 'Oh, I know that. Believe me, I know there's no easy way. There never is.'

And before he had a chance to respond she ducked past him and walked swiftly out of the room.

Luis stared after her. For a moment he just stood there, too distracted by what she'd just said to follow. What did she mean about there never being an easy way? It made no sense.

Some of his anger began to fade. To be honest, he hadn't expected to get that angry with Cristina. Why would he? By nature he wasn't given to outbursts of emotion, but seeing her in Bas's room had been too much for him to handle and he'd lost his temper.

Only he hadn't meant to scare her—and he didn't like the feeling of knowing that he had.

His chest tightened and, turning, he stalked out of the room. He had to walk fast to catch up with her.

'Cristina—' he began.

'Oh, there you both are! I've been looking for you.'

It was his mother. He felt the familiar rush of guilt, and remorse as he watched her walk slowly towards them. He had broken her, and she would never recover. But as she got closer he saw that she was smiling.

'Mamá. You should have sent Pilar.' He frowned. 'Is there something wrong?'

His mother shook her head.

'Does something have to be wrong for a mother to look for her son?' Reaching out, she tapped the camera in his hand. 'I thought you liked buying photographs, not taking them.'

Luis glanced down. He had forgotten the camera. Had almost forgotten why he was holding it.

As a flare of frustration kicked up inside him he turned to Cristina, just as his mother said anxiously, '*Querida*, did you get what you wanted? It was the painting of Luis and Baltasar, wasn't it?'

He watched Cristina nod. 'Yes. Let me show you. May I?'

She held out her hand, and as he handed her the camera their eyes met. He knew that she wanted him to be a witness to the moment. Gazing down at the screen, he watched as she clicked through the photos right to the end, so that there could be no doubt as to what she'd taken.

Stepping forward, Sofia slid her arm through his. 'In that case I suggest we all go and have some *apéritifs* before supper. Agusto and I are dining out tonight,' she said, turning to Cristina. 'But don't worry—Luis has promised to take good care of you.'

Cristina smiled mechanically, but inside her stomach plummeted. Given Luis's low opinion of her character, she was pretty sure that his version of 'taking care of her' was not going to be quite the same as his mother's.

Unless Sofia was also planning on dumping her into the sea at the first opportunity she had.

Dining alone with Luis would be the absolute last item on her bucket list, but there was no way she could get out of it, so at eight o'clock she found herself following Pilar out onto the terrace.

Luis had decided to eat outside, and it was difficult to find fault with his decision. The evening was warm, but not stuffy thanks to a faint breeze from the sea, and a vibrant orange sun was sinking below the horizon.

It was the most perfectly romantic setting she had ever seen. Or it would have been if the couple sitting at the table weren't more or less ignoring one another.

At least the food was heavenly, Cristina thought, swallowing a mouthful of the most delicious yellow *gazpacho* she had even eaten.

The soup was followed by lamb with smoked aubergines and then, for dessert, a *turrón* mousse. The wine was also delicious—a rich red Rioja with a streak of spice and blackberries—although she noticed that Luis stuck to water.

Perhaps he'd forgotten he was off-duty, she thought, her gaze drifting over his suit and tie—a mid-blue and stripe combination this time. She half expected him to hand her a memo, or start discussing the fiscal year.

In fact the absence of his laptop appeared to be his only concession to the informality of the occasion. Probably he wore a suit even when he went swimming. Or maybe he had a pair of pinstripe swim shorts...

'Sorry—'

She felt sparks jolt over her skin as they both reached for the bottle of water at the same time and his fingers brushed against hers.

'Please—allow me,' he said, breaking the taut silence.

Her eyes locked onto his long, slim fingers, curling around the bottle, and she felt her heartbeat ripple. They'd curled around her waist in much the same way as she straddled him and he'd gazed up her, his grey eyes dark and intent.

She steadied her breathing as he filled her glass, then his. 'Thank you.'

'I'm just following orders.'

'That must make a change from giving them,' she said sweetly.

Luis held her gaze. 'I'm not a monster, Cristina.'

Even though he had acted like one earlier.

He gritted his teeth. Everything she did made him question himself. Each time he thought he'd got her all worked out she did something to throw him off balance, so that his behaviour over the last few days now seemed not reasonable but over the top and unnecessarily brutal.

It didn't help that whenever he was within her orbit his body kept overriding his brain and reminding him of just how perfectly she had fitted against him.

Breathing deeply, he forced himself to tune out his libido and concentrate on the here and now.

Tonight she looked poised and demure, in a cream blouse that showed off the pale golden skin of her arms and a pleated navy skirt that skimmed her knees. Her beauty was undeniable, but he wanted to see beneath the beauty.

Finding her in his brother's bedroom, he had been convinced of her guilt. Or maybe he had *wanted* to be convinced, he admitted a moment later. To make her fit into the category he'd assigned her: sexy but unscrupulous female photographer.

So maybe she had been right. He did want to think the worst of her.

But it was easier that way.

Easier than admitting to the facts.

That he couldn't stop thinking about her.

That even now part of his brain seemed intent on imagining all the different ways they could be making love on this table.

Heat rushed across his skin and he felt his muscles— *all* of them—tighten.

'Are those boats racing?'

Luis blinked as Cristina's voice broke into his heated thoughts and he turned towards where she was pointing. Out on the sea five small yachts, some with brightly coloured sails and fancy graphics, were chasing one another. It was a regular occurrence over the summer, and something he and his brother had frequently done using their own dinghy.

A memory of the excitement and the intensity of those races popped into his head and suddenly he was pushing his chair back and walking round the table to where the stone parapet edged the balcony.

Leaning forward, he gazed intently at the little boats. 'Yes, they are. It happens most weekends here in the summer. A bunch of local kids take their boats and race round the island. It's what me and my brother used to do when we were old enough to sail on our own. When were little we used to make bets on which boat would win.'

Cristina edged forward, drawn in by this sudden shift in conversation, and by the unexpected softness in his voice.

'How did you choose?'

She tensed as he turned towards her, fearing that she'd somehow spoilt the moment and that her casual question would be enough to make him retreat back into his anger and contempt.

But after a couple of seconds he shrugged. 'Bas just picked his favourite colours. So basically red or yellow sails, or best of all a combination of both.'

Taking a sip of her drink, she frowned. 'Why red and yellow?'

'They're our family colours.'

Remembering the crest on the side of the limousine, she gave a nod of understanding.

'Right—so what about you? I suppose you did some incredibly complicated mathematical equation to work out the odds?'

She stared at him curiously, but she wasn't really expecting him to reply. Judging by the way he was managing the conversation, the chances of him answering a direct question with a straight answer were remote to non-existent. Just like her father, he knew the risk of sharing too much personal information. It was safer by far to guide the conversation into more neutral territory, or better still talk about other people.

He held her gaze. 'Actually, I used to choose the shabbiest-looking boat.'

'You did?'

He nodded. 'I've always had a soft spot for the underdog.'

Her pulse twitched, and she felt a flush of colour warm her cheeks. Unsettled by the effect his words were having on her, she stared past him at the boats.

'So prove it.' The words tumbled out of her mouth before she could stop them. 'Pick a boat.'

He raised an eyebrow. 'Fine. The boat with the white sails is mine. You can have all the rest.' Taking a step forward, he held out his hand. 'Deal?'

It was more than a wager. It was a dare.

She shook his hand, almost forgetting to breathe as his warm fingers curled around hers. 'Deal.'

He tightened his grip. 'So, will you stop jumping to conclusions about me if I win?'

She lifted her chin. 'Only if you do the same with me. But let's just see what happens.'

To Cristina's amazement, Luis won.

'How did you know that would happen?'

Luis shrugged. 'Simple. Whoever's crewing that boat doesn't care about showy sails, just about sailing.'

'That's it?' She stared at him in disbelief.

Watching her eyes widen and soften, he felt a sudden rush of longing like a punch to the chest.

'Well, that and the way they were hugging the coast. It meant they didn't have to fight the winds when they got past the headland.'

His smile curved up, and Cristina breathed in sharply as it hooked her somewhere low in her stomach.

Unsmiling, Luis was stupidly handsome. But when he smiled his beauty was like the sun itself—impossible to ignore, mesmerising, dazzling. It made her forget his lies and his accusations.

She was still thinking about that smile when she excused herself to check her phone. After Laura's call she had been too scared to answer it, choosing instead to leave it on silent. But she'd checked her phone at various intervals in the day, and each time there had been several missed calls and messages from Laura.

Her hands trembled as she deleted the messages without listening to them.

She would deal with it when she was back home. Or maybe she wouldn't. All she knew was that she couldn't cope with it now.

She heard voices in the sitting room. Agusto and Sofia had returned, and from the snatches of conversation she concluded they had decided to have an after-dinner *digestif*.

She was just about to join them when she remembered that she'd forgotten to switch on the volume on her phone.

Stopping outside the door to the beautiful living room, she reached into her pocket just as she heard Sofia say quietly, 'I showed your father Cristina's photos—he thought they were wonderful. Did you look at them, Luis?'

Body stilling, Cristina held her breath. She knew she should alert them to her presence—eavesdropping was wrong in so many ways—but her legs wouldn't move.

'Yes, Mamá, you know I did.'

Despite her nervousness, she couldn't help smiling. She

liked the way Luis spoke to his mother. He was so gentle with her.

'I must have forgotten—'

'Well, I did.' She heard Luis sigh. 'And I know you don't want to hear it, but I haven't changed my mind. I think she's inexperienced and that shows in her work—which is competent but unremarkable.'

Cristina flinched, and then as the full impact of his words hit her the phone slipped from her hand. She watched it fall, her heart tumbling after it in her chest.

It wasn't just that he found her work lacking, it was that he had looked at her photos—personal photos that it had hurt her to take—and dismissed them as 'unremarkable'.

'But, Luis—' Sofia's voice.

'Mamá, we already discussed this, and I told you if having Cristina makes you happy then I'm happy to overlook her limitations.'

Her phone smashed onto the tiles.

Crouching down, she picked it up.

'Cristina?'

There was nowhere to hide. Standing up, she met Luis's gaze. It had been painful enough hearing her life, her talent, her hopes damned with such brutal precision, but watching Luis's face as he realised that she'd heard what he'd said was worse—for her humiliation was no longer just hers.

'I think I'm going to go to bed now—please say goodnight to your parents for me.'

And, turning, she walked blindly in the direction of her room.

But it didn't matter where she went, she realised as the tears began to roll down her cheeks. There was nowhere to hide from the truth.

She was a disappointment. A let-down. Easily dismissed and effortlessly forgotten.

CHAPTER FIVE

IT SEEMED TO take for ever to get back to her bedroom.

Her legs wouldn't stop wobbling and she couldn't shake off the fear that Luis was going to come after her.

Not that there was any reason for him to do so, she thought dully as finally she reached the sanctuary of her room. He didn't like her. And now it appeared that he'd didn't respect her either.

Her stomach swayed.

Just like her father.

And she was so pathetic that she'd *still* let her head fill with fantasies of recreating that night they'd spent together. Still allowed herself to believe that there was something between them.

Her cheeks burned and, yanking open her wardrobe, she swiped at the tears filling the corners of her eyes. Well, now she knew the truth, she thought savagely, pulling out her suitcase.

Normally she hated packing. It reminded her too much of all the times she'd had to move home after her father had left, each time to somewhere smaller and more depressing and further away from the family life she'd taken for granted. Now, though, she didn't care. She just wanted to leave. To get as far away as possible from yet another man who had judged her and found her unsatisfactory.

Dumping her case on the bed, she began haphazardly stuffing clothes into it.

She had come here to turn her life around. To prove

that she was worthy of recognition. That she deserved to belong.

Only once again she had been found lacking.

Her mouth trembled and she clamped it tighter.

So now what?

Stay and know that she was there not on the basis of merit but because the Osorios felt sorry for her?

No, thank you.

She was done with people feeling sorry for her. At school, her classmates' curiosity about her father's disappearance had been bad enough. But it had been her teachers' sympathy—the carefully worded letters home to her mother, offering counselling and access to the hardship fund—that she'd found almost impossible to endure.

Then she'd had no option. Aged thirteen, there had been no escape from their pity. But she wasn't a teenager now. She was an independent adult with freedom to make choices, and she was choosing to leave with some of her dignity intact.

Panic was prickling her skin. For years now she'd hidden her fears behind several coats of mascara and a couldn't-care-less pout. But now she could feel them all seeping out of her pores—for Luis had tapped into the worst fear of all. That once someone got beneath the surface and saw the real Cristina they would find her a disappointment, a failure, a fraud—

'Cristina.'

She hadn't heard him come in. She'd been too lost in the mental fog of her misery and anger. But it didn't matter anyway, for she had nothing to say to him.

'Cristina?'

He had crossed the room and was standing behind her.

She ignored him. No doubt his mother had sent him after her. What other reason could there be? From the moment she'd stepped on to the island Luis had made it perfectly clear that he didn't want her there.

'You can't just pretend I'm not here—'

No, she probably couldn't. But she wanted to.

Ever since her father had climbed into that taxi and simply not returned she'd felt abandoned, rejected. And yet for some reason she couldn't quite explain Luis's careless dismissal of her hurt more than anything else. Probably because it wasn't just her photographs he'd rejected. It was her and that night they'd spent together. That beautiful, extraordinary night they'd spent in Segovia.

A night when he'd renewed her faith in men and more importantly in herself. When he'd made her feel beautiful and extraordinary. Her mouth twisted. Only of course none of it had been real. He'd been acting, playing a part. Just as her father had liked to do.

And she'd fallen for it.

Just as her mother had done.

And just like her mother, even though she'd had no reason to trust him, she'd let her guard down again. Tonight she'd stood beside him in the fading light, trying to concentrate on the flotilla of little boats racing around the island. But when he'd turned that dark grey gaze to her, his eyes slowly unpicking the buttons on the front of her blouse, she'd forgotten all about the boats. Forgotten too about his lies and the vile accusations he made.

The urge to reach out and run her finger along the length of his jaw had been so strong, so sharp it had hurt.

Her breathing was suddenly staccato.

But not as much as it hurt now, to realise that it had all been in her head. That was what men like him did. They made you *feel*, they made you care about them, so that like some stupid moth you kept banging into the flame even though you knew that it would burn you.

She'd known all this and yet she'd still let herself believe that the way he looked at her, the way his hand brushed against hers, had meant something.

Gritting her teeth, she tossed a jumper into the suitcase—what a complete and utter fool!

A hand reached past her and flipped the suitcase shut.

'Will you stop for one moment?'

It was the first time she'd ever heard him raise his voice, and it was that as much as his sudden intervention that caused her finally to turn and face him, to change her misery into anger.

'Why? So you can gloat about me leaving?'

Luis stared at her, his dark eyes narrowing in on her face, and she let her gaze rest on his beautiful curving mouth and the clean-cut lines of his jaw and cheekbones until she could bear it no more.

'What are you talking about?'

'It's fine.' She held up her hand. 'We both know you never wanted me here in the first place—' she gestured towards the suitcase '—so you really don't have to pretend that you're sorry I'm leaving.'

'You can't leave.'

The expression on his face was difficult to place. It should be relief—triumph, even—and yet it didn't look like either. Not that it mattered what he was feeling. It didn't change the fact that she wanted to get as far away as possible from him.

Slowly, she shook her head. 'There's a lot of things I can't do, Luis. Like algebra, and baking cakes, and apparently taking anything more than a "competent" photograph. But I can leave—and that's what I'm doing to do.'

Gritting his teeth, Luis watched as she turned back to the bed and began throwing more clothes into her suitcase. Despite the force and energy with which she was moving he could sense the numbness of despair spreading through her.

It was a numbness he knew only too well, for he had felt it too.

His mind looped back to the moment when he'd heard her phone smash to the floor. He'd known instantly that she'd heard his remark about her portfolio.

She might not have said as much, but the hurt expression on her face coupled with her swift, desperate retreat conveyed the truth as effectively as any words could have done.

And of course he'd felt bad—he had upset her, and he didn't like the way that made him feel. But he hadn't trusted himself enough to follow her.

Then he'd spoken to his mother.

His shoulders stiffened, and he closed his eyes.

What was it about Cristina that got under his skin?

For five years now his life had been orderly and meticulously planned. After his brother's death he had sworn never again to lose control. His days started with a workout and ended with sleep, and in between there was work. There were no spur-of-the-moment decisions, no acting on impulse.

Until Cristina.

And since then, for some reason, he'd ignored every rule he'd ever made, every instinct he had for self-preservation. From the moment he'd watched her walk past him in that square he'd been hooked.

At first he'd blamed his singular behaviour on his return. Even before he'd stepped onto the plane, he had known that coming back to Spain—to Segovia—was always going to be hard, unsettling, and sleeping with Cristina was surely demonstrative of that fact—one-night stands with sexy strangers were not his style and never had been.

Finding out she had deceived him—and, worse, that she had once been a *paparazza*—had been humiliating.

But he had told himself that it was a testament to his un-balanced state of mind.

He'd arrived at the island confident that he knew the 'real' Cristina—deceitful, unscrupulous, manipulative—and determined to expose her for what she was.

Only just when he'd thought he had proof—finding her snooping around his brother's bedroom—he'd had to re-vise his opinion of her. Not only had his mother given her permission to be there, but Cristina had been respectful and sensitive—not qualities he would have associated with the *paparazzi*.

His brain was still processing that thought as she slammed her suitcase shut.

Picking up the bag that held all her cameras, she swung round towards him. 'I'll go and say goodbye to your par-ents.'

'That won't be necessary,' he said quietly.

Her eyes widened with shock, and then her mouth curved into a contemptuous smile. 'Of course not. And you're right. You should be the one to tell them. You're so much better at twisting the facts than I am.'

Reaching down, he grabbed the suitcase from her hand and flung it on the bed.

'Nobody is telling my parents anything because there's no need. You're not leaving.'

Cristina stared at him. Her anger felt like a living thing, pulsing beneath her skin. She'd always known he was a control freak. Not just because of the way he'd insisted on overseeing the photo shoot, but because men like Luis and her father could only lead double lives by micro-manag-ing every detail.

So, even though he'd wanted her to leave before she'd even arrived, it had to be on *his* terms.

Her face felt hot as she lifted her gaze to his face. 'Yes, I am.'

She didn't want to leave. But it was better that she went now. Better to leave with what was left of her pride intact, given that Luis's opinion wasn't about to change and any reprieve would only be temporary. If she left now maybe she might be able to persuade Grace that it had been her choice—for what was the alternative? Being made to feel like a hopeless fraud until someone—probably Grace—finally put her out of her misery?

'I'm going home.'

He stared at her intently. 'I thought you didn't have a home.'

She frowned, caught off guard by his words. How had he remembered what she'd said that night?

'I—I don't.' Her heart gave a jolt as she pictured her mother's rooms in the staff quarters where she worked. 'But I'd rather sleep on a park bench than stay here.'

Her voice sounded too high—and thin, as though it were about to fray—and she glanced away, furiously fighting the tears that were building in her throat.

'Please don't do that,' he said quietly. 'I don't want you to do that.'

'I don't care *what* you want,' she snapped.

Luis took a deep breath. His chest felt tight as his gaze dropped from her small, pale face to the bag she was holding in front of herself like a buffer between them. 'Do you care that I'm sorry?'

Watching the flicker of response in her caramel-coloured eyes, he felt his heart beat faster.

She shook her head. 'Sorry for what? Sorry that I heard what you said? Or sorry you didn't get a chance to prove to your parents what a worthless person I am?'

Something in her voice made his heart clench inside his chest. His hands curled involuntarily. Her pain sounded old, and he wondered where it came from. And why did it matter to him?

His eyes drifted over her face. He'd known beautiful women all his life. Some were so confident of their beauty that they expected to be fought over. But Cristina was different—exceptional, really. Her beauty was more than just an aesthetically pleasing arrangement of features. In part it was her vulnerability, in part her pride.

It was a pride he knew he had wounded—not intentionally but carelessly. Gazing at her, he felt his heartbeat accelerate as he saw the mix of doubt and defiance in her light brown eyes.

He took a breath. 'Please don't leave. I am sorry—sorry for what I said and for upsetting you.'

Cristina looked up at him warily. He sounded sincere, and with his dark eyes softer than she had ever seen them it would have been easy to accept his apology. Her stomach muscles clenched. But it didn't really change anything. He was apologising for his thoughtlessness, not his actual opinion, and it still hurt that he thought so little of her photographs.

'You're entitled to your point of view,' she said stiffly.

He stared at her pensively. 'No, I'm not.'

Before she could respond, he sighed.

'Whatever I said to my mother, I'm not entitled to any opinions on your photographs. Especially not these.'

He lifted his hand, and for the first time she registered that he was holding her portfolio.

She looked at him, her eyes wide and wary. 'You haven't looked at them.'

It wasn't a question but he shook his head anyway.

'No. I spoke to Grace, but I didn't look at any of your work.' He hesitated. 'Until just a moment ago.'

She head was suddenly swimming with fear, her hands clammy. She wanted to snatch the portfolio from his fingers, tear the photos into tiny shreds—anything but hear him try and pretend that he hadn't meant what he said.

'I don't care. I don't want to know—I don't need to know,' she said quickly, panic hoarsening her voice.

He held her gaze. 'They're incredible. And I know you'll think I'm probably just saying that, but I'm not. Your photos are more than "competent". They're poetic and powerful. You have real talent, Cristina,' he said simply.

There was a charged silence.

Cristina could feel the blood buzzing inside her head. She felt dizzy, and suddenly she was fighting to get on top of her emotions. For so long she had wanted to hear those words. To know that she mattered.

'You do believe me?'

To her surprise, he sounded anxious. She nodded slowly. 'Yes. I do.'

And she did. Maybe it was the hesitancy in his voice, or the way his eyes were fixed on hers, but somehow she knew that he was telling the truth.

He took a step towards her. 'Look, we made a deal tonight to stop jumping to conclusions about each other and I meant it.'

'I meant it too.'

'Good.' He breathed out. 'So, my mother said that you exhibited these?'

He was watching her closely, and she felt her pulse leap as their eyes met. God, he was so handsome. She'd been so busy hating him, hating herself, that she'd forgotten what it was like to be this close to him. Heat as dark and glossy as an oil slick slid over her as she remembered the last time they had been so close.

Pushing aside memories of that night, she cleared her throat. 'I did. That's how I met Grace, actually. She came to the exhibition.'

Her skin tightened with the same prickling excitement that she'd felt that day, when Grace had come over to her, casually held out a business card and told her to call her.

It had only been later, sitting with her mother, trying to eat but still wound up with nerves and disbelief, that she'd realised Grace had written her personal mobile number on the back of the card.

Even now she still couldn't believe that she'd pulled it off—or that Grace was even real. But she was. And what was more she was the editor of the biggest news magazine in Europe. It was crazy. Meeting her had felt like one of those feel-good stories that got turned into films. She shivered. Except that in the movies her character wouldn't mess up her big break by having sex with the client's son.

Oh, yes, she would, she thought a moment later, as her eyes rested on Luis's handsome face. Unless for some reason she was trapped under a wardrobe during the entire film.

A very large and heavy wardrobe.

Dragging her gaze away from his beautiful, firm mouth, and the memory of what he could do with it, she forced herself to speak. 'She was kind to me. I didn't really have much experience...' Her cheeks felt warm, and she knew she was blushing. 'In portrait photography, I mean. But she gave me a chance.'

His dark eyes lingered on her face. 'Grace is smart and honest. And she's a very busy woman. If she gave you a chance it's because you deserved it. She must have seen something special in you...'

He paused, his gaze penetrating deep inside her, and then took a step closer.

'Just like I did.'

She felt her stomach lurch sideways in response to his simple statement. Nothing he'd said before had suggested that to be the case. Certainly there had been nothing in the way he'd behaved towards her to imply that he thought anything of her at all beyond his superficial and mistaken belief that she had shamelessly seduced him to further her career.

'What do you mean?'

Her eyes fluttered over his face. And as his gaze locked onto hers her body stilled. She knew exactly what he meant, for even now she could still recall the intensity of his focus. And the way she had responded. There had been no boundaries between them. Even fully clothed she had felt naked.

As if he could see inside her head, Luis took another step closer, his dark grey gaze homing in on the pulse at the base of her throat, and her own eyes dropped to his mouth—that beautiful firm mouth—and instantly she was imagining how it would feel pressed against her bare skin.

Luis sucked in a breath. Around them the air was vibrating, tiny ripples of tension flaring out in waves. But what was he doing? He hadn't come here for this.

The blood was pounding in his veins, but somewhere deep inside his head he could hear a voice telling him to leave. To turn and walk away. Only for some reason he didn't move. It was as though his body was acting on instinct—like a boat slipping free of its moorings and following the swirling currents beneath the surface of the sea.

As if to prove that point he took another step closer, and now he was close enough to feel the heat of her skin like a caress.

'I mean this,' he said softly and, leaning forward, touched his mouth to hers lightly.

He felt a jolt like lightning—felt his breath spinning out of him at the softness of her lips—and the intensity of his desire almost knocked him off his feet.

With an effort he lifted his head, and as her eyes collided with his they stared at one another in the pulsing silence.

Cristina felt dizzy. Not the fainting, falling over kind. The kind you got when you went on the Waltzer at the funfair. A tingling, shivering rush of endorphins that mixed fear with excitement and pleasure.

She didn't want to feel like this. Deep down she knew that she should be fighting it. But whatever logic and common sense arguments she should have in her head had been eclipsed the moment his lips had touched hers.

Her heart seemed to slide sideways. She could still feel Luis's gaze, his dark grey eyes seeking her out, impossible to ignore, futile to resist.

She turned towards him, her breath hot and scratchy in her throat. He held her gaze and then slowly lowered his mouth back to hers, kissed her again.

Cristina moaned as heat exploded inside her. Her lips parted and she was kissing him back, her hands seeking out the warm muscles of his arms, her fingers curling into the fabric of her shirt.

It would have been a lie to say that she had forgotten what it felt like to be kissed by him. She hadn't. She'd dreamed about it so often and so intensely that some mornings she'd woken and reached across the bed to find him. But she saw now that no dream could match the reality of Luis's warm, firm body against hers.

She shook with need as he opened her lips, deepening the kiss, his mouth claiming hers, his hand curving around her waist and pressing her against the hard breadth of his chest. And then his fingers splayed against her back, anchoring her closer, and he was tipping her head, kissing down her neck.

Her stomach tensed and she squirmed against him, wanting more, feeling the pulse beneath her skin and between her legs urgent now.

As though reading her thoughts, Luis tightened his

hands around her waist and in her hair, and then they were stumbling backwards towards her bed.

Panting, she pulled him closer, her fingers curling into his belt, clumsily plucking at the buckle. His low groan made her legs start to shake.

Breathing unevenly, he dropped the portfolio on the table by the bed and began pulling at the buttons on her blouse. She felt cool air on her skin and, whimpering, let her head fall back, her eyes seeking something solid to combat the dizzying effect of the heat soaking her skin.

She blinked. Her portfolio was lying on the table, where he'd dropped it, but some of the photos had fallen to the floor. Her heartbeat slowing, she stared at them dazedly.

Suddenly her breath felt like concrete in her chest. She wanted to look away but she couldn't. Her eyes wouldn't let her.

Maybe if it had been another photo… But how could she expect to block that image out?

She stared miserably at the photograph. That briefcase had changed her life. Or rather opening it had. Had totally destroyed everything she had believed to be true. Two letters and a snapshot had been all it took to stop her world from turning.

Her body must have frozen, for she felt Luis grow still against her and she breathed in sharply, her hands shrinking back from his body.

Where moments earlier there had been sweet pulsing heat, now panic was rising inside her.

What the hell had she been thinking?

Had she really been going to have sex with Luis again?

Last time had been stupid, but forgivable. She hadn't known his real identity. Or that he was happy to lie about who he was. But she had known the truth since the moment he had walked into his parents' sitting room.

Briefly she closed her eyes. So either she was stupid or she was genetically determined to follow the disastrous path her mother had taken. Either way, the outcome would be the same. Pain, humiliation, rejection.

'Cristina—'

The urgency in his voice cut into her thoughts and, gazing up at him, she took a shaky step backwards. 'This is wrong.'

Luis stared at her in confusion. Wrong? *Wrong?* What did she mean? Her words didn't seem compatible with the painfully aroused state of his body.

Somewhere inside what was currently functioning as his brain, he tried to make sense of what she'd said.

'Ah, you're not protected?' He frowned. 'I have condoms in my room…'

Cristina felt heat spread over her face. She had been so frantic, so lost in her own responses, that she hadn't even considered whether she was protected or not. That had *never* happened—ever—and it was one more reason why this had to stop. Now.

She shook her head, trying to focus on something other than his handsome face. It didn't help that her longing for him was still clawing inside her like a frightened animal.

'No, it's not that. It's this—us. We shouldn't be doing this—'

Because…?' he said slowly.

She stared at him blankly. What was she supposed to say? The truth? That she don't want to become her mother. Or be with a man like her father. That she didn't want to get hurt and that although having sex with him would be incredible it would also ruin her life—the life she'd only just got back.

Her throat felt tight with panic.

No, she couldn't tell him the truth, for that would mean

revealing more about herself than she had ever shared with anyone.

'Because I don't want it. I don't want *you*.'

An ache was building in her chest. She wanted to change her mind. To rewind back to the moment before she saw that photo and to close her eyes. But it was too late.

'But I thought—' he began.

'Then you thought wrong,' she said curtly, wincing inside as she spoke. 'I don't want you here and I'd like you to leave. Please.'

She watched his face twist, harden.

'You don't want me?'

He said it slowly, as if he didn't believe her, and judging by the look on his face he didn't. For that she could hardly blame him. She didn't believe herself either.

'So this…' He gestured towards his unbuckled belt. 'This was you not wanting me?'

She cleared her throat. 'You misunderstand me.'

Her voice sounded too clear, and too high, but she didn't care. She just wanted to get the words out so that he would leave before she fell to pieces.

'I do want you—but only because you're here.'

He took a deep breath. 'Is that right?'

Words failed her and she nodded. Suddenly she was hanging on by a thread. 'Yes. I'm sorry.'

But her apology went unheard. Before she had even finished speaking he had turned and stalked out of the room, closing the door softly behind him.

She collapsed onto the bed.

Some men would have lost their temper. One or two might even have ignored her protests and carried on. Most of them would have slammed the door.

But not Luis.

Her eyes were burning. People said that the truth hurt. And it did. Only nobody ever said that lying hurt more.

Worse, she clearly had a natural propensity for deceit, so that after years of believing she was her mother's child it turned out that she was actually more like her father.

Overwhelmed with confusion, and misery, she fell back against the pillow, and began to cry softly.

CHAPTER SIX

STRIDING INTO HIS BEDROOM, Luis resisted the urge to slam the door and instead began pacing frenetically across the floor. He felt as if he'd been hit by a truck. He could see his body and yet it seemed unconnected to his brain. Or rather the mass of tumbling, incoherent blink-and-you'd-miss-them thoughts that appeared to be all that remained of his brain.

What the hell had he been *thinking*?

Glancing down at the hard outline of his erection pressing against his trousers, he gritted his teeth. Not much, apparently. Or at least nothing that had anything to do with logic or common sense. His entire being had been focused on the need to take Cristina in his arms.

And not just for some hot, feverish kisses either.

The truth was that he had wanted her in the most basic, primitive way. Needed her in the same way that a starving dog needed a bone.

He started pacing again, his footsteps matching the thumping of his heart. It had been just like that night in Segovia—only this time the storm had been beneath his skin, a whirlwind of heat and desire, spinning out of control, whipping his senses until he'd had no choice but to reach out to her.

His chest was burning and he realised that he'd been holding his breath, his rapt body caught up in how it had felt to touch Cristina again, to lose himself in the sweetness of her kiss.

Remembering how she'd pushed him away, and the distance in her voice as she'd told him that she only wanted him because he was there, he felt his stomach clench. Not with anger—for that would have meant he thought she was telling the truth, and he knew without question that she had been lying to him.

Except, of course, the part when she'd told him that she wanted him to leave. She *had* wanted him to leave, but only because she didn't want a witness to her pain. A week ago he would have believed her cover story—would have been drawn by the apparent confirmation in her words of who he thought she was: a hustler he had every reason not to trust.

Now, though, it wasn't Cristina he was struggling to trust but himself.

An image of her face—pale, strained and young—slid into his head, and he felt his breathing quicken. Suddenly he was moving again, as though by doing so he could put some space between himself and that picture of her looking so tense and wary.

Had she wanted to, she could easily have seduced him. It would have been the perfect moment, for there was no way he could have resisted her. She had brought him to his knees…reduced him to nothing more than a rippling mass of impulses. His face felt suddenly hot with an almost adolescent shame as he remembered how effortlessly she had robbed him of his reason and resistance.

But hadn't it been inevitable that it should happen? They'd been alone in her room, and they'd been tiptoeing around one another since the moment she'd stepped foot on the island, the attraction between them invisible and yet omnipresent, heavy and taut—like rain about to fall.

So why, then, had she stopped?

A beat of blood pulsed inside his chest.

Every time he'd imagined just such a scenario in his

head it had played out in many ways, but each time the outcome had been the same. With the two of them alone in her room, Cristina lifting her mouth to his, her breath whispering against his lips, her body blurring beneath his fingers...

He'd expected her to offer herself to him, slowly peeling off her clothes in front of his unfocused gaze, only for him to push her away, demonstrating his resolve before casually turning his back on her.

Only none of that had happened. It had been she who had stopped it—not him. He'd been wrong, so maybe he'd been wrong about her in Segovia. Maybe she really *hadn't* known who he was.

His mouth twisted.

Or maybe she was playing the long game? Using her body to mess with his head.

How was he supposed to know?

He'd thought he understood Cristina but he didn't know the woman who had pushed him away, and her sudden physical and emotional retreat was not just baffling, it had got under his skin.

It was all deeply unsatisfactory. And confusing. And he hated it. He disliked and distrusted anything he couldn't classify and contain. But it was proving impossible to do either with Cristina, or any decision involving her.

Even his presence on the island now seemed rash and irrational; he was there because he'd thought she had set him up and he didn't trust her to be near his parents. Now, though, that image of an unscrupulous, manipulative Cristina just didn't match up with the panicked woman he had watched retreat into herself. He no longer knew what was real and what was just him being paranoid.

What he did know was that being around her all the time was no longer necessary on his parents' account. If she was a threat to anything it was to his sanity and—he glanced down at the outline of his erection—to his self-control.

He couldn't function with Cristina constantly in his thoughts. And she *was* in his thoughts all the time—at breakfast, during every single lap he swam in the pool, and as he was lying wide-eyed in his bed every night.

He needed distance and discipline. Not easy when he was stuck here with a woman who could so easily bypass his defences. The only woman, in fact, ever to do so.

His lip curled. The less time he spent with her the better—and not just because his physical response to her was instant, extreme, and quite frankly painful. She threatened his equilibrium in other ways. Feeling her withdraw from him, watching that flicker of vulnerability in those beautiful brown eyes, had moved him more than he was willing to acknowledge.

He blew out a breath. Cristina had got inside his head and she was proving impossible to dislodge. But there was a solution—an obvious one. Work had never let him down, and in having decided to stay in Spain he had created an ample backlog for himself. He would speak to his PA and soon he would be too busy to think about Cristina Shephard.

For now though, a cold shower should help dull the ache in his groin and, turning, he walked determinedly towards the bathroom.

On legs that still shook Cristina walked across the room and closed her window. She knew logically that it wasn't cold. She could see the sun and feel the warm air on her skin. But that didn't seem to matter. She felt cold to the bone and brutally tired—as though she'd run a race.

Her mouth trembled. A race she'd clearly lost.

Maybe it would always be like this. Maybe it wouldn't

matter how fast or how far she ran she would never escape her past. Somehow it would always pull her back.

Reaching down, she picked up the photographs from where they'd fallen. She carefully pushed them back into the portfolio and sat down on the bed.

It was her own fault. She should have told him to leave sooner. Or better still left herself.

She shivered, a pulse of fear and longing beating beneath her skin. But how could she have done either?

Being so close to him had rendered her not just incapable of speech—it had deprived her of any sense of self-preservation. Why else had she acted so recklessly? Letting him kiss her like that and then kissing him back...

Remembering the feel of Luis's mouth and hands on her body, she breathed in sharply, a ball of heat rolling over inside her. Despite suggesting that she had only wanted him because he was there, the truth was that she had been prepared to risk *everything*—including her future—in order to satisfy her desperate need for him.

And if she hadn't caught sight of that photograph—

Her breathing stalled in her throat.

It she hadn't come to her senses, then what?

Would she have gone all the way?

Her mouth slanted upwards in a not-quite smile. *All the way.* She sounded like a teenager. Her smile faded. Except that your average teenager was actually pretty savvy and switched on, whereas *she* had been like a leaf tossed in the wind, with desire driving her actions, not just disregarding the consequences but failing even to acknowledge them.

How could she have been so stupid? So short-sighted?

She steadied her breathing.

But she wasn't completely to blame. If Luis hadn't come to her room—

Her throat started to prickle. She knew she was overly

sensitive, and she despised herself for caring about other people's opinions—particularly his—but it had hurt hearing him dismiss her portfolio like that. Only then he'd come to find her, and apologised, and then—

Her thoughts were running away from her like meltwater in the spring. With an effort, she slowed her breathing again.

It was his gentleness that had messed with her head. Coming so soon after he'd been so cold and cutting, it had caught her off balance and broken down the walls she'd built around herself. He had made her feel as though he cared, that she could trust him.

Trust.

Her mind snagged on the word.

Luis couldn't be trusted. She knew that. The cool-eyed biker she had met in that club was the antithesis of the sober, suit-wearing heir to the Osorio fortune—and who knew how many other versions of him there were?

She'd learned from her father that living more than one life was an addiction that overrode everything—family, finances, even the laws of physics—for how else had he managed to be in two places at once?

Her mouth twisted. All of which meant that she could never trust Luis. Oh, she'd thought he was different once. In Segovia she'd believed that he was gritty and real, but she knew now that he was just like her father—all stubble and no soul.

Yes, he wanted her—but only in the way that she'd claimed to have wanted him, because she was there. No doubt he would distance himself as soon as he found something more interesting.

Slowly Cristina stood up and pulled her suitcase across the bed. There was nothing to be gained from picking over everything again and again. If she was going to stay—and she was—then she needed to focus, not waste time or energy wanting something from him that in reality couldn't ever exist.

The next day she was relieved to discover that Luis was not at breakfast. She would have faced him, of course, but even thinking about seeing him again made her skin feel hot and tight. Thankfully, the photo shoot was finally going well, and the glow of everything coming together absorbed her all morning.

There were many reminders of Baltasar around the house, but in the end Agusto had chosen a yachting medal and Sofia her son's favourite book. Their choices were not just proof of his life, they were charged with a deep, unwavering love, and perfectly captured both Bas's unalterable absence and his continued presence in his family's life.

Of course the living were harder to forget, and as the morning lengthened Luis was still absent. From feeling grateful that he was no longer watching her every move, some of her elation started to ooze away. In fact by lunchtime his absence was making her feel on edge in the same way that his presence once had.

Glancing at the table, she felt almost lightheaded as she saw that it was set for three. 'Is Luis not joining us?'

The question was out of her mouth before her brain had a chance to censor it.

She steeled herself as Sofia looked up at her, praying that her expression showed no trace of any intimacy between herself and the older woman's son.

'No, *querida*. He's popped over to the mainland. Something to do with business. He'll be away for a couple of days.' Looking across to where her husband was talking to Pilar, Sofia lowered her voice. 'He works so hard. Too hard, we think. But...'

She shrugged—a wordless gesture that somehow managed to imply both regret and confusion.

Cristina swallowed. She had grown fond of the older woman, and hated seeing her look so sad. Forcing brightness into her voice, she said quickly, 'It's not that surprising, is it? Your husband is still working now. Probably he worked even harder when he was younger.'

Sofia gave her a small, tight smile. 'He did. But it was different. Agusto was different.' She sighed. 'He worked for his family and to remind himself of his heritage.' Her smile stiffened. 'Luis works to *forget* that heritage.'

But why?

The question formed on Cristina's lips, but just as she opened her mouth to ask it Agusto turned towards them and the conversation moved on to the options for dessert.

The next day followed the same pattern—work interspersed with periods of trying not to think about Luis. Mealtimes were the worst, and despite enjoying spending time with Agusto and Sofia, she missed him so much that it hurt like a bruise just above her heart. Not that her heart was actually involved in their particular dynamic. Probably the ache was just a phantom memory—a reminder of how she had felt when her father had left.

As usual, thinking about her father made the breath rattle in her throat, and with a pure effort of will she forced herself to blank all thoughts other than work from her mind.

At first it worked.

She spent the afternoon playing around with the photos on her laptop, but her focus of a few days earlier had evaporated. The screen might as well have been blank for all the attention she gave it. Instead she couldn't stop thinking about what Sofia had said about her son, and her sadness. Her words played inside Cristina's head as images of Luis looped through her mind. His dark eyes as she'd asked him to leave, that blank look on his face the moment before he'd turned and walked out...

Her downshifting mood and diminishing concentration weren't helped by her phone vibrating with persistent regularity in her pocket.

Finally, it was time to wander up to the main house for supper.

She hadn't been expecting to see Luis, but even so the sight of the table once again set only for three gave her a jolt. The meal seemed to last for ever, and by the end her face was aching with the effort of smiling. Finally, pleading tiredness and a need for an early night, she excused herself and, back in her room, she lay down on her bed, willing herself to fall asleep.

It didn't work.

Her body felt impossibly restless. There was a sharpness beneath her ribs, and her breathing faltered in her chest. And she knew why she was feeling like this now. It was because he wasn't here.

She was missing him.

Rolling onto her back, she gazed up at the ceiling in confusion.

That made no sense at all. For the last few days she'd been desperate to escape his cool, critical gaze, so why should she be missing him now?

She should be celebrating, or at least feeling grateful that she wasn't having to spend time with him, for it was clear that despite praising her photos he still thought she was shallow, devious and not to be trusted. His barely concealed contempt for her had left her as breathless as his lovemaking.

Her pulse gave a twitch, heat flaring inside her as she remembered how Luis made love. The cool touch of his fingers, the heat of his mouth, the hard thrust of his body against hers, the feeling that when finally he pulled away she had lost a part of herself...

Her phone vibrated on the bed beside her and her body

froze, her thoughts abruptly eclipsed by a shifting and by now familiar apprehension. Glancing down, she felt almost winded with relief as she saw it was her mother calling.

'Hi, Mum.'

Pressing the phone against the side of her face, a rush of homesickness hit her head-on as she pictured her mother in her room.

'Oh, Chrissie—thank goodness.'

Hearing the agitation in her mother's voice, Cristina felt suddenly nauseous. Her mum was usually so good at hiding her emotions, but she wasn't even trying.

'What's the matter?'

Her heart seemed to drop inside her chest. Could Laura have contacted her mother? It seemed unlikely, but not impossible.

Trying to keep her voice steady, she said, 'Has something happened?'

'I've been leaving you messages for days. I thought something had happened to you. I know it's late, and I wasn't going to ring, but I couldn't bear it—'

Her mother's voice wobbled and Cristina gripped the phone more tightly, guilt coursing through her. After her father had left both she and her mother had become scrupulous about staying in touch. Even when she'd been at her worst—bunking off school, staying out all night—she'd still called her mum and answered every text from her.

'I'm *so* sorry, Mum.' She spoke quickly, desperate to reassure the one person in her life who had been constant and caring. 'The signal here isn't great,' she lied. 'And my phone keeps losing charge.' Another lie. 'It's been a crazy few days.' That was true—although not in the way she was making it sound.

The rest of the conversation was much easier. Her mum was a good listener, and so partisan in support of her daughter that Cristina found herself relaxing for the first time in days. But even as she said goodbye she could feel her earlier tension returning.

Gritting her teeth, she gave up all thoughts of an early night and, standing up, unzipped her dress and let it fall to the floor.

Ten minutes later, with a full moon above her, she was running along the cliff path, a light breeze in her face. Usually in London she wore headphones, to block out the noise of the traffic, but here there was no need. It was the first time she'd run in weeks, and the absence of any noise and the taste of clean air and sea spray was as exhilarating as neat alcohol.

Slowing down slightly, she zig-zagged through a clump of pine trees down towards the beach, her gaze following the pale path beneath her feet. And then she was on the beach, her trainers sinking into damp sand and the sound of the surf filling her head.

Hands on her hips, she breathed out slowly, enjoying the relentless motion of the waves and the sheer, dizzying pleasure of being so close the sea. She looked longingly down at the water. It would be so lovely to go for a quick swim. But then again…

She sighed. Swimming alone at night in a sea she didn't know was probably not the most sensible idea. Maybe she'd get up early and come back tomorrow—

Glancing up the beach, she stopped mid-thought, her attention snagged by a movement on the dark rocks—a flash of white.

Was it a bird?

Frowning, she walked swiftly across the sand. Up close, the rocks were slightly steeper than she'd anticipated, but she managed to grapple her way to the top. It was higher up than she had thought, but on the plus side she could see that there was a less arduous way back through the pine trees.

For a second she gazed at the path, mentally tracing it

up the hill. Heart still pounding, she made her way cautiously over the rocks—and then abruptly stopped.

Gazing down, she felt a tug of excitement. It was a tidal pool, almost circular, maybe ten metres wide, carved out and fed by the sea and perfectly hidden. Pulse twitching, she watched the waves lap over the edge of the rocks—and then, without warning, her breath caught in her throat and she took a step back.

Beneath her, swimming with smooth, effortless grace was Luis.

He was on his front, wearing nothing except a pair of blue swimming shorts with a flash of white. Feeling like a voyeur, but unable to stop herself, she inched forward, her eyes locked on his muscular back and the smooth, sleek lines of his limbs.

She knew she should move, but her feet seemed to be embedded in the rock beneath her. All she could do—all she wanted to do—was stare. And then, just like that, he was pulling himself out onto a terrace of rock, smoothing his hand over his wet hair, and it was too late for her to do anything.

Pulse soaring, she watched mesmerised as he made his way up towards where she standing. Right at the last moment he looked up and froze.

Cristina stared at him mutely, her skin on fire as though the moonlight was burning her. Sea water was trickling down from his shoulders over his chest and stomach, and his eyes were deeper and darker than the pool behind him. He looked like some mythological hero. Her gaze dipped to his mouth. But he was real.

Luis felt his muscles contract.

What the hell was she doing here?

He'd thought he was alone, and judging by her next remark Cristina had clearly been thinking the same thing.'

'I didn't know you were here. I thought you were on the mainland.'

Blood singing in his ears, Luis stared at her dumbly. Having made up his mind after their catastrophic kiss not to spend any more time with her than necessary, he had been avoiding her masterfully—even going to the trouble of arranging a meeting with a business colleague on the mainland.

His mouth tightened. *If it wasn't so tragic it might almost be funny!*

He'd gone away ostensibly to work, in reality to forget her. But he'd done neither.

Her name, her face, her body, even her voice had been impossible to forget, for she was inside his head. He could taste her in his mouth, feel her swimming through his blood just as he had swum across the pool.

And it wasn't just his memory and his body that seemed determined to remind him of her at every opportunity. The flowers on the table had conspired against him too, their scent reminding him of her and causing him to lose track of what he was saying on more than one occasion during lunch.

He gritted his teeth. He'd tried to stay away, but he couldn't. His need to see her, to be near her, kept pulling deep inside him, strong and relentless, like a marlin on the end of a line. And even though he'd known that returning to the island was an admission of weakness he'd come back anyway.

But seeing her like this, *here*—

His breath felt suddenly too low in his chest. This place was almost sacred to him. Bas had taught him to dive here. They'd tried their first and only cigarette sitting on these rocks. And it was where they'd always come to trade their fears and hopes.

Now he was here with Cristina. A woman he didn't fully

trust and yet who reminded him so much of his brother—not just in her beauty but in her effortless rapport with people even his parents. Usually they were quite formal and reserved with anyone except immediate family and longstanding friends, but they were both already clearly fond of Cristina, and she was delightful with them.

He might have been—*would* have been—suspicious of her motives had she only bothered to sweet-talk Sofia and Agusto, but he'd watched her with Pilar and with Gregorio, the estate's elderly and quite deaf groundsman, and she behaved with exactly the same easy empathy.

Behind him a wave splashed loudly against the rocks and, aware suddenly of his own stillness and silence, he cleared his throat. 'I decided to come back early...'

He hesitated. Having started to speak he now realised that not only did he not have a reason for coming back ahead of schedule—or at least not one he was prepared to share with Cristina—he also hadn't considered the possible interpretations of his change of heart.

'I was planning on meeting with some potential investors tomorrow, only my team are still working on the pitchbook so—'

He broke off as Cristina looked up at him blankly. 'What's a pitchbook?'

'A pitchbook is a presentation we give to investors. It outlines the firm's strategy, its principles, performance and terms of investment.'

'Oh, I see.'

Watching her nod slowly, he gritted his teeth. For some reason he wished that they hadn't started talking about work. Maybe it was because he was wearing swimming shorts, not his suit, or perhaps it was just that—weirdly—it didn't seem that important right now. Either way, he knew that he wanted to make it clear to her that his life wasn't all meetings and memos.

His eyes met hers. 'And, of course, I wanted a swim.'

'You did?' Her chin jerked up, brown eyes widening with surprise.

'Is that such a shock?'

He held her gaze, and it was as if a pulse beat in the air between them.

Cristina blinked. 'Well, yes...kind of. I mean, I haven't seen you out of a suit since I arrived. I just thought maybe you didn't *do* beaches or swimming or getting wet.'

She glanced furtively at the line of fine dark hair disappearing into his shorts, trying not to remember what lay beneath.

'I got pretty wet in Segovia,' he said quietly. 'Or have you forgotten?'

No, she hadn't forgotten. Remembering how he'd stripped off his sodden T-shirt in her bedroom, she felt her pulse began to beat out of time.

Shaking her head, she waited for her heart to slow before she replied. 'Not at all.'

A warm breeze was catching the ends of her hair and grateful for the chance to distract herself—and him—from the conversation, she ducked her head.

Grabbing the wayward curls, she said, as casually as she could manage, 'I'm sorry for interrupting your swim. I just needed a run, and... Anyway, I'll get out of your way—'

For a moment she thought he was simply going to nod and walk back to the pool, but instead he stared at her in silence, his grey eyes fixed on her face.

'Why did you need a run?' he said finally.

Her throat tightened.

Good question.

Unfortunately the answer was not so straightforward.

Her mouth felt dry and, stalling for time, she shrugged. 'I don't know... It's so beautiful here, and I like running.'

Luis stared at her. His question had been innocuous enough, and yet she looked not just startled but dismayed.

'It *is* very beautiful,' he said slowly. 'And I'm glad you like running. But that doesn't answer my question. Why did you need to run?'

Cristina felt a familiar panic rising inside her. Her ribs seemed to be closing, so that it hurt to breathe. How was she supposed to answer him? One thing was certain: it wouldn't be with the truth. She could just picture his face changing, pity overshadowing his curiosity as quickly as a cloud blotting out the moon.

And yet his voice was gentle. 'I run too. Back in California. I have a house by the beach, and when I can't sleep I go for a run there.'

The painful sensation beneath her ribs was fading.

'I run to escape.'

The words were out of her mouth before she'd even realised she'd spoken, and she felt a rush of fear. But, looking up at him, she saw that there was no pity in his eyes, no contempt curling his mouth.

'It doesn't have to be running. I just need to be moving. Otherwise I get these thoughts and I can't do anything.'

'What thoughts?'

'That I'm stupid. That I fail at everything.' Her mouth twisted. 'That even though I run I'm always the runner-up.'

Luis felt his heart twist. Even without the sight of her hands clenching he could hear the strain in her voice, and he wanted more than anything to take away her pain. But he didn't know what to say. Bas had always been the one who knew the right words.

'You're not a runner-up,' he said gently. 'You got this job on merit. Justifiably. Because you're extraordinarily talented. You need to believe in yourself.'

Her mouth slanted upwards, but her smile was taut and unhappy. 'That's easy for you to say.'

Pressing the toe of her trainer into the unforgiving lime-stone, Cristina felt her body stiffen as he took a step to-wards her.

'No, it isn't.'

Something in his voice made her look up.

'Every day I miss my brother so much.' He glanced past her, his face clouded with emotion. 'That's why I come here. It was *our* place. It's where I feel closest to him,' he said simply. 'We used to sneak out at night. Even when he was really young Bas was a rule-breaker. He loved tak-ing risks.'

Suddenly it hurt to look at his eyes, and she thought her cheeks might crack with the effort of keeping her expres-sion even. 'And you don't?'

His gaze switched to her face. 'No. I tried...' He gave her a small, tight smile. 'After Bas died I thought that if I acted like him then maybe I could somehow keep him alive. So I started to take risks. I surfed the biggest waves I could find. I jumped out of planes—'

He made it sound ordinary, but she could feel the pain beneath his words.

'What happened?'

He shrugged. 'I had to stop. My parents...' His mouth thinned. 'They had enough to deal with as it was, and it was upsetting them.'

Around them, the air was heavy and silent. Even the waves seemed to have stilled.

'But you still ride motorbikes?'

He shook his head. 'That was a one-off. I was keeping a promise to my brother to take the road trip we always said we'd do.'

She nodded, but there was a choking feeling in her throat and she felt suddenly sick with herself.

Luis hadn't been playing at being a biker in Segovia. He'd been grieving for his brother.

Without thinking she reached out and took his hand. 'I'm sorry, Luis. About your brother. And about all those things I said—'

He shook his head. 'I deserved them. I was being self-righteous and unfair.'

His fingers tightened around hers, and she felt her stomach squeeze. 'And I was stubborn and short-tempered,' she said.

'Sounds like we're made for each other,' he said softly, and she felt her heart clench as he leaned forward and kissed her.

Luis could hardly breathe. He hadn't intended to kiss her, but feeling her mouth soften against his made it impossible to still the longing in his blood. Deepening the kiss, he curled his arm around her waist and pulled her closer, his fingers threading through her hair. She tasted so sweet, and he wanted her so badly, and yet—

From somewhere deep inside he felt a ripple of panic rise to the surface, and slowly, dazedly, he kicked back against the relentless tide of his longing.

Gently, he broke the kiss and took a step backwards. 'I can't do this. I'm sorry.'

Her eyes widened and he swore silently, for the expression of shock and hurt on her face tore him up inside. But there was nothing he could do.

Cristina made him lose control, and he couldn't afford to lose control. She had the power to turn his life upside down and that wasn't something he could allow to happen—particularly now.

'Please forgive me...'

Her mouth quivered, and he knew that if she spoke, or touched him, he would change his mind. He'd surrender to the desire beating in his blood whatever the consequences.

But she didn't say anything. Instead she backed away

from him and then, turning, she ran lightly across the rocks.

He watched her head towards the pine trees, waiting until she'd disappeared before he breathed out.

It was the only choice, he told himself firmly. And the *right* choice. So why, then, he wondered as he started to walk slowly back towards the forest, did it feel as if he was making a mistake? And why did it hurt so damn much?

CHAPTER SEVEN

'To Sofia, my beautiful wife, *mi corazón*.' Lifting his glass of champagne, Agusto gazed at his wife, his dark grey eyes tender. *'Feliz cumpleaños.'*

Across the table, Cristina raised her glass and echoed his words.

'Happy Birthday, Mamá,' Luis said softly. 'Are you enjoying yourself?'

Sofia nodded, her eyes dropping to the beautiful sapphire necklace that had been her husband's birthday present to her. 'How could I not be, *cariño*?'

She ran her fingers lightly over the gleaming blue stones.

'This is one of my most favourite places in the world, and I've had the most wonderful day of being spoiled with all these beautiful gifts. But having you back, Lucho, is the best present of all. I'm so glad you could be here.'

Cristina felt her heart bump against her ribs. It was the first time she'd seen Luis properly since their encounter by the tidal pool the night before, so that was no doubt one reason why her nerves were humming. But it was also the first time she had heard Sofia call her son by that particular name, and the shock made swallowing the mouthful of champagne difficult.

For so long it had been easier to imagine that Lucho didn't exist except in her memory, but now her cheeks tingled as she realised that he was real. Real and sitting next to her.

Luis smiled. 'It's lovely to be here.'

Watching his face soften, Cristina held her breath. His smile was spectacular, but it was lucky that he didn't smile often, she thought. It was hard enough trying to keep control of herself under normal circumstances, but when he smiled—

She shivered, remembering the kiss they'd shared at the pool last night, and how simply and carelessly she had responded to the hard press of his body. How it had been Luis who had pulled away.

Her pulse quickened. Stumbling back over the rocks and through the pine trees, her self-control in shreds, she had tried telling herself that she'd had a lucky escape. That he shouldn't matter more to her than any man ever had or should.

Her fingers tightened around her glass.

In other words, too much.

He might have ended the kiss, but she had seen his face—seen that he was torn, barely controlling himself. He wanted her as badly as she wanted him, and suddenly, with an intensity that hurt, she wished that she could turn back time. Go back to that shabby little hotel room in Segovia when it had been just him and her and a bed, and no past or doubt or confusion.

Her heart gave a jump. Except that she still wouldn't trust herself not to try and make that chemistry between them into something more.

Her breathing stilled and, suddenly aware that the swell of conversation around her had stopped, she looked up and found three pairs of eyes watching her.

She blinked. 'Sorry—I was miles away.'

'It must have somewhere you were very happy.' Sofia smiled at her.

Glancing over at Luis, she found him watching her meditatively his dark gaze reaching inside of her. 'It was.'

Meeting Sofia's gaze, she smiled. 'But I'm very happy to be here too.'

How could she not be?

La Almazara was not just a restaurant, it was a gastronomic legend. Despite its rural location on a tiny Balearic island, the converted olive mill attracted visitors from all over the world—she'd read somewhere that every year several hundred thousand people tried to reserve a table there but only a lucky few managed to get one.

Glancing down at her starter of bean soup and *jamón jabugo*, Cristina felt her pulse accelerate. It wasn't the exclusivity of the restaurant, or even the incredible food that made her feel like one of the lucky ones. It was the fact that Sofia, and Agusto had included her in their private family celebrations.

Her shoulders stiffened as she remembered back to the birthdays and Christmases after her father had left. Her mother had *tried*—they both had—but it had been such a struggle.

As an assistant housekeeper at one of the embassies in London, her mother worked long hours for a salary that had to support both of them and never quite did. On the plus side, her job was live-in, but the rooms had never felt like a home, and it had been difficult for either of them to relax there. And the nature of her mother's job meant that any private celebration always seemed secondary to the needs of the family in residence.

Oh, how she'd envied them—those people with their birthday cakes, their turkey and their tinsel, their board games. It had made her feel like the little match girl in that story, shivering outside in the cold, her nose pressed against the glass. And being a *paparazza* had only exacerbated her sense of being uninvited and unwelcome.

Only now here she was. A guest of the family.

She hadn't expected to be asked, and had initially de-clined. But Sofia had refused to accept her answer, and Agusto had backed her up, and in the end she'd capitulated.

Of course that hadn't stopped her worrying about what Luis would think when he found out. But ever since breakfast, when Sofia had invited her, she'd had other, more pressing concerns. Such as what the hell was she going to wear?

Glancing down at the green silk dress that skimmed her body and left her shoulders bare, she suddenly wanted to smile and keep on smiling. It hadn't taken long to answer that question. This trip was a work assignment, so she'd brought work clothes. Smartish trousers, shirts, a couple of skirts, some T-shirts, and—yes—one dress. Only it was navy, knee-length, and she'd only packed it because it didn't need ironing.

It certainly wasn't something she would have chosen to wear to an elegant restaurant like La Almazara, where presidents and painters mingled with Hollywood A-listers. She'd actually noticed an action movie star and his latest girlfriend on the way in.

It all felt slightly surreal—but not as surreal as returning to her room and finding this dress and a pair of beautiful gold ombré heels in her wardrobe, with a note from Sofia entreating her to wear them.

It was such a sweet gesture—and so generous. Even from just looking at the label inside the dress, and the red soles on the shoes, she had known that this outfit had cost more than her mother's monthly pay packet. And, although she had already thanked Sofia and Agusto, she wanted to make sure that they understood how grateful she was.

'It really was very good of you to invite me,' she said quickly. 'And so kind to give me this dress and the shoes. It was such a lovely idea.'

'Querida!' Leaning forward, Sofia smiled. 'You really don't need to keep thanking me. But, actually, it wasn't

my idea.' Turning to her son, her face softened. 'It was Luis who suggested it this morning, when we were talking about the meal.'

Cristina froze, the other woman's words sending shock waves down her spine.

'Luis…?' She swallowed. 'But I thought—'

Sofia shook her head apologetically. 'I know you did, and I wanted to tell you the truth only Luis asked me not to—'

She broke off as a waiter approached the table with another bottle of champagne and spoke softly into her ear.

Turning towards her husband, she said, '*Cariño*, apparently Felipe and Isabella Alba are here tonight, and they have ordered this beautiful bottle of champagne for us.' She smiled at Cristina. 'Would you excuse us for a moment? We should go and thank them.'

Cristina nodded, and then, as they made their way across the restaurant to an elderly couple, she turned towards Luis and said quietly, 'Why did you do that?'

His grey gaze rested on her face. 'This place has got a reputation for being swanky, and obviously you didn't know you were coming here…' He hesitated. 'I didn't want you to feel uncomfortable.'

His voice was gentle, but that wasn't why her skin grew warm. It was his words. There was nothing dramatic or striking about them. But they didn't need to be because they were true, and that was the most important thing. *She* had mattered to him, and he had cared about her enough to actually do something.

She steadied her breathing. 'Thank you for doing that for me. It was really thoughtful.'

He met her eyes and she felt her skin start to prickle. His smile might be spectacular, but that gaze… It seemed to pierce her skin, hold her still so that she couldn't move, couldn't look away, couldn't even breathe properly. No one had ever looked at her like that, with such intensity of focus, and her body tensed with fear and fascination.

'My pleasure.'

Caught off guard by her unaffected expression of gratitude, Luis felt his pulse skip a beat with guilt. It was true that he had been worried about her feeling uncomfortable, but that wasn't the only reason he'd talked to his mother. In so many ways Cristina reminded him of his brother. Like Bas, she was an odd mix of confident and vulnerable, and she was also stubborn and proud like him too. It had been all too easy to imagine her deciding that none of her clothes were suitable for going out in public with his parents and simply excusing herself.

And he'd wanted her to be there.

His jaw tightened. After he'd pushed her away last night he'd found it impossible to sleep. He'd just kept picturing the expression on her face—the hurt and confusion—and the way he'd let her leave. All night he'd been on the verge of going to her room so that he could explain. But of course that would have meant telling her why his brother was dead, so instead he had spoken to his mother.

'I'm glad you like it.' He gestured towards the dress. 'I was a little worried about the sizing, but…'

Her pulse skipped a beat. She gazed up at him, her eyes widening. '*You* chose it?'

The corner of his mouth slanted upwards. 'Well, my mother's been a valued customer of that designer for years, so they were happy to give me a little advice. But I had a kind of idea of what I wanted.'

He felt his groin harden. Not just *a kind of* idea. It had been more like a full-blown Technicolor fantasy, and in that she'd actually been wearing very little. His breath caught in his throat as images of Cristina spilled again in his head—her long auburn hair tumbling in disarray over a crumpled pillow, her fingers tugging at buttons and zips—

Flattening down the ache of desire rising inside him, he cleared his throat. 'I wasn't sure about what colour to choose, and the general consensus seemed to be that black would be the safest option.'

Her face creased, but her honey-coloured gaze was steady on his as she said slowly, 'So you chose a green dress because...?'

He studied her face, seeing both curiosity, and vulnerability in her eyes. 'I suppose I don't think of you as the *safe* option,' he said softly. His eyes rested on her face and the air seemed to shimmer between them. 'Black is boring and sensible and unobtrusive, and the little black dress is a cliché. You're an original, *cariño*, and you deserve to be noticed.'

Cristina stared at him, his words tugging at the armour she had built around herself. For so long she had craved attention, but most of her life she had got it for the wrong reasons. And now Luis was telling her that she was an 'original'—not only that, she knew he meant it.

'Thank you.' Swallowing the emotion that was filling her chest, she lifted her chin. 'It's nice to know I'm not invisible to you any more.'

His eyes gleamed, the grey almost black beneath the restaurant's low-key lighting. 'You were never invisible to me, *cariño*.'

'You didn't notice me at the club. Or are you saying you walked into me on purpose?'

He smiled then—a long, slow, masculine smile that made her feel as though she'd drunk an entire bottle of champagne on her own.

'If you hadn't been wearing those shorts I might have been concentrating on where I was going.'

It was the first time he'd admitted what had really happened in the club, but it was more than just an admission of guilt. It was an olive branch.

Her heart began to thump jerkily against her ribs. 'So…
are you concentrating now?'

His gaze flicked intently over her bare shoulders and
down to the slight V of her cleavage and the curve of her
waist.

'Of course I am.'

Watching his jaw tighten, she felt a jolt of heat punch
her in the stomach.

'You're the most beautiful woman I've ever seen,' he
said hoarsely.

Not as beautiful as you, she thought, her breath suddenly too light.

And she wasn't the only one to think so. Across the restaurant, other female diners kept oh-so-casually glancing
in his direction. But it wasn't only the women who were
aware of him. When they'd followed the maître d' to their
table there had been a sudden alertness among the men in
the room, a recognition that they were in the presence of
someone who commanded not just attention but respect.
Why else would they all twist towards him like heliotro-
pic flowers turning to face the sun?

She could feel herself doing it too, feel her body pulling towards him, beyond any kind of conscious control.

Their eyes met.

'You look—' she began, and then she frowned. 'You're
not wearing a shirt and tie.'

Glancing down at his black polo shirt, he shrugged. 'I
felt like a change.'

This sudden switch from smart to casual was disori-
entating—or it would have been had Luis not chosen that
moment to take her hand under the table. As she felt his
fingers weave through hers it suddenly didn't seem to matter what he was wearing.

Dry-mouthed, she stared at him mutely as Sofia and
Agusto sat back down—

'Excuse me, *señorita*. Would you like sparkling or still water?'

Startled, she looked up at the waiter and smiled mechanically. 'Still, please. Just a drop,' she added as he also went to fill up her champagne glass. 'Are you not drinking?' she asked Luis. She'd noticed that he was once again sticking to soft drinks.

He shrugged. 'I've got a couple of conference calls tomorrow, so I need to keep a clear head.'

She nodded, intrigued. Surely his mother's sixtieth birthday was a special enough occasion to have a glass of champagne?

His mother smiled. 'Champagne used to give me such a headache when I was younger. Do you remember, Agusto, those cocktails your parents used to love so much?'

Taking his wife's hand, Agusto laughed. 'Not really, *cariño*, but I think that was the point.' Turning to Cristina he said, 'They used to mix champagne with sherry. It was absolutely lethal.' His eyes gleamed. 'Wouldn't you agree, Luis?'

Beside her, Luis groaned. 'I was young and naive—'

'What happened?'

She twisted towards him. Her pulse was dancing, and she knew that her pleasure at hearing about his life was all over her face, but just for once she didn't feel the need to hide her emotions.

He shook his head. 'I must have been about sixteen. My grandparents were having a party, and all the little old ladies were drinking cocktails, one after another. Bas and I thought they must be harmless, so we had one, and then two, three—' He grimaced. 'Harmless! I don't think I've ever felt so ill!'

'Were you sick?'

Shuddering, he shook his head. 'No. But neither of us

could stand up, let alone speak. In the end we had to go to bed.'

His father laughed. 'What my son is failing to mention is that they went to bed at half past eight, and the bed in question belonged to my parents' elderly mastiffs.'

Cristina burst out laughing. 'I can't believe you slept in a dogs' bed.'

'It was only the once.' Sofia smiled at her son affectionately. 'Luis has always been cautious. Even when he was a little boy he liked to do things properly, to do the right thing. And nothing's changed—has it, Agusto?'

There was a short, strained silence, and Cristina could almost feel the atmosphere around the table shift.

'He's a very good son,' Agusto said stiffly. 'But I'm not sure if deliberately living on the other side of the world from your family can ever really be described as doing "the right thing"—'

'Agusto…' Sofia said softly, but Luis interrupted her.

'It's fine, Mamá.' He met his father's gaze. 'Papá, I know you're upset with me, and I totally understand why you feel the way you do. But you have to understand and accept that my life is in California now.'

He spoke quietly, but with calm determination, and Cristina knew that this was not the first time he'd had this conversation with his father. Nor, judging by the glint in Agusto's eyes, would it be the last.

Her hunch was quickly confirmed as the older man said stubbornly, 'But that's just it. I don't understand. This is your home, Luis. Your life should be *here*. You have a family who loves you and needs you.' He frowned. 'And a legacy that has—'

Cristina felt her pulse jump as abruptly Luis pulled his hand free of hers.

'Ah, *now* we're getting to the truth.'

Luis drew a breath. He was deliberately stoking his anger, but beneath it he could already feel the old familiar guilt rising inside him.

Desperately he tried to hang on to his fury. 'It's not actually about family at all and it never has been. It's about the business.'

'They're one and the same.'

Despite having heard them since he was old enough to understand, his father's words still had the power to catch him off guard—but it was the sadness in Agusto's voice that made him grip the edges of the table.

Wincing inwardly, he shook his head. 'Not to me.'

Watching his father's shoulders slump, he felt a dull ache spread through his chest.

'I'm an old man, Luis. I can't run the business for ever.'

Hating himself, he reached over and gripped Agusto's arm. 'I know. But, Papá, we've been over this a hundred times, and each time I've given you my answer—'

His father shook his head. 'No. What you've given me is an excuse, Luis, and I don't understand why you feel that way. But I will accept it.' Lifting his hand, he patted his son's hand. 'And your mother's right. You are a good son, and we both love you very much. We're proud of what you've achieved.'

'I know. And I love coming to visit.' Frowning, he turned to his mother. 'Sorry, Mamá.'

'I'm sorry too, *cariño.*'

Sofia seemed more resigned than anything else, Cristina thought. No doubt she was used to it—and, given how close Luis and his father were, it probably sounded worse that it had seemed to her.

Clearly that was true, for moments later they were all chatting easily about Luis's ranch. But, despite the fact that conversation flowed smoothly for the rest of the evening, she couldn't shift the feeling that Luis had been lying to his parents.

Worse, she was pretty sure he'd been lying to himself too.

When they returned to the island Sofia and Agusto excused themselves, and Cristina found herself alone with Luis.

Given what had happened the previous night, she had supposed he would follow his parents and turn in, so she was surprised when he turned to her and said, 'I'm going to have a drink—would you care to join me?'

'Oh.' She gazed at him uncertainly. 'Well, that—'

She broke off as he raised his hands placatingly.

'I just meant coffee or tea.'

'So no champagne cocktail, then?' The urge to tease overwhelmed any caution she might have had about being alone with him.

His eyes gleamed, and she felt a tiny flicker of excitement as the corners of his mouth tugged upwards.

'Sadly we don't have any dogs, and the floors look awfully hard and cold.'

'Tea would be lovely, then.'

It was the first time she'd been in the kitchen. Although it was large, it felt surprisingly homely. 'This is lovely.'

He glanced over at her. 'We seem to have every flavour of tea imaginable, so—'

'Actually, builders' would be fine.'

'Builders'?' He raised an eyebrow.

She laughed. 'It's what English people call breakfast tea. I like it strong with lots of milk. Thank you.'

After Luis had made the tea, they sat on opposite sides of the breakfast bar. She had thought she would have to do the talking, but it was Luis who spoke first.

'Did you enjoy the meal?'

'Yes, it was incredible. I've never eaten food like that.'

Remembering the tension between him and Agusto, she hesitated. Then, 'Do you think your mother enjoyed herself?'

There was a tiny pause. Luis stared at her. 'Of course. It's her favourite restaurant.'

She waited for a moment, and when he didn't say anything else, just stared pointedly past her, she felt her cheeks start to tingle. She could just back off, talk about the food, or maybe the design of this kitchen, but she was still struggling to make sense of what had happened over dinner.

Luis was fiercely protective of his parents, and yet even though his father had as good as asked him to stay he'd refused. In fact he'd shut the entire conversation down even though she knew it had hurt him to do so. She didn't know how she knew—she just knew that it had. And that it had hurt her to feel his pain.

She bit her lip. Her heart started to race. 'She loves having you here.'

'I love being here.'

There was a definite warning tone in the coolness of his voice, but for some totally illogical reason that only made her more determined to talk to him about what had happened.

'But what about when you go back to California?'

He looked over at her, his grey eyes suddenly cool and hostile, as though she was some kind of intruder.

'I'm not sure why you think that's any of your business, but even if it were I don't want to talk about it.'

The expression on his face made her skin freeze to her bones. It was as though they were back on that balcony and he was that same man who had accused her of being a cold-hearted, self-serving parasite. But wasn't that what *she* always did when she was upset and scared? Lashed out at people, pushed them away...

Striving to stay calm, she said, 'I know. And I get that.

But what I don't get is why you don't want to talk to your father about it.' Her breath was weaving in and out of her lungs too fast, as though she'd been running. 'I'm not judging you—it's just that I don't have that kind of relationship with my father, and—'

And I'd kill even to hear his voice, much less have him tell me he loves me and needs me.

She finished the sentence in her head, her stomach churning with panic at the thought of having revealed the truth, even obliquely. The truth that she hadn't mattered to the one man whose love and protection should have been unconditional.

Luis felt his muscles tighten. He felt ashamed of the way he'd acted at dinner. Yes, maybe his father shouldn't have brought it up, but he'd handled it badly. Or rather he hadn't handled it at all. Instead he'd done what he always did when his parents discussed the bank, or him returning to Segovia, he'd got irritated and defensive. And tonight he'd let it get completely out of hand.

It was unforgivable. He shouldn't have done it—and wouldn't have except that he hadn't been thinking straight.

And it was her fault. He glanced over to where Cristina sat watching him, and suddenly it was easier to blame her than himself.

'You don't need to "get" it. You're not here to practise your amateur psychology. You're here to photograph my parents. *Allegedly*, anyway.'

'What does that mean?' Her eyes were suddenly narrow and blazing with anger.

'It means that just because I bought you a dress it doesn't mean that I've bought that whole little-girl-lost-on-the-streets-of-Segovia act. Do you really think I believe in that kind of coincidence?'

She stood up so fast that the stool she'd been sitting on spun away from her.

'*What* kind of coincidence?' She was practically shouting now.

'Oh, you know, Cristina—the sort where we end up in bed one night and then the next day it turns out that you just happen to be taking my parents' photographs.'

The blood drained from her face. 'It wasn't like that and you know it.' She took a step backwards, her body trembling with anger. 'And you know something else too. You might not believe in coincidences but I don't believe in *you*. I think everything that comes of your mouth is a lie. Not just about me. But about yourself. About who you are, and what you want.'

Her hands curling into fists, she picked up the stool and slammed it back under the counter.

'And, whatever you might think of me, your parents don't deserve that. What's more, you don't deserve *them*!'

The room fell silent.

Cristina breathed out shakily. She wanted to say more, but one look at his still, set face told her there was no point. And, really, why should she waste any more time on him? It might not have sounded like much to him but she had laid her soul bare and—

'You're right.'

She glanced up at him and felt her stomach lurch. His skin was no longer taut but shifting, like ice cracking on a frozen lake, as pain rippled across his face.

'I *am* lying,' he mumbled. 'I don't think you're that person and I shouldn't have said I did. You didn't deserve it.' He looked past her, his eyes dark with shame and unease.

But it was his voice as much as his words that startled her. The strain she could hear in it was heartbreaking.

'And they don't deserve a son like me.'

He stopped short, as though it hurt too much for him to go on, and looking across at his stricken face, Cristina felt her anger start to evaporate.

'Look, I shouldn't have said that. It's nothing to do with me. Your father will find someone else to run the bank—'

His face twisted. 'You don't understand. It's not just the bank.'

She stared at him, her body stiffening as though she was bracing herself for a blow. 'What do you mean?'

His face tightened, the skin taut across his cheekbones. 'I did something unforgivable.'

Shaken, she shook her head automatically. 'I doubt that. Whatever it was your parents would forgive you. They *would*,' she repeated as he shook his head.

'No, they wouldn't. They couldn't. You see, it was my fault. Don't you understand? None of it would have happened if—'

Only she didn't see. Or understand any of what he was saying. But she knew instinctively that it was what he wasn't saying that was really important.

'If what?'

He ran his hand tiredly over his face. 'It doesn't matter—'

Reaching out, she grabbed his arm. 'It does to me.'

Looking into her eyes, Luis felt his breathing trip in his throat. She was telling the truth. It did matter to her. But still he couldn't speak.

As though sensing his silence was beyond his control, she said quietly, 'If you're not happy in California why do you stay there?'

He looked up at her slowly. 'I never said I wasn't happy there.'

'But you did.' Her fingers tightened on his arm. 'You said you don't sleep. That you have to run.' She hesitated. 'What is it, Luis? What are you running from?'

The directness of her question caught him off-guard. And, looking up into her eyes, he suddenly wanted to answer her—for he could see that she was worried.

About him.

And that she cared.

About him.

But… 'I don't know when to start,' he said slowly.

Or maybe he meant *how* to start, for he'd spent so long trying not to think about that night that he didn't seem to have the words to tell his story.

Thinking about her own pain, Cristina felt a knot in her stomach. 'Usually it's not *when* that matters—it's who.' She glanced around the kitchen. 'And sometimes where. Let's get some air.'

It wasn't a question, but after a moment he nodded.

Away from the house Luis immediately felt calmer, and as they walked down to the beach it suddenly seemed the most natural thing in the world to start talking about his brother.

'Bas and I went to this party up in the hills. I didn't really want to go. I'd just finished my master's, and all I wanted to do was sleep. But he wouldn't hear of it and my mother thought I needed to relax.'

They had reached the beach, and as he stopped and stared at the sea Cristina felt a sudden panic that he'd changed his mind. That he was going to clam up, lock himself away.

Clearing her throat, she said quietly, 'Did you have fun?'

He shrugged. 'Not really. I liked my brother's friends but I was four years younger than them. We didn't really have a lot in common, and I felt a bit left out. I drank a bit too much—' The corner of his mouth dipped. 'And I was tired, a bit fed up, so I was just about to leave when…' He paused, his jaw tightening. 'When I saw her. She was already watching me.'

Glancing down, Luis pushed the toe of his shoe into the sand, wishing it was as easy to push away the past.

'Afterwards I couldn't believe how naive I'd been.'

Even now he could still remember the shock, the disbelief, and then the breathtaking shame of his vanity and stupidity.

Sick with misery, he turned, but Cristina stepped in front of him.

'After what?'

The guilt and despair on his face almost split her in two.

'After I found out she was *paparazzi*. Only by then it was too late. I'd already slept with her,' he said woodenly. 'And told her that my brother had hooked up with a Hollywood actress who was in town, making a film. She told her grubby little mates and that's how he died—crashing his car, trying to escape a bunch of photographers.'

His face was stiff with misery and pain.

'I was the last person to speak to him. He called and told me to have fun, and he said—' he was suddenly struggling to speak '—and he said that he loved me.'

Cristina couldn't speak. Her mouth wouldn't open and there was a hard lump in her throat that seemed to be stopping the words from coming out. But she couldn't just say *nothing*.

'I'm so sorry, Luis.'

Her words sounded trite, but Luis didn't even seem to hear them.

'If I'd been more careful—'

'But you didn't know—'

'No, because I was too drunk and too busy thinking what a man I was.'

'You're not like that.'

Her hands clenched together as she remembered him drinking water at his mother's birthday dinner. It wasn't just champagne or wine he didn't drink. It was all alcohol.

'You can't blame yourself.'

He looked at her then, his eyes unfocused and dull with

pain. 'But I *am* to blame. And that's why I have to live in California. I can't live in Spain and not take over the bank. That was *Bas's* birthright and I took it away from him. I took him away from my parents and I don't deserve their love.'

'Yes, you do.' She took a step closer. 'You made a mistake, and nobody gets through life without making mistakes. What happened to Bas was a terrible, tragic accident, but you can't keep punishing yourself for being young and naive.'

She hesitated.

'Sometimes it's easier to judge yourself harshly than to look at the bigger picture. But turning in on yourself doesn't solve anything. It just damages everyone around you.' Her heart contracted as she pictured her mother's anxious face. 'And if they're around you it's because they care.'

Luis stared at her in silence. After their initial shock at his story most people would surely be wrapped up in their own dismay or disgust. But Cristina seemed to care about him and his feelings—not hers.

'None of us can change the past. It won't matter how unhappy you make yourself, or how much you think you deserve to feel unhappy, you can't bring your brother back.'

Reaching out, she took his hand.

'You taking over the bank would not be disrespectful to your brother's memory. It would just be you taking care of your parents. Being their son—the son you were before Bas died, and the son you will always be.'

She knew she was right, but she'd been wrong about almost everything else. Luis was nothing like her father—a man who had never taken responsibility for his actions, let alone acknowledged them. He had not only accepted the blame for Bas's death he had punished himself for it, even going so far as to exile himself from his homeland and his parents.

She felt his fingers tighten around hers.

'I miss him so much…'

'I know. But forgiving yourself doesn't mean forgetting Bas. Your parents love you, Luis, and they need you. So you need to forgive yourself and come back home.'

Luis nodded, and then, leaning forward, he cupped her chin in his hand and tilted her face upwards. 'Were you always this smart?'

She smiled. 'Of course. Hadn't you noticed?'

Yesterday he had pushed her away, but now, with her warm body so close to his, it was hard to remember exactly why he'd felt he should do that. Her eyes were soft and light and, feeling his heart start to beat faster, he shook his head.

'I guess I was distracted.'

'By what?'

Her voice was shaking slightly, and he could see the pulse twitching at the base of his throat.

'By this,' he whispered and, lowering his mouth to hers, he kissed her.

Behind them the waves splashed against the sand, as he slowly wrapped his arms around her and deepened the kiss. Still kissing, they stripped each other naked, and then they slid down onto their discarded clothes.

His fingers were slipping over her bare skin, their touch light and yet electric, and his mouth was warm and hungry against her lips. His body felt hollow with desire as she pulled him closer, curling her hand around the curve of his neck, their clothes twisting beneath them as she turned her face into the hard muscles of his chest.

She felt his hand between her trembling thighs, his fingers gently parting her legs, their touch setting her adrift from her body.

'Look at me,' he whispered. 'I want to see your eyes.'

Breath quickening, she looked up at him, and he cupped her buttocks and thrust into her. And then his body was stretching hers and she was pushing back, tugging him deeper, until heat flowered inside her and she arched upwards as his shuddering body surged forward again and again, like the waves that were breaking against the beach…

CHAPTER EIGHT

LUIS WOKE TO the sound of his alarm. Eyes closed, he fumbled across the bed, his fingers reaching for his phone on his bedside cabinet. Only his phone wasn't there.

'What the hell…?' he muttered, rolling onto his side.

But of course he wasn't in his bedroom, and now he was actually awake he realised that it wasn't his alarm either.

'Sorry, sorry—did it wake you?'

Emerging from the bathroom, a towel clutched in front of her throat, another wrapped turban-style around her head, Cristina rummaged in the small clutch bag she had taken to the restaurant and pulled out her phone.

Holding it up, she swiped the screen. 'I meant to turn it off last night, but I…'

'You what?' Luis said softly.

His eyes dropped to the towel and he felt his fingers twitch as he wondered how she had managed to arrange it so that it seemed to both hide everything and yet hint at the spectacular body that lay beneath.

Her face stilled. 'I got distracted.'

'Oh, is that what happened?'

His muscles tensed, and a pulse began to beat beneath his skin as she walked towards him. He was still struggling to come to terms with what had happened last night—not just the fact that they'd ended up naked and making love on the beach, but that he'd told her about Bas, and about his part in his brother's death.

He hadn't planned to tell her. Hell, he hadn't planned

on telling *anyone*, ever—let alone a woman who barely knew him. But Cristina had surprised him by actually listening to what he'd said. More surprisingly, her words hadn't simply been catch-all platitudes. He had felt as if she knew him—almost as if she'd known him for a long time.

'I don't know. Is it?'

Her light brown eyes were watching his, and it was suddenly difficult to manage his breathing, let alone his thoughts. And, to be fair, it wasn't a question he'd ever been asked before?

But then he'd never done this before. He'd had a couple of one-night stands, both of which had been short and satisfactory but neither of which had required post-coital conversation. And in his other, more serious relationships sex had happened after the ground rules about intimacy and commitment had been established.

That first time in Segovia it had been simple. Just raw, powerful sexual need, no speaking required. It had been about bodies, and skin, and sweat, and one sole aim—his need to take her. He had practically torn her clothes off her, such had been the frenzy of his desire.

But last night—this morning—had been more than just sex.

His throat tightened. He could just be honest and tell her that. Tell her that it had felt good, incredible. And not just the sex but holding her against him and feeling her arm curled over his chest. He could tell her that part had felt better than good. That it had turned him inside out, and that no woman had ever made him feel like that.

Only he wouldn't tell her any of that—not without knowing what she was thinking.

'It was sensational, whatever it was,' she said.

He nodded, heat sweeping through him as she unwound the towel from around her head and began rubbing it slowly over her hair in a way that made his fingers itch to unwind the one around her body.

'So what happens next?'

The words were out of his mouth before he'd even known he was going to say them, and it was too late to take them back. Too late to do anything but meet her gaze.

Glancing over at his lean, naked body, Cristina felt heat pool low in her pelvis. Waking beside him in the darkness, his legs entwined with hers, she had thought she was dreaming, and it had taken several moments before her stunned brain could accept that Luis was there in her bed. Heart pounding, she had watched him sleep, mesmerised by his beauty, wishing silently that it could last for ever. That it could be just the two of them together and one endless night.

Listening to Luis talk about his brother, knowing that his loyalty and love for his family were absolute, she'd felt a fierce protective urge towards him, and more than anything she had wanted to take away his pain. But then at some point he had taken away her pain too.

She had never felt so completely desired. Or so needed.

It should have felt wonderful, and it had—it did—only...

Her breath felt suddenly leaden in her chest. Only facts were facts, and nothing could last for ever. Sooner or later Luis would discover that not only was she a mass of insecurities but she also had a humiliating past. And then that would be that.

She felt a ripple of fear snake across her skin. What if no man ever made her feel like that again?

Her pulse trembled.

That was, of course, a rhetorical question, for how could she ever recreate the last few days? All this—the island, the *fortaleza*, Luis—it wasn't real life. Or not her real life anyway. Soon she would be back in London and then her time with Luis would be nothing more than a beautiful memory.

But they were both adults, both single, and the sexual spark between them was powerful enough to light up the entire Iberian peninsula.

So why not make the most of it?

Looking down at his gorgeous body, she swallowed hard. 'I don't know, but I do know that I like you. And I think you like me.'

Luis felt his breath catch a little. The simplicity of her words as much as the proximity of her warm, near-naked body was making his pulse jump in his chest, and it took a moment to steady both his breathing and his expression.

Right now, being with Cristina felt like a no-brainer. No one had come close to making him feel like she did, but—

'You're not looking for something serious?'

She shook her head. 'I'm not.'

'My parents—'

'Don't need to know,' she said quickly. 'This is just between us.'

And if he'd been close to losing control before he almost lost it there and then as casually she undid the towel and let it drop from her body.

'Just you and me,' she said huskily.

Kneeling on the bed, she straddled him, her naked body pressing against his erection. Instinctively his hands slid up around her waist, then higher to her breasts, and he gazed up at her, his breath stilling in his throat as he felt her shiver.

Slowly he stroked her nipples, his heart kicking against his ribs as he felt the tips swell and harden beneath his fingers. Watching her soft brown eyes dilate, he lifted his head and kissed her.

'You're so beautiful,' he whispered against her mouth.

Breathing shallowly, Cristina reached down to steady

herself, and at the touch of her hands he broke away from her mouth, his head falling back against the pillow, the breath hissing between his teeth.

His eyes were fixed on her face, intent and impossibly dark, their grey swallowed up by the black of his pupils. Muscles clenching, she rolled back and forth on his body in time to the pulse beating between her thighs.

'Luis…' she murmured and, bending her head, she kissed him, brushing her lips over his, her fingers stroking his arms, his chest, down over the furrows of muscle on his stomach, then closing over the length of his erection.

He jerked against her and, maddened by her touch, he caught her fingers, tightening his hand around hers as she fed him into herself.

'Ah, Cristina…' He groaned, his pulse accelerating. She was so tight and warm and wet, and suddenly he knew he could wait no longer.

Rocking against him, Cristina felt the change, felt his body growing harder and tauter even as the ball of heat rolling inside her moved faster and faster. And then, just as she knew she could take no more, he grabbed both her hands and, pressing them into the mattress, thrust upwards as she arched into him.

Later—much later—she lay and watched him as he collected his clothes from the floor, where she'd stripped them off him earlier that morning. They had made love again, then taken a shower together, and ended up making love until the water had run cold, and they had stumbled, laughing, back into the bedroom and into bed.

Even just thinking about him moving against her made her skin prickle, for she knew how it felt to have him deep inside her, to have his mouth and hands roam at will over her body.

Her eyes rested on his hands—those same hands that had given her such pleasure—and she felt a pang like hunger.

And then, just like that, her brain jumped forward and she frowned. 'We missed breakfast.'

Luis glanced over at her from where he was buckling his belt. 'I'm sure Pilar will be happy to make you anything you wish, *cariño*.'

She shook her head. 'I'm not hungry—well, I *am*, a little—but what about your parents? Won't they wonder where you are? Where *I* am.'

'No and maybe. I quite often don't eat breakfast with them when I'm here, and they probably think you're having a lie-in.'

She relaxed slightly, and then felt her heart give a jolt as he picked up his shirt.

'But you're wearing the same clothes as yesterday. They're going to notice that, and then—'

Crossing the room, Luis sat down on the bed beside her. 'Then what?'

Reaching forward, he pulled her onto his lap, his dark eyes resting on her face, his bare muscular chest brushing her breasts.

'I'm thirty, *cariño*, not thirteen.' He held her gaze. 'I thought you were okay about all this?'

'I am,' she said quickly. 'I just don't want them to get the wrong idea.'

He smiled then—a slow smile that made her body surge back to life—and she wanted him again, so badly that she could hardly remember what they were talking about.

'No, you don't want them to get the *right* idea.'

He gazed down at her, eyes narrowing, and she felt her breath catch as his fingers began caressing her hipbone. Quickly, before her greedy body could override her brain, she wriggled out of his grip and stood up.

'Luis, stop... I need to get some clothes on and go and do some work, and so do you.'

She dressed quickly, expecting him to do the same, but

when she returned from cleaning her teeth he was still sitting there, his shirt dangling from his fingers.

Her heart seemed suddenly to be beating too fast. 'What is it? What's wrong?'

He was silent a moment, and then he said quietly, 'I've decided to talk to my parents.'

She heard the tension in his voice before she registered the implication of his words. 'You mean about Bas?'

He nodded. 'I need to tell them what happened. What I did.'

Reaching out, she pressed her hand against his cheek and stroked it gently with her thumb. 'I know you do. And this is the right time.'

'Is it?' He looked up at her, his grey eyes searching hers.

'Yes.' She nodded. 'Get dressed, and I'll come with you.

Cristina watched Luis walk away, and then, turning, she walked quickly outside, towards the terraced gardens. Her heart was bumping against her ribs—but not because she was worried about what Agusto and Sofia would say.

Blinded by guilt and grief, Luis had been unable to see the obvious. But she knew that his parents loved him unconditionally and would forgive him anything.

Why, then, did she feel so hollowed out? So empty. So alone.

The heat of the flagstones was burning through the thin soles of her sandals and, ducking into the marble folly at the end of the path, she breathed out with relief. It was cool and still inside, but while she might have escaped the sun there was no escape from the turmoil of her thoughts.

Gazing out across the smooth blue Mediterranean, she felt her throat tighten.

Other men had wanted her. But just for a moment Luis had needed her. She had been in his life for more than just sex.

Only now that moment had passed and she would go back to being an outsider.

Remembering the day when she'd finally realised that that was what she was, and would always be to her father, she shivered. His rejection had been total. Worse, it had been public too.

But so what if it had? Her mother loved her and that should be enough.

Except that it wasn't.

And there didn't seem to be anything she could do about it.

The blood was singing in her ears.

Or was there?

Reaching into her pocket, she pulled out her phone and scrolled down the list of calls on the screen. It was the same number. Laura's number.

A girl—a woman now—whose voice had upended her life.

Her half-sister.

They had never met—you couldn't call screaming abuse in front of someone a meeting. But Cristina knew who Laura was.

She'd stalked her on social media—knew that they were the same age and that Laura's birthday was exactly three months after hers, that they looked alike. Or they would if Laura dyed her hair red and swapped her preppy chinos and loafers for frayed denim and sky-high stilettos.

But that didn't seem very likely. Unlike her, Laura had been a high achiever at school, studied History of Art at Bryn Mawr College and now had a job at the Metropolitan Museum of Art.

Cristina's hands were trembling.

Laura was everything she'd wanted to be and everything her father had wanted from a daughter. There was nothing to be gained from talking to her.

Maybe. But there was infinitely more to be lost by burying her head in the sand. For hadn't she encouraged Luis to face his worst fears? If she was too scared to speak to her super-successful and cool half-sister then she was not only a coward, but a hypocrite.

She lifted her chin and pressed Laura's number.

It rang twice, then—'Hello? Cristina?'

Her pulse soared. For a moment she almost hung up, and then, biting back the panic filling her mouth, she said, 'You wanted to talk to me.'

'Yes.'

There was a short, stunned silence, and she could almost picture the expression of shock and disbelief on Laura's face.

'Yes, I do. I just can't believe you called me back.'

There was a noticeable shake in her voice, and it occurred to Cristina that Laura sounded more nervous than she did. Even though that made her feel marginally better, it still took courage for her to ask the question that had been bothering her ever since her half-sister had started calling her.

'How did you get my number?'

She heard Laura clear her throat.

'It wasn't that hard. I found you on social media, and you were tagged in a photo with some other *paparazzi*. So I rang round all the agencies and someone told me you were working for Grace.'

Cristina flinched inwardly. She felt suddenly horribly exposed—almost as though she'd been caught on camera herself. 'You know Grace?'

'No, but obviously I've heard of her, so I rang the magazine.' She paused. 'I didn't say anything about us, I just said that I wanted to talk to you about that photo you took of Bornstein. We're doing an exhibition of his sculptures next year...' Her voice trailed off.

Feeling calmer, Cristina said slowly, 'So why do you want to talk to me?'

'I'm sorry… I don't know really know how to tell you this so I'm just going to say it. Papá is in hospital.'

Christina said nothing. Still clutching her phone, she stared blankly at the sea, a choked feeling in her throat. Having more or less stopped talking about her father, it was a shock to hear Laura referring to him so naturally. But more shocking still was the news that he was ill.

Only really why should she care? When had Enrique Lastra last cared about *her*—if ever? She'd had her appendix out when she was nineteen, where had he been then?

'Well, thank you for telling me,' she said woodenly. 'But I don't really see what that's got to do with me.'

There was a silence, then Laura said quietly, 'I thought you'd want to know. He's your father too, Cristina.'

'Not for a long time he hasn't been. Actually, make that never.' She hated hearing the bitterness in her voice but it was impossible to stop it.

'I know how you must feel—'

'I doubt that. In fact I'm pretty damn sure you *don't*.'

She knew she was being unfair. Laura was not responsible for their father's actions any more than she was, but she couldn't help herself.

'You're right. I don't, and it was a stupid thing to say. But I really think you should see him.'

'I'm not going to fly to America to see a man who's barely—'

'He's not in America, Cristina. He's in Spain. Just like you. In Madrid. And he's dying.'

Dying!

Her heart felt like a lump of ice. The breath in her throat had turned to lead.

'He can't be…' she whispered.

'I'm sorry. But he is.'

Cristina could hear the ache in Laura's voice.

'That isn't why I've been ringing you, though.' She hesitated. 'He wants to see you.'

Cristina covered her mouth with her hand. She had waited so long to hear those words. Played out so many scenarios inside her head. But now that it had happened she didn't know what to say.

'I don't know,' she said finally. 'I need to think about it.'

'But there's not much time—'

She cut through Laura's pleading words. 'I can't talk about this now. I'm working and—'

'Surely they'd understand?'

From somewhere outside she could hear the sound of footsteps and she stood up hurriedly.

'Look, Laura, I'm not like you. I need this job.' She thought of her mother, and the fold-out bed she used every time she visited her. 'I need the money. So please don't call me again. I'll ring you when I can.'

She hung up, and turned just as Luis stepped into the folly.

For a moment he just stared at her, his eyes dark and intent, his shoulders blocking the entrance. 'So,' he remarked in a voice that made a chill slip over her skin, 'who was that on the phone?'

He'd been looking for her for at least half an hour.

It had been a gruelling but ultimately rewarding morning. Telling his parents had been easier and less painful than he'd imagined it would be.

Easier because he'd already confided in Cristina, and less painful because both Agusto and Sofia were so distressed by the fact that he had not only felt responsible for Bas's death but coped with his guilt alone.

'Of *course* it wasn't your fault, Luis.' Agusto had shaken his head. 'Whatever you told that reporter, Baltasar was a grown man. He could have simply stopped the car. Or let the *paparazzi* follow him. Your brother's death was a terrible accident, and your mother and I agreed on that a long time ago.'

He'd felt calmer then, and lighter, as though something had been eased from his shoulders. And it was all thanks to Cristina. If she hadn't been there—

His heart had contracted and he had known he needed to find her and thank her.

Only she hadn't been in the house, and Pilar hadn't seen her either. He'd tried calling her, but her phone had been engaged. It was only by chance that he'd caught sight of her as he was striding past the folly.

But as she'd turned to face him his anticipation of talking to her had given way to a mix of doubt and disquiet, for even if he hadn't heard the urgency and panic in her voice, her cheeks were flushed with guilt.

'Who were you talking to?' He spoke calmly, but watching her trying to compose that beautiful face—that beautiful, disingenuous face—into a mask of innocence, he felt as though a hurricane was raging through his body. He remembered all the times her phone had rung and she'd ignored it.

She gave him an awkward shrug. 'Oh, it was just Grace. I sent over some of the shots.'

'What did she think?'

It was difficult to say what was more impressive, he thought savagely. Her ability to lie so efficaciously or the detachment in his own voice.

The flags of colour on her cheekbones grew darker as she smiled. 'She hasn't looked at them yet.'

Cristina thought her lips might crack with the effort of smiling. It felt wrong, lying to Luis, but what was she supposed to tell him? The truth?

Her stomach lurched. No, anything was better than that. Particularly as his mood seemed to have shifted.

Glancing at his face, she let her brain loop back to earlier that morning, and her heart thumped as she realised why he was acting so oddly.

'So how did it go with your parents? Was it okay?'

He held her gaze. 'Is that what this is about? My family secrets? If so, I hope they're paying you well, because by the time you step off this island I'll have made certain you never work again.'

The stone floor seemed to ripple beneath her feet and she took a step backwards. 'What are you talking about? I don't understand—'

'Then let me enlighten you.'

He stepped forward and, taking the phone from her hand, swiped the screen. Then, eyes narrowing, he thrust it in front of her face.

'According to your contacts list you were talking to Laura, *not* Grace, and that makes you a liar.'

Watching the shock and then resignation on her face, Luis thought he might throw up. He had believed her. Not just believed her but confided in her.

'It— It's not what you think,' she stammered.

'No,' he said coldly. 'It probably never is with you, Cristina.' His mouth curled with contempt. 'Now, I could make some accusations and you could deny them—but, frankly, I don't want to waste that much time on you. So I think I'll just call this Laura and find out which grubby little rag she's working for—'

'No. You can't call her!' Cristina lunged for the phone but he held it out of her reach.

'But I can.'

His eyes were blazing with anger, and to her horror she realised that he was serious.

'Please—she's not a reporter. She works at a museum.'

He glanced over at her but didn't lower his arm. 'And she's ringing you because…?'

She stared at him dumbly, pain swelling in her chest. 'She's my half-sister.'

Luis stared at her. No one except maybe a professional actress could fake the shock and pain in her eyes. She was telling the truth, but…

'But why didn't you answer her calls?' He glanced down at the screen. 'She must have rung you a hundred times.'

She was looking at him, but he could tell that she wasn't really seeing him, maybe not even hearing him. Incredibly her shock and distress outweighed his own.

He lowered his arm. 'I didn't know you had a sister— half-sister, I mean. You haven't mentioned her. Are you not close?'

Cristina shook her head. 'Actually, I've never met her.'

Looking up at him, she saw the confusion in his eyes and quickly looked away. What had possessed her to tell him the truth? It had been stupid—but she wasn't thinking straight.

'So why does she keep ringing you?'

Her heart began to thump, but there was nothing left now but the truth.

'She's been trying to get in touch with me because… well, because my father's in hospital. In Madrid.' She took a breath. 'He's dying.'

'Dying—?'

He sounded not just confused now, but stunned.

'Why didn't you tell me?' His eyes were wide with shock and remorse. 'Look, take the helicopter—please. Tomas will fly you wherever you need to go—'

'No, thank you,' she said stiffly. 'That won't be necessary.'

'Cristina, your father's dying.' He moved towards her. 'Right now nothing matters more than you seeing him.'

'I'm not going to see him.'

She couldn't look at him any more.

'Cristina.'

His voice was so gentle. Too gentle. It was making the ice in her heart melt.

'It's okay, *cariño*, I understand. You're in shock…you're not thinking.'

He reached out to her but she batted his hand away.

'No, you *don't* understand.'

She was almost shouting, and her body was shaking not with anger but despair—for his good opinion mattered to her, and whatever she said or did now he was going to end up thinking badly of her.

'How could you? Your parents adore you. They are so happy just to be with you. I'm nothing to my father.'

Luis flinched inwardly. He couldn't understand how this beautiful, vibrant woman should think something like that, and yet he could hear the lost note in her voice, could feel it piercing his heart.

'You're his daughter.'

She shook her head. 'I'm his dirty little secret.' Her mouth twisted. 'Laura's his real daughter. Her mother is his wife, and she always has been his wife—even when he decided to marry my mum.' Her hand balled against her chest. 'That makes him a bigamist and me illegitimate.'

Illegitimate and therefore grotesque to a man like Luis Osorio. A man whose ties to his family were sacrosanct. A man who could trace his family back hundreds of years. He even had a castle—and a crest.

Luis took a deep breath. The pain in her eyes was like a band around his chest, and automatically he reached for her. She tried to back away but he gripped her shoulders and held her still.

'So what? I don't care.'

Her eyes widened with shock but, ignoring the expression of blatant disbelief on her face, he pulled her closer.

'Half the thrones of Europe have been filled by illegitimate children. My family's just the same.'

Thinking back to her childhood, she bit her lip. 'Your family is not the same as mine, Luis. My father led a double life for fifteen years. He lied to my mum, and to me, and when we found out, he just left us. He just disappeared. It was like he'd never existed. But then I suppose he hadn't really.'

Looking up, her mouth twisted.

'I know what you're thinking. You think there must have been some signs. But there weren't. We were just really naive, and he was a very convincing liar.'

He held her gaze. What he'd actually been thinking was that now he understood why Cristina had reacted so strongly to finding out he was heir to the Osorio fortune. Given her father's deceit, it was hardly surprising that she had been so suspicious and distrustful of him—a man who appeared to live two very different lives.

'How did you find out?' he asked gently.

He felt her shoulders stiffen. 'He went to the airport and left his suitcase in a taxi. The driver dropped it back at our house, and when my mum unpacked it she found a letter to his accountant about a trust fund for his wife and daughter.'

Her face was rigid.

'Only it wasn't me and my mum. It was Laura and her mother. There was a photo of them too. When he rang, my mum tried to talk to him but he just hung up.'

'Did he never try to contact you?'

She shook her head. 'I found out later that he'd moved to New York. I did see him once, though.' She hesitated. 'About a year after he left. He came to London with his family. His *real* family, I mean. I'd been stalking Laura on the internet and she was all excited about the trip. I spoke to his secretary. Pretended I was Laura. She gave me the address of the hotel where he was staying and I went there.'

Her mouth dipped at the corners.

'He didn't even want to acknowledge me at first. And then, when I wouldn't leave, he pulled out his wallet and gave me a bunch of money. I threw it in his face.'

Luis squeezed her shoulders. Her voice was so steady, so matter-of-fact, but somehow that made everything worse. 'He got off easy.' It was a poor joke, but he had to say something to ease the pain in her eyes.

Cristina looked up at him, and tried, and failed to smile. 'He's my dad.'

He pulled her into his arms and suddenly it felt like the easiest, most natural thing in the world to bury her face against his chest.

'I'm sorry,' she mumbled. 'For lying to you about the phone calls. Especially after what you told me about that reporter.'

He closed his eyes 'I'm sorry too—for accusing you of all those terrible things.'

She felt his arms tighten around her.

'So what happens next? Are you just going to ignore what Laura told you?'

Lifting her face, she looked up at him, confused. 'I don't know—' she began.

But he just carried on talking as though she hadn't spoken. 'I suppose the easiest solution is just to pretend it never happened but...'

Her eyes narrowed. 'Nice try! But I'm not going to see him. I don't want to.'

'And I understand that. But I think you *should* go—no, hear me out,' he said as she started to shake her head. 'You told me that nothing can change the past, and you were right. But you also told me that letting the past ruin your future is wrong. So go and see him and free yourself. Otherwise you'll put your life on hold forever just like I did.'

Her hands squeezed the fabric of his shirt. 'I don't think I can face him. Not on my own.'

'You won't be on your own.'

'But I can't ask my mother—'

Tipping her head back, he kissed her forehead gently. 'You won't have to. I'll be there.'

She stiffened. 'I can't ask you to do that.'

He smiled. 'You're not asking me. I'm telling you that's what's happening.'

'But why would you do that?'

Heart thumping, Luis gazed down at her. Had she guessed? Could she possibly feel the same way?

For perhaps a fraction of a second he thought about answering her truthfully. Telling her that he couldn't bear the idea of her not being there, and that he wanted to be there for her when she met her estranged father.

That in fact he wanted to be there for her always.

But, looking into her eyes, he knew it was not the right time. She needed his support—not some out-of-the-blue emotional outburst that he couldn't really explain to himself let alone her.

He shrugged. 'I pushed you into telling me about your father. That makes me kind of responsible.'

'For me?'

Cristina gazed up at him. For so long she'd had to be tough, to fight for what she wanted, and now here was Luis, offering to go into battle with her like some fairy-tale prince.

He tucked a stray strand of hair behind her ear. 'For what happens next. Now, I think we should go back to the house. You need to pack, and I need to tell Tomas to get the helicopter ready.'

As they walked back up to the house she felt dazed. She couldn't stop thinking about the look in his eyes as he'd offered to come with her. He had seemed so serious, so intense—it had felt almost as though he was offering her something else...something more than just sex.

Her breath caught.

Like a future together.

For a moment she thought about what that would mean. What it would feel like to have a place in Luis's life and in his heart.

Her pulse stalled. It would be incredible. He was smart and sexy and sensitive, and she liked him. She liked him a lot. And it seemed like a harsh twist of fate that at the very moment she realised that fact there was no time to think, let alone act on it.

But after so many years of waiting and hoping, and pretending that she didn't care one way or another, her father finally wanted to see her—and right now that came first.

CHAPTER NINE

'WOULD YOU LIKE to go round the block one more time?'

Looking up at Luis, Cristina felt her heart thump inside her chest.

Laura had emailed her the address of the private hospital where her father was staying, and up until the moment the limousine had pulled up in a side street she had thought she was making the right decision.

But now even just looking at the gated entrance to the Hospital Virgen de la Luz in Madrid was making her throat constrict, and the palms of her hands felt damp against the leather of the bag she was clutching in her lap.

'It's okay,' Luis said, his voice gentle. 'I can text Laura… tell her we're going to be a little late—'

'No.' She shook her head. 'I've already messed her around enough. All those days of not picking up the phone—'

'Come here.' He curved his arm around her waist and pulled her against the hard muscles of his chest. 'You haven't messed anyone around. And another couple of minutes isn't going to make much difference.'

The tension eased from her face.

'That's not what you said this morning,' she said softly.

Her expression was innocent but her eyes were anything but, and desire rose inside him, swift and strong, his body hardening faster than quick-dry cement as he remembered how he'd pressed her against him in the shower.

Lifting her chin with his hand, he held her gaze. 'Are you accusing me of being inconsistent?'

'I think insatiable might be a better fit.'

He grinned, and Cristina shook her head, but she was smiling too. How could she not? He was just so gorgeously handsome and sexy. She liked it that he was wearing a polo shirt again—this time it was grey, perhaps a shade darker than his eyes. Liked, too, the way it clung to the hard definition of his muscles.

But now was not the right time to be giving in to the heat pooling inside her. Laura and her estranged father must take priority now.

Her pulse jumped and a flurry of fear spiralled up inside of her. Was she doing the right thing?

'Yes, you are.'

She looked up at him, startled.

'No, I can't read minds. But I'd have to be completely devoid of feeling not to guess that you're nervous about this.'

And then before she could respond he bent his head and kissed her, and kept on kissing her until his lips had blotted out the fear and the doubt inside her.

As he lifted his mouth she breathed out slowly. 'Was that for luck?'

He shook his head. 'No. I'm just insatiable, remember?' Leaning forward, he tapped on the glass behind the driver's head 'You, however, are the smartest, sexiest and strongest woman I've ever met. So come on—let's go and introduce you to the other side of your family.'

As it turned out, even before Laura tentatively stepped forward to greet her, Cristina was surprised to find that meeting the woman she'd alternately envied and despised for so many years was easier than she'd anticipated.

In fact, although both women were clearly on edge, their main reaction to one another seemed to be not resentment and hostility but surprise.

Maybe that was down to the fact that they were alike in so many ways. Weirdly alike. Same height, same eyes, same way of standing with one foot turned out.

It was still awkward, of course—how could it not be? And perhaps if Luis hadn't been there they might have carried on making polite but wooden conversation about Laura's hotel and Cristina's journey. But something in his quiet, calm manner seemed to ease the tension between them, so that both she and Laura began to relax, and the three of them spoke easily for five minutes or so before Laura offered to find a nurse and tell her that Cristina had arrived.

While she was gone, Luis pulled her close. 'You two seem to be getting along okay.'

Cristina nodded. Her skin felt too tight, and she didn't seem to be able to breathe properly.

'I didn't think I'd like her,' she said shakily. 'Or that she'd like me. I was just so hung up on the fact that we were only half-sisters.'

He drew a finger over her cheek. 'Two halves make a whole.'

Her mouth trembled, but when she looked up at him, his eyes calmed her.

'It's going to be all right.'

'Is it?'

He nodded automatically, but as she looked up at him the expression on her face stayed his heart. 'Your father has asked to see you, *carino*. Let's just start with that.'

'Cristina!'

It was Laura. Beside her stood a young woman dressed in a pale blue tunic and trousers.

'We can go in now.'

The short walk to her father's private room seemed to take for ever. Her heart was beating painfully fast, and if it hadn't been for Luis's hand firmly gripping hers she might well have turned and run.

But in him there was something reassuringly solid—not just in his grip but in his manner. It was nothing overt. On the contrary, he was quiet and courteous. There was, though, a subtle natural authority about him that seemed to resonate with those around him.

Watching the busy hospital come to a virtual standstill, she felt warmth swell in her chest. She had never imagined trusting a man—and right now she had never felt more vulnerable—and yet with Luis by her side she felt safe in a way that she'd craved since her father had ripped any ability to trust away from her at the age of thirteen.

And now she was going to see him for the first time in eleven years…maybe for the last time.

She hadn't seen him since that terrible scene in the hotel. Enrique Lastra had been stocky then, with a broad, square head like a bull and mass of thick black hair that had earned him his nickname—Mino, from *minotauro*, the half-man, half-bull of Greek mythology.

But there was nothing imposing about the man in the hospital bed.

True, he had that same mass of hair. Only now it was almost white. An ache was building in her chest and she stared at him dazedly, barely registering Laura's hand on her arm as her sister pulled her towards the bed.

'*Holà*, Papá. It's me… Laura.'

Cristina felt her stomach clench as her father's eyes opened, for they hadn't changed. They were still the same dark brown she remembered, and that only seemed to make her chest ache even more. His eyes might not have changed but everything else had—not just his appearance but in their relationship too.

'Laura…' His voice hadn't changed either. It was still a distinctive rasp—the legacy of a life spent smoking, first cigarettes and then later cigars.

She watched as her half-sister smiled. 'I'm here, Papá,

and I've got someone here with me. Someone I know you want to see.'

Cristina's pulse rippled as her father turned his head slowly towards her. But if she'd been expecting a tearful gasp of recognition she was to be disappointed.

Enrique stared at her blankly. 'I don't—'

'It's Cristina, Papá,' Laura said quickly. 'She's come to see you.'

His eyes narrowed then, and Cristina waited for him to acknowledge her, but instead he turned back to Laura.

'What does *she* want?'

Laura glanced over at her but Cristina said nothing.

It was clear from her sister's stricken face that Enrique had not wanted to see her at all. Probably it had been Laura's idea—a misguided desire to reunite her dying father with his estranged daughter—but they both knew without having to say it out loud that he had nothing to say to her.

If only that she could tell him that she didn't want anything from him, and that he was as big a disappointment to her as she had obviously been to him. But the words stuck in her throat, and she was scared that if she pushed them out then the tears she was also holding back might burst free too.

She couldn't see Luis's face, but she felt his hand tighten around hers, could feel the hard breadth of his chest at her shoulder, and more than anything she wanted to turn and bury her head against it. But to do that would mean showing how hurt she was.

How hurt and humiliated.

Biting down on the howl of anguish filling her lungs, she turned and walked swiftly towards the door, just as a nurse pushed a trolley through it. Sidestepping it, she heard Luis curse and Laura call out her name, and then she was running through the corridors and down the stairs, out into the street and then into another street, and then another, tears streaming down her face.

Finally she could run no more and, whimpering, she crouched down in a doorway like a wounded animal and cried—just as she'd cried eleven years ago when she'd realised that her father wasn't coming back and that he didn't want or love her.

Striding into the living room of his family's apartment on the exclusive Calle de Velázquez, Luis tugged off his jacket and punched Cristina's number into his phone for perhaps the twentieth time. His mouth tightened as it went straight to voicemail again and he didn't leave a message. There was no point. He'd already left a whole bunch of messages and she hadn't responded to any of them.

Where *was* she? More importantly, was she okay?

Remembering the look of devastation on her face as she'd left her father's room, he felt a rush of anger towards the man lying in the bed.

How could anyone be so cruel as to turn away from their own child?

His heart was pounding in time with his headache. It was nearly two hours since she'd fled from the hospital. In between calling her phone he'd tried to find her, stopping in bars and cafés, convinced that he would somehow catch sight of her just as he had that first night.

But he hadn't and so, knowing that sooner or later she'd have to go back to the apartment, he'd decided to wait for her there.

Too impatient to wait for the lift, he'd taken the stairs three at a time, and as he'd walked in he'd half hoped she might have returned. But she wasn't waiting for him in the living room, or the bedroom. Nor had Elena, the housekeeper, seen her. Everywhere was silent and empty.

It was a silence that reminded him painfully of his family home in the days and weeks following his brother's death and, suddenly unable to bear the memories of that time, he reached for his jacket. He couldn't just stand here doing nothing.

His heart jolted in his chest as somewhere in the building he heard a door close.

'Cristina?'

He was halfway across the floor when she walked into the room.

'*Cariño*. Thank goodness.' Pulse racing, he pulled her against him, touching her hair with his lips, feeling her exhaustion.'

As his arms tightened around her Cristina leaned into his chest, the scent of his cologne and the warmth of his body enveloping her. It would be so easy just to stay there for ever in an eternal embrace...

But he was not hers to hold.

Breathing out slowly, she shifted backwards.

His arms loosened, and as she looked up at him he said, 'I went looking for you and I tried calling—'

His voice was steady but she could feel his pulse leaping beneath his skin. He had been *worried* about her, and the fact that he cared made her want to cry all over again.

But instead she managed a weak smile. 'I put my phone on silent when we went into the hospital...' Her voice faltered. Her skin felt numb and her brain seemed to be working at half-speed, but she could picture it still—her father's face as he'd turned and looked at her. Or rather looked through her. As though she wasn't there. As though she didn't matter.

Her stomach gave a lurch.

She had gone to see him, believing that he wanted to see her. That he wanted to talk to her, make amends, maybe even ask for forgiveness.

Forgiveness? What a joke!

Suddenly she was perilously close to tears again.

He hadn't even known she was coming, and he certainly hadn't wanted to see or speak to her, much less ask for forgiveness. Nothing had changed. He still didn't love her or want anything to do with her.

An ache of misery was spreading inside her. It had been crushing to realise that fact when she was thirteen. More crushing still a year later, when he'd turned his back on her in that hotel foyer, for that time his rejection had been public.

But at least then her pain and shame had only been witnessed by strangers. This time Laura and Luis had been there to see that she was not worthy of love—not even from her own father.

'Cristina?'

She felt Luis's fingers curl around her hand.

'You have every right to be upset. But your father's very ill. He didn't know what he was saying.'

She shrugged. 'I know that, and I'm fine. Really, it doesn't matter.'

Like hell it didn't.

To Luis, the aftershocks from that encounter with her father were palpable. Her face was pale and set, and she had obviously been crying, His stomach muscles clenched and he felt anger spike inside him for he hated seeing her so upset.

But he was just going to have to keep his feelings under wraps. Right now, Cristina came first.

Realising that he needed to tread carefully, he glanced at his watch. 'Look, it's nearly three o'clock Let's have something to eat now, and then maybe we can pop back to the hospital tomorrow—'

Her head snapped up.

'Or we could go back today,' he said.

Slowly she shook her head. 'I'm not going back today

or tomorrow or any other day. Don't you understand, Luis? I don't want to see my father again. Not now. Not ever.'

He held up his hands placatingly. 'I know you feel that now, but—'

'But what?' Cristina looked up at him challengingly. 'Do you seriously think it will make any difference how many times I go back to that hospital? You saw him today—he didn't even want to look at me.'

'I know. But he was probably in shock. He wasn't expecting to see you—'

'So what are you saying? That this is *my* fault, somehow?'

He frowned. 'No, of course not. I just meant that he'll have had a bit of time to think—'

She cut him off before he had a chance to finish his sentence. '*A bit of time?* How much does he need? He's had eleven years.'

She shook her head. She was breathing too fast and the ache inside her chest was building.

'You just don't get it, do you? I could wait *one hundred* years and it wouldn't change the way he feels about me.'

'You don't know that,' Luis said quietly. 'You came here to face your past, Cristina, not to run away from it.'

She threw his hand off hers, her eyes blazing with anger and hurt. 'How dare you?'

Her words were barely above a whisper, but he could feel the force of them as though she were shouting.

'I was upset—'

'And you were right to be.' Reaching out, he grasped her hands in his. 'Totally and justifiably right. But that doesn't change the fact that if you walk away now all this will have been for nothing.'

He took a step towards her, keeping his grey gaze steady on her face.

'I know you don't want to hear it, but trust me, *cariño*. You can't run away from this. I know because I tried.'

She stared at him mutely, the truth of his words silencing her. He was right, but knowing that didn't seem to make any difference. She still felt sick with fear.

Trust me. It was so easy for him to say, but a virtual impossibility for her to do. She had loved her father, trusted him unconditionally. He had helped her with her homework, dug sandcastles with her on the beach, taught her to ride a bike, and none of it had mattered. When it came to it he had simply turned his back on her.

Her body began to tremble. The first time she had been a child. It had been out of her control, and the same had been true about their meeting at the hotel. But what had happened today at the hospital was different. *She* was different—older and in control of her life. She was an adult now, and if she let this happen again—if she let him reject her again—then it would not be bad luck, or a mistake. It would be a choice.

A choice she was *not* willing to make.

'I know you're trying to help, but it's not the same,' she said flatly. 'You and I are not the same.'

Her heart began to beat faster as she remembered how she had allowed herself to imagine being not just in Luis's bed but in his life. Maybe if Luis had been a different man from a different background, and they had met under different circumstances, she might have let herself be swept away by his tenderness and support, given in to some kind of romantic fantasy.

But there was no point in reading anything into his gesture. Luis might be loyal and strong and handsome like a prince, but he was also wealthy like a prince too. Wealthy, privileged, and with all the expectations of his birth.

Her mouth tightened. Expectations that would never include her. This wouldn't last. It couldn't. Not just because they came from opposite ends of the social spectrum, or even because she was illegitimate. It had to do with her, and what she knew deep down to be true and immutable about herself.

That beneath all her bravado she was a let-down.

'I'm not going back to see my father. There's no point. I'm done with that part of my life now. It's time to move on and...' She hesitated, but only for a moment. 'And I'm not going back to the island with you either.'

It had been hard enough saying the words inside her head. Speaking them out loud made her stomach turn inside out with misery. But that was nothing to the pain she would feel if she went back with him and waited for him to end it—as he surely would.

Luis stared at her in shock, his hands tightening on hers involuntarily. She had stilled, her body tensing, and he could sense that already she was retreating—just as she had before.

The breath in his throat felt thick and cloying, and panic rose up inside him as he imagined the island without her— his life without her.

He'd seen the doubt and fear in her eyes when he'd asked her to trust him, and he knew that he needed to do something, say something to calm her, to stop her closing off and withdrawing from him. To make her trust him.

'I know how much your father's hurt you, Cristina. He's hurt you and that's why you don't want to go and see him again. You don't trust him not to hurt you more.'

He paused, the doubt and fear on her face staying his words for a moment, and then he breathed out slowly.

'I know you don't trust me either, and you think I'm going to hurt you too. But I could never hurt you, *cariño*.' Heart thumping, he held her gaze. 'I love you, Cristina.'

Her brows drew together and she looked up at him uncertainly.

It wasn't that he was lying. She knew with absolute certainty that he believed what he was saying. Just as her father had believed it when he'd stood in front of a room full of witnesses and told her mother that he'd love and cherish her for ever.

But the problem was that she didn't believe it.

Worse, she knew how it would play out, for she'd been in this exact place before, with previous boyfriends. Only she had never felt like this before, and that was what was scaring her the most.

She already cared far too much about Luis. Soon she'd panic like she always did, about losing her place in his affections and then it would just be a matter of time before he realised that she wasn't worthy of his love, his time or his attention.

Better to get out now, with her dignity and her heart intact.

Gently, she slid her hands from beneath his. 'One day you are going to find the woman who will make you happy.'

There was a long, loaded silence. He stared at her, a flicker of confusion in his eyes, as though he hadn't quite understood what she had said—as though she had spoken in a foreign language.

'I have found her,' he said finally.

She shook her head. 'I like you, Luis, and I'm grateful—'

'Grateful!'

The word sounded harsh as it echoed around the beautiful room.

'Yes, for everything you've done, for your help and support. But that's all I feel.' She clenched her jaw, biting down on the lie. 'We said we didn't want anything serious. Don't you remember?'

She watched his face shift and harden as anger replaced confusion.

'Yes, I remember. But that was before all this.'

'This doesn't change anything.' She spoke quickly, for with every passing second it was getting harder to believe that leaving Luis was the right thing to do. 'I'm sorry if you thought it did, but it doesn't. My life is a big enough mess right now—I don't need or want any more complications.'

'And that's what I am, is it?'

His voice was steady, but the expression on his face made her want to curl up somewhere dark and private.

'A complication?'

Luis stared at her in silence. His head was spinning; anger and misery were rippling through him in waves, tangling up with his breath so that his chest felt full of knots. He knew she was scared of being hurt, and that she found it hard to trust. So he'd offered himself and his feelings up like a sacrifice to prove that he could be trusted.

He'd thought it would be enough.

But he'd been wrong.

Trust wasn't the issue. She just didn't want him.

For her this had only ever been a fling. A short-term sexual liaison.

His anguish felt like a living thing.

Not just because he was losing her but because he saw now that he'd never really had her.

Something seemed to fall forward high up inside him.

He'd fallen in love and he'd wanted her to feel the same way—so much so that he'd trusted his emotions over the evidence, put feelings before facts. It was the emotional equivalent of a HALO jump without a parachute. The ultimate gamble.

And he'd lost.

He hadn't heard her leave the room but she must have done, for suddenly she was standing there with her bag.

'I'm going to stay in a hotel.'

'There's no need,' he said flatly. 'There's no reason for me to stay now, so you might as well use the apartment.'

Cristina shook her head. Her body was so rigid with misery that it hurt to make that tiny sideways movement, but she didn't care. In fact she was grateful, for it gave her something to concentrate on aside from the crack opening up inside her heart.

'Thank you, but no. I'd rather stay at a hotel.' She hesitated. 'I'll write to your parents.'

He nodded. 'What about your things? On the island?'

She shrugged. 'Throw them away. I have everything I want.'

It was a lie. The thought of walking away, of leaving Luis behind for ever, was like staring into a star as it exploded. She knew that afterwards she would be left blind and broken, but there was no alternative—or none that she could imagine. It was like trying to picture what lay beyond the horizon.

To stay would only prolong the agony.

There was nothing left to say.

As she lifted her bag and walked towards the door Luis watched, his body frozen, his brain silently pleading with her to stop and turn around. His heart aching for her to change her mind.

But she didn't so much as hesitate, and he was still standing there when he heard the door close behind her and felt the silence of the empty apartment rise up around him.

CHAPTER TEN

SCOOPING HER HAIR up into a ponytail-cum-bun, Cristina sat down on the bed in her Madrid hotel room and breathed out slowly, trying to control the irregular beat of her heart as she looked down at her phone.

She scrolled slowly through the messages and missed calls. She'd already checked twice that morning, and she knew—*knew*—that there was no point, but she couldn't stop herself from doing it.

Just in case by some miracle Luis had texted or called her.

Don't cry, she told herself. *You promised that today you wouldn't cry.*

She blinked furiously.

Switching off her phone, she swallowed past the lump of misery wedged in her throat. It had been the same every day since she'd walked out of the Osorios' apartment. No text, no message. Nothing.

That had been a month ago.

A month spent trying not to think about Luis.

Trying and *failing* not to think about Luis.

Her chest felt heavy and tight. Even now she could re-member that look on his face as she'd left, his hurt and confusion as he'd tried to hold himself together.

Suddenly she was fighting to catch her breath, fight-ing not to give in to the tears that had fallen ceaselessly since that last day with him. She'd even woken at night and found her face wet and her pillow damp.

She had never felt more miserable and desperate, and the fact that her misery was self-imposed was no consolation at all. Life—hers and other people's—had just stopped mattering, and she wanted to do nothing but lie in bed in her pyjamas with the curtains drawn.

It was Laura who had helped her. Her half-sister and now her friend. It had been Laura who had booked her into the same hotel as her. Laura who had fed her and forced her to get dressed, listened to her talk and cry—sometimes both at the same time.

She breathed in shakily. At least she had been able to support her half-sister when their father had died quietly in his sleep ten days ago. It was the main reason she had chosen to stay in Spain. And even though she hadn't gone back to see Enrique again Laura had understood. Just as she had understood Laura's need to be by his bedside.

Since his death Laura had been tied up with arrangements for the funeral, but they met for breakfast or lunch most days, and supper every evening, and Laura had already begged Cristina to come and stay with her in America.

America.

She stared lethargically across the room. Six weeks ago she would have killed to do something as glamorous and exciting as go to New York. And she was excited about going, but also a little nervous too—for Laura wanted to introduce her to her mother, Nina, the woman who had been her father's wife and then ex-wife.

Cristina had been shocked to learn that Nina and Enrique had been divorced for seven years. Shocked too by how that made her feel. Given everything that had happened with her father, it would have been logical and completely understandable for her to feel that he'd got his comeuppance. Instead, though, she simply felt sad.

But it was a sadness that she could contain, for Enrique

had been absent from her for so long that it felt as though she'd already spent almost half her life grieving for him.

In contrast, Luis's absence felt like a raw wound, an ache that would never heal. How could it? He had been a part of her, and without him she would never feel whole again.

She felt the sting of tears and, brushing at her eyes, stood up quickly and looked round for her handbag. As she did so she caught sight of her reflection in one of the gilt-framed mirrors on the wall and, pausing, reached up and touched her hair.

It had been auburn for so many years but now it was what her mother called 'mouse'.

She looked familiar, yet different. It was like meeting someone from the past, and in a way she was. 'Mouse' had been her father's nickname for her, and that had been one of the reasons she had decided to dye her hair in the first place. It had been a teenager's angry response to being forgotten—a way of standing out and mattering.

It had taken a long time, but it had worked.

Grace had been delighted with her photos of Agusto and Sofia. So delighted that she had instantly commissioned Cristina to do an interview with an award-winning *madrileño* actor, and to shoot the French-born striker who had just won his third Golden Boot trophy for a cover.

But despite earning herself a permanent position at the magazine, and loving spending time with Laura, she still felt listless—numb, almost.

And lonely.

Her throat tightened. All her life she had been chasing a dream. A dream of being accepted. Of belonging. But now that her dream was a reality she realised that it wasn't enough. That there was only one person whose acceptance she craved. Only one person to whom she truly wanted to belong.

Only he wasn't here. She had pushed him away and then walked away from him. And now she would never see Luis again.

She breathed in, consciously refusing to let her thoughts spiral down again. It was done, and she'd had no choice. Letting Luis get close to her was too big a risk to take.

All she could do now was focus on the positive—her job and her sister.

Her sister! Glancing at her phone, she swore softly.

The sister she was supposed to be meeting for lunch in fifteen minutes.

If she left now, she thought, she might just get there on time. And, snatching up her bag and room key, she ran towards the door.

She was hot and sticky by the time she arrived at the café.

'Sorry,' she said, throwing her bag down onto the spare chair and then kissing Laura on both cheeks. 'I completely forgot the time.'

Her sister rolled her eyes. 'It's fine. I only just got here myself.' Leaning back, she squinted up at the sun. 'I thought we had long meetings at the museum, but I honestly thought the one I had this morning would never end.'

Cristina felt a pang of guilt. Following Enrique's death, Laura had been saddled with meeting the various lawyers and bankers that her father had employed to manage his business affairs.

She frowned. 'Can I do anything? Oh, thank you.' She glanced up as the waiter put two bottles of water, some bread and olives on the table. 'I know I've been pretty useless lately, but I want to help.'

Tearing at a piece of bread, Laura shook her head. 'I know you do. But I'm just whining, really.' She glanced at the menu. 'Is there anything you particularly want? Or shall I just order for us both?'

Cristina glanced inside the café to the counter, where dark grey slates were piled up high with grilled chorizo and white asparagus wrapped in Riojan cheese.

'No, you choose. But be quick.' She grinned at her sister. 'I'm starving.'

The *tapas* arrived before they'd finished the bread. They were hot and moreish and full of smoky flavour.

As the waiter arranged the small terracotta dishes efficiently over every available space on the small table she felt her mouth start to tingle. Despite the family atmosphere of the café, some of the *tapas* were so beautiful they looked like canapés at some upmarket party, or starters from a Michelin-starred restaurant.

Her fingers tightened around her fork.

Damn. She had promised herself that she wouldn't think about Luis over lunch, but her brain had made the leap from Michelin-starred restaurant to that meal with his parents with astonishing speed.

'Are you okay?' Laura was looking at her anxiously. 'Did you burn yourself?'

Cristina shook her head. 'No, I was just thinking—'

'About Luis.' Her half-sister finished the sentence for her.

'Not really—' Catching sight of Laura's expression of disbelief, she sighed. 'Well, okay—yes, I was. But it has been at least three minutes,' she joked weakly. 'And, on the plus side, I haven't cried at all today.'

Reaching across the table, Laura squeezed her sister's arm reassuringly.

'I'm fine—honestly. And if eat everything on this table I'll be in so much pain I won't be able move, let alone cry. So pass me the *alcachofas*...and I'll have some of that *mojama* too.'

Looking over at Laura, she felt her smile fade from her face. She had expected to see her sister smiling back at her, but instead Laura was gripping the edge of the table, and her light brown eyes were watching Cristina with a mixture of uncertainty and fear.

'What is it? Has something happened?' She felt a rush of panic and remorse. Laura was always so calm, so steady. 'Did something happen at your meeting?'

Her sister shook her head. 'It's nothing to do with the meeting or with me.' She hesitated. 'It's about you. Only—'

'Only what?' Cristina breathed in sharply, trying to shift the knot of fear lodged in her chest as her sister's fingers clenched and unclenched against the table.

'I want to tell you, only I'm worried it's going to upset you—'

'What are you talking about?' she said hoarsely.

There was a short, tense silence, and then Laura reached into her bag and pulled out an envelope. Cristina felt her mouth turn dry as she spotted the familiar crest above Laura's name and the address of their hotel.

She stared at it numbly as Laura cleared her throat.

'It's from Luis. It came a couple of days ago.' She bit her lip. 'I know I should have given it to you right away, Chrissie, but you've been so upset. And then, when you started to seem a bit happier, I didn't want to make it worse again.'

Looking up into her sister's anguished face, Cristina drew in another breath, still trying to stay calm.

'Why did he write to you?'

Laura held her gaze steadily, but when she spoke there was a quiver to her voice.

'He came to the hospital the day after…you know…' A flush of colour spread over her cheeks. 'After you left him. He asked to see Papá alone.'

'Why? What for?' Now it was Cristina's cheeks that were burning.

'Just read the letter, Chrissie. Then you'll know why.'

Laura held out the envelope, and after a moment or two Cristina took it.

She stared at the cursive handwriting on the front, watching the letters slip in and out of focus, and then with hands that were surprisingly steady she pulled out the letter and read it.

Dear Laura,

I was so saddened to hear about the death of your father. Please accept my condolences. I know from the short time of seeing the two of you together that you were close, and that he loved you very much. But you don't need me to tell you that. You were at the heart of your father's life.

Sadly, however, the same was not true for Cristina.

She believes that she meant nothing to her father, and that she had nothing in common with Enrique.

But she is wrong on both counts.

When I spoke to him at the hospital I discovered that he was just as proud and stubborn as she is.

He told me that he regretted not speaking to Cristina when she visited him. That he had always loved her and wanted to reach out to her but was too scared of being judged for the actions he had always regretted but never had the courage to face.

He also told me how very proud he was of Cristina—not just her career but her courage—and that had he been brave enough to do so he would have been proud to call her his daughter.

Unfortunately, as we both know, Cristina did not get a chance to learn of Enrique's true feelings for her. Nor would she believe me if I told her. I feel, though, that she would believe you. I therefore ask

if you would share this letter with her so that maybe,
finally, she can believe in herself.
    Please take care of her for me.
Yours sincerely,
Luis

The words were swirling in front of her eyes. She knew that Luis loved her. He had told her so. But what she hadn't realised until now was that she loved him too. Loved him so much that her heart felt as though it would burst.

'Oh, Laura.' She looked up, tears spilling over her cheeks. 'What have I done? What have I *done*?'

Stopping at the edge of the cliff, Luis gazed out towards the horizon. The sun had already burned away the early-morning haze of cloud and was now shimmering like a huge golden orb in the sky. Past the dark grey rocks, white-topped waves were slicing through the smooth blue surface of the water. It was going to be a glorious day.

He glanced at the sea longingly. Maybe next time he would take the boat out—right now, though, he wanted to go swimming.

Stepping back, he made his way down the cliff path towards the tidal pool. The beach was his usual destination for an early-morning swim, but he was feeling lazy today. Today he simply wanted to enjoy the delicious and still novel feeling of playing truant in the sunshine. And what better way to do that than by lying on his back and gazing up at this cloudless sky, buoyed up by the warm Mediterranean water?

The last four weeks had been some of the busiest and most chaotic in his life. Having decided to move back to Spain permanently, he had finally sat down with his father and the lawyers yesterday and formally taken over as chairman of Banco Osorio. And last week he'd flown back to California to sort out his business affairs and arrange the sale of his properties.

Returning to Segovia, he'd known immediately that he'd made the right decision. Even without his parents' joy it had felt as if he was coming home.

But, although he was happy to be back, he felt Cristina's absence every minute of every hour. At times he thought he was losing his mind with the misery of losing her. Just like with Bas, he felt as if a part of him was missing— almost as though when she'd walked away she'd taken something with her.

His legs slowed to a halt and, closing his eyes, he let the pain wash over him.

That was why he'd returned to the island alone. To face the pain head-on in the place where he and Cristina had become lovers.

He might have met her in that club in Segovia, but that night had been about sex and oblivion.

This was where the miracle had happened—where the barriers he'd built between himself and the world had started to crumble. And this was where he needed to be to start the long process of rebuilding his life.

Without her.

Opening his eyes, he breathed out slowly. Cristina was gone from his life, and only by exorcising the memory of her and his hopes for what might have been could he hope to move on.

The ache inside his chest was suddenly so big that he thought it might break through his skin. He didn't *want* to move on. He wanted to go back in time—go back to the moment when she'd needed him.

Except that wouldn't work, for even if he could stop time it wouldn't change the eventual outcome. Cristina didn't love him, and however painful it was to accept that fact he needed to do it.

Bas's death had taught him that.

Life was for living, not for grieving.

But he did just want one last moment before he reset the clock for ever...

From somewhere nearby he heard a splash, and the sound pulled him back to the present. Theoretically he could stay here for as long as he wanted, but he'd made a deal with himself. One last swim and then he would go home.

Turning towards the oval of clear blue water set into the rocks, he made his way across the warm limestone slabs—and abruptly stopped.

A woman was swimming smoothly beneath the water.

He couldn't see her face, but then he didn't need to. Even with the sun glaring off the water, dazzling his eyes, the curve of her back was unmistakable. Unforgettable.

Staring down at her, he felt his stomach seem to go into free fall, just as though he'd dived off the rock to join her. He watched, dry-mouthed, as she slow-crawled to the side and pulled herself up onto one of the flat plateaux that edged the pool, blinking water out of her eyes, leaving her hair—*her brown hair*—clinging to the contours of her skull.

Cristina.

He forced himself to say her name inside his head, and just as though she'd heard him she turned and their eyes met.

For the longest moment neither of them moved. They just gazed at one another. And then suddenly she was walking towards him.

His skin was prickling with shock.

It must be a dream. Or some kind of optical illusion. Maybe he was hallucinating...

He stared at her in silence as she picked her way across

the rocks, his breath catching fire in his throat as she stopped in front him.

Since she'd walked out of his life he'd thought about her endlessly, replayed every glance, every word they'd shared, imagined whole conversations inside his head, and he knew that he should say something—that he *needed* to say something. Yet now she was here both his mouth and his brain seemed to have stopped working.

But as he looked down into her face it suddenly didn't matter what he said, for he could see her tears mingling with the drops of seawater and he knew that no words were needed.

Her heart belonged to him just as his heart belonged to her.

And, reaching out, he tugged her to him, an ache of love and longing swelling inside his chest.

'You came back,' he said softly, fighting back his own tears. He felt her nod against him. 'But how did you know I was here?'

Cristina swallowed. 'I spoke to your father.'

'My *father*?'

She almost laughed at the shock in his voice.

'He was so sweet. And kind.'

'He likes you.'

She felt Luis's lips brush against her hair.

'And I like him. But I like you more—so very much more.'

His heart gave a thump as she tilted her head back and he saw that fresh tears were sliding over her cheeks.

'I love you, Luis. I have done for ages, only I was too scared to let myself feel it. And then, when you told me that you loved me, I was too scared to trust you. I just couldn't believe I could have a place in your life.

'So what changed?' he asked shakily.

She smiled weakly. 'I realised that you *are* my life.'

Her eyes were soft and unwavering.

'I've missed you so much. Every day I woke up thinking of something to tell you, and you weren't there. Every street I walked down I'd reach out for your hand, and you weren't there. And every night when I fell asleep I wanted to feel you next to me, but you weren't there.'

Luis could hardly breathe. She was baring her soul to him, proving not only that she loved him but that she trusted him too.

His arms tightened around her. 'I felt the same way. Nothing matters without you, Cristina. You're my life. My world. *Mi corazón.*'

And, taking her face between his hands, he kissed her fiercely.

Finally he raised his head, fixed his grey eyes on hers. 'I love you.'

Cristina felt her heart contract. He sounded so serious. So full of certainty...

She glanced up him, her lips trembling—and not only from the force of his kiss.

'Enough to marry me?' The words scrambled from her mouth before she could stop them.

He drew back, his eyes widening with shock and surprise, those beautiful grey eyes that she had missed so much searching her face.

'Are you asking me to marry you?'

Cristina held his gaze. The certainty she had craved for her entire life rose up inside her and she nodded. 'Yes. Yes, I am.'

She held her breath, her pulse jumping with hope and love, and then with joy as relief and happiness spread across his face and he kissed her again.

'Is that a yes?' she croaked, when finally he lifted his mouth.

He pulled her closer, steadying her body against his, his eyes as dark and damp as the surf-splashed rocks beneath their feet.

'No. But *this* is.'

And, lowering his mouth, he kissed her again, pressing her so close that nothing could come between them.

* * * * *

MILLS & BOON

Coming next month

KIDNAPPED FOR HIS ROYAL DUTY
Jane Porter

Before they came to Jolie, Dal would have described Poppy as pretty, in a fresh, wholesome, no-nonsense sort of way with her thick, shoulder-length brown hair and large, brown eyes and a serious little chin.

But as Poppy entered the dining room with its glossy white ceiling and dark purple walls, she looked anything but wholesome and no-nonsense.

She was wearing a silk gown the color of cherries, delicately embroidered with silver threads, and instead of her usual ponytail or chignon, her dark hair was down, and long, elegant chandelier earrings dangled from her ears. As she walked, the semi-sheer kaftan molded to her curves.

"It seems I've been keeping you waiting," she said, her voice pitched lower than usual and slightly breathless. "Izba insisted on all this," she added, gesturing up toward her face.

At first Dal thought she was referring to the ornate silver earrings that were catching and reflecting the light, but once she was seated across from him he realized her eyes had been rimmed with kohl and her lips had been outlined and filled in with a soft plum-pink gloss. "You're wearing makeup."

"Quite a lot of it, too." She grimaced. "I tried to explain to Izba that this wasn't me, but she's very determined once she makes her mind up about something and apparently, dinner with you requires me to look like a tart."

Dal checked his smile. "You don't look like a tart. Unless it's the kind of tart one wants to eat."

Color flooded Poppy's cheeks and she glanced away, suddenly shy, and he didn't know if it was her shyness or the shimmering dress that clung to her, but he didn't think any woman could be more beautiful, or desirable than Poppy right now. "You look lovely," he said quietly. "But I don't want you uncomfortable all through dinner. If you'd rather go remove the makeup I'm happy to wait."

She looked at him closely as if doubting his sincerity. "It's fun to dress up, but I'm worried Izba has the wrong idea about me."

"And what is that?"

"She seems to think you're going to...marry...me."

Continue reading
KIDNAPPED FOR HIS ROYAL DUTY
Jane Porter

Available next month
www.millsandboon.co.uk

LET'S TALK
Romance

For exclusive extracts, competitions
and special offers, find us online:

f facebook.com/millsandboon

📷 @millsandboonuk

🐦 @millsandboon

Or get in touch on 0844 844 1351*

For all the latest titles coming soon, visit
millsandboon.co.uk/nextmonth

Want even more
ROMANCE?

Join our bookclub today!

'Mills & Boon books, the perfect way to escape for an hour or so.'

Miss W. Dyer

'Excellent service, promptly delivered and very good subscription choices.'

Miss A. Pearson

'You get fantastic special offers and the chance to get books before they hit the shops'

Mrs V. Hall

**Visit millsandbook.co.uk/Bookclub
and save on brand new books.**

MILLS & BOON